THERE WAS A SCREAM . . .

and then a series of screams and yells from directly ahead, near the great complex of buildings that was the central home of the Eagle *calpulli*, the clan to which Cuauhtemoc, Motechzoma, and the Snake-Woman all belonged.

Don looked up sharply. This sort of thing was unknown, so far as he knew, in Tenochtitlan. He started forward at a run.

Some forty persons were streaming away in all directions as fast as they could make it. Some stumbled and fell, hustled up again, continued the retreat.

Now he could see what it was. An Indian, naked save for a loincloth, had obviously gone amok. He was wildly swinging a *maquauhuitl* in each hand and dashing here and there in an attempt to get at new victims. He had already downed or viciously slashed a half-dozen.

A child, certainly less than a year of age, sat in the middle of it all, screaming fear. A young woman, hardly more than a child herself, came dashing in, bent low. She snatched the baby up, turned to run, screaming. She slipped on blood already shed and came to her knees and the berserker was on her, flailing his Indian swords wildly.

And Don shot him between the eyes.

THE OTHER TIME

MACK REYNOLDS

WITH

DEAN ING

A BAEN BOOK

THE OTHER TIME

Copyright © 1984 by the literary estate of Mack Reynolds.

A Baen Book

Baen Enterprises
8-10 W. 36th Street
New York, N.Y. 10018

First printing, December 1984.

ISBN: 0-671-55926-5

Cover art by Kevin Johnson

Printed in the United States of America

Distributed by
SIMON & SCHUSTER
MASS MERCHANDISE SALES COMPANY
1230 Avenue of the Americas
New York, N.Y. 10020

A MESSAGE TO THE READER

Before his death in 1983 after a long illness, Mack Reynolds had taken several novels to first-draft stage and then, perhaps driven by a sense of mortal urgency, gone on to the next. When it became clear that Mack would be unable to bring them to completion, I, with Mack's and later his estate's approval, commissioned Dean Ing to take the entire group to a fully polished state. Dean's purpose has not been to collaborate posthumously, but to finish them exactly as Mack Reynolds writing at the utter top of his form would have done.

We believe that Dean has succeeded to an almost uncanny degree. For any writer, and particularly one of Ing's stature, to so subordinate his own authorial personality is a remarkable achievement.

Requiescat in pacem, Mack.

—Jim Baen

I liked Mack; I liked the way he lived; and I liked his tequila. That's why . . .

—Dean Ing

Chapter One

Donald Fielding went through the barrier and from his own space-time continuum to the other time without knowing it.

He had left the Land Rover camper, possibly two hours earlier, to strike out on foot over territory where even that rugged vehicle couldn't go. Although it was early August, the mornings in the area of Mexico where the States of Tlaxcala and Vera Cruz meet can be cold and he had left his sun helmet back in the car, not thinking he would need it. But now the sun was nearly overhead and he could definitely feel its rays. Old Sol can be brutal in the clear Mexican air at an altitude of ten thousand feet.

So it was that he blamed his feeling of faintness and the nausea on sunstroke. There seemed to be a sort of shimmering effect in the air, a hazy blurriness, and for a time, he decided, he must have blanked out. He looked about him and couldn't recognize his surroundings. He must have stumbled around a bit, only semiconscious. His brain felt melted.

He shook his head in an attempt to clear it, brought forth his bandana, and tied it over his short cropped hair. He had better get back to the Land Rover and drive into nearby Jalapa, or possibly Vera Cruz, if he could make it.

He had evidently got quite a bit of sun and it wouldn't hurt to check it out with a doctor before continuing his explorations. He had been a fool not to bring his hat; he had been on enough field expeditions in various parts of Mexico to know better. However, he hadn't figured on being away from his vehicle this long. One thing had led to another.

His theory was that the archeologists had miscalculated on their maps the extent of the domains of the Tlaxcala Confederation and portrayed the area the four tribes occupied as considerably smaller than these traditional enemies of the Aztecs really occupied. He was seeking proof that some of their towns had extended down this far toward the coast and into what was now the State of Vera Cruz. With luck, he hoped to run into ruins of one of the minor Tlaxcalan villages. But thus far the luck eluded him and his Mexican vacation was about over. He would have to get back to his teaching job in Austin.

Assistant Professor Donald Fielding had taken his doctorate in ethnology and was a specialist in Mexican cultures. He had also studied quite a bit of archeology and usually spent his vacations in various areas of Mexico.

He came to a rise in the ground and stared out over the barren countryside. He still couldn't place his location. And he couldn't spot the Land Rover. Damn it, how far had he wandered while under the effect of the sun?

He looked out over the horizon and distinguished the almost nineteen-thousand-foot former volcano, Mt. Orizaba, some miles to the south and west. Well, that gave him direction. He had walked west from the car. He brought out his small pocket compass and double-checked. All right, the Land Rover must be over that way.

Don Fielding had always prided himself on his sense of direction. So it was that he must have spent two hours looking for his camper before admitting he was hopelessly lost.

Well, not hopelessly. He knew the area he was in enough to be able to strike out in the general direction of the town of Coatepec which he was using for his base. Sooner or later, he would run into a path or minor road. Sooner or later, he would get to Coatepec where he could hire a truck or something to take him to get his camper. It was damned irritating was all, and he still felt nauseated.

He hadn't even had the good sense to bring his canteen along on his tramp. Undoubtedly, the touch of sun had brought on his current thirst. Lank and on the lean side—he looked like Gary Cooper but didn't know it—Don Fielding didn't usually perspire very much. Well, in an hour or so he'd probably run into some sort of human habitation. He'd have to take his chances with the water, running the risk of getting the Aztec two-step, since it hadn't occurred to him to carry his halazone tabs along with him.

Even as he walked toward the east, he checked what he did have. His clothes, of course. Good heavy-duty stuff, including a khaki bush jacket. His friends laughed at him, claimed he wanted to look like Papa Hemingway, especially when he wore the sun helmet. However, he was interested in the practicality. The bush jacket had four big pockets and you could stash almost as much in them as you could in a small pack.

Right now, there was precious little in them. He hadn't carried any food at all. Not even a candy bar for quick energy. He had a pack and a half of cigarettes, two folders of book matches, his wallet with both Mexican and American money, his wristwatch, a Swiss-army-type pocket knife with its multiplicity of blades and tools and minor gadgets, and his pocket compass. On his left hip he carried an army surplus entrenching tool in its khaki case and on his right a holstered .22 automatic, the very small Italian Beretta type. The entrenching tool unfolded in such a manner that you could utilize it either as a spade or a hoe. He used it for digging around such ruins as he found. The gun was for snakes. He had a box of shells for it in his shirt pocket; about forty-five rounds were still left, counting those in the gun.

He came to a dirt path, mentally flipped a coin, then turned right on it.

Fifteen minutes later he came over a hill and discovered a village next to a minor stream.

Calling it a village was stretching a point. It was actually one large building, reminiscent of some of the ruins of the Pueblo Indians in the American Southwest. It was obviously adobe, quadrangular, about two hundred feet to the side, with a courtyard in the center. One story high, the fifty or so rooms all opened into the courtyard.

He stood there for a moment and took it in. It was unbelievably primitive. No windows, no doors, no chimneys. In one corner of the courtyard was an improvised outdoor kitchen, women bustling around it. Other women were coming up from the stream, carrying water in the pots on their shoulders or atop their heads. He had seen similar dress in the back areas of Yucatan and Chiapas, but never this far north. They all wore the *cueitl*, an ankle-length undershirt, and the poncho-like *huipil*, a rectangular piece of cloth with a slit through which the head passed, the sides sewn except for armholes.

There was a multitude of children running and screaming in their play or rolling about in the dust. There were a few dozen turkeys pecking around, but, to Don's surprise, none of the moth-eaten dogs, which usually abounded in a Mexican village, to come forth and bark and growl their defiance of the stranger, though not usually brave enough to attack. The children were naked, and as he approached he noted that they were almost universally afflicted by an eye disease.

There were but a few men around, most of them old. Don imagined that the able-bodied were out in the fields.

As he came closer, he realized that he could not see a

single item of store-bought clothing or shoes—surprising even this far back in the hills. Denims and work shoes had come to Mexico with a vengeance years before. You seldom witnessed the picturesque homemade costumes of the past. Automated textile factories had taken over.

So far as shoes were concerned, everyone went bare-footed. No, that old man, seated up against the wall, wore what looked like sandals made of maguey fibers.

A ten-year-old spotted him and sent up a cry. All eyes zeroed in on the stranger and activity slid to a halt. He came to the large gate which opened into the courtyard and stood there politely. The Mexican, even the most backward, is long on the amenities.

A younger man came out of one of the rooms, a staff in one hand. When he came closer, his eyes popping at Don Fielding, it could be seen that the end of the staff had been sharpened and charred in the fire. It was, Don supposed, meant to be a weapon, a spear. Evidently these people were too poverty-stricken to afford even a few shotguns for game.

Don said in Spanish, "Good afternoon; I have lost my way. Could you tell me how to get to Coatepec?"

The other stared at him blankly. He took in Don's clothing. He had obviously never seen such an outfit, including the paratrooper-type boots Don wore.

It came to Don Fielding that they were even. He had never seen an outfit like the other's either, even in the backwaters of Chiapas or the Yucatan jungles where the natives still lived as had their ancestors and still largely dressed the same. He recognized the other's garb, but only through his studies. The man wore a *maxtli*, the Mexican version of the loincloth, a cincture that was passed between the legs and brought up about the waist, its two ends hanging in front and back. This one was embellished fairly attractively. He also wore a *tilmantli*, a mantle, which was a rectangular piece of woven cloth tied over one shoulder.

It was probably made from the coarse fibers of the maguey, Don decided.

He decided also that he had hit upon an absolute treasure. He would wow them up in Austin. They would send an expedition down to research the place. This was by far the most primitive settlement he had ever seen in Mexico. In the backwaters of the country were some fabulously primitive communities, but he had never seen anything like this. It was an anthropologist's dream.

He said again, in Spanish, "Good afternoon."

He doubted that he was in any physical danger, even if he hadn't had the gun. The Mexican peon is a passive type. The crime rate in the smaller hamlets was all but nonexistent. Except in Guerrero, of course, and some parts of Chihuahua.

The other was still blank.

It came to Don Fielding, with another thrill of surprise, that he had stumbled upon one of those communities where Spanish was not spoken. He had heard about them, had even been in one or two where Spanish was little understood, compared with the old Indian tongue, but if this young man didn't have Spanish, he doubted if anyone else in the village did.

Texas University at Austin supported the world's finest array of pre-Columbian studies. Even so, Don's Nahuatl dialect was tentative and ragged.

He said carefully in Nahuatl, "I am a stranger. I have become lost and wish to have directions to Coatepec."

The other said, in Nahuatl, "Magician, *this* is Coatepec."

Don shot a quick look around. Possibly the whole area was called Coatepec, as well as the town, something like the name "Travis County" back home. Or possibly he wasn't getting through. However, on some of his other field expeditions he'd had no difficulty using Nahuatl among Indians. There were tens of thousands of people within a hundred miles of Mexico City who spoke no other language even in this day. He wasn't particularly happy about the other calling him a magician. It was the equivalent of witch or warlock. They still believed in witches in wide areas of Mexico, and feared them. And a fearful man is a dangerous man.

Don said, "I am not a magician, only a stranger from *los Estados Unidos*, the United States. I seek only some water, perhaps something to eat, and the directions to the *big* town of Coatepec."

By this time at least two hundred others—women, children, and a few elderly men—had gathered and were pop-eyeing him. They were largely silent and, it came to him, fearful. Fearful of a solitary stranger? Inwardly, he shrugged.

The other made a gesture that would have done credit to a gentleman of the Renaissance. "You are a traveler. Coatepec is yours."

He turned and led the way and Don Fielding followed.

Almost ten years before, while he was still a student, he had made a trip through Turkey, spending a summer researching the Hittites. He had found incredible hospitality in isolated villages. Invariably he had been taken to the local headman's home, and invariably all the hospitality available had been extended to him. He was a traveler, and hence a gentleman, and was put up at the headman's home, fed, and otherwise refreshed, the otherwise including the presence of one of the maids to warm his bed at night with such treatment as he had never known in his own land. In primitive societies hospitality is the rule. It must be. The host today might be a traveler tomorrow.

His guide said, "I am Cuatlazol, Magician."

Don had expected him to be Manuel, or Jose, or even Jesus, but he said, "I am Don Fielding."

"A rare name," Cuatlazol said, nodding his head politely. "I will take you to the Tlachochcalcatl."

Don Fielding knew the term, though he had never been

exposed to it before in a Mexican town. It meant, roughly, the head chief, but he hadn't expected it to be applied to as small a settlement as this. He would really wow them in Austin when he reported this community. Jerry Black would go green.

The Tlachochcalcatl sat, cross-legged, on a mat in a room which was probably larger than most of the others in the pueblo. The only light was that which came through the doorway. He was a man of forty-odd which, Don Fielding knew, was beyond par for a Mexican in these primitive towns. He was gray of hair, wrinkled, and had an air of apprehension when Don was presented.

What was there about the aborigine that his eyes shifted in discomfort upon meeting the more civilized man? Don Fielding had run into it before. There is often a dignity, possibly beyond that of a city-reared sophisticate, but there is also a discomfort.

Cuatlazol said, respect for his chief in his voice, "The stranger magician is named Don Fielding, O Tlachochcalcatl. He says that he seeks Coatepec."

The older man nodded, but a frown came to his wrinkled face. "But this is Coatepec, Magician. Why should you seek us?"

Damn. It would seem unlikely that two villages would have the identical name in the same vicinity. Don grimaced and thought about it.

He said finally, "I am no magician, simply a traveler. But then where is the nearest big town?"

The old man nodded again and pointed. "A day's journey toward the sea, Zempoala."

Cempoala! The chief had given it the *old* Nahuatl pronunciation. Why, it must be thirty miles.

"Not Jalapa?"

The village chief looked over at Cuatlazol, who shook his head, then back at Don Fielding.

"I have never heard of this Jalapa, Magician."

Don sighed and gave up. He said, "May I have water and perhaps a little to eat? Then I'll go on."

Behind them, the inhabitants of the community building had crowded not too far from the doorway; though highly curious, they evidently did not wish to be too unsafely near the mysterious stranger.

The old man clapped his hands. "Food and drink for the magician!"

Evidently they were sticking to their guns. A magician he remained, no matter how he might deny it.

Several of the women scurried away to return in moments with an earthenware jug of water, a platter of the largest tortillas that Don had ever seen, and a bowl which, by the aroma, contained chili and beans.

There was no furniture in the room whatsoever, not to speak of table and chair, nor were there any utensils. Don brought forth his Swiss gadget knife and opened up the spoon. He took the jug of water first and, with a sigh for his halazone pills, drank down a considerable quantity. He could worry about getting *turista* later. He needed the water, particularly if he was going to take off across the country again.

They watched, wide-eyed, as he took up one of the tortillas, folded it into fours, dipped into the bowl of beans and peppers with his spoon, and began to eat. It came to him that they were probably so backward that they had no eating instruments and probably dipped up their food with a tortilla. Well, he had seen that before, further to the south.

The beans were surprisingly good and well flavored, although there didn't seem to be any meat or fat whatsoever. He wondered at the fact that they didn't seem to have pigs. He couldn't recall ever having seen a Mexican settlement, no matter how small, without a host of scrawny, tick-ridden hogs rooting around.

He stood there, eating out of the bowl which the Indian

woman still held for him, until he was satisfied. He folded
two more of the large tortillas into small rectangles and put
them into a top pocket of his bush jacket just for luck. He
folded the spoon back into the overgrown knife, returned it
to his pocket, and turned to the chief.

He brought his wallet forth and extracted a ten-peso
note. That should be plenty, a few cents American but
probably a small fortune here. He handed it to the chief.

The other looked at it and blinked. He turned it over and
looked at the other side, then up at Don again.

"But what is this, O Magician?"

Don said, "A slight gift, in return for your hospitality."

"But what is it, Magician?"

Then it came to Don. He had run into this once in the
rear areas of Chiapas where he had been investigating
some Mayan ruins. They didn't trust paper money. He
took the bill back and fished into his pants pocket and
came up with four pesos, a fifty-centavo piece, and three
twenties. He handed them over. It was the total of the
change he had.

All in the vicinity who could see the money gasped. The
chief's eyes shone like obsidian. You would have thought
he had been given a treasure.

"I'm sorry I don't have more," Don told him. Could
these people be that poverty-stricken? Surely they had to
have *some* money for such things as salt, thread, needles,
nails. You can't have a completely self-sufficient economy,
even on this level.

He said, "It grows late. I shall have to be on my way.
Thank you for your hospitality, old one."

Cuatlazol led the way back to the courtyard and to the
gate. They were trailed by the whole village, save for the
chief, who remained, in dignity, in his pathetic throne
room.

At the gate, Cuatlazol pointed. "Zempoala is that way,
O Magician. A large town of the Totonacs."

Don was vaguely surprised that he hadn't been directed toward Vera Cruz; it couldn't be much further from this point. He checked his compass, the other staring at it wide-eyed. Cuatlazol had obviously never seen one before.

Don bade him farewell and took off in the indicated direction. In actuality, he had no intention of attempting to get all the way to Cempoala. Sooner or later, if he stuck to a straight course, he would run into a road, no matter how small. Follow it long enough and he'd run into either a town or a bigger road with vehicles. In this country, any car or truck he hailed would stop and give him a lift.

However, he didn't come to a road, nor even much in the way of paths. He certainly was having the luck of the Irish, damn it. The day was getting toward dusk. Not a town, not a hamlet, not even isolated farms. This was insane. There had to be *some* roads.

He wasn't particularly worried. He'd parked the Land Rover out in the open, but in this area there was small chance that anyone would run into it. Even if they did, the inhabitants of the vicinity were painfully honest. It was quite unlikely that they would pilfer its contents. It was simply irritating, and time was running out on him. He wanted to get to his explorations and wrap things up in time to return to Austin and his job.

Night caught him in a mountain pass, and "caught" was the only apt term. The wind blew chill and he could make out snow on the nearest peak. Happily, he was able to scare up enough mesquite to build a fire, and he snugged himself into a small cave, under a ledge. The tortillas he had put in his pocket were a godsend; so also were two of his cigarettes. He dozed a bit before dawn, but it was the most miserable night he could ever remember having spent.

He took off groggily at first dawn, as soon as he could see well enough to walk without falling. There was a narrow path now and he was going downhill, so he made good time. Finally, far ahead, he could make out the sea and a fairly large community. The buildings gleamed almost like silver from this distance; highly whitewashed, he assumed. It was undoubtedly Cempoala. He had never been in the town, which was noted for being quite an archeological zone, but he would have thought it to be larger than this. It was located on the edge of a small river, and shortly he was proceeding along the stream, the path somewhat wider by now.

As he got nearer and was able to make out individual buildings and even some of the people, he realized that he had stumbled on a movie set. He had heard, vaguely, that one of the big American producers was in Mexico making an historical film that rivaled *Cleopatra* in its all-out expense. At least it would be interesting to see. He could take a taxi or bus back to Jalapa and the real Coatepec later in the day and reclaim his vehicle.

As he got closer to the environs of the town, he began scowling in puzzlement. Various things didn't fit. The buildings on the outskirts didn't ring true. He had no idea that movie sets were this permanent-looking. He could see no movie equipment, cameras, lights, or sound equipment, and though he had never been on a movie set, it didn't look right. Or rather, he thought with a prickle of gooseflesh, it looked *too* right.

He began to pass various extras, who seemed to be conducting themselves as though they were on camera—but they weren't: children playing in the street, costumed women going up and down carrying water jugs or produce from the market, Indian warriors beplumed and with primitive weapons in their hands. And then he rounded a corner and almost ran into three soldiers done up in the costume of sixteenth-century Spain.

A cold finger went dit-dit-dit up his spine.

This was no movie set.

Chapter Two

Or, if it was, these three were going overboard in their attempt to achieve authenticity. The two bearded ones wore helmets, breastplates, and swords and carried pikes, or perhaps they were halberds. Don wasn't particularly up on medieval weapons. The younger one, possibly in his early twenties, wore a velvet cap rather than a helmet and was without armor. His sword seemed lighter and was more highly decorated than those of the others. He was darkly handsome in the Latin tradition, almost to the point of being pretty.

They wasted no time. The younger man's rapier flashed out. The two pikes were presented, quickly, efficiently. The sword's point was at Don Fielding's throat.

"By my soul, a stranger," the young one lisped in Spanish. It wasn't the deliberate Castilian lisp of the educated Spaniard but evidently a slight impediment in speech. He had an open enough countenance; chestnut hair curled close to his head, and his frame seemed strong and sinewy. He could have been one of Don's students, save for his get-up. There was a certain undefinable insolence in his eye, a mocking.

Don said evenly, "What is all this about?"

"Ah-ha, so you speak our language. Who are you, my

sky-high friend? Where are you from? What manner of garb is that?''

Don said, ''If you'll take that damned pig-sticker away from my throat, I'll answer your questions. I am lost. I'm trying to find transportation back to my vehicle. My name's Don Fielding.''

''*Don* Fielding. Then you claim to be of gentle blood?'' The point of the sword withdrew slightly.

''Why . . . why I suppose so.'' Don must remember to speak the other's Castilian, rather than the Mexican dialect with which he was more familiar. His Spanish was excellent; it had been his major language when a student and he'd had a lot of practice since. The swordsman's own terminology seemed somewhat archaic but was perfectly understandable and obviously his native tongue.

The other came to a sudden decision and slipped the sword back into its scabbard.

He took the feathered velvet cap from his head and made a sweeping bow—Errol Flynn couldn't have done it better. ''Gonzalo de Sandoval, your servant, Don Fielding. And now if you will accompany me to the Captain-General, we shall have more of your story.''

He turned and headed off, leading the way. There was nothing else for it, and Don followed. The two soldiers, silent all this time, brought up the rear. He was still under guard.

As they progressed, Don took in more of the town. No, this was no movie set. He didn't have the vaguest idea of where he was, or what was up—but *this was no movie set.* It was all very real.

The houses were largely similar to the community building he had seen the day before. That is, they were single-storied, many-roomed, and invariably built about a courtyard. Even the smaller ones had a good many rooms. There were no doors, no windows, no chimneys, but all was spotless, even the streets. The place had a peculiar smell—

not unpleasant, but rich with exotic promise. The smaller places were thatched with palm leaves and there were usually colorfully decorated mats or rugs over the entries to the rooms. Flowers and trees were everywhere. It was an extremely beautiful town, no matter how strange.

The throngs of people in the streets were all in costume and of the same type he had seen the day before, save of higher quality. The women, in particular, had highly colorful cotton dresses and bodices which were embroidered in such fashion as to remind Don Fielding of the dress of bishops and abbots of the Roman Catholic Church. A great many of the less richly dressed were barefooted; those who seemed to be in better circumstance, or were wearing their best, for whatever festive reason, wore sandals of leather, some quite ornate. Some of the men wore ear plugs, or even lip plugs. How far out in primitive costume could you get?

They passed an open area containing a market. It seemed literally to overflow with produce. Largely, it was similar to a score of other Mexican town markets Don had witnessed in his time, though, strangely, some of the products he would have expected were not evident. Bread, for instance, or chickens; nor, for that matter, did he spot either beef or pork in the section devoted to meats. And where were the inevitable ice-cream vendors? Whoever heard of a Mexican market without ice-cream vendors? And, now that he thought about it, there were no refreshment stands selling beer.

But it was the costume that threw him off. The market contained thousands of both sexes and all ages, and every single one was in costume. Why, in the name of anything holy?

As they progressed, from time to time they passed small groups of others in the armor and costume similar to that of his following guards and the lad who had named himself Gonzalo de Sandoval. All were armed and all were armored; most wore helmets, though some were bareheaded. Almost all were black- or red-bearded. They would look after Don and his escort curiously, but none addressed them. Don got the feeling that they thought him a strange sight, but they were used to strange sights.

In the center of town was a large walled enclosure which he estimated to be several acres in area. As they approached, he could make out sentries patrolling the walls, pikes in hand. There must have been some twenty of them.

They entered through a large gateway, walking briskly. Immediately inside was a guard of ten and two small cannon, each about four feet long. Don was no authority on muzzle-loading cannon, but unless he was mistaken they were falconets. They were mounted in as primitive a manner as he could have imagined.

Two of the guard carried matchlock arquebuses, two others crossbows. The rest, except for one who was obviously an officer, were armed with pikes.

Sandoval said, "San Tomas," and continued on his way. Don followed. The enclosure seemed to teem with soldiers in the same costume as those with whom he had already come in contact, hundreds of them. All over again, his reeling mind considered the possibility that this was one great movie set.

To his left was the most beautifully reconstructed pyramid Don had ever seen. But, no, it couldn't be a reconstruction. Not even in Chichen Itza had he come into anything like it. It *had* to have been built comparatively recently. There were some fifteen pyramids, temples, and other buildings within the enclosure, all done with the utmost authenticity, so far as he could make out without further investigation.

They headed briskly for the largest of the temples. At least, he supposed it was a temple. It reminded him of various Mayan ruins, including the House of the Governor in Uxmal, though on a smaller scale. It was set up on a platform and they had to mount the stone steps. To the right was another pyramid and to the left what looked like an altar. Don looked about as they mounted the steps. Besides what he quickly estimated at about three hundred of the medieval-clothed white men were possibly a hundred Indians, both men and women. Some of them were dressed in black. Priests?

At the top of the stairway was a long rectangular building with various doorways, highly ornate in the decoration of the stone facing. Don Fielding was reminded of some of the late Aztec reliefs in the National Museum in Mexico City.

Before one of the entries were two more sentries, both armed with crossbows. The weapons seemed to be in mint condition. Whoever was behind all this, whatever *all this* was, was a demon for authenticity. Don couldn't imagine what could have motivated this breathtaking reconstruction.

Sandoval lisped to the sentries, "San Tomas." It was obviously the password of the day. He and Don Fielding entered; the two pike men remained behind.

They were in a room about twenty-four feet long and twelve feet wide. It had no connections with the rooms on either side. It was easily sixteen feet to the ceiling and was naked of furniture except for an improvised wooden desk in its middle behind which, on a folding wooden chair, sat another Spaniard—Don assumed they were Spaniards. Certainly that was their language, as well as their costume.

There was also present, standing, a girl of about twenty or so. She was an Indian and one of the most attractive Don Fielding could ever remember having seen. She was more than averagely light of complexion and her features were quite Caucasian. Her dress was similar to the Mayan. She wore the *kub*, a single piece of decorated woven cloth with holes for the arms and a square-cut opening for the head. Underneath, she wore a longer petticoat-like dress highly decorated and fringed. Don was reminded of the sack-dress style of some years ago in the States. She was barefooted.

There were also present a priest garbed in robes and a youngster of possibly eleven who was done up in costume approximating that of his elders, even to a light sword.

The one behind the desk said, while staring at Don Fielding, "*Hola*! Gonzalo, what have we here?" In Spanish, of course.

The youthful Sandoval chuckled. "I have brought him here in hopes you would tell me, my Captain." He turned back to Don and made a flowing gesture of his hand in way of introduction.

"Captain-General Hernando Cortes, Don Fielding."

And the cold finger traced its way up the spine of Don Fielding once again.

The other was a man somewhere in his middle thirties, pale of complexion, large dark eyes in a small head with a weak jaw. Though he was seated, the man was less than average in stature, though, for that matter, so seemed all of the rest of the white men he had seen today, not to speak of the Indians. He was obviously a man of vigor and one of intelligence. Or would you say cunning? He was richly dressed, compared to the others, and wore a gold chain around his neck. He radiated command, cheerful temperament, good will.

And Don Fielding did not like him.

Beyond the desk Cortes nodded, made a gesture of his own toward the priest, and said, "Fray Bartoleme de Olmedo."

Don said, "My pleasure, Father." He looked emptily at the girl.

"And this is Malinche," said Sandoval.

Hernando Cortes said, in surprise, "Doña Marina. She has been baptized. But although you are a stranger, evidently you have heard of me, *Don* Fielding."

"Yes," Don said, his minding reeling. "I have heard of Hernando Cortes."

Sandoval said, "He claims that he is lost and wanted transportation back to his . . . vehicle."

"Vehicle?" Cortes repeated. "But there are no vehicles in all New Spain. What kind of vehicle?"

Though his mind was spinning with the impossibility of it all, Don Fielding knew he was going to have to play this with care. With great care.

He said, "In my land we call them campers."

"And where is your land?"

"Far to the north. You know nothing of it. It is not even on your charts."

"But you speak Spanish. A somewhat oddly accented Spanish, but surprisingly good."

"There are some Spanish in my country. They have come from . . . Puerto Rico, in particular."

"Ah," the priest said. "Poor shipwrecked souls, undoubtedly."

Don didn't answer that aloud, though he muttered in English, under his breath, "In a way."

Cortes was staring him up and down with continuing amazement. He said, "This vehicle of yours, where is it?"

"About a day's journey to the west."

"To the west! Toward the lands of the Tlaxcalans?"

"On the border of Tlaxcala."

The eyes of the Captain-General narrowed. "You name yourself a gentleman, yet you carry no sword. Not even in this country of savages who have never heard of our Saviour."

"I am a scholar, not a soldier."

"My faith, you must be a madman to travel about without a weapon and by yourself. What is that?" He pointed to the entrenching tool which hung from Don's belt on his left hip.

Don said, "A tool which I use in my scholarly research."

The Spaniards evidently assumed that the small holster on his right hip contained the same. None asked him about it.

Cortes thought for a moment. He said, "This far land of yours—what is its name?"

"The United States of America. And it is very far—in more ways than one, I fear."

"I see. Is it a rich land?"

"It is the richest land in the world, Don Hernando."

"My faith," the other said, his eyes narrow again. "Perhaps one day we shall visit it, eh, Gonzalo?"

Young Sandoval chuckled.

Cortes said, "However, for the present we are interested in the domains of Montezuma, which lie to the west and beyond those of Tlaxcala. You must understand, Don Fielding, that we are an exploring expedition from Cuba with the intention of opening up trade with this area."

Fray Olmedo said, a touch of reproof in his voice, "And to convert the heathen, my son."

"Yes, of course," Cortes said. "On my faith as a gentleman, that is the most important feature of our expedition. Within a few days we plan to take up the march inland toward this fabled city of Tenochtitlan to meet with Montezuma. The route will take us through Tlaxcala. Perhaps you will join us, Don Fielding; we may recover your vehicle on the way, though I doubt that your animal will have survived for such a period of time."

Don didn't bother to tell him that his particular vehicle was a horseless carriage and that, so far as he knew, it was a very long distance away in more than just space.

He was under no misapprehensions about why he was being invited to join the expedition. The Captain-General wanted to hear more of this rich land far to the north. He was evidently capable of already planning beyond Tenochtitlan.

Don Fielding hesitated. He was without food, trans-

portation, or locally acceptable funds. He was without
employment and without any idea whatsoever of how to
acquire a position. In short, he had no alternative.

He said, "You are much too kind, Don Hernando."

Cortes said briskly, "Very well, it is done. Gonzalo,
see that Don Fielding is given quarters and provisions."

All this time, the girl, Doña Marina, as they called her,
had remained quiet, her intelligent dark eyes taking Don
in. She was evidently set back by his height. He towered
more than a full foot over her. It occurred to Don that she
didn't speak Spanish and had been unable to follow the
conversation. He opened his mouth to say something in
Nahuatl, but then closed it again. No one present knew
that he was acquainted with the language and he doubted
that any of the Spanish spoke it. It wouldn't hurt to keep
the fact to himself; it might be an advantage on some
occasion. He could use advantages.

Instead, even as he turned to follow young Sandoval, he
said to Fray Olmedo, "Padre, could you tell me the exact
date?"

The priest said, "Why, it is the tenth of August, in the
year of Our Lord, 1519."

"I was afraid you'd say something like that," Don
Fielding said emptily.

Chapter Three

Don and Sandoval walked side by side, without benefit of guards this time. At the bottom of the steps they turned left and headed toward another large temple, this one with some strange constructions that looked like nothing so much as chimneys out in front. The temple itself was raised up on an extensive platform and to its right was a large rectangular building, obviously living quarters.

Sandoval was saying, a mischievous element in his slight stammer as he glanced at Don from the side of his eyes, "And what did you think of our Captain-General? We come from the same town, you know, Medellin, in Spain."

Don said carefully, "I think him the type of man who succeeds in life."

The young dandy chuckled. "By my soul, that he is. Though hell should bar the way."

He gestured around the large courtyard at the various temples and the living quarters of the priests. "The Captain-General is a stickler for discipline and care. Upon reaching Cempoala and seeing the nature of this enclosure, he immediately marched the priests and their assistants out of here and the army took over. We are all quartered within the walls. None is allowed to leave without permission, and none alone, though these Totonacs are not a warrior people. It is no wonder that the Tenochas milk them of tribute. Besides Cempoala, there must be some fifty villages in this land. By my soul, I am unable to understand why the Great Montezuma does not annex the whole area outright.''

"Because he doesn't know how," Don muttered.

"I beg your pardon, Don Fielding?"

Don said impatiently, "I told you that I was a scholar. One of the things I have studied is the governmental system of the Aztec Confederation.''

The younger man looked at him. "The who?"

"The nation you are about to move against. It is composed of three tribes occupying three cities in the Mexican valley, and all are of a common heritage. But having primitive institutions, they have no manner of assimilating new towns, towns with other heritages, into their society. They can defeat others and wrest tribute from them, but they don't know how to bring them into their government.''

Don grunted. "They could learn a few lessons from the Incas in that respect.''

Sandoval shook his head and laughed. "A scholar you must be, Don Fielding, for I cannot understand aught you say. But here we are. Since you are a gentleman, I will quarter you with Diego de Ordaz, one of our captains of foot. An excellent soldier. During the battle of Ceutla, by my soul, he killed more Indians than the plague.''

They ascended the stone stairs and entered the building through an archway. This opened into a patio surrounded by the many-roomed buildings to which Don was becoming accustomed. Sandoval led the way to one of them, brushed aside the mat curtain which served as a door.

"*Hola*, Diego!" he called.

The room, perhaps twelve feet square, was, as always in Indian architecture, windowless, and the door was the sole source of light. It was also furnitureless, unless a Spanish leather trunk, about the size of a footlocker, up against one wall, was to be counted. However, there were colorful rugs on the walls, and mats and bedding on the floor; all was spotlessly clean.

On the bedding, in armor, was sprawled a husky, red-bearded Spaniard, his sword drawn in hand. He didn't look comfortable, but he did look tough, Don decided.

His eyes had shot open upon Sandoval's call, and now he sat up, staring at Don Fielding.

Sandoval laughed. "Your new roommate, Diego! Don Fielding. A mysterious stranger from a fabulously rich nation to the north!"

The other growled, "Why not put him with the other prisoners?"

Sandoval turned to Don. "See? There is no chivalry in this world. It is a wonder our brave Diego does not wish to throw you to the mastiffs."

Ordaz, like all the others before him, ran his eyes up and down Don's outlandish clothing in extreme puzzlement. Obviously, this was no Indian, especially in view of the blue of Don's eyes and relative lightness of hair and complexion, in spite of his suntan.

Don attempted a bow, although he had never bowed before in his life, save in a grammar school play in which he had done a sloppy job of being Launcelot.

"A pleasure to meet you, Don Diego," he said in his best Spanish.

The other was taken aback all over again. "By my beard," he snorted. "You speak our tongue!"

Sandoval said, still amused, "Don Fielding is a noble-man from a far land to the north where a ship from Puerto Rico was wrecked. Thus he was able to learn Spanish. It teems, so he tells us, in wealth. The Captain-General has added him to our expedition."

"By my beard!" the other repeated, astounded.

Sandoval said, "He will eat in our soldier's mess and be

. . . in your charge. The Captain-General would know more of this United States from whence he comes. Perhaps, one day, we shall journey there.''

"If you live to be four hundred, you might," Don Fielding said under his breath. "And I wonder how this conquering army would react to a battle tank."

Diego de Ordaz had come to his feet and now returned his sword to its scabbard, after his eyes had automatically checked and found that Don was unarmed.

It came to Don Fielding that this was not the day of the handgun. Matchlock arquebuses, yes; slow-loading muskets that took an age to operate and were, in actuality, less effective than the more common crossbows. Until he used it for the first time, these people would have no idea of what his modern little Beretta .22 automatic was. He had some forty-five shells all together. It behooved him to nurse them. In spite of the smallness of the caliber, a .22 rifle cartridge was deadly when accurately placed, and he was a fairly good shot.

Sandoval said to him, "You have eaten?"

"Not since yesterday."

"By my soul, you must hunger. Diego, will you take our new comrade to the kitchens? Undoubtedly, the Indian wenches will still have ample for Don Fielding's needs. I must continue my patrol of the town." He turned back to Don, took off his cap, and made another flourishing bow. "Your servant, Don Fielding." There was a mocking twinkle in his eye. He turned and left.

The husky redbeard said, "Come. We will see what we can find. This Indian food, you'll discover, is less than civilized. I yearn for the oil and garlic, the meat and fruits, the wines of Spain. But at least it is filling."

He lead the way through the mat-covered door and Don followed. They exited into the patio and hence onto the terrace and to the left. The kitchens, so called, were out in the open. Long poles supported a thatch roof; otherwise there was no protection against rain or wind. The Cempoalans had obviously not advanced to the point that their buildings provided for fireplaces, not to speak of stoves. The Indian women had improvised rocks to support large pots which bubbled over the fires. Over others were flat ceramic pans.

Ordaz, as they came up, called to a couple of them, "Food, you ugly wenches! Food!" He pointed at the pots and then at Don Fielding. "Food!"

Undoubtedly, they couldn't understand a word he said, but his gestures were obvious. One of them, a middle-aged drab, squatted down next to a pile of what looked like coarse dough, took up a handful of it, and began to pat out a tortilla. She was deft, and in moments it was round, paper-thin, and about a foot and a half across, the bread of the Mexican Indian. She put it on one of the flat pans over the fire and started another one.

Ordaz took up a bowl and handed it to Don. He indicated one of the pots of stew. "Try this, Don Fielding. Not too bad. Fowl in a thick sauce containing various rare foods of this cursed land, including what they call chocolate and a ground nut unknown in Europe."

There were some wooden ladles. Don took one up and plunged it into the thick stew. It was, he discovered, an early version of turkey *mole*, the national dish of Mexico. The sauce was almost black in color and it turned out that the red-bearded Ordaz had been correct. It contained not only several kinds of peppers, both sweet and hot, but chocolate and peanuts as well. It was excellent.

Don had delved into his pocket and come forth with his Swiss knife. He extracted the spoon, picked up the now-done tortilla from where it had been baking, and sat down on a block of worked stone which formed the first step of the platform of the house in which they were quartered. He began to eat. The tortilla was certainly the real article, complete with grit from the stone grinder. Don soon learned to chew carefully; some of that grit could chip a tooth.

Diego Ordaz was staring at the knife. "By my beard!" he said. "Now that is a new one. May I see it, Don Fielding?"

Don demonstrated the knife, including several of the blades and gadgets. It even had a small set of scissors.

The other was delighted. "'Tis a small miracle. The most delicate craftsmen of Toledo produce no such thing. From whence comes this mechanism, Don Fielding?"

It was no use telling him Switzerland. The question would then arise how Don had gotten it into his possession. He said, "From my own far land. We have highly trained craftsmen there."

Ordaz handed the knife back so that Don could continue his meal.

The Spaniard said thoughtfully, "So you do. Tell me, Don Fielding, are your armies advanced to the point where they utilize swords of steel, armor of steel, arquebuses, and crossbows?"

Don finished a leg of the stewed turkey and tossed the bone into a nearby wicker scrap basket. "Well, no," he said deliberately. "Our armies are not armed with such weapons. Frankly, Don Ordaz, I was surprised to see them in the hands of your own army."

The other was not a devious man. He could not keep the gleam from his eyes. He said, "And tell me, Don Fielding, what do you use for money in this far land of yours? By my faith, these Indian dogs use none at all. They trade only by barter."

Don Fielding was well aware of the trend of the other's thoughts, but the good food was working on him to the point where his spirits had risen.

He said absently, "Why, in our land the currency is based on gold. Tons of gold which the government holds in reserve."

"Tons!" the Spaniard blurted. "You exaggerate to make your point, surely."

"No," Don said, accepting another tortilla from the Indian woman who brought it over to him. "I meant tons. And our government is making every attempt to secure still more. They think they possess not enough."

"Your mines must be rich!"

Don made an expression to indicate he was considering that. "Well, not so rich as they once were, since we have mined them so extensively." He sighed deeply. "It is necessary for our government to import gold from still further lands so as to provide plenty for the rings, bracelets, and necklaces our women love."

The Spaniard's eyes were narrow now and Don was reminded of Cortes, whose expression had also gone greedy when told that the United States, to the north, was the richest land in the world.

Ordaz said, "Your women wear much jewelry, eh?"

Don said idly, "Practically every adult woman wears at least a gold ring. It is a custom. And most often another ring, one set with a diamond. Part of the prestige of her husband is determined by the size of the diamond he buys her upon their betrothal."

The other's eyes were bulging. "On your faith, Don Fielding?"

"On my faith," Don said, finishing the last of his turkey stew and folding up his knife. Suddenly the weariness hit him. The past two days had not been easy and he had slept hardly an unfitful moment the night before.

He said, "If you will pardon me, I think I shall return to our quarters, Don Diego, and rest for a time."

Ordaz cleared his throat. "Very well. I will not disturb you. Indeed, it is necessary that I go to the Captain-General to report. Ah, that is, to see if he has any orders for me. I am in charge of the night watch."

He turned and hurried off in the direction of the Cortes command post.

Don looked after him and cursed himself inwardly. Why had he felt it necessary to prod the other in that manner? Shooting off his mouth for the sake of amusement would get him nowhere. The cupidity of these mercenaries had already been whetted by what he had told Cortes and Sandoval; there had been no point in increasing it. That was the difficulty in having a sense of humor. He snorted inwardly as he came to his feet. A squad of Green Berets armed with automatic rifles would take the whole Spanish expeditionary force, had there been any chance of meeting between the two eras.

He walked his way back to the room in which he was quartered with Diego de Ordaz, made a bed for himself out of three or four of the mats and rugs, and flaked out on it. However, in spite of his extreme weariness, or perhaps because of it, he didn't find immediate sleep. There was too much on his seething mind.

Assistant Professor Donald Fielding had been no more exposed to the concept of time travel than is the average man. It had simply never occurred to him to consider it seriously and he had never, as a social scientist rather than as a student of the physical sciences, delved into what serious material there was on the subject. He had never even heard of the theory of alternate universes, or space-time continua, or considered the nature of time. It simply flowed, didn't it? Everyone knew that.

As a boy, he had read the usual time travel classics such as Wells's *The Time Machine* and Mark Twain's *A Connecticut Yankee In King Arthur's Court,* and he vaguely remembered a movie he had seen revived on television entitled *Berkeley Square*, in which Tyrone Power had mysteriously returned to the age of Doctor Johnson in London and attempted to introduce the steam engine, the locomotive, and the electric light. However, it had not even remotely occurred to him to find anything but entertainment in such stories.

He tried to be logical in facing the reality of the situation in which he found himself, and couldn't. There was no place from which to start in trying to think it all out logically.

He must face the fact that *somehow* he had been transported, if that was the word, to the early sixteenth century. He had to accept reality. Here he was. He was existing in the camp of Hernando Cortes, immediately prior to that adventurer's march inland toward what is now—he caught himself there—Mexico City and was then—he caught himself again—Tenochtitlan.

He had come through time, or crossed the time barrier, or had been reincarnated backwards, or whatever had happened to him, and here he was.

No, he had to reject that reincarnation bit. He was in possession of physical items such as his gun and wristwatch. So it wasn't a matter of only his mind, or psyche, or whatever, crossing the void. *He*, clothing and all, had crossed it.

Now that he thought about it, he vaguely remembered reading an article about two female English schoolteachers of the early twentieth century who had written a book claiming that they had been walking through the gardens of Versailles when suddenly they were thrown back into the time of Marie Antoinette. At the time he had thought it utter nonsense and hadn't even finished the article. If they had written a book on the matter, in their own age, it meant that they had not only traveled into the past but had returned to their own present.

Could that happen to him? That is, was it possible that he might slip back into his own era as easily and quickly as he had slipped into this one?

He traced back his memories of the day before. That shimmering of the air, that supposed sun stroke. That must have been when it happened. No wonder he couldn't find his Land Rover camper. It wasn't there. And no wonder Coatepec hadn't looked like the Coatepec he had known. Far from the modern village, complete with Pemex gasoline station and all the rest, he had found the original primitive Indian pueblo, a fairly large adobe community house with some six or seven hundred inhabitants.

But *what* had happened? He simply didn't know. One moment he had been in the latter part of the twentieth century. The next, he was in the early part of the sixteenth. How and why, he hadn't the vaguest idea and he strongly suspected he never would.

It occurred to him, sourly, that as a student of Mexican ethnology and archeology he had the most unrivaled opportunity of all time. But to what end? Who would ever know? And then the thought came to him that he could emulate Sir Boss in Twain's *Connecticut Yankee*, that is, write it all down and stash it away somewhere where future generations could find it. But what good would that do him? Scholarship for scholarship's sake? He grunted. All his instincts now told him, *survive, survive;* nothing else mattered. And he had a sneaking suspicion that survival was not going to be easy. He didn't trust the gold-hungry Spanish, and since he was familiar with what was to happen in the next few months, he had no reason to believe that the Mexican Indians were going to have much regard for any white man in the near future.

His mind went back, nagged, to the time travel paradox. How *could* this be happening? It simply made no sense at all.

Suppose that, driven by self-defense, he killed one of these Indians. It would mean that all the descendants of that Indian would never live. There were four hundred years or so between his period and this. Say, some twenty generations. How many descendants would a man have in twenty generations? He didn't trouble to figure it out mathematically, but he assumed it would be at least hundreds of thousands, possibly millions. Presidents of Mexico, famous generals such as Pancho Villa, world-known artists such as Diego Rivera. Rich men, poor men, beggars, and thieves, all would have had this Indian's genes in them. Nor was Mexico alone involved. How many of the descendants of the Indian had gone back to Spain, the blood slowly to be diffused into tens of thousands of Spaniards? How many had gone to the United States to breed there? How many to Europe? In four hundred years a bloodline could be diffused all over the world.

Now that he thought about it, it needn't even be an Indian or, for that matter, a Spaniard. Suppose he shot a rabbit? As a result, the literally millions of descendants of that rabbit would never be born. Perhaps, as a result, thousands of coyotes, who largely feed on rabbits, would be kept from their ordinary diet. Perhaps, as a result, they would turn to pulling down lambs or kid goats. And, as a result of that, the owners would be thrown into destruction— with all the developments that might mean, including revolution.

To take it from another view, suppose he managed to survive and impregnate one of these Indian women, or Spanish, assuming there were any Spanish women in the camp and he vaguely recalled from his history that there were a few. That would mean that his descendants, by the time the twentieth century rolled around, might number hundreds of thousands. Hundreds of thousands who hadn't been there, actually, when he lived in the twentieth century. Might some of them be presidents, great inventors, statesmen, generals, or others who shaped the destinies of men? If so, his world would no longer be the world he knew. They would have altered it.

And suppose . . .

He drifted off, at long merciful last, into sleep.

Chapter Four

He was awakened by a fumbling at the holster of his pistol.

Taking a note from the fact that the burly Diego de Ordaz had seen fit to sleep fully clothed, even to his steel breastplate, and with sword in hand, Don Fielding had retained all of his own clothing, save his bush jacket, which he had folded over his head in the way of a pillow. The weather in August, in this part of Mexico, was hot and humid since, after all, it was the tropics. There was a cooling breeze off the sea, but it was still hot.

For a brief moment, when he awoke, he didn't know where he was and the room was pitch dark; however, before he thought it out, he grabbed the hand before it could wrestle the gun out. At least he grabbed a wrist, and his first thought was that it must be that of a woman due to its size.

"Who's that?" he barked.

A tremulous voice answered, "It is Orteguilla, page of the Captain-General, Don Fielding. He has sent me to invite you to dine with his captains."

Don held on to the wrist for the time. His eyes were already becoming used to the dark. Outside, it was night, but there were plenty of stars in the sky and the mat at the door had been pushed aside for more air. He could make out the other now. It was the eleven-year-old who had been present when Sandoval had introduced him to Cortes and the others. He had thought at the time that the youngster's eyes had a shifty something in them.

The boy whined, "Please, Don Fielding. It was so dark; I knew not where I was touching you." He tried to pull his arm away.

"You lie, *niño*." However, he turned the other loose and sat up on his improvised bed. "Where is this supper to be?"

"In the room next to the one in which you met the Captain-General. It is to begin in half an hour, Don Fielding." The boy scampered to his feet and darted out the door.

The night was cooling off. Don stood and got back into his jacket. Nature was beginning to call and he wondered what the Indians did in the way of providing toilet facilities. Certainly, there couldn't be any sewage system in a building as primitive as this. He was to find later that they used ceramic slop buckets, the contents of which were taken each day out into the fields to be utilized as fertilizer. The Spanish, however, had dug latrines, military-style, not liking the stench of the buckets in the rooms in which they slept.

He left the room and walked around behind the rectangular building without meeting anyone along the way, although he could still see a considerable number of the Spanish soldiery milling about the enclosure. For want of a better place to do his business, he relieved himself up against the wall.

In half an hour he would be confronting Hernando Cortes again. Meanwhile, he had time to kill. There was a set of stone steps leading up to the top of the wall which enclosed the giant courtyard. The night was cooling and beautiful. He ascended the steps with the idea of looking out over the town and getting a clearer picture of it. He could make out a figure at the northwest corner. One of the sentries? But, no, the other wore a woman's clothing.

He shrugged and approached. One of the natives, undoubtedly. He was somewhat surprised that the Spanish allowed them on the walls. He was going to pass her and walk on.

She turned and looked at him and he realized that it was Malinche, or, as the Spanish called her now that she had been baptized, Doña Marina. She acted as an interpreter for Captain-General Cortes.

Before thinking, he said to her in Nahuatl, "Good evening. It is a beautiful night." Then felt like biting his tongue. He had intended to keep his knowledge of the language a secret, at least for the time being.

She was surprised and cocked her head slightly to look at him. "It is the newcomer, Don Fielding. But you speak my mother tongue."

"Yes," he said. For some reason he knew not, he decided to be frank with her. "However, I would rather you not tell the Captain-General, or anyone else, for that matter."

She frowned. Now that he was more used to the night light, he could make out the beauty of her face. She had a generous, good mouth, eyes as soft and dark as those of a deer, braided hair, its very blackness accented by the fact that her complexion was almost as fair as Don's own and considerably more so than a good many of the Spanish. Beyond good looks, she had an elusive attractiveness Don couldn't quite put a finger upon, something possibly based on pride, but it added to her desirability.

She said, "But why do you not wish my lord, the Captain-General, to know? He would be delighted to have your services as an interpreter. I am afraid I am inferior, since I know so few words of Spanish."

"Possibly because I am not sure that I trust these

Spaniards. They are greedy, rapacious, vicious, and cruel. And they are here in Mexico for no good cause . . . from the viewpoint of you inhabitants of this land.''

''But you are Spanish yourself!''

''No. I am a white man, but not Spanish. I am an American.''

''I have never heard of that tribe. But you are wrong about the Captain-General, who does me the honor of having taken me to his bed. He comes to this land to bring the new gods, Mary and her Babe. The old gods were evil, especially those of the Tenochas such as Huitzilopochtli to whom the priests sacrifice large numbers.''

Don Fielding considered himself an agnostic, to which he usually added *with atheistic tendencies*. He said, ''All gods are evil, since they are the inventions of men. If they do not begin evil, they are soon corrupted by their priests who supposedly interpret their desires.''

The girl's chin went up slightly. ''Not Mary and the Babe. They are pure.''

''Perhaps,'' Don said sarcastically. ''But at this very time, over in Spain, hundreds of people are being tortured and burnt to death in the name of your Mother and Child. They call it the Inquisition. In their name, also, dozens of wars will be fought by rivaling sects and hundreds of thousands killed—men, women, and children.''

The chin was higher. ''I do not believe it.''

''No, of course not. However, let me tell you. Primarily, your Spanish are here for gold, which they value above all else, in spite of their religious protestations. They also seek land to convert into feudalistic fiefs and to enslave your people.''

''Enslave?'' she said.

''An institution you are not as yet aware of in this country, although the germ of it is beginning to appear in the *tlacotli*. Your more advanced societies are just beginning to establish classes. They aren't quite here yet, but you're on the verge.''

She frowned. ''I do not understand.''

''No, of course not. No more than an ancient Greek could have understood feudalism or than a feudalistic baron could have understood the workings of the classical capitalism of the early twentieth century. It just didn't make sense to them.''

''I . . . I do not understand, Don Fielding, even though you speak Nahuatl, some of the words . . .''

''I'm sorry,'' he said.

She said worriedly, ''Even though I interpret for my lord, the Captain-General, some of the things he wishes to explain I do not understand. What is a vassal? What is a king? What is a noble? What is a fief? What is an emperor?''

Don Fielding snorted despair. He looked at his watch. ''Doña Marina, Malinche, it would take me a dozen evenings to begin to explain the differences between your ways and those of the Spanish—if I ever could. How long have you been with them now?''

''Many moons. I was born in Jaltipan, where we speak Nahuatl. However, when I was but a child, I was stolen by some wicked *pochteca* traders who were on their way through the town and taken to Tabasco and traded to become a *tlacotli* servant girl. There they speak the Mayan tongue, and of course I learned it. Then I was given to the *teteuh*.''

''The who?''

''The *teteuh*, the gods.''

''Ah. The Spanish. I thought the word was *teules*.''

''So the Captain-General and the other Spanish pronounce it. We say *teteuh*.''

''Go on.''

''With the Captain-General was Aguilar, a countryman who had been shipwrecked in the Mayan country years ago and who had learned the Mayan tongue. So now he speaks both Mayan and Spanish, and I speak both Mayan and Nahuatl, the language of most of this land. So it is that my lord, the Captain-General, can communicate by telling Aguilar what he wishes to say, in Spanish. Aguilar tells me what he said in Mayan, and then I am able to translate that into Nahuatl.''

Don Fielding closed his eyes in pain. "What a way to communicate. Have none of these bravos bothered to learn the language of the country they are trying to conquer?''

She looked at him, her face blank. "But they are *teteuhs*.''

He said urgently, "Now listen to what I have to say, Malinche, because your future depends upon it. The Spanish place more importance on what they call noble birth than anything else. More than ability, or achievement, or education, even more than money, although those who achieve enough money usually wrangle a way to become aristocrats.''

"Aristocrats?''

"The same as nobles. Now listen to me. You must let them know that you are a princess.''

"Princess? What is a princess?''

He groaned. "Something you don't know about here in Mexico.''

"Mexico?''

"Listen to me, damn it.'' The "damn it'' was in English, but he had no equivalent term in Nahuatl. "You are going to have to tell them that you are the daughter of nobles, rulers. You are a princess. When you were a child, you were the heiress of large areas, but your jealous mother, wishing to marry another man after your father's death and give him your inheritance, sold you into slavery. You are a princess.''

She was at sea. "But there is no such thing as a 'princess' here.''

"Don't worry about that. The Spanish will invent the equivalent. They can't think in other terms. There *have* to be kings and queens and nobles and princesses and all the rest of it. That's the way it is in Europe and they simply can't think in any other terms. That's where all these words that confuse you come from. In their viewpoint, there have to be vassals and nobles, kings and commoners, kingdoms and empires, rather than just tribes."

She was utterly confused.

He pursued it. "Haven't you seen that some of the *teteuhs*, as you call them, consider themselves better than others? How some rule it over the others? Men like Cortes and Sandoval and Ordaz are nobles, are dons. The others are commoners and must obey them."

"Yes," she said worriedly.

"In your society, your chiefs are elected. In theirs, they are born into command. So what you must tell them is that you, too, are noble. You are a princess. You were sold into slavery by a cruel mother."

"My mother was not cruel."

He groaned despair. "That has nothing to do with it. This Spanish generation is that of Cervantes. . . ."

"Cervantes?"

"A Spanish storyteller who satirized his generation of romantics in a book called *Don Quixote*. That means nothing to you. However, if you establish yourself as a Mexican princess, then, when it comes time for marriage, you will be able to wed with a noble. Believe me, it makes a difference. You are on top of the social heap, rather than the squaw of a drunken foot soldier. Believe me, Malinche, you now share the bed of Hernando Cortes, but he will betray you as he will betray everyone to his own ends. He will throw you contemptuously to one of his junior officers, or someone even lower, if they think you less than an Indian noble."

"How do you know?"

"History tells me so."

"Who is history?"

He looked at her in frustration. "I am afraid I can't explain."

"You are a magician that you can see into the future?" She held her arms tight against her sides in a feminine reaction to something she feared.

He remained silent for a long moment. Then: "Yes, I suppose that in your eyes I am a magician. I can see into the future . . . I think."

In truth, he didn't know. Was this world in which he found himself *exactly* the same as his own? Was everything going to happen exactly the way it had in *his* history? If so, how explain his own presence here? How explain the things he had gone over to himself before dropping off to sleep the night before? What would happen to world history if he pulled out his automatic right this minute and shot the famed Malinche, "the tongue," as the Indians called her, of the conquering Cortes, the alter ego behind the Spanish occupation?

"I am afraid of magicians, Don Fielding," she said.

"You need not be of this one," he said gently, even as he looked at his wristwatch. "I'll have to go now. I am to have dinner with the Captain-General and his officers."

He turned and went over to the stone steps and down them. As he walked toward the temple where he had met Cortes earlier in the day, he wondered if the girl, had she truly known what lay ahead, would have deserted the Spanish. Or was she so infatuated with them that she would be willing to betray her own race to its destruction?

There were still a few Spanish wandering around the enclosure, but no Indians. He soon discovered why. A monstrous mastiff came bounding toward him, growling ferociously. He dropped his hand to the butt of his gun, but even as he did so, he knew that the small calibered bullet the weapon fired would never stop the heavy dog in time. Not unless he, by pure chance, hit it in some such spot as an eye.

He spoke, as soothingly as he could, in Spanish, and the dog skidded to a halt and puzzlement came over its ugly face. It obviously didn't recognize the clothing, but the voice and possibly the smell were those of its Spanish masters. Undoubtedly, Don realized, these dogs were turned loose at night in the enclosure, and pity any but the Spaniards that were caught by them. He imagined that Malinche and the Spanish women were the only exceptions. The trainers undoubtedly had gone to pains to introduce her and the other women to the war dogs.

He walked on, keeping a watch on the animal from the side of his eyes. However, he had been accepted.

He ascended the steps to the temple and found two footmen with pikes standing guard at one of the doors. Inside, he could hear the noises of a group.

He entered a room possibly forty-five feet long by fifteen deep, somewhat larger but otherwise identical to the one where Cortes had received him earlier. The furniture consisted of an improvised table and folding wooden chairs, obviously military rather than Indian, to seat possibly twenty. The room was lit by two large candles, undoubtedly Spanish, sitting on the table.

Standing about the room, cups in hand, were the twenty—eighteen soldiers, including the Captain-General, and two in the robes of priests. Don recognized one of the latter as Fray Olmedo. He also recognized Sandoval and Ordaz. The others, except for Hernando Cortes, were strangers. All wore armor and carried their swords. Sandoval half raised his cup in a gesture of greeting to the newcomer.

Cortes came up, his face radiating amiability, and patted Don on the arm. "Ah, our good Don Fielding." He turned to the others. "Gentlemen, I present Don Fielding who comes from that far country to the north."

They had fallen silent at his entrance and Don got the feeling that they had been discussing him. That was hardly surprising.

Cortes himself took up another cup from the table and poured from a glass decanter into it. He handed it to Don and raised his own again.

"A sip of wine before we eat, Don Fielding. My faith, there is little enough of it left. This cursed land has no wine, save a horrible concoction they call pulque, and no spirits at all. This wine comes all the way from Spain. To be exact, from Jerez de la Frontera in Andalusia."

Don Fielding took a sip and found it nutty and strong. An ancestor of sherry, it would be, if it came from Jerez.

The Captain-General took him by the arm and led him about, introducing him to the others. There were too many of them for Don to retain all of the names, and most of them, with their beards and almost identical armor, looked so much alike that they were hard to distinguish as individuals. However, a few stood out.

There were five of the Alvarados, but Pedro de Alvarado, who was evidently second in army command, was the only one that particularly impressed himself upon Don Fielding. He was in his early thirties, taller than the average of the Spaniards present, going possibly five foot eight, was crowned with as flaming red hair as Don could ever remember seeing, was more flashily dressed than his companions, and had a swaggering, swashbuckling air. His bow, when Don was introduced, was a grand flourish.

Then there was Alonzo de Avila, noteworthy because of his quiet dignity, and Cristobal de Olid, aggressive and fierce in appearance. Don got the feeling that this one would be as dangerous to tangle with as anyone present. The second priest was Padre Juan Diaz, a younger man and obviously the junior of Fray Olmedo so far as the expedition was concerned.

Introductions over, Cortes waved them all to the table, occupying the head of it himself and insisting that Don Fielding take the place of honor at his right side. The American couldn't help feeling a certain tenseness in the air. Covert glances were shot at him from time to time, particularly by Alvarado and Olid. Sandoval, to the contrary, seemed to be secretly amused.

Dinner, served by Orteguilla and another page, consisted of considerably more in the way of variety than Don had enjoyed earlier from the Indian women. After the blessing by Olmedo they set to work on roast venison, roast turkey, roast duck, various broiled fish, boiled beans done Indian-style with chili, avocados, and various tropical fruits. The Spanish were meat men and obviously scorned other fare.

And, being soldiers, as they ate they complained. The tortillas, as a type of bread, they sneered at. When it came to fruit, they yearned for the citrus of southern Spain. When they came to the fowl, they hungered for the chickens of Europe as opposed to the dry flesh of the turkey. The wild duck presented was not up to the domesticated varieties of the land of their birth. They wished for their fish to be fried in oil, rather than broiled.

Don was moved to wonder, inwardly, why the hell they hadn't stayed home.

Sandoval called down the table to Don, "Don Fielding, by my soul, I am astonished that you were able to lose your vehicle."

"So was I," Don said sourly and in self-deprecation.

All laughed. Pedro de Alvarado's had a contemptuous quality. How could a grown man lose his means of transportation, even in a strange land, was the implication.

Fray Olmedo said sympathetically, "You brought it all the way from this far land from whence you come?"

"Yes." Don took up another tortilla from the platter in the table center and wrapped some of the duck in it. The table was laid with small knives and two-pronged forks, but he enjoyed the Indian method of eating.

"My faith," Cortes said, beaming amiable charm. "Just how far is this far land?"

"Some five hundred leagues to the nearest border,"
Don told him.

"Five . . . hundred . . . *leagues,*" one of the others got
out. "And you come all that way without a weapon?"

"Not exactly," Don said truthfully to that. "I left my
weapons in my vehicle." He'd had a twelve-gauge shotgun in the camper.

Cortes said idly, "Diego Ordaz tells me your country is
rich in gold."

Damn it. Why hadn't Don kept his trap shut! "Yes," he
said.

The fierce-looking Olid said, "Are your people a warlike one?"

Don finished his tortilla and duck and said, "Well, we
like to think of ourselves as a peace-loving nation."

"As all should be," Fray Olmedo said softly. The
others ignored him.

"However," Don added, taking up an avocado, "there
are some who would debate that."

"But you don't utilize such weapons as steel swords,
crossbows, arquebuses?" Alvarado pursued.

"No, we don't."

Ordaz looked about the table with an I-told-you-so
expression.

Dinner was over. It had been eaten with a speed and
gusto that Don would have thought would have led to
immediate indigestion. The Spaniards wiped their greasy
hands on their clothing.

Hernando Cortes leaned back in his chair and smiled his
friendship at Don. He put a hand over his mouth politely
and belched. He said, "Don Fielding, I have a treat for
you."

He turned and called to one of the pages, "Ochoa, go
forth and summon Botello Puerto de Plata."

The page scurried out.

Cortes turned back to Don, "We have among our host

an astrologer, or seer, if you will. Surely we must find what he will tell you. Perhaps he will foresee your return to your own land.''

"My son," Padre Diaz said in a chiding voice, "astrology is a heathen abomination and a device of the devil. It is said that the Pope, the Holy Father, will soon rule upon it.''

Cortes chuckled it away. "Good Father, we do not take it seriously, of course. We are educated men. Only the saints can foresee the future. But it is known that Botello has a touch of *gitano* blood in him and all know the reputation of the gypsy.''

The page, Ochoa, reentered, followed by one of the guards who had been stationed without. He was a shifty-looking, black-bearded man with abnormally long arms and pig eyes. His face was smallpox-marked and he looked like a stereotype villain out of a television show.

All eyes went to him, and Cortes chortled, "My good Botello, observe! Here is the stranger about whom the camp has been abuzz. What do your arts tell us of him?''

"My son," the priest said again, reproach in his voice.

But Botello approached Don, his small eyes smaller still.

What was he going to do? Don wondered. Read his palm or something? He knew this was an age of superstition, and in spite of what the Captain-General had said to the priest, he suspected that all present, probably including the two men of God, believed in soothsaying.

The foot soldier scowled at the newcomer and his mouth worked as though in puzzlement.

"Well, Botello?" Cortes urged.

The soldier said slowly and flatly to Don Fielding, "You are not of this world.''

Don said, "Of course not. I come from way to the north.''

The other shook his head in puzzlement. "No. You come from another world.''

Chapter Five

Don Fielding awoke, but from no deep dream of peace, in the early morning, and once again he had to orient himself. The happenings of the past few days were so bizarre that he simply couldn't accept them. For long moments, lying there on the floor, his bush jacket under his head, he stared up at the triangular ceiling. It was an arch without a keystone, with the faces of the stone beveled and forming a perfect vault, and reared some twenty feet high above him. He wondered how many Indians had occupied this room before Ordaz, and now he, had taken over. Probably a couple of families of them. They crowded in, as their ancestors must have into caves. In fact, these rooms in Indian towns were little more than man-made caves. Windowless, dark, they were simply a shelter, no more, the most primitive type of architecture basically, no matter how ornately decorated with reliefs on the outside.

He groaned and came to his feet. He felt sticky. It was three days, now, since he had been out of his clothes. What did the Spanish do in the way of laundry? The manner in which they had nonchalantly wiped their hands on their clothes the night before indicated they must have some way of having them washed. He assumed that the

46

Indian women did it. He would have to find out. His socks felt absolutely stiff.

The night before came back to him. Cortes and his captains had done all they could to pump him about his native land. It would have been laughable, if it hadn't been so damned serious. Their cupidity was obvious. They drooled at the idea of a country as wealthy as he had reported only a thousand or so miles away. Did they picture themselves marching over the desert to its conquest? Obviously, they did—once they had disposed of Montezuma and his Tenochas, or Aztecs, as they would one day be called.

The story of Coronado and his search for the Seven Cities of Cibola, came back to him. Was it a result of what he had told the Spaniards last night that Coronado's expedition had taken place? He shook his head in despair at the paradoxes. Had history been formed by his return here to the Mexico of 1519 and by his stories of riches to the north? He didn't know, and thinking about it brought him nothing but confusion.

He took up his jacket and shrugged into it and was about to leave the small room just as Diego Ordaz entered. The other was obviously tired.

The Spaniard growled, "This night watch is an abomination, by my beard. Why doesn't the Captain-General let that pet of his, Sandoval, take it over for awhile? Not that it's even necessary. These Totonacs haven't the guts to scratch their own fleas."

His speech was nonchalant enough, but Don Fielding detected a slight element that hadn't been there the day before. Diego Ordaz was incapable of dissimulation; his face clearly reflected his inner thoughts. Something was wrong, and Don didn't like it. What?

He said, "How do I go about getting breakfast?"

"Breakfast?" the red bearded husky snorted. "You rustle up your own. This cursed land has but one meal a day,

ordinarily. Go out into the kitchens and see what you can
scrounge. It has been all that we could do to arrange for
the Indian bitches to prepare two meals a day for us. Aiii,
when we've fully taken over, there will be some changes
made!''

Don was about to leave but Diego Ordaz said, an edge
of cunning in his voice, ''Is it true, Don Fielding, what
you told us last night? That is, your nation is rich with
gold and jewels but unwarlike in nature. What prevents
your neighbors from attacking you?''

Don sighed inwardly. He said, ''Our neighbors to both
the north and south have long been at peace with us. They
are no more militarily inclined than are we. Perhaps less.
We do not even have fortifications along our borders.''

The Spaniard shook his head in wonder. ''And they too
are rich?''

''Especially those to the north,'' Don told him and
pushed aside the mat which shielded the door.

He'd like to see this bunch of rag-tail bandits take on a
troop of the Royal Canadian Mounted.

The early part of the morning passed uneventfully. He
had gone around to the improvised kitchens and liberated a
couple of large tortillas and some more of the turkey stew
to wrap up in them and, finishing that in the way of
breakfast, had located some water in which to wash his
socks. That wasn't particularly easy since the Indians had
no soap, and if the Spanish had brought any along with
them from Cuba, they had evidently by now used it all up.
He had asked one of the Spanish footmen and received
only a laugh in return.

He sat on a lower step of one of the minor temples, his
socks stretched out on the stone to dry, his bare toes
absorbing the sun's rays. His feet felt good to be out of the
paratrooper boots for the first time in days. He looked at
the socks and shook his head. They were of heavy nylon,
but it was just a matter of time before they wore out, and

they were undoubtedly the only pair in the country. Well, so would all his other clothing wear out. Sooner or later he was going to have to adopt the clothing of the Spaniards—or that of the Indians.

That brought to mind the fact that eventually, if not sooner, he was going to have to join up with Captain-General Cortes and his expedition. Malinche had been right. Cortes, when he discovered that Don spoke Nahuatl, could use him as an interpreter. He didn't really approve of this buccaneering expedition, or hadn't when a student of it, but it was simply a matter of rationalizing his beliefs. The conquest of Mexico was inevitable. If Cortes didn't do it, the next expedition would. If the Spanish didn't pull it off, the English or the French or some other European country would. The Europeans were several ethnic periods ahead of these Neolithic Indians; it was inevitable that they be sucked into the cultural vacuum. All in the name of world progress, wasn't it?

A voice said, "Good morning, my son."

Don looked up. It was Fray Bartolome de Olmedo. For some reason, he had taken to this priest more than he had Padre Juan Diaz. Perhaps it was because the night before the eyes of the younger priest had gleamed just as avidly as anyone else's at the table at the mention of gold.

Don began to come to his feet, but the other made a gesture of negation with his right hand. "Remain seated." He looked at the drying socks and then took in the rest of Don Fielding's clothes. "Truly, the clothing of your country is remarkable, my son. However, it seems very practical."

Don said, taking up the socks to see if they were dry and finding them so, "We do not dress in this manner all the time. It is clothing suitable for tramping in rough country."

"The boots in particular seem sturdy," the priest nodded. "Tell me, my son, are you of the Faith?"

Don knew he was on thin ice now. Even as he drew on his socks, he let his mind race for answers. This was the age of the Inquistion. Heretics could be burned at the stake. So far as he knew, the Holy Office had no representatives with the Cortes expedition, but that didn't mean that sooner or later, particularly after more of the Spanish appeared on the scene, there would not be such representation. If he recalled his history, the Inquisition had become notorious in New Spain shortly after Cortes had come to power.

He said carefully, "As you know, Father, I am from a distant land. Those who think as I do have not received the message of Rome."

Evidently, it didn't occur to the older man to ask where Don Fielding had heard of Rome.

He said, "I am willing to baptize and to instruct you, my son."

Don was *really* on thin ice now. He knew that the two priests burned with the desire for new converts, with the desire to baptize the inhabitants of this whole country. The cynicism of a later age did not apply here. These men were zealots and fanatics.

Sooner or later, once again, Don knew he was going to have to toe the line if he was to survive. The Reformation had not as yet come to Europe and not even in Germany and England were Protestants to be found, not to speak of atheists and agnostics. However, for the present he rebelled.

He shook his head. "No, Father. Truly, you would not want it so, nor would I. It is one thing to take a barbarian, a slave, such as these people are, and baptize them without their truly knowing all the ramifications of your religion. But I am an educated man. You would not want me to accept your faith without truly understanding it and coming into it with both heart and brain, but for now we have not time for you to instruct me thoroughly."

The priest sighed. "Perhaps you are right, my son.

When and if you do join us, I anticipate that you will be a strong arm of the Church, since, as you say, you are a man of education in your own land.'' A twinkle came to his eye. ''However, do not let Padre Diaz know. He would pester you into baptism before you so much as learned the names of the Holy Trinity.''

A trumpet blasted from the entry to the enclosure and then a drum rattled—a military drum, not one of the Indian kettledrums.

Don and the priest looked in that direction. A procession was entering.

It was headed by two young men dressed in barbaric splendor, complete to highly colorful headdresses of Quetzal feathers. There were ornaments aplenty, but Don Fielding noted that they still wore the basic *maxtli* breechcloth, no matter how ornate, and the *tilmantli* mantle. And their legs were bare. Their sandals were rich with gold and stones, but they were still sandals. In their right hands they carried flowers which looked like roses, at least from this distance, and from time to time they smelled daintily of them. Don Fielding was reminded of movies he had seen portraying aristocratic fops in the French court of Louis the Fourteenth. Each of them had an attendant to one side and a bit to the rear, equipped with a fan to brush aside the flies.

Following these came four older men, perhaps in their forties, still richly dressed but not so much as the two leaders, who seemed to be in their early twenties. The elders wore no feather headdresses but had their glossy black hair tied in a knot of the top of the head.

And following these came some twenty barefooted porters clad only in loincloths and bearing burdens.

At a stately pace the procession headed for the main temple which housed Cortes and his captains.

From the temple, also at an unhurried pace, came Captain-General Cortes done up in what was probably his richest best, his breastplate agleam, his helmet ashine. Flanking him, also in their finery, were Sandoval and Olid and, bringing up the rear, Malinche and an unarmed Spaniard Don didn't recognize but soon decided must be Aguilar, the other interpreter. Padre Diaz was with them.

The two groups approached each other and a page scurried forward with Cortes's folding chair. He placed it and the Captain-General seated himself with controlled dignity, as though a king holding court.

"Now, who is this?" Fray Olmedo muttered. He put his hands in the sleeves of his robe and, walking slowly, proceeded to join the Spanish group.

Don hustled into his shoes, came to his feet. Others of the Spanish soldiery came up and stood at a respectful distance. Don joined them.

The procession came to a halt and one of the two young leaders stepped forward. He had considerable sangfroid, and it came to Don Fielding that these were most certainly not the easygoing Totonacs.

Malinche and Aguilar came forward and stood one to each side of Hernando Cortes.

The Indian said, in Nahuatl, "I am Cuauhtemoc, of the Eagle *calpulli* of the Tenochas, and hence nephew of Motechzoma, the Tlacatecuhtli. And this"—he gestured to his companion—"is Axayaca, also of the Eagle clan. We come as a delegation from the high council of Tenochtitlan to enquire of the *teteuh* gods as to their purpose in this land and why they have turned the Totonacs against us."

Malinche made a light obeisance to him, then turned to Aguilar and spoke to him rapidly in, Don assumed, Mayan.

Aguilar, who seemed a colorless nonentity and not particularly bright, turned to Cortes and said in Spanish, "He says he is the nephew of the Emperor Montezuma who has sent him to demand why you have taken over Cempoala and the fief of the Totonacs."

Don groaned inwardly. His first inclination was to step

forward and offer his services as a translator directly from Nahuatl into Spanish. In the first place, the title *Tlacatecuhtli* didn't by any means mean "Emperor." It meant "One Who Speaks," or could be translated the "First Speaker," indicating that in Tenochtitlan, at high council meetings, Motechzoma spoke first. There were other things completely wrong with the translation as it finally got through to the Captain-General, but Don Fielding held his peace. He still thought it just as well to keep to himself his knowledge of what was going on.

Hernando Cortes came to his feet, smiling hospitably. He stepped forward and gave the somewhat startled Cuauhtemoc a warm Spanish *abrazo*, then turned to Axayaca and gave that young man a similar embrace. The Indians looked surprised; obviously physical contact between men was not their custom.

The Captain-General returned to his chair and said to Aguilar, "Tell our friend that we welcome the nephews of the great monarch Montezuma to our camp and that my liege lord, Charles the Fifth, King of Spain and Emperor of the Holy Roman Empire, the greatest monarch in the world, sends his warmest greetings and prays that the great Montezuma will accept the true faith and, with all his subjects, be baptized into the Holy Mother Church."

Aguilar had listened carefully. Now he turned to Malinche and spoke in Mayan. She in turn looked to Cuauhtemoc and said in Nahuatl, "The *teteuh* says that he welcomes you and that his chief, Charles, who is the greatest chief in the world, sends his greetings and wishes all the Tenochas to embrace the new religion which comes from over the seas and which is the true religion of the three gods."

Well, Don decided inwardly, that didn't come through quite so badly, though the girl didn't seem to have a very clear picture of the new religion she embraced. He wondered if the three gods were the Holy Trinity—Jehovah, Jesus, and Mary. The two young Tenochas looked puzzled.

However, Cuauhtemoc turned and clapped his hands and some of the porters hurried forward.

The four older chiefs took from these various articles and piece by piece unwrapped them. They consisted of gold and silver art objects and ornaments sometimes bejeweled, rich cotton stuff elaborately embroidered, beautiful mantles of the *plumaje*, the famous feather embroidery, and various other gifts which, Don suspected, though it might be great Indian art, would be consigned to the junk pile by the Spanish as soon as the others were gone. But the eyes of the Europeans glinted at the gold and silver, and there was an expression, even in the face of the priest, Juan Diaz, of quick estimation of its value. Piece by piece the treasure was offered to Cortes, who invariably expressed his delight and then had it sent off by his soldiers to the temple in which he was housed.

When all had been presented, the Captain-General in turn clapped his hands. Sandoval leaned down to hear his words.

Cortes said, even while beaming at the Indians, "Get these dogs a few handsful of the green beads, some of the red ones, and two or three of the hand mirrors. And, let me see, perhaps a string of the artificial pearls. That should be sufficient."

Sandoval went off and shortly reappeared with the page Orteguilla impressively bearing a tray with the ordered gifts.

Cortes personally took them up and presented them to the Indian spokesman, who seemed impressed by the quality of the gifts, if not by their number. He turned and proffered them to one of his older subchiefs who wrapped them up with care in some of the cotton cloths in which their own presents had arrived.

Cuauhtemoc turned back to Cortes.

That worthy had evidently decided upon a show of force. He made a gesture with his hand, evidently a prearranged signal, because in split seconds Pedro de Alvarado came dashing around from the back of the major temple at the head of fifteen other horsemen, all of them in full armor, all of them bearing lances.

They rode at full tilt down the length of the enclosure, Alvarado at the lead, the others in three lines, five abreast. At the enclosure's far end they wheeled, reassembled into one long line, lowered their lances and charged. The horse's hoofs whirled up the dust and made an impressive drumming, thunderlike roar. They wheeled again, charged back again, this time with their swords out and flashing on high.

They paused now and formed ranks again, and two of them galloped forth alone, Pedro de Alvarado and one of his brothers, Jorge de Alvarado, if Don wasn't mistaken. He wasn't nearly as spectacular as his swashbuckling older brother.

They rode to opposite ends of the enclosure, spun their horses, and headed toward each other, lances couched. Both lowered the visors of their helmets. They came together with a great crash. Jorge was swept from his saddle and hit the earth with a rattle-bang of armor. Don winced, but the soldiers around him laughed and put up a great shout in Pedro's favor.

But Jorge was back onto his feet and whipping his sword out, even as his horse ran off.

Pedro vaulted out of his own saddle, brought forth his sword, and they had at it, with a great banging of the steel weapons on armor. It soon became obvious to Don Fielding that they were faking it, working for the effect rather than attempting to wound the other. He suspected that the Alvarados had done a considerable amount of this type of jousting in the past. However, the show must have been impressive to the Indians, who were watching round-eyed, in spite of their attempts to retain dignity.

After a few minutes of this fervent battle, the two stood

back and laughed at each other, put their swords away, and embraced. They secured their horses, returned to the troop, and all rode off to whence they had come, the improvised stables behind the temple.

The army had fourteen cannon in all. Four of the small falconets and ten larger brass ones. Two of the falconets were at the gate, and one of the heavier guns was mounted on each corner of the wall. The rest of the artillery was parked approximately in the center of the courtyard.

Cortes called out now to the group of guards at the artillery park, "Load up a lombard and direct it at that temple." He pointed.

The temple in question was one of the smaller ones and mounted atop a minor pyramid which had about a score of steps leading to the top.

A large stone ball was dropped down the muzzle of the gun. An artilleryman laid the gun and another touched the breech with the smoldering tip of a short piece of rope. There was a sputtering and then a great crash and gush of smoke and flame. The ball came thundering forth and smashed into the tiny temple, completely collapsing it.

To a man, the Indians had staggered back a step or two and Cuauhtemoc himself lost caste by barking out an exclamation.

Cortes called to one of the musketeers, "Rodrigo, load your piece with shot and bring down that flock of turkeys over there."

The soldier poured powder into his clumsy matchlock, added a sizeable quantity of shot from his belt pouch, and rammed it all home. He leveled the gun with care. The turkeys his commander had indicated were several hundred feet away and numbered about twenty. The gun went off with a satisfying boom and a great discharge of black smoke, and the turkeys went down to a bird. A few of them continued to kick and squawk, but none remained on foot.

Cortes turned back to the Tenochtitlan delegation and said, "A slight demonstration of our weapons for your edification."

Aguilar and then Malinche translated, though it was hardly necessary. The Indians were impressed, despite all efforts to hide their near-consternation. The porters were terrified.

Cortes said, "And now to the purpose of your embassy. You must realize that, though this principality of the Totonacs was formerly vassal to your great monarch Montezuma, they were dissatisfied with his rule and pleaded with us to accept their pledge of obedience to His Majesty, Charles the Fifth."

By the time that got through the interpreters, it was a mishmash so far as Don could see, and the Indians looked confused.

Cortes said, "However, I bear great affection for your king and shortly will pay my respects to him in his capital, where all misunderstandings between us can be readily adjusted."

That came through a little better but wasn't very well received by the nephews of the First Speaker of Tenochtitlan. Cuauhtemoc consulted briefly with his companion and then turned back to Malinche.

"Tell the *teteuh* that the way is hard and long and there is little food and that there are many enemies. It is not well that he try to approach Tenochtitlan."

That went through the translation process and Cortes laughed in gentle reproof.

"But tell our ambassador that my master, His Majesty, has ordered me to pay his compliments to the great Montezuma and that he would never forgive me if I failed, no matter how long and difficult the path. Besides"—he gestured at the two priests—"it is most necessary to reveal to him the new faith and bring him into the Holy Mother Church."

"Amen," the priests intoned.

Malinche and Aguilar went through their process again. The Indians looked dismayed and their eyes went back to the artillery.

Cortes stood. "But now is the time for refreshment. The hour for the midday repast is upon us and my servants have prepared as luxurious a banquet as the inadequate facilities of Cempoala provide for such noble guests. Pray join me, honored lords."

He took Cuauhtemoc by one arm, Axayaca by the other, and in the most friendly of fashions led them toward his temple headquarters, even while Malinche and Aguilar translated his words. The two Indians still obviously didn't like to be handled.

The four older subchiefs began to follow, but Sandoval, a mocking in his eyes, held up a restraining hand and pointed in the direction of the outdoor kitchens.

One of the foot soldiers next to Don said, "If these Indian dogs think they are going to eat before us, they are daft."

The balance of the Indian procession, which had entered so bravely an hour before, now looked bewildered. Some of them squatted down on their heels and simply waited for whatever was to come.

Alvarado's troupe came up, horseless now, and also made their way to the temple, along with the interpreters, the priests, and Sandoval and Olid.

Don, it seemed, was not invited. He shrugged and turned to head, along with the Spanish soldiery, to the kitchens. He grimaced wryly. Listening to any more of that chaotic translating would have given him a sour stomach anyway. He doubted that half of what got through was understood by either side.

As they headed for their lunch, the soldier next to him sized him up from the side of his eyes and said, "You are Don Fielding, the giant stranger from the north."

Don looked at him. "That's right," he said. The other seemed to be about twenty-eight, of middle height by Don's standards, but probably tall by contemporary Spanish ones. He seemed open-faced, active, quick, and stacked up into a well-made soldier. In fact, he had a certain elegance and grace beyond the average in this army. He evidently had a curiosity quality; most of the others largely ignored Don, as though suspicious of his intrusion into their ranks.

This one said, "Bernal Diaz del Castillo of the town of Medina del Campo in Castile."

Don stared at the historian-to-be. "I have heard of you." In his eighties, approaching blindness, this honest man was to write the only accurate story of the conquest. He didn't look like a writer. He looked like an honest man.

The other frowned. "Heard of me? From whom?"

Don Fielding backpedaled quickly. "Uh, I don't know. I have talked to so many these past two days. Perhaps Diego Ordaz, with whom I am quartered."

"He is a brave captain," Bernal said.

"Evidently, he also thinks well of you," Don said, covering.

They had reached the kitchens and joined the line of footmen, military-fashion in chow line. It was a cafeterialike arrangement. Each man helped himself to the tortillas, the steaming cauldrons of stews, roast fowl, and the fruit. As a soldier reached his turn, he took up a bowl, or sometimes two, and dished up his own quantity. The food was at least plentiful and Don wondered how much of a strain was put on the town's economy by these additional three or four hundred voracious Spaniards.

Bernal growled, "On my faith, this food is not fit for dogs and there is no wine. Sometimes I wonder why I ever left my home." But then he laughed. "Obviously, to gain my fortune. When we have taken this land, we will bring the olives, the beasts, the foods, the grapes of Spain. And

then we will see. With the Indians for slaves, all will be
paradise for us veterans.''

"Undoubtedly," Don said, dryness there. If history
bore him out, a man in the ranks of this army was not
going to do nearly as well as Cortes and his higher-ranking
captains had promised.

They reached the head of the line, took up bowls, and
made their selections. They stayed together, wandering off
aways to where they found seating room on one of the
stone steps of a temple. Evidently, Bernal Diaz was interested in continuing Don's company. At least he had intel-
lectual curiosity, which seemed a quality the others didn't
possess.

Between bites, Bernal said, "The rumors about you go
through the camp. It is said that you come from a land
many days' journey to the north."

"That is correct," Don said around his mouthful. And
now, he thought, come the questions about the gold.

But Bernal said, "Is it true that in those lands there are
people with but one leg and their mouths in the tops of
their heads?"

Don looked at him sarcastically. "Possibly in Texas,"
he said. "Anything can happen there."

Chapter Six

Bernal chuckled. "You jest," he said. "But I did not believe it anyway. Is your land La Florida?"

"No."

"I once spoke to a sailor of the expedition of Juan Ponce de Leon, who journeyed to La Florida in the year of our Lord 1513. He reported that there were unicorns in that strange land." Bernal took in his companion. "But he did not mention natives who spoke Spanish or were so well attired or accomplished as you seem to be."

Thin ice again. Don said carefully, "They're inclined to dress very informally in Florida. For one thing, the heat is such that too much clothing is not practical."

"And the unicorns?"

"If unicorns existed, it would undoubtedly be in Florida, or possibly California, another of our states, but in sad truth they don't. It is a superstition."

The other was fascinated. "He also reported that there were great lizards as much as twenty feet long which live in the water and are very ferocious. Of course, I did not believe that, either."

"Alligators," Don told him. "No. He was correct. They aren't particularly dangerous on land, but I wouldn't want to be in the water with a hungry one around." Don

61

Fielding tried to remember whether or not alligators would attack a man, even in the water. He knew crocodiles would. But alligators? He didn't know.

He said, "What was all this today?"

Bernal chuckled. "These Indian dogs have met their match in the Captain-General. They do not know if they are in retreat or charge. A few weeks ago, when we first landed, we pushed north here to Cempoala in this minor principality which was held in fief by the great Montezuma."

Bernal took another bite and went on. "The Captain-General, informed that Montezuma's tax collectors appropriated large quantities of the best products of the area, told the local cacique that they need no longer deliver these things. That he would protect them. So it was that when five of the official tax collectors turned up, ah, arrogant they were, Don Hernando so incensed the Totonacs that they rose and threw the collectors into the stocks."

Bernal laughed again. "But this is where our Captain-General proved his wiliness. Secretly, he released two of the collectors, brought them to his quarters, expressed his high regard for them and for the great Montezuma, and gave them presents and let them escape, to return to Tenochtitlan. He then pretended anger at the Totonacs for letting the two escape and took the remaining three out to our ships and later allowed them to depart for their capital as well."

"What was the point?" Don said.

Bernal wiped up the balance of his stew with a tortilla. "Can't you see? The great Montezuma is now indebted to us for releasing his officers. But the Totonacs are terrified that he will take his revenge upon them. Thus it is that they have sworn allegiance to His Majesty and become a Spanish fief."

"Machiavellian," Don muttered, tossing his head in a gesture of wonder.

"What?"

Don was about to explain who the Florentine was but then drew quick rein on himself. Niccolo Machiavelli, the devilish statesman, was probably still alive and active in the Florence of these days. Bernal Diaz might even have heard of him. But Don, in his present guise, couldn't possibly have had.

"Nothing," he said. He too was finishing his meal.

They both stood and Bernal was about to make off to his duties, or whatever. He hesitated and looked at the newcomer to the camp. He said, "One word, Don Fielding—I noted you in the company of Gonzalo de Sandoval, who is the closest intimate of the Captain-General. Perhaps I should not speak thus to a stranger of a comrade in arms, but though he is the most charming of young men—he is a viper. There, I have said it and should not have."

Don looked after him as he strode away. He grunted surprise. Bedamned! It looked as though he had made a friend.

With the Spanish soldiery all fed, some of the Indian women who worked in the kitchens took bowls of food over to the subchiefs and the porters, who ate it, squatting on the ground. Don watched them for awhile. So these were the famous Aztecs, most warlike of all Mexican Indians. They were not done up in the paraphernalia of war of course, but even so, they didn't look particularly prepossessing. He estimated that their average height was about five foot two, about the size of Napoleon Bonaparte. By his own standards they were little more than midgets; however, they were well muscled and wiry.

He then drifted over to some temple steps and sat and watched the soldiers drill. The show was obviously intended to impress the visitors. Diego Ordaz presided as drill master and ordered the three hundred footmen up and down the enclosure. To the left flank, march; to the right flank, march; about face! They were no troop of West Point cadets, Don decided, but they weren't bad. Certainly,

such discipline must pay off in combat with a mob of
savages.

As he sat, he thought it over, all over again. He was
going to have to offer his services as an interpreter to
Captain-General Cortes. There was no alternative. For one
thing, the situation was impossible. How could Cortes and
Motechzoma communicate when the war chief thought
the adventurer was a god and the adventurer thought the
Indian war chief an emperor?

But then the thought came to him: what if he did take
over the interpreting? In that case the historic mistakes that
had taken place would not have occurred and history would
be revised. Could he revise history? But how could he? If
he did, then very likely he would never have been born.
And here he was. He shook his head in black, sick despair.

Shortly he saw the two Indian ambassadors, accompanied by Cortes and his people, emerge from the temple.
Still projecting the utmost amiability, the Captain-General
conducted his guests back to the others who had accompanied them from the Tenocha capital and the procession left
the enclosure still trying to maintain its shaken dignity.
Don wondered bitterly how Charles the Fifth would have
reacted to a demonstration of an explosion of an H-Bomb.

Even from this distance Don Fielding could see the
expression on the face of Hernando Cortes. Obviously the
Spaniard had only contempt for his Indian foes. He turned
with his group and re-entered the temple.

He might as well get about it. Don stood and made his
way in that direction. He ascended the stone steps and
headed in the direction of the room where the army head
made his offices.

Two soldiers armed with pikes stood guard. One of
them was Botello, the alleged astronomer and seer. He
seemed to pull a lot of guard duty, Don thought. At his
approach they crossed their pikes, barring the way.

Don said to the pockmarked footman, "I have a message for Don Hernando."

The other's small eyes shifted. He said, "The Captain-General is in conference with his captains and does not wish to be disturbed."

"It is an important message."

The eyes shifted again, uncomfortably, and the other licked his upper lip. He said stubbornly, "His orders were specifically that he not be disturbed. Important issues are being discussed."

There was something wrong about all this, but Don Fielding had no clue to just what it was. There was nothing for it; he turned and marched back down the steps. He had the uncomfortable feeling that not only was the Captain-General not available to him now but perhaps was not going to be later, though Don had nothing definite to go on in the way of evidence.

He walked back to his quarters and, on looking through the door, saw that Diego Ordaz had retired, in full armor and with sword in hand, as usual. No need in disturbing him, so Don withdrew.

He thought about it and decided to go for a swim. Washing facilities were at a minimum here in the camp and he was beginning to feel clammy with dried sweat and dust.

He walked over to the gateway, with its guard of ten, nodded to the captain of the watch, who turned out to be Alonzo de Avila, the handsome, young officer who had impressed Don with his quiet dignity at the dinner with Cortes and his officers. He began to exit through the gate, but Avila called to him.

"Just a moment, Don Fielding. Where do you go?"

Don halted. "I was thinking of going down to the river for a swim. I haven't washed for days."

The other shook his head. "It is the Captain-General's

command that no smaller number than three ever leave the enclosure and even then only upon his permission.''

"But I am not of your army. The command doesn't apply to me.''

There was an element of embarrassment in Avila's voice. "I am afraid that it does, Don Fielding. The Captain-General mentioned your name in particular when giving me his orders.''

"I see,'' Don said. "Very well. Undoubtedly, the order is well taken. There can be no trouble with the Indians if we all remain within the safety of the enclosure.''

He turned and headed back in the direction of the conglomerate of temples and pyramids. He didn't like it. He got somewhat the same impression from Avila that he had from Diego Ordaz the last time he had spoken to his roommate. Something was offbeat. Well, the only thing he could do was to see Cortes, offer his services, and if anything was wrong, try to rectify it.

To kill time until the conference of officers was over and he could again attempt to see the army head, Don Fielding decided to inspect the pyramids and such temples as were not being used as living quarters or to fill the other needs of the Spanish forces. He approached the largest of the massive structures, the one that he had at first thought a remarkable job of reconstruction when he had originally entered the large courtyard. The steps were steep and many, and he could feel the sweat coming through his shirt by the time he reached the top.

He had looked forward to inspecting the interior of the small temple that crowned the great pile of stone. After all, he was still an anthropologist and archeologist and, in spite of the situation in which he found himself, still fascinated by the possibilities that presented themselves to him in the way of research.

But he was to find that the interior had been stripped of its original contents of native gods and whatever, washed down, and whitewashed. In the center was an altar and atop it a carved Madonna and Child, richly robed. Crosses were hung on the walls. Evidently, the good Fathers had taken over with a vengeance.

He peered at the Madonna and decided that it must have been imported from Spain, or at least Cuba. The robes and ornaments, gaudily ornate as they were, could never have been produced in this country. The local religious decorations were ornate, but of a different culture.

Although the single room was whitewashed, some of the Indian reliefs could be made out. It was while he was studying these that she found him.

He heard a sound and turned, expecting to confront one of the soldiers who had come up for prayer. But it was Malinche.

She said to him in Nahuatl and urgently, though in low voice, "I must speak to you quickly, Don Fielding, for someone else may come."

He frowned. "All right, but what is all this?"

"You are in great danger."

"But . . . why?"

"You spoke too much of the great wealth of this land of yours to the north."

He swore inwardly. What an ass he had been.

"What has happened?"

She said, "I do not speak this Spanish tongue but I can understand more of the words than they know. My lord, the Captain-General, and his captains . . . they discussed you. It was decided that you suspected their desire to march north, after subjecting Tenochtitlan and add your own country to the realm of Charles, the great chief in the lands across the sea. They are afraid that you might escape and return to your country to warn them there. They would rather appear as a surprise. There is great advantage in surprise."

"They'd be the ones to be surprised, all right," Don growled. "They'd never find my native land."

She frowned puzzlement. "Is it, then, so hard to find?"

"It is impossible," Don said. "You were correct. We are all, my people, evidently magicians, since all but I have disappeared. But tell me, what did they decide?"

"I do not know. My lord, the Captain-General, ordered me on an errand before they had come to decision. Padre Diaz wished to have you arrested for being a heretic and brought to trial. But Captain De Leon objected to that. For some reason, he does not wish there to be religious trials in this country. Then Tonatiuh, the Sun . . ."

"Who?" Don said.

"Alvarado. The Indians call him the Sun because of his brilliant hair. He laughed at De Leon and said that he was part Jew, whatever that is, and that one day the Inquisition would get him. Whatever the Inquisition is."

"All right," Don said. "I understand that. But then what happened?"

"I do not know. It was then I left. You must flee, Don Fielding. I have told this to you since you tried to aid me with your words last night about being a princess. I have since told Aguilar what you informed me to say and he, in turn, has repeated it to the others. He is not a man of great mind. You should have known that there were no such things as princesses in all this land, but he seems to have learned little of our ways in the seven years he spent in the Maya country."

"But what are they going to do? I can't flee. They won't let me out of the enclosure."

"I do not know. But you are in great danger and now I must leave."

He put a finger under her chin and tilted it upward. Don Fielding was not much of a lady's man, but this girl had risked her own life in an attempt to save his. He bent down and kissed her on the lips. "Thank you, Doña Marina."

She brought her head backward in surprise and touched her fingers to her mouth. It came to him that in spite of the fact that she was the mistress of Cortes, she had never been kissed before. Could it be that the Spanish leader was actually so contemptuous of her that he refrained from kissing, as one usually refrains from such an embrace with a whore?

She shot a quick, startled look at him from the sides of the dark eyes, spun, and darted away. He couldn't help but note her figure, even through the sacklike clothing.

A fine time to be thinking about a woman's figure! The fat was in the fire.

He made his way slowly down the steps of the pyramid. It was already beginning to grow dark.

Over at the kitchens, the Spanish footmen were lining up for the evening repast, but he could feel no appetite within him. *Survive! Live!* But how? Should he attempt to gain an audience with Cortes? To what end? By this time the other had decided what to do with Don Fielding, native of a land to the north which teemed with gold. All over again, Don castigated himself. Why couldn't he have described the slums of Newark rather than the contents of Fort Knox?

He went to his quarters—there was nowhere else to go. Diego Ordaz was no longer there. The husky commander of foot was probably already about his duties as captain of the night guard. Don wondered what his orders might be in regard to himself. Probably to shoot on sight, he decided sourly.

Well, for the present there was nothing he could do. He kicked together a bed of the mats and blankets. He took a lesson from Ordaz and first threw the magazine from the butt of his Beretta automatic and checked the contents. It was full. He rammed the clip back into the gun and jacked a cartridge into the barrel. He flicked the safety with his thumb, returned the gun to its holster, and made sure it rode loosely there. He was no quick-draw expert by any means, but he didn't want the thing sticking if he got in the crunch. "A .22," he growled. What he needed was a .45.

He stood there a moment in thought and then brought out his entrenching tool from its canvas cover on his left hip. He unfolded it, so that now it was a spade. Back to him came a bit of early reading, *All Quiet on the Western Front*, by a man named Remarque who had fought in the German army. He had mentioned, in passing, that the German infantryman, in trench warfare, had often found that the entrenching tool was more handy than the clumsy rifle and bayonet when it came to close quarters. Don Fielding had no idea how near his own American war surplus was to Remarque's German tool of the First World War. It had a somewhat pointed steel shovel attached to a heavy wooden handle about two feet long. He would hate to get whacked with it.

He stretched out on the improvised bed, the entrenching tool in his right hand, with no intentions of sleeping but with the idea in mind of trying to think his way out of his predicament. Shortly he would confront Cortes and try to iron it all out. Should he confess that he had exaggerated? That actually there was nothing in this age to the north but wide deserts and then animal-covered plains. The other would probably have him skewered on the spot.

He had miscalculated his weariness. In spite of his fairly good slumber of the night before, the past several days had exhausted him, both physically and mentally, not to speak of the psychological drain. He fell off into sleep almost immediately.

But his subconscious was on the alert. He *expected* something to happen to him and hence woke to immediate action when it did.

It was dark outside. On top of that, the mat at the door

parlayed the gloom of the small room. The first sword thrust missed him entirely and dug only into his bedding.

Don frantically rolled. The handle of the entrenching tool was in his hand. He swung with it and missed. He could make out his assailant, hulking above him.

The other disentangled his blade from the bed clothing, swore, *"Por Dios,"* and lunged again.

Don Fielding, on his knees, scampered away and found himself with his back to the stone wall, cornered. He swung wildly as the other stumbled forward, swearing still at the impossible darkness of the room.

Another lunge which pierced Don's clothing and carried through to the wall, the point of the sword striking into the stone.

Don was now fully awake, the adrenaline surging in him. To his later astonishment, he was perfectly cool—the reaction would come in fifteen or twenty minutes. He had never been in personal combat before, save for the usual fist fights of his grammar school days and teens.

He chopped with the entrenching tool at the other's extended arm and hit at the wrist. His would-be assassin screamed in pain.

Already, Don's eyes were accomodating themselves to the dark. He swung desperately upward and caught the other under the chin. And it came to him now why the German infantrymen had favored the entrenching tool over the bayonet. He could feel it cut halfway into the other's head.

It couldn't have taken more than fifteen seconds. His attacker was on the floor, gurgling his life away.

Don Fielding's first reaction was to bolt, simply to flee. To where, he didn't know. He tried to capture himself. He forced himself to stand firm for a moment. Perhaps the small patio outside teemed with other opponents. But then, if it did, he didn't have a chance. *Stand firm for a moment. Think.* And then, incongruously, at a moment like this, to his mind came the slogan of International Business Machines. Think! Ha.

He debated, momentarily searching the body of the fallen man.

For what?

What could the other have that made any difference to him?

Nothing.

He stooped and picked up the sword. He brushed the door's mat aside and stared forth. No one else was in sight. He scurried through.

To his mind came the thought, *have I left anything behind?* But no. He had gone to bed wearing everything he possessed. This time he hadn't even used his bush jacket as a pillow. He had been a fool to allow himself sleep. But he was proving Don Fielding a fool over and over again in this impossible, insane situation in which he found himself.

Sword in hand, he proceeded, unconsciously humped as though trying to present as small a figure as possible. He hurried through the patio, through the gateway, to the left, to the left again, and to the stone stairs that mounted to the wall.

Whatever agnostic gods there might be, he prayed to them that there be no sentries at the top.

The agnostic gods came through. At the wall's top he tossed the sword over, got down on his knees, lowered himself by his hands, and dropped to the ground, twelve feet or so below.

Part Two

Chapter Seven

For a moment Don Fielding stood up against the wall, listening. Had he been spotted by one of the sentries? If he had, then a shout would go up immediately. No shout. For the moment he was safe.

One of the large community houses loomed across the way, possibly a hundred feet distant. Now here was the crucial point, so far as the sentries on the battlements of the enclosure were concerned. He doubled over and sprinted for the shade of the wall of the house. Luck again. No challenging shout.

He made his way around the side of the building so that now the wall sheltered him completely from sight from the camp. He dug into his pocket and came forth with the compass. He could hardly make out its face in the gloom. He set a course due west and started off at a rapid walk.

The town wasn't as large as all that. He estimated it at about ten thousand citizens, even considering the manner in which the Indians packed themselves in. As he recalled history, Cortes, in his letters to Charles Fifth, had claimed it to be thirty thousand, but Cortes was a soldier and the soldier who didn't exaggerate the number of his enemies and the size of the towns he captured had yet to be born. He hadn't upped it by more than three times.

73

Don worked his way around and about the sprawl of community houses, the market place, the pyramids and temples. There wasn't a soul on the streets at this hour. He looked at his watch. Almost eleven o'clock. He'd had quite a sleep before his would-be assassin showed up. He wondered who the man was. Possibly nobody he knew. He had not recognized the voice when the other had sworn. Possibly, on the other hand, it might have been one of the Cortes staff. The Captain-General might have wished to keep the army as a whole from knowing about the killing. There might be some who would think the less of a commander who resorted to personal assassination without legal cause. Though, come to think of it, from what Don had seen, they were as vicious a bunch of cutthroats as had ever come down the pike. The sole exceptions he could think of—and he wasn't even sure they were exceptions—were Fray Olmedo, Bernal Diaz, possibly Alonzo de Avila, and Malinche, of course.

He came eventually to the outskirts of town and headed in the direction of the river. He wanted to find the path by which he had entered so few days ago. And, yes, here it was. He set off at a jogging run.

Time was important now. Whoever that man was he had killed, someone was undoubtedly waiting for him to report. When he didn't, someone else would be sent to find out why. How much time would elapse, Don couldn't know, but it wouldn't be too much, and already perhaps fifteen minutes had elapsed since the attempt.

He had to put as much territory as possible between himself and Cempoala before the pursuit began. He groaned when he remembered that they had horses while he was afoot. They also had dogs—mastiffs for fighting, greyhounds for speed, and two long-eared dogs that might qualify as bloodhounds.

It was perhaps a mile out of the city, on the river path, that he came upon them. There were about fifty camped on the river's edge. It took him only a moment to realize that here was the delegation from Tenochtitlan.

Yes, there must have been half a hundred Indians, all together, a larger number than had participated in the procession into the enclosure in Cempoala. Obviously, on approaching the city, they had made a camp here and the leaders had regarbed themselves for the parade to meet the Spanish.

He approached, his mind desperately seeking a gimmick.

There were half a dozen or more small camp fires and he went from one to the next. Those about the fires looked up at him questioningly, but none spoke nor did any stand. He could see weapons about—bows, quivers of arrows, lances, and *maquauitls*, the vicious Indian equivalent of the sword, a sort of flat paddle of hard wood with pieces of razor-sharp obsidian sunk into the edges. However, no one took them up.

He found whom he sought at one of the fires around which were the six leaders of the expedition.

Don Fielding said, "Cuauhtemoc, nephew of Motechzoma Xocoyotzin, the Tlacatccuhtli, greetings."

The young ambassador looked across the fire to where the one who had been named Axayaca sat, before standing. Cuauhtemoc's eyebrows were high in surprise. He was a handsome man, Don realized again, and bright-looking, intelligent; his features were more delicate than those of most of his fellows and the body, well, less squat. He and the others had changed from the rich trappings of the procession and the meeting with Cortes and were now dressed in much the same garb as were all the others.

"You know me and you speak our tongue."

"Yes, I speak Nahuatl. I saw you today in Cempoala when you met with the commander of the Spanish." He had to use the English word for Spanish, since he knew there was none in the Nahuatl of this period.

"Ah, yes. I recognize you. The giant who towered

above the others, even though he wore no hat of metal on his head, and who wore different clothing. I thought you perhaps a priest of the teteuhs. Why do you come? Perhaps to bear me a further message from Malintzin, the chief of the teteuhs?''

"Malintzin? His name is Cortes."

"But already the inhabitants of these lands have begun to call him Malintzin, from the name of the girl Malinalli who acts as his tongue and is sometimes called La Malinche for that reason. To her name we have added *tzin* which, of course, means chief.''

"I see," Don said. "But, no, I do not bring a message from Malintzin."

The Indian was puzzled, and said, "If you speak our language so well and that of the teteuhs, why did you not translate for us this day?''

"Because I did not wish the Spanish to know I spoke your language.''

Axayaca, across the small fire, had also stood. He said, "But you are a teteuh yourself. How could they *not* know?"

"No, I am not," Don said to him definitely. "I am a white and hence of the same race, but I am not Spanish. I come from a distant land and once we even fought a war with the Spanish." He hesitated, then added, "And defeated them completely and took some of their lands from them.''

"Your people defeated the teteuhs!" Cuauhtemoc blurted. "But one cannot win in a war against teteuhs." He scowled puzzlement again. "But then, of course, you too are a teteuh. Do then the gods fight among themselves?''

"I am not a god," Don said grimly. "Nor are they gods. They are men like yourself."

"I have seen today the terrible weapons of what you call men, but they are the weapons of the gods.''

"No. They are terrible weapons but made by men. Gods do not have weapons. They do not need them.''

The Indians stared at him.

Axayaca said, "Why do you come here now with your strange words? Is it to spy upon us?"

"No. I come seeking refuge. The Spanish made me a prisoner and then attempted to kill me. Instead, I killed him who came after me and escaped."

"You killed a teteuh! But that is said to be impossible," Cuauhtemoc said.

"It is not impossible," Don said grimly. "As someday you will find when you fight them."

One of the subchiefs, still squatting at the fire, shook his head. "We will never fight the teteuhs. The Tlacatecuhtli, Motechzoma, fears them. He would never lead us against the teteuhs."

Don said to Cuauhtemoc, "Nevertheless, I seek refuge in Tenochtitlan where I can tell your leaders much about the Spanish and their plans." Precious lot of good it would do them, but this, now, was his sole chance of survival.

Axayaca said stubbornly, "No. You wish to spy upon us. Motechzoma has ruled that none of the white men shall enter Tenochtitlan. He has sent them much metal, for which they have such a strange love, to bribe them to return across the seas from whence they come."

Don snorted. "The worst thing he could have done was to send those presents. As Cortes himself once said, the Spanish have a malady of the heart which can only be cured by gold. They will never rest now, not until they have come to your city and scoured it of every ounce of gold you have."

One of the subchiefs said, "Why should we care? It is of no value save as ornaments, baubles for the vain. Let them have our gold, if they will but go away."

"But they won't go away," Don told him. "They will kill you, enslave your women, and make your children work in the mines for still more gold."

He shook his head and looked back at Cuauhtemoc.

Though the boy was probably the youngest Indian present, he had an air of command and dominated the others. A natural-born leader, Don Fielding thought. Well, the Indians were going to need some leaders in the near future. Not that it would to them any good.

But he must survive. He said, "I have much to tell your Tlacatecuhtli and his high council."

Cuauhtemoc said, "It is not his high council, it is the Tlatocan, the council of chiefs. He is but a member of it. We continually get the impression in our contacts with the teteuhs that they think Motechzoma alone is the government of Tenochtitlan, and all other cities and lands, for that matter. He is merely the war chief of Tenochtitlan, Tetzcuco, and Tlacopan, the three cities of our united league. He can do nothing without the concurrence of the Tlatocan."

"Very well," Don sighed. "However, I have much to tell your people and request that you take me with you."

Axayaca, frowning still, said, "No. It is forbidden for a white man, even though you say you are not a teteuh, to enter our city."

But Cuauhtemoc was obviously thinking about it. He said, "You are not a warrior?"

"No. I am a scholar."

Cuauhtemoc was surprised. "But you are not an elder."

"No. Nevertheless, I am a scholar. A teacher of the . . . young."

"You are a priest, then?"

"No. I have no gods. Our customs are different than your own."

"Obviously." The Tenocha thought some more.

Finally, he looked about the fire. "I am in favor of taking him to the Tlacatecuhtli. It is for Motechzoma to decide. It is as though we were bringing in a prisoner. He can tell us much about the teteuhs. We would make a great mistake if we were to lose this opportunity."

Axayaca repeated, "No."

But the four subchiefs thought about it. They seemed to have some method of communicating among themselves that Don didn't catch. One of them finally said, "Very well, we shall take him."

From a distance, Don could hear the clatter of horse's hoofs. He snapped, "They are searching for me."

Young Cuauhtemoc was a man of quick decisions. "Out of your clothes!" he rapped.

Don could do nothing but put himself in the hands of the others. He stripped.

"And your strange sandals," the other said. He snapped something else to one of the porters.

Don's things, gun and all, disappeared into one of the loads. Another porter hurried up with Indian garb, including a large poncholike *tilmantli* mantle, such as all the others wore. They made no attempt to find him sandals; none would have been large enough. There was no time to get him into the breechcloth. Cuauhtemoc himself helped him into the *tilmantli*, tied it over his shoulder in standard fashion. The Indians had neither buttons nor pins.

The Indian leader pointed at one of the fires around which porters were sleeping. The fire was almost out. "Sit there, the *tilmantli* over your head, looking as though you are asleep as the others."

There was nothing to do but comply. Don Fielding squatted down, brought the mantle over his head, as some of the others had it. How they were able to sleep sitting up, he didn't know, but some of them were doing it. He realized that his feet were white, a sickening white by Indian standards, and tucked them inside the blanket-sized serapelike mantle—and prayed still once again to his non-existent agnostic gods.

The horses came up in a charge.

Gonzalo de Sandoval, bareheaded and without armor, and in a fury, led them. His bare sword was in hand.

There were four others, including one of the Alvarado brothers—which one, Don couldn't remember. He pretended to be asleep but watched through a tuck in his covering.

The horsemen slammed to a halt.

Sandoval shrilled, "The stranger! The tall one! Have you seen him?"

The Indians looked at him blankly.

He shot his eyes around the camp, swore, "By my faith! Such a filthy group!" He dug his spurs into his animal and was off with the others, up the path toward the mountains.

When they were gone, Cuauhtemoc looked at Don Fielding in thought. There was an element of humor in the Indian's face. He said, "I begin to believe you, my giant friend. You are not loved by the teteuhs."

"They aren't gods," Don said wearily. "They're some of the biggest bastards ever to hit this world."

They hadn't brought the dogs. Not yet, at least. They would have been too slow, perhaps. Evidently, several groups of horsemen had set out in various directions, probably north, west, and south, along what inadequate roads—paths would be the better term—existed, in hopes of rounding him up immediately. He wondered again who it was he had killed with his entrenching tool.

Don remained where he was. He knew very well that Sandoval's troop would be back shortly. He hadn't had the time to get more than a couple of miles distance from Cempoala. The Spanish would go up the road that distance and then decide that if he had come in this direction, he must have headed cross-country. He wished that he'd had the presence of mind to keep his gun. He could have concealed it under the mantle. He doubted that he could bring all five of the armed men down before they got to him, rode him down, or skewered him with their lances, but he could have given them a bit of trouble.

He was right. In about fifteen minutes the horsemen came charging back. This time they didn't bother to pause at the Indian camp but dashed on.

Cuauhtemoc came over and said to him, "They have gone."

Don let the *tilmantli* mantle slide back from his head and looked up.

"They'll be back," he said. "In the camp two of those large dogs you saw are what are called bloodhounds. They are able to follow a trail by smell. They will know my smell from the blankets on which I slept in the priests' quarters in the temple."

Cuauhtemoc thought about it. "Very well," he said finally. "We will hasten on." He gave a shout to the camp and in moments there was a great bustle as the porters took up their baggage and kicked out the fires.

Cuauhtemoc in the lead, they swung out across the fields at a trot. Barefooted on the gravel, twigs, and rough vegetation, Don Fielding's feet were shortly bruised by stone and sore. At this rate, he would be lamed in half an hour.

He called a halt finally, put a hand on the Indian leader's arm, and said, "I can't go on like this. I'll have to have my footwear."

Cuauhtemoc himself wore sandals as did the other chiefs, although the porters were barefooted. He stopped and sighed. "My giant friend, you are more trouble than I had bargained for. Perhaps we should have left you here."

However, he called for the porter who had hidden Don's things in his bundle. In moments, Don had fished out the shoes and socks, sat down on the ground and hurried into them. He stood again and fished his gun, holster, and belt from the pack and belted it about his waist, under the mantle. They were off again.

They ran two abreast over the rugged way, Don and Cuauhtemoc in the lead. He had spent the whole summer tramping around in the back areas of Mexico and was now in fairly good shape, though the Indians were setting quite a pace. He wondered how long they could continue like this.

He gasped to the other, after a mile or so, "Where do we go?"

Cuauhtemoc grinned at him. "There are many advantages to having such deer as the teteuhs ride . . ."

"They are called horses," Don got out.

". . . however, there are disadvantages as well, for it is obvious that there are places a man can go that they cannot."

Shortly, to Don's relief, the trot was slowed to a walk. He realized that the porters were holding up the pace of the group as a whole. Their burdens looked as though they must average at least fifty pounds and a man does not run with a weight of fifty pounds for long. They walked briskly for about another mile and then Cuauhtemoc led them into a trot again.

By the time they slowed to a walking pace once more, Don was thankful. He wondered if the young Indian leader planned to continue this all night. He didn't know if he could take it. If they'd only had a road to follow—but this overland thing was rugged.

He realized now why the dogs hadn't yet manifested themselves. They would assume that he had headed north, in an attempt to return to his own country. So they would have sent the dogs north, first. Undoubtedly, later on, when they failed to pick up his scent in that direction, they'd bring them down here. Well, at least he was getting a good head start.

Toward morning, they came upon the road—narrow though it was—he had prayed for and their pace was speeded. Nevertheless, to the rear, far back, he could hear the baying of the dogs.

He looked over at Cuauhtemoc. "Those are the blood-hounds. They are on our trail."

He said to Don, "We'll forge ahead. Just you and I."

"They'll catch up with your column here."

"But it will not occur to them that there is any connection. The scent which the dogs follow will indicate that we are ahead."

The two took up a faster pace and had soon outdistanced their party.

Don was beginning to blow.

The Indian looked over at him and grinned. "Your giant body does you little good at a time like this, my friend. It takes too much strength to push it along."

Don didn't take the breath to answer. The baying was considerably closer and an unhappy thought came to him. Were the trainers managing the dogs mounted, rather than on foot? If they were, then they would be held back only by the speed of the running bloodhounds, now well on the scent and making good time.

But then the meaning of what Cuauhtemoc had said earlier about the disadvantages of riding the "deer" came through. They had arrived at a steep hill, rugged with great boulders, and the narrow road dribbled away to a path, along which they had to ascend single file.

"Ha," the Indian chortled. "We have defeated their pursuit."

"We hope," Don puffed.

The dogs couldn't have been more than a quarter of a mile behind now and the pace of the two had slowed considerably as the path steepened. The baying grew less questioning and more excited. Undoubtedly, the dogs could sense the nearness of their quarry.

The path became increasingly rough and Don decided that the horsemen were going to have to call it off. They couldn't possibly get their animals up here. The dogs, yes, but never the horses.

Evidently, the pursuers had no intention of calling it off. Shortly, Don and his companion could hear their shouts behind them.

"Faster," the Indian gasped. His breath too was now short, almost as short as Don's own.

But Don Fielding was rapidly reaching the end of his endurance. They had been on the march, on the run, for hours, without a single real rest. He was amazed, in actuality, that he had been able to continue even this long. Only the fear of death had allowed him to rise to the occasion.

They puffed on. Dawn was breaking. Behind them they could hear both dogs and soldiers, the dogs out ahead. The soldiers, who had been riding, as Cuauhtemoc and Don ran and walked, were considerably fresher than their game. The dogs broke into excited barking when they spotted their quarry and the soldiers shouted success. They must have wondered who the individual was who ran with Don Fielding.

The dogs sped up their pace now, outdistancing the men. They were only a couple of hundred feet behind and below the scrambling fugitives.

Don sank down behind a rock. "I can't go any further," he gasped, his chest heaving. The Indian looked down at him in dismay.

"There are four of them and well armed with the weapons of the gods."

Chapter Eight

Don brought forth his own weapon of the gods and thumbed off the safety. He doubted that so small a caliber would penetrate the Spanish armor, but he'd go down trying.

He held the gun in both hands to steady it and balanced it on the top of the rock. The dogs were no further than fifty feet below them and coming in fast, their teeth bared now. Obviously, they were trained to take on the objects of their chase.

When the lead one was no more than twenty feet away, Don gently squeezed the trigger. The gun snapped and the animal yelped, but continued on, frenzied now with blood lust. There was a *twang* and a feathered shaft buried itself in the beast's chest and he went down, an almost human scream coming from his mouth.

Don didn't bother to look over his shoulder at his Indian companion. He fired again and again into the second animal. He hit it twice out of three shots, and the bloodhound collapsed. Gallant at its job, it tried to work its way to its feet once more and come on. But another arrow whizzed past Don's head and sank into its carcass and down it went, this time to rise no more.

Cuauhtemoc was staring at the gun. "It is one of the weapons of the teteuhs but much smaller."

Don saved his breath. The Indian had leaned his lance against the cliff side and held his bow in his right hand, another arrow already notched on the bowstring. The quiver was over his right shoulder, handy to access.

About a hundred feet down below, the Spanish, undoubtedly astonished at the sound of gunfire, had come to a halt. They took shelter behind rocks, and although Don Fielding couldn't make out their words they were jabbering in obvious confusion.

He doubted very much that they had brought any arquebuses with them. The heavy matchlocks were simply too awkward. They were undoubtedly armed with swords alone.

But at that moment a crossbow quarrel spanged into the rock behind him and ricocheted off with a whine.

Oh, oh. At least one of the enemy had brought one of the smaller size crossbows with him, the type that could be handled on horseback.

Cuauhtemoc, an edge of apprehension in his voice, demanded, "What was that?"

"A type of bow which shoots a small metal arrow. Stay well down. They are very dangerous, though clumsy and slow to load. However, he cannot fire at us without exposing himself."

The Spanish, although probably bewildered at the fact that they had heard four shots, one right after another, must have decided that Don, too, would take considerable time to reload. They probably thought he had some fancy four-barreled gun of some sort. Such were not unknown, particularly in Italy. At any rate, they made a rush.

Don fired just once, got a satisfying scream of pain from the target, who must have been hit in an arm or some other body area not protected by armor. The four assailants dropped down behind rocks again.

Don had noted the one who carried the crossbow and waited for him. Sure enough, in a minute or so the bearded, helmeted soldier, his teeth bared, reared over the large rock behind which he had been crouched and tried to take a bead. Don fired twice. One bullet missed by inches, whining off the stone cliff behind the other. The other splatted dead center in the soldier's breastplate. Don had his answer. A .22 Long Rifle bullet would not penetrate the chest armor of the enemy. He was going to have to aim at more vulnerable portions of the body. And although he wasn't a bad shot, he was no expert marksman.

The crossbowman sank down quickly without getting off his bolt, and Don could hear excited jabbering again.

Cuauhtemoc whispered, "Come. They will follow us no more."

He was right. Now that Don had caught his breath, it was possible for them to sneak away. It would be considerable time, he suspected, before the Spanish tried another rush. No man likes to attack, in the open, against weapons he doesn't understand, particularly firearms. They left as quietly as possible and resumed the trail, taking full care to tread in such wise that no rocks were sent clattering back down the trail.

It was but a short distance to the top of the steep way and within ten minutes they emerged on a plateau. There were more hills beyond and mountains in the distance.

Don looked back thoughtfully. He said, "Between the two of us, we might be able to push a large boulder over and start an avalanche that would destroy them."

The Indian looked at him strangely. "No. The Tlacatecuhtli and the high council have not declared them enemies. It is one thing to defend oneself, even against gods, if one's life is in danger, but to attempt to destroy them when one is safe is not proper."

Don couldn't have brought himself to it at any rate. Last night he had killed a man. It was the first time he had ever seen a man die and he had done it. It had not been an easy experience. Self-defense, yes. It was his life or the other's. Just as had been that shoot-out down below. But he was no killer at heart.

Cuauhtemoc said, "Come, let us be off. They will never find us now, not without the gigantic dogs that smell one's trail."

They hit off over the plateau.

Cuauhtemoc seemed to know the way in spite of the fact that he avoided the path. They headed for the far mountains at a walk. Both were too exhausted for more. And now that it was over, Don was beginning to get the reaction to the high excitement and the fray. He was no man of action. There had been two wars in his time, but he had considered himself a conscientious objector in both cases and had pulled every string he could to escape the draft.

Cuauhtemoc looked at him from the side of his eyes, an amused element there. He said, "Your hand trembles, teteuh. You are obviously not a warrior, though you conduct yourself in emergency as a true man must."

"I am not a warrior," Don said. "I am a scholar. And I am not a god."

"Then what does one call you?"

"My name is Don Fielding. And my thanks for your assistance, particularly when you thought you were fighting against gods."

"Don Fielding. All of you gods have strange names."

Don sighed.

As they walked, he checked the magazine of his gun. He cursed himself for not having thought of bringing his partially full box of cartridges along with him when he had gotten into his things to retrieve his shoes and gun. He had only three shots left; one in the barrel, two in the clip. If the Spanish resumed the chase, he was done for.

He said to the other,"And how will you explain all this

to your uncle, the First Speaker? It is not usually the
activity of an ambassador.''

Cuauhtemoc laughed and said, "I won't. The first lesson an ambassador must learn is diplomacy. What my
uncle knows not will worry him not. Already, he worries
too much when it comes to the teteuhs.''

"They are not gods,'' Don Fielding sighed again. He
must get this idea over, he believed. If the Tenochas
continued to think the Spanish gods, then there was no
refuge for him in Tenochtitlan. He would be handed over
to his foes upon their demand. One does not oppose gods.

The other did not reply directly to that but said, "Tell
me more of these three gods from across the seas which La
Malinche mentioned.''

Trying to keep his own viewpoint as an agnostic neutral,
Don Fielding explained as best he could in Nahuatl the
Christian belief. It wasn't as difficult as he had expected to
get the fundamentals over to the Indian. In Tenochtitlan,
too, they had gods who were born of virgins and native
gods also often had more than one aspect. The Father,
Son, and Holy Ghost, three, still only one, did not bewil-
der Cuauhtemoc.

"But what are your own beliefs, Don Fielding?'' the
Indian asked, after assimilating what he heard.

How did you explain the agnostic viewpoint to a super-
stitious native?

Don said, seeking out his words carefully, "Man is the
only thinking animal.'' He remembered the recent—for
him recent—experiments with the porpoises and added,
"So far as we know.''

"Animal?''

"Yes, animal. For we too are animals, though the most
advanced.

"Go on, Don Fielding. This I do not understand.''

"Being a thinking animal, a reasoning animal, he seeks
answers for everything he sees. Unfortunately, he cannot

always find them. His intelligence is not *that* great. So what he cannot answer he ascribes to some greater power, some mystery. He invents gods. He cannot understand such things as lightning, storms, rain, so he ascribes them to gods. He rebels against death and invents an afterlife, a heaven or a hell, or both. The priests, often with selfish ends in mind, lay out a code which must be followed, supposedly, if the gods are to be appeased. And if they are able, they punish those who do not conform here on earth—not waiting for the gods to handle the punishment in an afterlife.''

"You make my head ache, Don Fielding. One thing I may warn you about.''

"Yes?''

"Do not let Xochitl hear such things from your lips when we arrive in Tenochtitlan.'' The Indian chuckled deprecation.

"Xochitl? Who is he?''

"The High Priest of Huitzilopochtli, the Hummingbird God, who is the chief god of the Tenochas. Speak thus and you will wind up on the altar, your heart torn from your chest. It is said to be a worthy way to die; however, I personally have never so regarded it though tell no priest I said so.'' The other laughed his deprecation again.

Don Fielding liked this one. In his Mexican travels he had found the Indians largely on the dour side, but it came to him that the Indians of his period had plenty to be dour about and it was probably brought out in them especially in the presence of a white man. Cuauhtemoc was more often smiling and there was a good deal of laughter in his conversation. Cuauhtemoc, Cuauhtemoc. He searched his memory. He seemed to have heard the name before, or at least read it. Although he was a Mexican specialist, he hadn't particularly made a big issue of the conquest of the Aztecs, though he was reasonably familiar with it. Cuauhtemoc? Possibly it was pronounced differently than the manner to which he was accustomed. Lord knows, he had already run into several different ways of pronouncing Montezuma.

They came upon the road again, if road it could be called. It was little more than six feet wide and consisted of packed dirt. But at least it was considerably easier to navigate than the open field. They walked side by side.

Don Fielding said, 'Where does this lead?''

"To Tenochtitlan. It is the main road from our city to the eastern area. From there it turns south along the coast to Xicalango, the great trading center where our *pochteca* traders meet with those of the Mayans.''

Don had once visited the ruins of Xicalango, which were about twelve miles south of Vera Cruz.

He said, "And how far are we from Tenochtitlan?''

"Perhaps nine days travel.''

"Nine days! Without food? Without even water?''

The Indian looked at him in surprise. "How could you have traveled so far from this land of yours to the north without knowing more of our roads?''

Don couldn't think of an answer to this and it sounded irrelevant to their problem, but he was in no position to try and explain to Cuauhtemoc his manner of appearing on the present scene. Particularly when he didn't know himself.

The other's question made more sense in about half an hour when they came upon what Don Fielding at first thought was a small settlement of adobe houses along a narrow stream. On their approach, however, it turned out that they were deserted. There were about twenty rooms in all, most of them on the small side and all grouped around the inevitable central courtyard.

After they had both drunk at the stream, they entered the enclosure and explored several of the rooms which they found spotlessly clean—as all the Indian habitations seemed spotless—but all but barren of contents. One room was evidently that for which Cuauhtemoc sought. It, an exception, contained quite a few baskets with lids, several leather bags, and quite a few pots of varying size. He explored around in them and came up shortly with a handful of what turned out to be dried venison, Don realized when he tasted it. Jerky, they called it in the American Southwest. There were also various empty pots and bowls and Cuauhtemoc handed him one of the former which was smoke-blackened about the bottom.

"Water," he said.

Don took it and went down to the stream, gnawing on the venison as he went. It tasted as good as anything he could ever remember having eaten. The last meal had been nearly twenty-four hours before and he'd had a good deal of exhausting exercise since then. He dipped the pot half full of water and returned with it to his companion.

Cuauhtemoc had also located a supply of mesquite wood cut up into handy sizes and began laying a fire in a corner of the courtyard where there were rocks, making an improvised open-air stove. Don put the pot down and watched him. The Indian had located fire-making equipment as well. A small bow with a loose string, a block of soft wood, nearly punk, and a spindlelike stick of what was evidently some very hard wood. He took it up, inserted the spindle in the loose string of the bow, and began to saw back and forth to twirl it point-down in the wood block.

Cuauhtemoc sawed away with his bow making the spindle whirl. He had the fire going in surprisingly short order. He heaped sufficient wood on it and then placed the pot of water above.

Both of them then returned to the storeroom and investigated the baskets further. There were beans in some, dried peppers in others, a considerable quantity of what looked like some type of sweet potato Don had never seen before, quantities of dried fish and dried shelled corn, as well as various other staples. Cuauhtemoc dug out a selection, handed part of it to Don to carry, and led the way back to the fire. He tossed the whole conglomeration into the stew pot and stood back to look down on it with satisfaction.

Don said, "Who supplies all this?"

The young Indian looked at him, frowning slightly. "Those who live in this vicinity."

"Well, why?"

"But it is the custom. The wayside shelters are maintained by the inhabitants of the area. Thus it is along every road in all the land from the far north to the far south and from the east sea to the west. How, otherwise, could the *pochteca* traders and any else who travel, survive? One cannot carry sufficient food to last more than a few days."

Don said, "You mean that anyone who comes along is free to help himself to as much of this food as he wants?"

The other looked at him as though Don was out of his mind. "Why not?"

"Your uncle, Motechzoma, enforces this? He requires all the tribes to do it?"

"No, he does not *require* it. Why should he have to?" Cuauhtemoc said, mystified.

"But suppose enemies of the local tribe come along? They too are free to help themselves?"

"The *pochtecas* are enemies of no man. They are traders; and what could any of us do without trade? If one tribe annoys the *pochtecas* of another, it means war. Others who travel are ambassadors. They too are touched by no man; it is unheard of."

"Well, other travelers."

"What other travelers?"

Cuauhtemoc had him there. He supposed that other than traders and ambassadors, practically no tribesman had any reason to go from one area to another, save during wartime and then, Don assumed, all bets were off. Actually, it made a lot of sense. What you lost when somebody crossed your territory you gained when you crossed someone else's.

They squatted Indian-fashion next to the fire until the stew was done.

Cuauhtemoc was no chef but the mess was at least filling and they emptied the pot without strain. Following their meal, the Indian thriftily put out the fire and led the way with the dirty cooking pot and the bowls from which they had eaten to the stream. They washed them out, using sand, and returned them to the storage room.

This too made sense, Don decided. Each traveler cleaned up after himself so that the next man along would find everything equally spotless.

Following that, they returned to the stream, shed their clothing, and bathed in the icy water, to Don's relief.

He said, "How far between are these wayside shelters?"

"Half a day's journey."

Probably about fifteen miles, Don decided. You should be able to do thirty miles a day on a level road. He imagined that they were closer together in the more rugged areas, such as the mountain passes. Fifteen miles should be near enough that you could make it to the next shelter in case you were overtaken by rain, snow, or whatever.

They returned to the shelter and sat up against one of the adobe walls, taking in the sun. Don Fielding wished he had one of his few remaining cigarettes, but they were with all the rest of his things in the porter's bundle. He looked at his watch. It was pushing noon. He wondered if Cuauhtemoc planned to spend the balance of the day here. Not that Don Fielding was in any hurry; the exhaustion was beginning to catch up on him and his body ached.

The Indian was staring at the watch. "What is that?"

Don unstrapped it and handed it over. "Put it to your ear."

"It makes a chewing sound! There is a tiny worm inside!"

Don said, "It is a very delicate mechanism of metal. You see the tiny arrows on the face there?" He pointed.

"This one moves!" He was talking about the second hand.

"Yes, all three move at different speeds, all at a steady pace. According to their position you can tell the time."

The other was astonished. However, he pointed up at the sky. "But what is wrong with the sun?"

Don said, "For one thing, when it is very cloudy, you can't see the sun. And you can't see it ever at night."

"But who cares what time it is at night? What makes it run; what makes it eat? A small animal inside? A small devil?"

Don Fielding shook his head. How did you go about explaining a watch's mechanism to a Neolithic barbarian?

He tried, but without success, and finally gave up. Cuauhtemoc decided it was all magic and gave up too.

"You are a magician?" he asked finally.

Don denied it, but he doubted that the denial was going to stick. How else to explain such things as guns and wristwatches?

The train of the fifty others caught up with them about two hours later. They filed into the shelter and immediately set up camp. They didn't seem to be particularly surprised to find Don and Cuauhtemoc. Don wondered if they had spotted the two dead dogs or if they had come by another route.

Axayaca said merely, "The teteuhs who rode the deer after you returned to Zempoala." He looked at Don Fielding expressionlessly. For some reason, this one had taken a dislike to him, Don decided. He didn't know why.

For the first time, he realized that three of this expedition were women. Muscular, vigorous girls, who had obviously been brought along to do some of the chores usually relegated to women. They were tiny, by American standards, possibly four foot eight. They entered the storeroom, came forth with corn and hollowed out stone *metates* and began to grind corn flour with stone rollers. When they had a quantity, they brought water and made the paste-dough which was the basic ingredient of tortillas.

Don had sought out the porter who had his things and now rescued the clothes and his other few possessions, leaving for the time only the Spanish sword he had appropriated from the assassin. He took them into one of the empty rooms and changed with a sigh of relief. The Indian garments had been no great treat to him. They didn't even protect you from ants when you sat on the ground. He belted the holster back on, fished out his box of .22 cartridges, and reloaded the clip of the gun.

He took the discarded Indian garments out and returned them to the porter.

One of the Indian women had laid four fires in the outdoor kitchen. She took up the small bow and the other fire-making equipment and began to twirl.

Don came up and said, "Here." He brought forth a book of paper matches and struck one of them, knelt, and lit the fire.

She goggled at him. So did Cuauhtemoc who was standing nearby.

Cuauhtemoc said accusingly, "You said that you were not a magician."

"Yeah," Don muttered in English and then in Nahuatl, "This is a device that all have in my land. It is not magic."

The other grunted contempt of that opinion. Don could see how his mind worked. Fire had sprung from the white man's fingers. The hell with it. There was no way of explaining.

The group had evidently shot several rabbits along the way with their bows. They went into the community stew. In spite of the fact that he and Cuauhtemoc had eaten only a few hours ago, the smells of the dishes the women were preparing were appetite-provoking with a vengeance. When the time came to eat, he and his companion of the night before were both in line. The food was dipped out of the pots and distributed by the women. Then the men retired to squat on their heels, tortillas in hand, and ate off to the side by themselves. The women evidently ate later.

Don had assumed that they were to stay here for the balance of the day and night and get a fresh start in the morning, but after a short rest following eating, the porters began to reassemble their things again and shortly the train was under way.

Cuauhtemoc looked at him and said, "Malintzin informed me, in spite of my protests, that he would soon march to Tenochtitlan to meet with my uncle. We would not wish them to overtake us after the events of last night."

Don said, "Is this the road to Tlaxcala?"

"No. That lies further north. We are enemies of the Tlaxcalans and it would be ill to travel through their territory, even though we are ambassadors."

"Then you need not worry about the Spanish overtaking us. They go first to Tlaxcala."

"How do you know?"

What could Don Fielding say? He knew because history told him so. The Spanish marched first to the land of the long-time enemies of the Tenochas, enrolled them in their forces, and then marched on Tenochtitlan. But could history be altered? Hadn't he already altered it? The night before he had killed a Spaniard. If that soldier had remained alive, in what manner would he have participated in the conquest? For all Don knew, it was Cortes himself, or possibly Pedro de Alvarado, who played such a big role in the destruction of Tenochtitlan. But how *could* that be? So far as he could see, if he swatted a single mosquito, history would be altered. The mosquito's descendants, all the millions upon millions of them, would then never exist. And how many of that insect's descendants had, in their time, bitten human beings and given them, say, malaria or yellow fever? If those mosquitoes failed to be born, they would never have bitten their victims and the victims would have survived. Survived to do what? To become the ancestors of generals, statesmen, artists, inventors, and what-not. And hence alter the history of the world. His mind reeled. Nothing, nothing of all this made sense! It couldn't be happening. If history had been altered by his presence here, he simply wouldn't be here. But he was here. A dream? Ha! It might have seemed a dream the first day, the first few hours, but he had been in the past, fully conscious, for the better part of a week now. It was no dream nor fantasy. He was here, in 1519, in the world of Cortes and Montezuma.

He said simply, "I know."

Cuauhtemoc thought about it. He was obviously no lightweight. He said finally, "Nevertheless, we will march. The sooner I report to The First Speaker and the Tlatocan the better."

So resume the march they did, and for the next nine days. Some three hundred miles, Don Fielding estimated. He had never walked such a distance before and most certainly hoped never to have to in the future. The *distant* future, he corrected himself hopefully, with its nuclear weapons and penicillin, freeway congestion and Poulenc in stereo. But was this future now all in his past?

The journey was broken up twice a day at the shelters. In the morning they would eat a bit of the tortilla leftovers from the day before. At noon they would stop and have the real repast of the day, the women preparing it from the basic supplies in all the Indian equivalents of inns spaced some fifteen miles along the way. In the evening they had meager leftovers from their midday meal, which had been brought along, and tortillas which the women made freshly. Evidently, in Indian society, one meal a day, one major meal, was the rule. Don Fielding had his troubles getting used to it. He was used to three a day, not to speak of snacks or raiding the refrigerator before bedtime. How they achieved their stamina was a mystery to him. However, they had it. Their endurance was beyond his.

They had left behind their view of the sea from the mountain crest, left behind the rich growths of the tropics, and ascended into the dark belts of pines in the higher altitudes. The summer rains were upon them and the road became so muddy as to hold up their progress. To make their thirty miles a day, they had to slog along from dawn until dark and to shorten their midday rest period. The aspect of the country was as wild and dreary as the climate.

They passed through some areas that showed abundant traces of volcanic action where acres of lava and cinders proclaimed the convulsions of nature, while numerous shrubs and moldering trunks of enormous trees among the crevices attested to the antiquity of these events.

They went through various passes, snow-topped mountains on both sides, the weather so cold now that Don was forced again to take one of the Indian mantles to ward it off.

There was a branch-off of the road and Cuauhtemoc pointed and said, "Cholula."

Cholula? Then they weren't so very far from their destination. Don said, "Don't we go through there? I thought it was one of your cities."

"Our cities? No. It is not even in the valley. Sometimes they ally themselves with the Tlaxcalans and the people of Huexotzingo and war against us. Sometimes they ally themselves with us to fight Tlaxcala."

The next day, Don Fielding could recognize two of the mountains, Popocatapetl to the left of their march, Iztacciuatl to the right, both of them soaring higher than seventeen thousand feet. There was a feather of volcanic smoke above the former, Don noted. In his own day—his former future day?—the volcano was seldom active.

They pressed on through the pass, through the heavily

wooded slopes that now materialized—noble forests of oak, cedar, and sycamore—and eventually, turning an angle of the mighty sierra, they came suddenly on the view of the valley of Mexico. And there in the lake was Tenochtitlan.

Chapter Nine

Don Fielding had often viewed Mexico City and the valley which lay below, in his own time, from approximately this spot. There was a super-highway going through the pass to the city of Pueblo. However, he recognized nothing. In the twentieth century, Lake Texcoco was all but completely gone. The Spanish and modern Mexicans had drained it.

Now, the lake covered what seemed to be most of the valley floor. It was ringed, so far as his eye could see, with villages and towns, some of them in the lake itself. Largest of them all was Tenochtitlan, located on the far side, not too distant from the shore line of a bay and approached by three causeways; four, if you counted one which made a juncture with another before reaching the city proper. In the distance, on the edge of the lake and nearly screened by intervening foliage, he could barely make out what must be Tetzcuco, the sister city and friendly rival of Tenochtitlan. As Don recalled, it was said to be at least the same size.

Cuauhtemoc said proudly, "Tenochtitlan."

"Yes, of course," Don murmured in awe. He could make out the temple area, the soaring pyramids, the huge buildings, even from this distance, and the distance was great; at least another day's march. But the air was clear.

101

The blinding smog of his own day was unknown here. It might not be so bad, he thought—and firmly directed his mind elsewhere.

It was a city of canals, of greenery and other color everywhere. So covered was the area with vegetation that Don could only wonder where the people lived.

They started to descend at a stronger pace now, since the way was downhill. For that matter, the road was better. Obviously, it was more utilized this close to the capital. Shortly it became paved with some type of pink pumice traprock composed of silica and volcanic ash from what Don could see. It was wider now.

Although all had perked up at the sight of their goal, they still had a long way to go. They'd never reach the city this night, no matter that it was magnificently in view.

Don said to Cuauhtemoc, "I have been curious. How is it that your uncle and the council sent such young men as you and Axayaca as ambassadors to Cortes?"

"But we are of the Eagle *calpulli*."

"What difference does that make?"

"Why, it is well that while we are still young men, we gain experience so that later, if we are elected to office, we will know how to conduct ourselves."

"Why shouldn't this apply to any other clan?"

"It does, but in lesser degree. Each *calpulli* must elect its own chiefs, of course. But we of the Eagles are particularly trained to hold high office in both the city and the confederation. We have long been noted as warriors and administrators. For many generations our clan has supplied the office of Tlacatecuhtli to the city, and that of the Cihuacohuatl, as well."

"Cihuacohuatl?" Don said. The word meant, literally, snake-woman.

"The head chief of the Tenochas," Cuauhtemoc explained.

Don Fielding looked at him. "But I thought your uncle, Motechzoma, was head chief of the Tenochas."

The other shook his head. "No. You don't understand. Motechzoma is the head war chief of our confederation of Tenochtitlan, Tetzcuco, and Tlacopan. Tlilpotonque is the Snake-Woman. It is a title that goes so far back that we know not its origins. He is not a woman, of course."

In a way, Don Fielding was amused. Cortes, in his so badly translated dialogue with Cuauhtemoc, had assumed Motechzoma to be emperor, or at least king, of what amounted to all Mexico. Now it turned out that he wasn't even head chief of the Tenochas.

As they descended, the woods became thinner and patches of cultivated land appeared more often, wherever in fact, there was level enough a plot to work. From what Don could see of the valley, that need was obvious. Population explosion there was in the area in this era, though not as bad as in his own. However, in his time the Mexicans were able to bring in food and other necessities by railroad and truck. But in this age a porter's back, over these long stretches and these rugged roads and conditions, didn't make much sense. You might be able to requisition food from as far away as fifty miles from Tenochtitlan, but after that the amount of food that the porter consumed, coming and going, started giving you diminishing returns. Shelled dried corn, of course, a concentrate, wasn't so bad. But other staples of Indian diet—squash, melons, tomatoes, green peppers, and so forth? It simply didn't make sense. Largely, the overcrowded inhabitants of the Mexican valley would have to raise their own food.

They spent the night in a town Cuauhtemoc told him was named Ayotzico, which was located at the southernmost part of the lake. Evidently, the Indians considered the lake to be not one, but five, although they were all joined. This was Lake Chalco, evidently named after the largest town which bordered it and which was located somewhere over to the right.

Ayotzico itself spread out into the lake. That is, some of

the town, resting on piles and reclaimed land, overflowed into the water.

Cuauhtemoc was not on home territory, it seemed. Ayotzico was allied to the Tenochtitlan league. He was met with full honors by the local chief and they were escorted to the quarters in one of the larger community houses. It was at least as big as anything in Cempoala, and Don realized that if and when the Spanish saw it, it would be dubbed a palace.

In the morning they arose at dawn and set off alongside the edge of the lake. Cuauhtemoc informed Don that the night before the local chief had sent a runner ahead to Motechzoma and the high council to inform them of the return of the ambassadors. Undoubtedly, they would be summoned to appear and report immediately upon arrival.

As they proceeded, the towns became thicker and were even more inclined to extend out into the lakes. They were half dry land villages, half *chinampas*. Don Fielding, in his wanderings about Mexico, had been in the town of Xochimilco more than once, the largest of the remaining *chinampa* towns in the country.

It was an interesting method of agriculture. Driven by necessity to achieve more land for cultivation, the inhabitants of the Mexican valley had created it. The lake was quite shallow, so the Indians had been able to dredge up mud from the bottom and dump it into huge baskets, in which they planted crops. The roots would soon grow out of the bottom and sink themselves into the lake floor. Each year, new baskets would be added and more rich lake bottom mud added to the top. When a fairly large area was thus covered, even trees could be planted, and in time the land would become quite permanent. Dredging up new soil to place on top each year gave somewhat the same result as the flooding of the Nile in Egypt. That is, the old land was continually fertilized by the new mud and it was possible to wrest several crops a year from the soil.

Yes, Don Fielding knew all about the *chinampa* towns, but it was fascinating, as an anthropologist cum archeologist, to witness them at their peak of glory. In actuality, these people were gardeners rather than farmers. They had no field agriculture, no beasts of burden, no domesticated animals save the turkey, and a small hairless dog they bred for food. Yes, fascinating, but fated to go. The Spanish would introduce the plow and draught animal, and field agriculture would be here.

It all came under the head of progress, he admitted. This *chinampa* system was primitive. He could see the Indians working them, with their ancient *coa* digging sticks; considerably wider at the digging end than the handle, it was somewhat reminiscent of a very early form of shovel.

Cuauhtemoc named the towns and villages as they progressed. Here was Xochimilco, the very town Don had known in another age, here Tlalpan, here Cuicuilco, and here Coyoacan, which was somewhat larger than most of the others and must have boasted some five thousand inhabitants.

At Coyoacan they branched off onto one of the causeways that led to the great city in the lake. It was of stone and gravel and periodically they crossed over bridges made of removable wooden beams. Cuauhtemoc, obviously prideful of his city, explained that the water breaches had three purposes. They permitted the movement of canoes through the causeway, allowed for the ebb and flow of water which might otherwise have damaged the causeway, and in case of danger, the beams could be removed so that an enemy couldn't attack the city. An ancient horizontal form of drawbridge, Don decided.

Don Fielding could see the obvious need for passageways for the canoes. The lake was aswarm with them—dugout canoes, holding one, two, or three persons, seldom more. They were limited in size due to the fact that they were carved out of single tree trunks, undoubtedly brought down from the surrounding mountains.

After about a mile, they reached a small island which was fortified with both towers and walls and where they joined a larger causeway which came up from the south.

"Acachinanco," Cuauhtemoc told him. "We have fortified it against our enemies of the city Huexotzingo."

They halted here long enough for Cuauhtemoc and Axayaca and the subchiefs to get into their formal attire as ambassadors. Then they went on. The causeway, now, was some twenty-five feet wide and aswarm with Indians coming and going between the mainland and the city. All together, Don Fielding estimated the causeway must be some four miles long. The Indians bug-eyed him, but didn't stop.

The nearer they got to the city, the more *chinampas* they came upon. Evidently, Tenochtitlan was still growing, still sprawling out over the lake. History told him that originally, when the Tenochas had first moved out from the mainland, there had been only a few marshy islands and practically no dry land at all. Slowly, using the *chinampas* method, they had enlarged it until now, almost two hundred years later, it embraced some twenty-five hundred acres in all. The trouble was, where the lake ended and the city began was moot. The closer you got toward the center, the more the *chinampas* thickened, until finally what had been more or less open lake became patches of land, surrounded by canals.

Finally, the causeway merged into dry land and sizable buildings began.

"Xoloco," Cuauhtemoc said. "This is the *calpulli* of Xoloco. There are twenty *calpulli* in all and the city is divided into four sections, Teopan, Moyotlan, Aztacalco and Cuepopan, each containing five *calpulli*, each occupied by a clan. Then there is Tlaltelolco, our sister city to which we are attached to the north, and it contains six more *calpulli*. Ours is the greatest city in the world.''

Well, perhaps, Don thought inwardly. He wondered just what cities they might have in this age in China or India. In Europe, perhaps, they might not have quite this population, though he suspected that Venice, London, or Paris could give this Neolithic town a run for its money.

There were the usual community houses spread out over wide areas; there were temples and there were pyramids of smaller size.

Cuauhtemoc indicated one building. ''The *tecpan* of Xoloco,'' he said.

''*Tecpan*?''

Cuauhtemoc frowned. ''Where the *calpullec*, the chiefs of this clan, conducts its business affairs. Where the chief reside. Where . . .''

''Precinct station,'' Don muttered.

As they proceeded, it came to him that Tenochtitlan resembled Venice, or perhaps Amsterdam. It was a city of canals. There was as much, or more, traffic on water as there was on land. Every house seemed to have two entries, one on the street, one on the canal. It was actually possible to enter many of the larger buildings either way; that is, you could pole or paddle your boat right into the building.

Don was reminded of the gondolas of Venice. They even stood to pole or paddle them in gondolier fashion. Evidently produce and freight was moved on the canals; so evidently was even fresh water. He pointed out another canoe, laden down with what he knew not, and asked Cuauhtemoc about it.

The young Indian laughed and explained that the public latrines were unloaded into these canoes and the contents taken over to the mainland to be used as fertilizer. It made sense. If they'd dumped their sewage into the canals, they'd not only have a horrible stench in short order but possibly an epidemic as well.

Actually it was a beautiful town, Don decided. These people went in for flowers, gardens, and trees. There was color everywhere, in the clothes, in the painting of the houses, in the decorations of temples and public buildings.

The houses were single story, as in Cempoala and every other Mexican town Don had thus far seen; however, the second story seemed to be attempting to evolve. Some of the larger community buildings, now that they were on land that was of firmer foundation, would have an arrangement where there was a first floor, then a platform behind it. An exterior stone stairway would take you up to the second landing and there would be additional rooms.

They emerged finally at the end of the causeway to what in Don's day was the Zocalo of Mexico City and was in these days a complex of pyramids, temples, and governmental buildings of Tenochtitlan.

It was enwalled, completely surrounded by canals, and possibly the most impressive complex of buildings Don had ever seen, even in his own age. The area was far and beyond the courtyard in front of St. Peter's in Rome or the square before St. Mark's in Venice, and it was as abuzz as either of those.

Don Fielding had seen a model reconstruction of the great plaza of Tenochtitlan. He could make out the inaccuracies, but in actuality, it had been rather well done. He could recognize now, straight ahead, where one day the cathedral would be and where now reared a temple set atop the largest pyramid in the vicinity. Over there, to the right, where one day was to be the National Palace, the space was now occupied by a huge building with several entrances.

When he saw Don looking in that direction, Cuauhtemoc said with pride, "The central house of the Eagle clan."

"Then that's where your uncle, Motechzoma, lives?"

"No, the First Speaker, the Snake-Woman, and the other head chiefs of Tenochtitlan live there, in the *tecpan*."

The other pointed to another huge building on the other side of the great temple. "There they administer the city and the affairs of the confederation. There they entertain visiting delegations from the other cities. There they divide the spoils of war."

"City hall," Don muttered to himself in English.

His eyes went around the rest of the square, even as they proceeded in the direction of the *tecpan*. He winced at the sight of the great block of the skull-rack, where thousands of skulls, threaded on poles, were piled high in orderly symmetry. Nearby was a ball court in which some young men were kicking a ball about with hips and elbows, in an effort to bounce it through two rings set opposite each other on the walls that ran the length of the court. Nearby, too, was a stone altar Don recognized, to his surprise. It was the Tizoc sacrificial stone, hollowed in the center so that hearts from the victims could be burned there. And one day to be displayed in the National Museum.

And now he noted a stench in the air, similar to that of a foul butcher shop which rose above the odor of incense from the braziers which were so thick about the square that the air was almost smoglike in quality. In his association with Cuauhtemoc and the others over the past ten days, he had forgotten this aspect of the Tenocha culture.

Let the Spanish come! At least they would end this!

On the way down the causeway street, he had spotted black garbed priests on several occasions. Now their number increased considerably and he came close enough to several to get their stench. Their hair was long, obviously never cut, and matted with what must be blood. Don's stomach churned.

They reached an enormous gate leading into the courtyard of the building Cuauhtemoc had named the *tecpan*, and Don and the two younger ambassadors, followed by the subchiefs, filed in. The porters and women went off elsewhere, their portion of the expedition completed.

The building, sizable though it was and evidently containing literally hundreds of rooms, was aswarm with humanity. Some, either singly or in groups, were scurrying here and there, obviously on business. Some stood about, arguing, debating, discussing, sometimes laughing. Others squatted on their heels, doing the same. As always in these Indian buildings, there were no chairs. One could sit on the edge of a step, if he wished. Few of them seemed to. The Indian, like the Moslem, preferred to sit or squat on the floor.

Don followed Cuauhtemoc and Axayaca up a fairly steep set of stone stairs to where a moderately large set of rooms was set back on a platform—the nearest thing to a second story their architecture had thus far evolved, as he had noted before. This must be the official quarters of Motechzoma Xocoyotzin, Montezuma the Second, the First Speaker, but there were no sentries. By appearances, the Indians hadn't gotten that far in their military know-how. Come to think of it, save for their party entering the city after a long trip, he had seen no armed men at all. Tenochtitlan, like ancient Rome, must forbid arms within the city limits. Weapons, seemingly, were stored in some sort of armory until needed.

They were being awaited. Who was evidently Motechzoma himself sat on what was the nearest thing to a chair that Don had thus far seen in Mexico. It was of leather and had a back but no legs. The war chief was still sitting on the floor. Around him were seven others, standing.

The room was typical of all that Don had as yet seen in this era. About fifty feet long by twenty deep, aside from tapestries, rugs, and colorful mats, it was unfurnished. There were no windows, no fireplace, and no way of closing the door through which the only available light came.

The war chief stood, a somewhat startled look on his not unhandsome face. The relationship to Cuauhtemoc was obvious. He looked to be about forty, well proportioned though lean, was about the same height as his nephew, which made him slightly above the Indian average. He affected a thin black beard, had the same good eyes as Cuauhtemoc, and his complexion seemed somewhat lighter than those of most of his companions. Perhaps he was in the sunlight less often. He, like the others present, was dressed similarly to all the Indians of this country Don had seen thus far. Perhaps a bit richer but much the same.

Don said politely, "Greetings to Motechzoma Xocoyotzin." Montezuma the Younger, that meant, or Montezuma the Second; there had been another Montezuma several generations back.

All had been ogling the newcomer in amazement, but that really set them back.

The First Speaker blurted, "You speak our tongue!" His eyes went to his two nephews. "You did not inform me that the teteuhs used our tongue. Thus it has not been in our past relations with them. It was necessary to speak through this La Malinche and the other to converse with Malintzin."

Cuauhtemoc said defensively, "He is the only teteuh who speaks Nahuatl. He says he is not of the same nation as the other teteuhs. He denies that he is a teteuh himself, or even that *they* are. His story is that they imprisoned and tried to kill him but that he killed the assassin and escaped. He came to us and we brought him here." The younger man was properly respectful, but he didn't seem to have any particular awe for his uncle.

Motechzoma's eyes were going back and forth in utter disbelief.

"I did not instruct you to return with a prisoner."

"He is not a prisoner. He came of his free will. Besides, I doubt that I could take him prisoner if I so wished, since he carries one of the weapons of the gods."

One of the older chiefs came up with, "It is said that it is impossible to kill a teteuh."

Motechzoma said, "If you are not of the same nation as Malintzin, from whence do you come?"

Don gave him the story of his land to the distant north, and he could see disbelief in the other's eyes. He wasn't being overly impressed by the head war chief of the Mexico valley confederation. The other had a somewhat fearful quality about him. Fearful of Don Fielding, here in his own capital, here in his power? He had only to clap his hands and Don was a dead man. Nevertheless, there was no denying the other's confusion.

Axayaca said, "He claims that Malintzin marches on Tlaxcala."

"Tlaxcala!" one of the others blurted. "Then we are safe."

Cuauhtemoc shook his head. "Malintzin himself told me that he comes here to see the Tlacatecuhtli. That then all problems will be solved between you."

Don Fielding said, "He goes to Tlaxcala on the way here. He intends to make allies of them and then march on Tenochtitlan." He could have told them, he supposed, that Cortes was coming for no good, so far as the Indians were concerned, but why should he? He wished, above all, to continue living, and ultimately survival could only be through the Spaniards. Tenochtitlan's fate was already in the cards. Somehow, he must make his peace with Cortes and the Spanish army. How, he didn't know, but he would have to. Perhaps he could get to him through Fray Olmedo, Malinche, or Bernal Diaz.

One of the chiefs, the seemingly sharpest of them, said, "If you are their enemy, how should you know?"

Don lied, "When I was in their camp I heard their chiefs talking."

Motechzoma seemed in despair, but he got around, at

last, to introductions. He indicated the last Indian speaker. "This is Tlilpotonque, the Cihuacohuatl."

So Snake-Woman, head chief of the Tenochas, was possibly ten years the senior of Motechzoma and considerably his senior intellectually, if Don was any judge. This man had achieved his high office through his own endeavors, not just because he belonged to the Eagle clan. He hadn't the good looks of Cuauhtemoc and his uncle, but he had an intensity that came through in eyes and facial expression.

The war chief was introducing the others. Tlacochcalcatl, Tlacatecatl, Ezhuanhuacatl, Cucuhnochtecuhtli. Don didn't know if these were titles or names or both. The words meant, literally: man of the house of darts, cutter of man, bloodshedder, and chief of the eagle and prickly pear. If Don got it correctly, these four, all of whom were more elderly than the rest present, were the head chiefs of the four sections into which Tenochtitlan proper was divided.

The war chief was indicating the others. "And Tetlepanquetzaltzin, Tlachochcalcatl of Tlacopan; Cacama, Tlachochcalcatl of Tetzcuco; Itzcuauhtzin, Tlachochcalcatl of Tlatelolco, our sister city."

Evidently this was not just a meeting of the high council of Tenochtitlan, but of the confederated cities as well. If he had it right, it was strictly a military alliance. The three cities were united for the purpose of looting their neighbors—a bandit people whose raiding expeditions extended over half of Mexico and some three hundred cities, towns, and villages. Well, the Spanish would end that, too, with raids to end all raids. In fact, they had already begun. Cempoala had been one of the tribute areas and Cortes had taken it over in the name of his monarch, Charles Fifth.

There was only one other present, thus far unintroduced. He was black-robed, his hair matted and filthy; a seeming madness gleamed from his eyes set in a fox face.

Motechzoma said, "Xochitl, the Quequetzalcoa."

So this was the High Priest of Huitzilopochtli, the Hummingbird God, the god of war of the Tenochas.

His eyes burned and he screamed, "Sacrifice him to the gods!"

Chapter Ten

Don Fielding almost stepped back at the fury of the priest's voice. But he held himself. He couldn't afford to lose caste before these men. He held silence, not knowing what to say, but looked at Cuauhtemoc from the side of his eyes.

The returned ambassador said, "He is a teteuh himself, and possibly cannot be killed, even if we wished to sacrifice him to Huitzilopochtli. But more important, he is a magician who can tell us much about Malintzin and the way of the teteuhs."

"A magician?" Motechzoma's eyes shifted.

"I myself have seen him bring flame from his fingertips."

The young Tenocha could use some backing up at this point, Don Fielding decided. He brought one of the folders of paper matches from the breast pocket of his bush jacket and nonchalantly struck one of them.

A sigh went through the room. Motechzoma's mouth twitched.

Some war chief, Don decided inwardly. He would hate to follow this one into battle. Well, possibly the man was under pressures he was unaccustomed to. It was up to him, evidently, to handle foreign affairs. As the confederation's war chief, he was also Secretary of State, or at least of

Foreign Affairs. His shoulders carried the load of deciding what to do with the encroaching white men and his problems were intensified by the fact that everybody thought them gods, including himself.

"Sacrifice him," Xochitl screamed again.

The man was crazy as a coot, Don decided unhappily. That was all he needed, a crackpot priest.

Axayaca, not looking at Don, said to the chiefs, "Hold him for the teteuhs, if they in truth come. He is not a Tenocha. It is not a problem for us. Let Malintzin, who he claims is now his enemy, decide."

Motechzoma looked about at the others, obviously wanting more advice.

The Snake-Woman said, "Hold him as an honored guest, here in the *tecpan*. Let him wander about Tenochtitlan as he wishes, for there is nothing that he can do to harm us, and no place for him to go in all the land. If Malintzin comes, then he can decide."

Cuauhtemoc looked at Don and bit his lower lip slightly but he said no more. He had already stuck his neck out and he owed this white man nothing. In fact, it was the other way around.

Motechzoma looked about at the assembly of chiefs and said, "Very well, if there is no dissent, save that of Xochitl, the stranger shall remain here in the *tecpan* until we have decided further or until Malintzin comes." He looked at Cuauhtemoc. "He shall be your responsibility. Find him quarters. See that his needs are filled."

The interview was evidently over.

Cuauhtemoc said to Don, "Come," and turned and led the way.

They descended the stone steps to ground level and began making their way through the largest courtyard. They went through an archway and into another courtyard. The whole *tecpan* was a veritable labyrinth of courtyards, each with its rooms, most of them single and unconnected, set about them. Don wondered, in passing, whether this was actually similar to the original labyrinth. Had the ancient Cretans, at somewhat the same level of civilization, built a complex of buildings similar to the *tecpan*? Was that what the palace of Minos at Knossus really was? Well, he had no time to consider it now.

He said to Cuauhtemoc, "Why is the priest so anxious to have me sacrificed?"

Cuauhtemoc scowled. "Perhaps it is because Huitzil-opochtli thirsts for blood. It has been long since he has been appeased. When the disturbing news came from the coast of the eastern sea that the white gods had appeared on their floating hills . . ."

"Ships," Don said.

". . . Motechzoma was to the south in the lands of the Mexticas conducting war and taking many prisoners for the sacrifices. When he heard the news, he hurried back to Tenochtitlan and recalled our warriors from all the land, now knowing what must be done. So it is that no more prisoners arrive."

They had come to a courtyard, somewhat smaller than most of the others. Cuauhtemoc led the way to a room. It was remarkably similar to the one Don had utilized in Cempoala. In fact, Indian architecture in general seemed to lack anything in the way of variety. The quality of the tapestries, blankets, rugs, and mats might be somewhat superior here.

Cuauhtemoc squatted Indian-fashion on the floor and said, "I would like to rejoin my family, but there is probably much that you wish to know. And soon it will be the time for food and you will need to understand where to go."

"Family?" Don said. "You have a family? You seem very young for marriage."

The Indian smiled and said, "We Tenochas lose many of our people in the wars. Thus it is that we need children to restore the population. A boy becomes a man at the age of sixteen. At twenty he is ready for marriage, after undergoing his warrior and other training. A girl is ready to be wed at the age of sixteen. I took my bride from the ranks of the Turtle clan, next to the Eagles, the clan of the greatest prestige.''

"It is required that you marry a woman from some other *calpulli* than your own?" Don was, momentarily, again the ethnologist.

"Yes, of course." The other seemed to think that a strange question.

Don sat on the floor, too, less comfortably than his companion. He had as yet to master the squatting posture the Tenochas seemed to be able to hold for hours on end without strain of the muscles.

Cuauhtemoc said, "There is another reason, perhaps, that Xochitl would as well that all you teteuhs be driven from the land."

"Oh? What is that?"

"For long years, Huitzilopochtli, the Hummingbird, has been our chief god, since long past when the god Quetzalcoatl disappeared into the eastern sea, sailing off but vowing to return in the year One Reed. He was the chief god of the Toltecs, the people who preceded us here." Cuauhtemoc hesitated and then said, "He did not demand sacrifices, as does Huitzilopochtli."

The Indian hesitated again, then, "Some say that he was of white complexion and had a black beard, even as your own."

Don felt his face ruefully. He hadn't been able to shave in nearly two weeks and the stubble was getting on the long side. He understood that the Indians had razors made of thin slivers of obsidian. He would have to look into that; he didn't like a beard. On the other hand, they had no soap beyond a few shrub roots. How did you shave without soap? Would some sort of oil soften the beard sufficiently?

Cuauhtemoc said, still speaking carefully, "This is the year One Reed and Malintzin and his people have come. Xochitl fears it is the return of Quetzalcoatl, the feathered serpent god, come to demand that Huitzilopochtli be overthrown and that he be returned to power."

Don was somewhat acquainted with the story. Cortes had encouraged it as part of his scheme to confuse the Indians.

He sighed and said, "Cortes isn't Quetzalcoatl. He isn't any other kind of god either."

"How do you know?"

"As I told you before, there are no gods."

Suddenly eight or ten whistles began to sound and there was a rumble of drums.

Cuauhtemoc came to his feet. "The summons for the meal," he said.

Don followed him—some dinner gong, he thought—through another maze of courtyards and connecting arches, they joining the mass of men headed in the same direction. Well, in the future he wouldn't have any difficulty finding his way to where they ate. All he'd have to do was blend with the traffic.

He was taken aback by the size of the room when they entered it. It must have been the better part of a hundred feet long and some thirty-five wide. It was full of men; at least five hundred, Don estimated.

Women and boys were scurrying around, putting bowls on the floor. Some of the bowls were atop braziers to keep them hot. The men were dressed as always, loincloths and mantle; most of them were barefooted. They were very interested in Don Fielding, but avoided looking directly in his face—probably out of courtesy, he decided. Now that he thought of it, no Indian stared directly into your eye. It was a white man's trait.

Cuauhtemoc led him to the far end of the room where Motechzoma and his chiefs were gathered. Among them were some new additions to those Don had met at the meeting with the Tlatocan high council, but they weren't introduced to him in spite of their obvious curiosity.

Motechzoma sat in his version of a chair, but the others stood and most remained that way to eat, though some squatted. Before the war chief were spread a white cloth and several napkins. He pointed out various of the dishes, in their bowls on the floor; one of the boy waiters brought them to him. Two women approached with a basin and a ewer of water, and he washed his hands and dried them on the towels they provided.

One by one the other chiefs and Cuauhtemoc and Don, in their turn, did the same.

All through the room, men were inspecting the pots and making their selections. There must have been some three hundred dishes in all, Don decided, though many duplicated each other. A barbaric banquet!

Cuauhtemoc took up a bowl and handed it to him. "Try this," he offered.

There were stacks of tortillas about and other types of native bread which he didn't recognize, some of them sweet, probably with honey. All he could do was experiment.

Other women came in with jars of frothy chocolate. It wasn't sweetened, but they had seemed to add vanilla. It had been whipped into a foam and was excellent. They continued to bring in fresh supplies all through the meal.

The dish his Indian companion had given him was a stew. They went in for stews, perhaps because there was so little meat in the diet. Save for turkey and the small edible dogs, meat was either wild or you did without. Whatever this conglomeration was, it was delicious. The Indian cooks—he assumed they were women—had a way with spices and herbs.

Motechzoma motioned him to be seated at the royal side. Now that the decision as to what to do with Don had been made, the war chief was possibly relieved and now, of course, curious.

As he ate and drank the chocolate, he said to Don, "You say that Malintzin is not a god, but my messengers have brought me paintings of his hills that float in the sea, of his terrible weapons that thunder and knock down trees and houses. Of his deer, upon which they ride."

Don finished his bowl of food and took up a piece of fruit from a nearby tray.

He said, "In the land from which they come, across the sea, these things are the common property of all warriors. And in my own land, as well. They are not solely the property of gods. In time, I suppose, I could show you how to make them for your own use."

He thought about it. Could he? Vaguely, he knew that gunpowder was made from saltpeter, sulfur, and charcoal. They were ground to a fine powder and then combined. But in what proportions? And the gunpowder Don had seen was mostly brittle, glazed chunks, coarse for blasting powder, quite small for the black-powder guns of enthusiasts. Was it also necessary to press it into bricks and then crumble it again?

Well, one day he'd have to try and collect the materials and have at it. Though where he might find saltpeter was a real poser. . . .

Casually, knowing it might cause a sensation, he withdrew his pack of cigarettes. "You might find this amusing," he said, offering one to Motechzoma.

Don put his own in his mouth, brought forth his matches and lit up, inhaled gratefully and then blew a smoke ring—one of his very few party tricks.

Motechzoma blinked. All the other chiefs were staring at him—and at Don.

Motechzoma put the cigarette in his mouth and motioned to a boy with a light. Don anticipated him, struck another match, and touched it to the other's smoke.

The Indian cautiously sucked in. Then his eyes widened. "It is but tobacco," he said. And then, "It is the best tobacco that I have ever tasted."

Don nodded modestly. "Kentucky," he said.

The obsidian eyes of Motechzoma glittered like a Spaniard eyeing solid gold.

There was nothing for it. Sighing inwardly, he took out the pack with its remaining eight cigarettes and handed it to the First Speaker. Offhand, he couldn't think of anything else he carried that might be utilized as a present; things like his Swiss knife he wanted to hang on to. The Indians, he knew, made clay pipes. He was going to have to acquire one and a supply of native tobacco, if he was going to continue the habit.

Motechzoma expressed his thanks for the present of the tobacco of the gods and, the cigarette finished, rolled over on his side and promptly went to sleep. It could be seen that the institution of the siesta was not an invention of the Spanish alone. Most of the others in the lengthy dining hall were doing the same. The women and youngsters left, undoubtedly to go to their own meal, now that the men had been served.

Not for Don Fielding; he wasn't the least bit sleepy. He got up and headed for the nearest door. Cuauhtemoc, seeing him go, also stood and followed, although he looked as though he too could have enjoyed a nap. It was easily enough understood. With but one real meal a day, the Indians gorged themselves to the point of becoming groggy.

In the courtyard, Don said to his companion, "If it were not for me, where would you go now?"

"To the house of the Eagle clan, but my uncle has directed that you be my responsibility."

They started for Don's quarters. He said curiously, "And what are your usual duties, as a Tenocha chief?"

The other shook his head. "But I am not a chief. Upon occasion, my uncle or Snake-Woman utilizes me to give me experience, and of course, in times of war I become a leader of twenty since I am a *Cuachimec*." He said the last with pride.

Cuachimec meant, in Nahuatl, strong eagle or old eagle. So, in spite of his youth, Cuauhtemoc was already an Eagle Knight, as the Spanish called them—something like a corporal or sergeant.

Don said, "But otherwise how do you pass your time?"

The question evidently surprised the other. "Why—I work in the *calpulli*'s fields, in the plot that has been awarded me, upon my marriage, from the common lands."

It was Don's turn to be surprised. He said, "But you're a member of the Eagle clan and the nephew of Motechzoma himself."

Cuauhtemoc said, almost indignantly, "All members of the Eagle clan of my generation are nephews of Motechzoma, just as all members of his generation are my uncles. And who do you think would work our fields if we ourselves did not?"

He had Don there. As an anthropologist, he should have remembered that the institutions of slavery or serfdom hadn't appeared in this era as yet. The germ was there, but one man working for another was a rarity.

They had reached the room assigned him. Don said, "I am free to wander about?"

"Of course. As Snake-Woman said, there is no manner in which you can harm us and no place for you to go."

"Then, look. Why don't you go see your family? I'll look about. Tomorrow, perhaps, you can show me the city."

Cuauhtemoc favored him with a grin, gestured as if to say "you're on your own," and hurried off.

Chapter Eleven

Tenochtitlan took a lot of seeing.

There was no equivalent in the twentieth century any-where on earth, the nearest probably being some of the primitive towns of north central Africa, such as ancient Timbuktu. But even there civilization had made its imprint.

Sometimes alone, more often accompanied by Cuauhte-moc, he explored the Neolithic city—the temples, the pyramids, the larger and more elaborate community build-ings which housed most of the population. There was even a zoo; it consisted largely of birds, but to his surprise, there was even a bison. He knew that there was no such thing as a zoo in contemporary Europe. This was going to set the Spanish back when they saw it.

They walked along the causeway to Chapultepec, paral-leling the aqueduct which brought fresh water from the springs there to a huge basin in the great square. Many came to that point to dip up water, but this was not the only manner of distribution. At key points along the aqueduct, special canoes would come up. Water was dipped from the open ceramic pipes to fill containers in the boats which would then make off for deliveries. The aqueduct was about as big around as a man's body and was, Don knew from his reading, the Achilles' heel of the city. Cut the aqueduct and there was no fresh water for Tenochtitlan; the lake water was brackish and undrinkable.

He was particularly impressed by Tlaltelolco, the twin city of Tenochtitlan to the north. They were divided only by one of the large canals and Don Fielding was reminded of Minneapolis and St. Paul, of Buda and Pest. Aside from the fact that the pyramid there, which adjoined the marketplace, was the largest in the combined city and from its top a superlative view could be had of the whole area, the market itself was the largest Don Fielding had ever seen. It must have been larger than the Halles market of Paris of his own day and literally covered acres.

Surely this was not just the market of Tenochtitlan-Tlaltelolco, nor even, for that matter, the principal one of the cities, towns, and villages of the Mexican valley. It was the largest market over that whole part of Mexico dominated by Tenochtitlan and her allies. Food was only one of the items for which thousands bartered. There were téxtiles of a score of materials and a hundred styles, by appearance done by dozens of different tribes. There were stalls for leather goods, paper, stone implements; there were birds, to be eaten or made into pets; there were dealers in gold, silver, native copper, and even lead; there were whole streets of herb sellers and nearby apothecary shops where the herbs were made up into Indian medicines; there must have been at least an acre of ceramic vendors. It was all highly impressive.

Working through Cuauhtemoc, Don got his obsidian razors and a jar of oil which had evidently been extracted from some plant with which he was unfamiliar. There were barber shops in the square and he decided that he would have his first shave in two weeks at the hands of a professional so as to avoid butchering himself. Cuauhtemoc paid for both the razors and the shave with a few cocoa beans he took from a pouch slung over his shoulder.

They made some minor purchases, including paper, ink,

and writing quills for Don, and when his companion ran out of the beans, he bought another quantity with a shake of gold dust which he carried in a turkey feather quill. A very rude money was obviously evolving in this economy. Don worried over repaying him until the other explained that Motechzoma had ruled that any expenses involved in Don's stay be drawn from the city treasury.

So, he was a ward of the government.

It was when they reached the street of the woodworkers that inspiration hit him. Their stone tools, sometimes augumented with copper knives, axes, drills, and hammers, were crude but they seemed to get their products done with them.

Working still through his Indian companion, Don sketched a three-legged stool and then a simple table. Shaking his head in wonderment, Cuauhtemoc placed the order and gave instructions on where it was to be delivered. By the looks of it, he was well known to all and evidently well liked. Don could understand that; Cuauhtemoc, who was rapidly becoming a friend, projected good will. His always ready smile had a charm that worked on all, not just on Don Fielding. He ought to run for election; this young Aztec could have sent Cesar Chavez back to the barrio.

Another idea hit him when he came to a section devoted to shields. They were made on a circular wooden frame, then covered with very stiff animal hide which was in turn covered with highly colorful featherwork. Looking thoughtful, he had Cuauhtemoc, once again mystified, buy him one.

Cuauhtemoc said in puzzlement, "But that is the shield of the coyote clan of the Mixtecs. Our featherwork is superior to their own, so their *pochteca* traders buy them from here for those who can afford the quality."

"I'll show you why I want it later," Don told him.

When they returned to his room, late that afternoon— they had eaten in the market—it was to find, to Don's surprise, that the stool and table had already been delivered. Cuauhtemoc had witnessed Cortes's folding chair and had probably even sat in one when he had eaten with the Spaniards in Cempoala, but they obviously held no comfort for him. He had also seen how the Spanish sat at the table when they dined, so that article of furniture wasn't a completely new item either.

Don sat on the stool and put his newly acquired shield on the table. He stripped off the feather-covered leather to reveal the heavy circular woodwork beneath. He brought forth his Swiss army knife and opened up the awl. He laboriously dug a hole through as near to the exact center as he could make it and then opened up the largest of the knife blades and cut the hole larger and as smooth as possible.

He put the shield aside and got out his writing equipment and did his best to sketch a wheelbarrow. His best wasn't very good, he decided, and he tried again. In actuality, he had never had occasion to use a wheelbarrow in his life. He had seen them, of course, but it had never occurred to him to inspect one with thorough care. Why should it?

He finally came up with a sketch that was probably going to be as good as he could manage. He kept that one and did another, based on it, from another angle. And then from a third angle. He was no blueprint man by any means, but these would have to do.

It took him a full hour to explain to Cuauhtemoc, who had been squatting on the floor all this time, looking at him in amazement, just what he had in mind. Finally, he got it through.

The other stared down at the three sketches. He said finally, "But why?"

"Friend," Don told him. "The wheel has just been introduced to Mexico."

"But we put these things on little toys, clay dogs; our children push them around, playing with them."

Don nodded. "So I have heard, but it has never occurred to your engineers, such as they are, to use them as a tool. So now we'll go about developing the wheel as a tool."

It took them three trips to the woodworkers before they came up with a wheelbarrow sufficiently sturdy to be useful. They had no nails and wooden pegs had to do.

Don himself pushed it over to where some construction work was going on at a pyramid. Without bothering to give a talk of instruction and with Cuauhtemoc standing by as wide-eyed as the Indian workers they were interrupting, Don loaded four of the worked stones into the wheelbarrow and began pushing it about at a great pace. Holy smokes, it worked! The construction men had carried but one stone of this size at a time.

A temple priest, black-robed, filthy, was standing nearby, his face dark. He rasped to Cuauhtemoc rather than to Don Fielding, "What is this?"

Don answered, "It is a method whereby one man can do the work of four, and with more ease."

"It is not the manner in which a Tenocha carries stone."

"Not just stone," Don explained reasonably. "They can be made either smaller or larger, and anything to be transported for short distances can be carried."

"It is not the way in which our ancestors have forever carried their burdens!"

"That's too bad, because it is a better way!"

Cuauhtemoc was in-between. He was a good citizen of his city and a good Tenocha. He was also religious and didn't buck the priests of the temples in which he worshipped.

However, he rose to the occasion. He said quietly, "It is a method of carrying burdens which they use in the land of the teteuhs."

The black-robed fanatic shrank. He obviously wasn't of a mental caliber to answer that. How did a priest answer that?

Cuauhtemoc said evenly, "It is known that when Quetzalcoatl lived in Tula, capital of the Toltecs, he introduced many new ways." The young Indian paused, then added significantly, "Even the use of maize, which is our staff of life."

How did a priest answer *that*?

By this time, a multitude was surrounding them, staring at the new device from . . . from the land of the gods.

Don demonstrated several times, picking up expertise as he went along. He knew very well, though, that in a matter of days these laborers would have it down more pat than he ever could. It wasn't his field.

Eventually, he simply left his improvised wheelbarrow there and went off with his companion. They'd got the message. Unless he was sorely mistaken, there'd be a score of wheelbarrows in Tenochtitlan before the week was out, and hundreds in the valley of Mexico before the end of the Aztec month.

But even as they walked his shoulders slumped. Did the poor bastards have even a month before Cortes got here? He couldn't remember how long it had taken the Spanish army to get from the coast to Tenochtitlan. It had been fun and something to do in the absence of books and the various other things with which he usually occupied his time, but so far he had done the locals precious little good.

When they got back to his quarters, it was to find a message from Motechzoma summoning him to the First Speaker's quarters. He had seen the other on various occasions, but nothing of significance had been said. The head chief of the confederation was impressing Don Fielding less as time went by. He wondered if the man was a good leader in the field. As a handler of international affairs—*intertribal* was probably the better word—he was no Winston Churchill.

Cuauhtemoc accompanied him up the stone steps to where Motechzoma held sway. There they found the First Speaker and the Snake-Woman. The other chiefs of the Tlatocan were not present.

Motechzoma was jittery and looked wan. He didn't look as though he was getting much sleep. The Snake-Woman was considerably in better possession of himself and sharp as ever.

At their entrance, the war chief blurted, "You misinformed us. You said that the teteuhs were men, even as we are men, and that they could be killed in battle."

"They can," Don told him.

The Snake-Woman said, "We have spies and messengers. The teteuhs have fought battles with the Tlaxcalans. None of them died. Large multitudes of the Tlaxcalans died from the thunder weapons of the teteuhs, under the hoofs of the deer upon which they ride, from the fangs of the gigantic dogs and their other weapons. But none of the teteuhs died."

Don drew on his history once again. "Some of them died. They carried them from the field and buried them under the floors of the houses in which they were quartered, so as to pretend that they cannot be killed. They wish to throw fear into you by pretending that they are gods who cannot die."

He didn't know why he bothered to tell them. Tenochtitlan was fated to fall. This Stone-Age culture was fated to disappear under the onslaught of a society at least two ethnic periods above them. What was he trying to do—prolong the agony? The coming of the Spanish was progress. Vicious as they were, by the standards of the twentieth century, they were far in advance of this primitive culture with its human sacrifices and all the rest of it. But then, he was anxious to live, no matter what, and at this stage he had to butter up the Mexican chiefs.

Cuauhtemoc looked at him quizzically. "How could you know that they buried their dead under the floor?"

Don said, "I know."

The Snake-Woman said softly, "You are then a magician who can look over great distances?"

Don didn't answer.

The Snake-Woman said, "Then what do they do next?"

"They will make friends with the Tlaxcalans and then march on Tenochtitlan. But first they will stop at Cholula; and though at first they will fight the Cholulans, as at first they fought the Tlaxcalans, they will make allies of them and the Cholulans too will join their march on Tenochtitlan."

Motechzoma's face worked. "You claim then also to be able to look into the future?"

Cuauhtemoc sucked in breath and said, "I reported, O Tlacatecuhtli, that he told me the teteuhs would first march on Tlaxcala. And he brings fire from his fingertips, as you have witnessed, and bears one of the thunder weapons, though a small one, of the teteuhs. He has killed their war dogs with it. He also wears on his wrist a small container which has within a demon worm which tells him the time of day beyond the accuracy of the position of the sun."

Motechzoma closed his eyes and moaned softly.

The Snake-Woman went to a corner and picked up something and returned with it to Don Fielding.

"What is this?"

It was the sword which Don had taken from the man who had attempted to assassinate him in Cempoala.

"It is a weapon of the Spanish. It is made of a metal you have not as yet discovered in . . . Mexico. It is their equivalent of the *macquauitl*, the weapon you use for close-in fighting."

The Snake-Woman was standing near the doorway. He slashed out with the sword, banging it into the stone. He knocked out a sizable chip of the soft rock they used in their construction.

He said accusingly, "There is no such metal as this in all the land. See, it is not even dented. If this were a *macquauitl*, the obsidian which makes up the blades would be shattered. Even if it were made of copper, it would be badly dulled."

Don said doggedly, "Yes, this metal is in this land, but you have not as yet learned how to . . . wrest it from the mountains. You have gold and silver, and you have copper, particularly from Tarasca, to the north, but thus far you have not learned the use of this metal which is known as . . ." he used the English word " . . . iron. But *it is here*."

"It is a most deadly weapon," Motechzoma protested. "With it, the teteuhs cut down the Tlaxcalans in large numbers. In *very* large numbers."

"Yes," Don said. "Steel is far beyond obsidian for most purposes."

Cuauhtemoc said, "Could you show us how to find this new metal, in our streams, in our mines, so that we too can make these weapons?"

"No. I do not know how to find it. But it is not found in streams, as gold dust is. It has to be extracted from stone as is copper. I am not knowledgeable in this field."

Snake-Woman said, "You will not tell?"

"I do not know."

All three of them stared at him. Disbelief was possibly lacking in Cuauhtemoc alone.

The First Speaker said in argument, "But you are a magician."

Don gave that up. He said, "But I know nothing of the working of metals."

Even Cuauhtemoc now had the expression of disbelief. They *knew* he was a magician, and did not magicians know everything? But what could they do? It was obvious that Motechzoma, at least, was afraid of him.

Chapter Twelve

Partly to kill time, partly out of pure curiosity, he argued theology with Cuauhtemoc. And largely got very little out of it. The Tenocha religion had evolved to a complexity that became pure chaos to someone not born into it.

One afternoon, seated in his room after the midday meal, he asked about the human sacrifices.

The other said simply, "The gods are pleased with the blood and hearts of the victims."

"How do you know?" Don demanded.

That set the Indian back only momentarily. On the face of it, everybody knew that, surely. "The priests tell us so."

"Perhaps they lie. Throughout the world there are supposedly many gods, but nowhere except in this land do the gods thirst for blood."

"Perhaps that is why we Tenochas are so great, so powerful," Cuauhtemoc said strongly. "Because we placate the wrath of Huitzilopochtli, the Hummingbird god of war."

"The Spanish do not make human sacrifices to their gods and they are more powerful than you. A mere four hundred of them are marching on your city."

The Indian had to think about that one. He said finally, "They are gods themselves."

133

Don shook his head. "No, they are not! We have argued about that before. They are not gods and they die just as other men die. But about the sacrifices. You told me the other day that Quetzalcoatl did not demand sacrifices of human beings and that he was the strongest god of all, before the coming of your Huitzilopochtli. If he did not need sacrifices and gave so many things to the people, why should your Hummingbird god, who gives nothing, but takes?"

The other gave in slightly. He said, "In truth, I have thought about it on occasion, though never tell a priest I said so. It would be my death. But I have thought about it and this is my conclusion: When we Tenochas were still very poor and a very small tribe and lived far to the north, we were already a warrior people; we had to be to survive in that harsh land. So it was that sometimes we took prisoners in battle. What could we do with these people? If we turned them loose, they would live to fight us again. If we kept them alive, as captives, they would eat our food and we had little enough for ourselves."

"So you got into the habit of sacrificing them to the gods," Don said.

Well, at least they had evolved out of the still earlier custom of eating their captives. From what he understood, the priests went through an act of symbolic cannibalism, but that was evidently a leftover from the early days of the tribe. These Indians weren't the only ones to practice symbolic cannibalism in their religion. Even some of the Christian sects went through the act of supposedly eating the flesh of Jesus and drinking his blood when they took the wafer and wine.

"Yes," Cuauhtemoc said. "And Huitzilopochtli grew so to like the stench of blood that he called for ever more victims. And so it was that when there was no war, and hence no prisoners to sacrifice, it became necessary for us to provoke wars so that we could take captives."

"Which also gave you a good excuse to clobber your neighbors and wrest their property from them."

"Yes," the Indian said, not getting the sarcasm. "But there is another thing, too."

"How's that?"

"There are too many people in the land. In some areas there are more people than the land can feed. If great numbers are sacrificed on the altars of the gods, then those who remain have sufficient."

Don shook his head in despair. "That's one way of controlling the population explosion," he muttered. Then audibly, "The Spanish are going to introduce some even more effective methods. Wait until they put you to work, en masse, in their silver and gold mines."

Cuauhtemoc frowned and said, "What?"

"I was but looking into the future."

The Indian shook his head in his turn, then laughed. "And you claim that you are not a magician!"

The days passed rapidly. Cuauhtemoc, by the looks of it, took his position of responsibility for Don seriously and was seldom away from him during the daylight hours. He was continually amazed at his charge's ignorance of the most common facts of life. He knew nothing whatsoever about hunting, certainly not with the weapons of the Indian, the javelin and spear thrower, the stone propelled from a sling, the blowgun and its pellets. He knew nothing about fishing, at least with the toe-anchored throw-lines the Tenochas used in the lake, and could not even paddle a dugout canoe.

That last in particular flabbergasted the Indian. *Everybody* knew how to propel a canoe about the lake and about the canals of the city. Why, a child could hardly walk before it had the ability to punt a canoe around. You were practically born with the art. Not Don! The clumsy dugouts, usually round-bottomed, were completely unmanageable so far as he was concerned, particularly when you stood erect to either paddle or punt. He turned bottoms-up, drenching himself twice, before he called it quits. If he was to be boated around, let somebody else do the powering while he sat in the bottom.

Cuauhtemoc gave up on introducing him to the weapons of war, as well. He just couldn't get over the working of the *atl-atl* javelin thrower. And when he tried to explain the niceties of dueling, Indian-style, with the *maquahuitl*, utilizing practice weapons inset with the razor-sharp obsidian blades, he shortly rolled up his eyes in agony. The sling? Don couldn't hit the wall of a house—from inside— with the egg-sized stones the slingers used.

After a few days of this sort of chaff, Don Fielding had had enough. When he had been a boy in high school, there had been a school archery team, and although Don had never made the varsity, he had gotten the basics of the sport down pretty pat. And they had, of course, not only used an updated version of the English longbow; they'd been coached on techniques far and beyond any Robin Hood had known. Archery in the twentieth century was an art that approached science.

Don had noticed that the Indian bow was all but useless, particularly in the manner in which it was fired. The short bow, about four feet long, was held in the right hand, the arrow drawn back to the chest with the left hand and aimed without truly sighting.

He got out his drawing equipment and let the other know what he wanted. A bow, six feet long—he had Cuauhtemoc's height in mind, or he would have made it longer—and a pull as stiff as the Indian bow-makers could make it. And he wanted arrows half again as long as the Indians utilized. Once again he had mystified his friend, but Cuauhtemoc had learned by now to be inquisitive about any innovations this white man suggested.

The bow was ready in several days, as was a quiver of obsidian-tipped arrows of the length Don had requested.

They walked over to Chapultepec, across the causeway, to check it out. Cuauhtemoc brought his own bow as well.

Don found the glade he wanted. He pointed. "Let me see you hit that tree."

His companion frowned at first, but then made a shrug that would have done credit to an Armenian and began walking closer, pulling an arrow from his quiver.

"No," Don said. "From here."

Cuauhtemoc looked at him. "No man lives who could hit that tree from this distance, even if there was a bow that could reach so far."

The tree trunk was approximately the thickness of a man's body. Don brought forth one of his arrows, closed his eyes long enough for a quick prayer to his nonexistent gods, and notched the arrow, using the left hand to hold the bow. He raised the arrow to eye level. The bow had a good pull. He could have possibly handled more, but it was enough. He held the same stance that once the English yeoman had at Crecy and Agincourt when longbowmen had destroyed the power of French chivalry.

The arrow sped true and buried itself dead-center in the tree. Then and there, Don Fielding, who hadn't shot a bow in fifteen years, decided never to fire an arrow again. His reputation was made; he wasn't going to take any chance of it being destroyed!

With a great air of nonchalance, he led the way to the tree, Cuauhtemoc following, bug-eyed. It was a lengthy walk.

The arrow was implanted so deep that the Indian had considerable difficulty drawing it forth. The obsidian point, of course, was shattered, but that was not of importance.

"What kind of a magician's bow is that?" Cuauhtemoc demanded, an edge of indignation in his voice.

Don handed it to him, unslung the quiver of arrows, and handed that over as well.

He said, only mild condescension there, "I will give

you a few lessons in the proper manner of handling a bow, and then you can practice.''

The other stared at him, then at the bow, then at the—to him—outsized quiver of arrows. He threw his own bow away, without thought.

''But this is a fantastically better weapon than my own.''

''So the merry men in Sherwood Forest proved long ago,'' Don told him.

Nor was Don Fielding by any means done with the wheel, now that he had gotten his wheelbarrow built. He had spotted Motechzoma, in a ceremony evidently having something to do with a religious festival, being carried by four men in a litter, and his eyes had narrowed. The streets, here in Tenochtitlan, were paved. And well paved; some sort of mortar Don didn't recognize, but it was at least as smooth as asphalt.

He asked Cuauhtemoc about it and discovered that the Tenochas used litters ceremonially but not for cross-country travel. Don could understand that. The roads were too inadequate. It would be more comfortable to walk, and evidently that is exactly what happened. Even the Great Montezuma, as the Spanish called him, walked on his military expeditions.

Don wanted one of the litters. Again his companion was mystified but, as always now, perfectly willing to go along. The litter, canopy-covered, was produced and parked in the courtyard before Don's door.

He looked it over critically. The shafts, before and behind, were not as sturdy as he could wish, but they could work that out later, after sawing them short.

He sketched out what he wanted. Four wheels, each about three times as large as the one he had based on the shield. Then he diagrammed the axles. He knew precious little about wagons, had never ridden in one, but he knew that some sort of grease had to be utilized, at least if you were going to get any efficiency and eliminate ordinary wear. He was no Connecticut Yankee all-around-man such as Mark Twain had written about. He was a teacher and knew nothing about even the basic mechanics. Although he assumed he could mess around with it and figure out a method of turning the front wheels, for the moment it eluded him, and after trying to puzzle it out, he decided to hell with it. Give them the basics and let the Indian craftsmen work out improvements.

He had the litter hauled over to the street of the wood-workers and let Cuauhtemoc explain the sketches to them. By this time, the craftsmen were interested to a man in anything that Don attempted. Within days he had his primitive wagon. It was a litter mounted on four clumsy wheels, a shaft sticking out in front with a bar at its far end which two men could utilize to push. It amounted to a four-wheeled chariot, man-powered, since nothing else was available. He wondered, passingly, about goats. Didn't they have king-sized mountain goats in Mexico? Yes, he had seen two in the Tenochtitlan zoo. Was it possible to train them? He hadn't the slightest idea. And besides, the Spanish would take over before they'd have the time. And the Spanish would bring more practical animals than a trained mountain goat—oxen, horses, mules, burros.

The wheeled litter was an instant success, so far as those who witnessed its maiden voyage were concerned. Two porters, at first stunned by it all, took over the job of pulling the clumsy contraption. Don and Cuauhtemoc sat above on the mats that were in lieu of seats. They took off at a trot across the great square in front of the pyramid. Actually, since none of the spectators had ever seen wheeled transport before, it must have seemed fantastically efficient to them, though it took half the square to turn because the front wheels were as stationary as the back.

Don, in his amusement, failed to see Xochitl, the Quequetzalcoa, glaring down at them from halfway up the stairs to the temple atop the pyramid of Huitzilopochtli.

But Cuauhtemoc saw, and realized that undoubtedly the fanatic priest had already heard reports of the innovations which the white man was bringing that conflicted with the rituals and taboos of the Tenochas.

They finally headed the primitive wagon back to the street of the woodcraftsmen, and Don pointed out that the vehicle could be used as other than a wheeled litter to transport chiefs. Put sides on it and it made a conveyance that would permit much heavier loads than could be carried on a man's back or in a wheelbarrow. He was gratified to see gleams of understanding in the eyes of the men. Backward they might be, by the standards of European society of the time, but stupid they were not.

The rickshaw came next and that gave him more thought than anything that had come before. The original design wasn't so bad and his workers were rapidly gaining knowhow. Their wooden wheels were improving considerably. But the trouble was, he had no idea whatsoever of how to create some sort of springs. When his new vehicle was completed, it gave a terribly jouncy ride, smooth though the streets were, here in the city. On any kind of a rough road at all, the passenger would have been in danger of breaking his spine.

But then something came to him. He said to Cuauhtemoc, "You have balls of *olli* with which you play the ballgame *tlachtli.*"

"Yes, of course."

Don indicated the rim of the wheels, and even as he did so, he realized that he was going to have to introduce the spoked wheel. These were much too heavy, particularly for a single man to pull around at a dogtrot.

He said, "Would it be possible for the men who work the *olli* into balls and for whatever else it is utilized to make it into strips and glue it here, or however else attach it?" He knew that the rubber he was requesting came from the Tabasco area down on the coast.

"But why?"

"It will make the vehicle more comfortable in which to ride and easier to pull, as well."

"We can find out."

From time to time Cuauhtemoc or one of the chiefs would pass on information to him on the advance of the Spanish army. Thousands of Tlaxcalans were accompanying them now, in addition to the Totonac porters they had brought all the way from Cempoala. The march was becoming a triumph, and small towns and villages came over to the white men they thought gods.

Cholula was entered, and when the local chiefs proved stubborn and fell short on supplying the food and other demands of the Spanish, a massacre was precipitated. The numbers killed differed in the varying reports, but a chill of apprehension swept through Tenochtitlan.

Motechzoma again summoned Don Fielding and this time the full Tlatocan, the council of chiefs, was present, as was the high priest Xochitl, his eyes as mad as ever. The First Speaker, seated on his half-chair, was obviously on the verge of terror.

He blurted, before Don and Cuauhtemoc had hardly entered the room, "Malintzin is in Cholula where he has killed many of the chiefs and warriors. What will he do now, Magician?"

Don had given up the attempt to deny himself a wizard. He said, "He will rest his army for a few days, then march on Tenochtitlan. On the way he will recruit the warriors of the city of Huexotzinco, who will come over to him without a fight, since they hate you so much."

"No! No! He will not come to Tenochtitlan. I have sent another embassy with presents, to forbid him to come further toward the city."

Don sighed and said, "He will not listen. The Spanish are so greedy for gold that nothing could stop them now.

Cortes will be on the causeways before seven days have elapsed.''

Motechzoma moaned.

The Snake-Woman was looking at the war chief contemplatively. He said, ''Perhaps we should summon our host. Call upon our allies. Recruit every warrior in the valley. March out upon them.''

''No! They are teteuhs! They would destroy us all, as they destroyed the Tlaxcalans who resisted them. As they destroyed the Cholulans who fought.''

One of the other chiefs, whose name Don Fielding had forgotten, said, ''Each day that goes by, their force grows. And now this teteuh here, the white giant, tells us that Huexotzinco too will come over to them. At this pace, soon we will not have enough of a force to resist them.''

Motechzoma was as though crushed. ''We can't resist gods,'' he moaned.

Cuauhtemoc caught the eye of the Snake-Woman and they looked at each other deliberately, then thoughtfully back at their elected war chief. The Snake-Woman shook his head.

During the day hours and in the company of Cuauhtemoc, Don Fielding got by reasonably well. The city was so interesting and the innovations he was introducing so occupied his time that he had no opportunity to consider his situation. It was at night that the despair hit him.

He was able to tell himself that he would have to make his peace with Cortes. But how? He tried to delude himself into believing that the attempted assassination was the act of an individual who had come to rob him and that Cortes knew nothing about it. But he knew better, particularly after Malinche's warning. Cortes had undoubtedly ordered the execution. And now that it hadn't come off—and instead, one of his own men had been killed—Cortes would be that much more enraged at Don Fielding.

No; once the Spanish found him here, he was a goner.

He considered briefly heading north for the land of the Tarascans. Possibly, they would take him in. They were a people that the Tenochas had never been able to conquer and were at least as advanced as the Mexican valley confederation. Among other things they worked copper better than any other tribe in Mexico. Perhaps he could win them over with a few innovations. For instance, was copper tough enough to be used as a wood saw?

But no, he was kidding himself. Even if the Tarascans did take him in, rather than killing him on the spot or sacrificing him, within a short time after the fall of Tenochtitlan the Spanish were slated to send forth their expeditions to conquer the rest of Mexico. Mexico? Hell, within a few years they would extend from California and what were in his days the southwestern states all the way down to Chile! There was no place to run, no place to hide. The Coronado expedition was slated to go as far north as Kansas, in less than twenty years after Mexico City fell.

The messages came through that the Spanish army had left Cholula. He estimated that it would take them from three to four days to arrive. Their speed was held down to the pace of the heavily laden porters who carried the cannon, the other equipment, and the supplies of food.

For once, Cuauhtemoc was not around. Don understood that Motechzoma had sent him on one of the several embassies that the war chief was sending to Cortes in hopes of dissuading him from approaching any closer to Tenochtitlan. It had done no good for Don to tell him that the Spaniard would continue to march anyway.

Walking more or less haphazardly, Don strolled across the great square. He had been thinking about introducing the potter's wheel, although he knew precious well that his knowledge of ceramics was all but nil, and besides, he didn't have the time now. And what was the point? The Spanish would bring it in shortly anyway, as soon as European craftsmen came from the Old Country.

There was a scream, and then a series of screams and yells from directly ahead, near the wall of the great complex of buildings that was the central home of the Eagle *calpulli,* the clan to which Cuauhtemoc, Motechzoma, and the Snake-Woman all belonged.

He looked up sharply. There was a milling and continued shouts and screams. This sort of thing was unknown, so far as he knew, in Tenochtitlan—certainly here in the big square.

He started forward at a run.

The initial gathering of persons, possibly some forty in all, were streaming away in all directions as fast as they could make it. Some stumbled and fell, hustled up again, continued the retreat.

And now he could see what it was.

An Indian, naked save for a loincloth, had obviously gone amok. He was wildly swinging a *maquauhuitl* in each hand and dashing here and there in an attempt to get at new victims. He had already downed or viciously slashed a half-dozen, most of whom were trying to crawl away from the vicinity. It was a scene of chaos and carnage.

A child, certainly less than a year of age, sat in the middle of it all, screaming in fear.

A young woman, not more than sixteen or seventeen, hardly more than a child herself, came dashing in, bent low. She snatched the baby up, turned to run, screaming. She slipped on blood already shed and came to her knees and the berserker was on her, flailing his Indian swords wildly.

And Don shot him between the eyes.

PART THREE

Chapter Thirteen

Don Fielding looked up from where he sat on his three-legged stool at his rickety table.

In the doorway stood Cuauhtemoc. Behind him was Tlilpotonque the Cihuacohuatl, Snake-Woman, head chief of Tenochtitlan; behind him, a priest that Don vaguely knew as Panitzin, one of the priests of the Eagle clan.

Cuauhtemoc was in his regalia as an Eagle Knight, complete to the hooded headdress composed of feathers and the head of an eagle. Don had seen him dressed thus on only one other occasion, some sort of ceremony. The Snake-Woman was also in his finery, undoubtedly the costume of his office.

Don Fielding knew he was in ultimate trouble. He had killed a member of the Tenocha tribe—no matter what the circumstances. He realized, too, through his studies, that the institutions of the Tenochas resembled those of the Moslems when it came to the insane. These were *the afflicted of Allah*, and holy. The Mexican Indians, too, thought the insane to be in the power of the gods and thus not to be thwarted, whatever.

On top of this, Don Fielding was familiar with the workings of the primitive clan when it came to bloodshed. The blood right had to be paid. And he had no resources.

And the matter had to be handled, if it could be handled, between the chiefs of the two clans involved.

He didn't have a clan or a chieftain to handle his troubles. He had killed a man and he was, so far as they considered, without kin to protect him. He was a stranger in a strange land, and among primitives the word *stranger* is synonymous with *enemy*. All are enemies save the members of your tribe or confederation of tribes, if your society has evolved to that point. Don had neither confederation, tribe, nor clan.

He looked up at his once-friend, Cuauhtemoc, blankly. The other's face was expressionless, empty. So this was it. This was *it*.

Cuauhtemoc said, "Honored brother, we have come to invite your adoption into the Eagle calpulli, even though you are a teteuh, and thus far above us."

In his time, Don Fielding had often read about the jaw of a character dropping. When a fictional character was greatly surprised, his jaw invariably dropped. However, in real life Don had never actually witnessed it in another nor gone through the experience himself. Now he did.

Cuauhtemoc said formally, "The woman was *my* woman, honored brother. *The child was my only child*." In his eyes was something like fire. Pride, perhaps—or love.

Don Fielding looked at the Snake-Woman whose face was also expressionless.

And Tlilpotonque said, equally formally, "If you will honor us, teteuh. There has not been an adoption into the Eagle calpulli for many years, but it is part of our tradition."

The priest remained silent—Don Fielding was not getting along too well with the priests of Tenochtitlan—but he was obviously present as a clan representative.

The ceremony later was impressive. And fascinating to an anthropologist.

Don Fielding had to be born again. Into the Eagle clan.

And since a babe comes into the world naked, he was stripped nude for the ceremony.

The whole clan was present, even Motechzoma, complete in full regalia, including the jade lip plug and heavy earrings, including impressive headgear of green and golden Quetzal feathers, the holy bird of the Tenochas which lurked in the southern jungles. The whole scene was one of barbaric splendor. In the background was a hellish clamor of kettledrums, whistles, conches, rattles, and pipes. There were ceremonial dancers, ceremonial singers, the chanting of priests.

The ceremony itself was symbolic. The mother of Cuauhtemoc stood in such wise, her skirts held high, that Don was able to crawl between her legs—symbolically born again. He had read as a student that the ancient Jews had used the same ceremony in adoptions into their early tribal sibling groups. He would have given a good deal to have been able to present a paper on the subject to one of the anthropological journals. It would have made his name, until he was required to cite his sources!

Upon his emergence—born again—the ceremony went wild. The alleged music became a fire drill in Bedlam. Youngsters came rushing in with foaming jars and cups of what turned out to be pulque, the fermented juice of the maguey and ordinarily allowed for elderly people alone or during certain religious festivals.

Don quickly redressed, having felt like a fool, spanking naked before the multitude. They had been amazed at the whiteness of his skin where the clothing had prevented his acquiring a tan such as he had on his face.

Pulque Don Fielding had sampled before, though not in this age. He found that they had various mixtures unknown in his own time when it had become the swill of the Mexican poor. They mixed it with honey; they mixed it with nuts; they mixed it with vanilla. After the first two or three quarts, he decided it was delicious. Although a moderate drinker under ordinary circumstances, Don had been known to take a few martinis or highballs in his day. This parlayed up, over the hours that followed, into more than a few cocktails. He was obviously meant to get blind drunk, as was everyone else, especially Cuauhtemoc, his mother, and his wife.

They proceeded to do so.

He managed to get at least part of the story before his personal fog rolled in and before he had gotten to the point where he didn't care whether or not school kept.

Off to one side with Cuauhtemoc, who was now, it would seem, literally his brother so far as the Eagle clan saw it, he was told that his victim had not been insane, as he had thought, but under the influence of the hallucinogenic mushrooms which sometimes filtered up from Oaxaca. What did they call them? *Psilocybe*? It was forbidden the Tenochas and those who took it were drummed out of their calpulli and became kinless ones who had to find employment as common laborers, *tlacotli*—the nearest thing the Tenochas had come to slaves—for their subsistence.

The party evidently lasted until dawn. Not that Don knew it. For the first time in his life, he had passed out. For that matter, he had seldom enough even been moderately tight. The last time had been at a New Year's party.

When he awakened, his head was splitting. His mouth told him he had been eating mule hoof soup; his eyes were burning, and his stomach felt as though any minute it was going to launch whatever green concoction it contained. He groaned misery.

Where was he? He lifted his head just enough to allow him to look about. Next to him was his new blood brother, Cuauhtemoc, out like a light, but, even in sleep, his face flushed. And beyond him, his petite wife whom Don had met the night before. She was a pretty little thing and gushingly thankful for his rescue. What was her name? Centyautl, or something like that. All three of them were sprawled on the usual Indian beds, nothing more than mats and blankets.

Beyond the girl, in a highly decorated Indian equivalent of a cradle, was the baby, and it was beginning to stir. Save for some chests or trunks of wood and leather, the cradle was the room's sole article of furniture. The walls were decorated as tastefully as usual with tapestries, the floor with colored mats, but otherwise furniture was nil.

Don Fielding was obviously in the home of Cuauhtemoc, in the complex of buildings that were the principal residence of the Eagle clan of Tenochtitlan.

He rolled over and groaned again.

Cuauhtemoc looked up and had it in him to laugh. "Well, my giant brother, so you will drink the god pulque."

"The god pulque," Don protested in agony. "If you must deify even such things as an alcoholic drink, please be accurate enough to call this one a devil, not a god."

The Indian laughed again, turned, and spoke to his wife, who scrambled immediately to her feet, smiled shyly at Don in the way of morning greeting, and hurried from the room after pushing the tapestry which covered the door to one side.

Don Fielding was only slightly put off by her presence. He knew the lack of European- or American-type modesty among these people and that also several families would often pack into one room. Cuauhtemoc and his wife saw nothing amiss in his sleeping with them. He shook his head, closed his eyes, and groaned again. That was the last time he was going to overdo on pulque.

A warrior, wearing a maxtli loincloth decorated with the design of the Eagle clan, appeared at the door and spoke briefly to Cuauhtemoc in too low a voice for Don to hear.

After he was gone, Cuauhtemoc turned to his new blood brother.

"Malintzin and his army spent the night at Itztapalapa."

"Where is that?"

"On the edge of the lake, at the end of the causeway which leads south."

The girl came back bearing two small cups. She handed one to Don, one to her husband.

"Drink, giant brother," Cuauhtemoc said, knocking back his own.

Don looked at it suspiciously, then smelled it. It smelled horrible—by appearance, some concoction of roots and herbs.

"I could never get it down."

"Drink!"

Don shrugged, closed his eyes and gulped. It tasted as bad as it smelled. Worse.

He said, "What is Motechzoma going to do?"

The other grimaced. "Nothing. Come; we must get your things from the tecpan. The Snake-Woman has ordered that it be emptied so that the teteuhs and all their force can be accomodated there. It is proper that you move here, anyway, since now you are a member of the Eagle clan."

It came to Don Fielding, in a wave of shock, that his hangover had suddenly fled. His head was cleared of fumes, his stomach of nausea; even his eyes no longer stung. He was astonished. That brew, whatever it was, would have been worth a fortune in his own age.

He followed his companion from the room into the courtyard beyond and across it. Cuauhtemoc pointed out the room that was to be Don's new home. Evidently, a single room was all that anyone rated here in Tenochtitlan, save for officials such as Motechzoma and the Snake-Woman who, of course, needed extensive quarters for administrative purposes.

They exited from one of the various large gates that led onto the square. Over the arch was a huge stone eagle, totem of the clan.

As they walked toward the tecpan, Don said deliberately,

"If the Spanish and their allies are not resisted but allowed to enter the city, they will capture it."

Cuauhtemoc looked at him. "How do you know? Motechzoma believes that if they are not resisted but are given many presents, particularly of the gold and silver they love, they will go away, return to their large canoes of the sea and return to from whence they came."

"I know," Don said wearily. "But even if the Spaniards wished to, they couldn't return. Cortes scuttled their ships so that those who wished to turn back couldn't. When they see me—with four hundred Spaniards in this town, it's just a matter of time before they spot me—they'll have me under arrest."

The other looked at him in shock. "But you are now a member of the Eagle clan. The teteuhs can do nothing to you. That is one of the reasons I prevailed upon the Snake-Woman to permit your adoption into the clan."

Don said, "Thank you for your good intentions, Cuauhtemoc, but you will soon see how much concern Cortes has for the Eagle clan, or for the whole Tenocha nation, for that matter."

They rounded up a couple of the tecpan porters to help them transport Don Fielding's things back to his new quarters. And he realized just how scanty his things were. Stool and table, his newly acquired writing materials, a few odds and ends he had worked with when designing his wheels and vehicles.

Which brought to mind the fact that he was in rags. His clothing had not been new at the time the switch to this age took place, and since then he had put heavy wear on it. His socks he had long since discarded and his undershorts as well. His shirt was in tatters and his pants not much better. Only his bush jacket was really in reasonable shape.

As they headed back to his new home, he asked his

companion about having some of the Indian women copy his clothing in the cotton cloth they utilized.

Cuauhtemoc contemplated him thoughtfully. "Perhaps it would be better, giant brother, of you began to wear the garb of the Tenochas and then be unobserved by the teteuhs. We could have one of the medicine men stain your skin and perhaps even darken your hair."

Don shook his head negatively. "It would never work. I am a head taller than the tallest man in their army and weigh half again as much as any Tenocha in Tenochtitlan. I stand out like a walrus in a goldfish bowl."

"A what?"

"Never mind. But there is no hiding me, other than temporarily, from the Spanish. I'll go and meet them upon their arrival. There is little use in putting it off."

He stood and watched from the flat rooftop of his new home when the Spanish entered the square. They made a brave show, marching to the staccato rattle of their drums. Thousands watched them from the roofs of the buildings about the huge plaza.

Cortes led the parade, riding next to the litter in which Motechzoma had met him. Following were the fifteen other horsemen and then the footmen. Bringing up the rear were the thousands of Indians—Tlaxcalans, Totonacs, Cholulans, and various other tribesmen who had accepted the Spanish colors. The Indians were in war garb and paint, and bore weapons.

The Tenochas standing near Don Fielding took in the armed array glumly. For the first time, armed men were within the precincts of Tenochtitlan—blood enemies. By custom, the Tenochas did not bear arms within the city.

The warrior next to Don grunted deprecation.

Motechzoma conducted the newcomers to the tecpan and through one of the major gates. The Spanish on horse and foot, looking every which way in amazement at what they saw, followed, and the Indian allies as well. The tecpan was large enough to accommodate them all, particularly if the Indians were packed into the living quarters wholesale. Don Fielding could imagine the reaction of the Spanish. They were being given a palace in which to stay. The conception of any building this large not being a palace was beyond them.

Axayaca came up and stood next to Don. He was in his costume as an *Otomitl*, one of the "Wandering Arrow" warriors, a rank analgous to Cuauhtemoc's standing as an Eagle Knight, though with not quite as much prestige. The night before, the young Indian had been somewhat more friendly to Don than in the past. After all, they were now members of the same clan and hence brothers. Don Fielding got the impression that the other had been opposed to his adoption, but in view of the fact that it had taken place, they were now kin. In Indian society, kin was all-important. It was, literally, social security. If kin do not take care of each other, who will?

Axayaca said, "The teteuhs are to be given several hours to adjust to their new surroundings and to eat the midday meal they and the scum they have brought with them have carried from Tlaxcala, Cholula, and the other towns. Then the First Speaker of the Tlatocan and others of the chiefs will wait upon them. Motechzoma requests your presence since you speak both our tongue and theirs."

Don had already steeled himself to confronting the conquistadores. Why attempt to put it off?

"Very well," he said.

Axayaca looked at him from the side of his eyes and said, "You fear them?"

Don took a deep breath. He disliked losing face before this younger man. However, he said, "Yes. I am not a warrior."

Axayaca said, "All men of the Eagle clan are warriors, save the priests."

"I am not. I am a scholar and a teacher of the young."

The other looked straight ahead. He said softly, "Somehow it comes to me that in time of need you will become a warrior."

What could you answer to that? It was meant to be a compliment; it was the first kindly thing Axayaca had ever said to him.

The parade was over. He returned to his quarters and shaved and policed up his clothing to the extent he could. He also brought forth his automatic and checked the clip. Perhaps he was no warrior, but he wasn't going down before Cortes and his cutthroats without resistance.

Cuauhtemoc, in his regalia as an Eagle Knight, came for him an hour or so later. It would seem that his friend had also been selected as one of those who were to join the audience with the Spanish. Don was mildly surprised. The other was not a chief, nor even a senior warrior, though he was an Eagle Knight.

It turned out that Motechzoma, when the tecpan had been cleared out for their unwelcome visitors, had moved his establishment to these quarters of the Eagle clan, which was natural since it was his own clan. The Snake-Woman, too, Don supposed, would be in residence here, as well as most of the others connected with the city and confederation administration. He imagined that there would be a strain on accomodations, but the place was monstrous, and if worse came to worst, he assumed that some of the inhabitants could be switched to other Eagle clan houses or even to those of other clans.

The procession that was to confront the Spanish formed in the largest of the courtyards; Motechzoma and Tlilpotonque, the Snake-Woman, were both being borne in their ceremonial litters. All the rest were on foot, some twenty in all, besides Don and Cuauhtemoc. Porters bearing gifts brought up the rear. Don recognized a dozen, at least, of the chiefs and the total Tlatocan, high council, and the head chiefs of the confederate towns. None were armed.

Were they mad to submit their whole government to possible attack? To march into the lion's mouth?

He knew it was useless to protest. The Spanish power was fated to destroy this backward culture. Time was marching on with a vengeance. Within five years there would be hardly a vestige of the Tenocha left remaining and the city of Tenochtitlan would be but a memory. The Spanish would raze it in the names of God the Father, Charles the Fifth, and Gold the First. These primitive buildings were unuseable for Europeans, in spite of the highly exaggerated descriptions the conquistadores were sending back to Spain.

The procession swung out into the great square and headed for the tecpan.

As they came nearer, Don Fielding could see that the invading army had lost no time. Cannon were mounted on the flat rooftops; armed sentries were posted everywhere—crossbowmen and arquebusiers, pieces in hand, fingers in triggers.

Cortes was showman enough to make the grand gesture. He had placed himself in the center of what had once been Motechzoma's conference room, at the top of the stone stairs which Don had mounted on his various interviews with the war chief. The Captain-General did not deign to descend to welcome his reluctant host but sat there in his chair while Motechzoma and his chiefs ascended.

Hernando Cortes was the only one seated and the only one not to wear armor. He was dressed in rich black and wore a velvet cap. Malinche stood to one side of his chair, Aguilar to the other. Behind, in a row, were the two priests, Fray Bartolome de Olmedo and Padre Juan Diaz, and all of the captains of Cortes's little army. Don Fielding was surprised to see even Bernal Diaz, who had evidently been promoted to officer's rank since they had last spoken.

Don and Cuauhtemoc brought up the rear of the Indian

procession and it was Malinche who spotted him first. She sucked in air in a gasp.

The eyes of Hernando Cortes widened in a shock of recognition, and behind him the red-headed Alvarado swore; his hand went to his sword and half drew it from its scabbard.

Without need to look around, Cortes said grimly, "A moment, Pedro."

He looked coldly at Don Fielding. "You are under arrest for the murder of Gomez de Alvarado and will be hanged in the morning at first dawn."

Don said, "Would you lay hands, then, on a member of the royal family of Tenochtitlan? I am a nephew of the Emperor Montezuma."

Chapter Fourteen

If he had told them he was the Second Coming of Christ he couldn't have astonished the Spanish more

"My faith, are you mad?" Cortes blurted.

Don stared him straight in the eye but held his peace

The Captain-General snapped at Aguilar, "Ask them about this!"

The interpreter spoke to Malinche in Mayan. She in turn, her eyes as wide as those of her master, spoke to Motechzoma in Nahuatl, saying, "This giant white man claims to be of your family."

The Tenocha war chief, who was obviously completely befuddled in the presence of these men he had so long feared, said uncomprehendingly, "But yes. He has been adopted into my clan. He is the blood brother of my nephew and hence my nephew as well."

Malinche looked at Don and blinked. However, she turned to Aguilar and spoke in Mayan.

Aguilar, as surprised as any of the rest, turned to Cortes. "The Great Montezuma says yes. Don Fielding is his nephew."

Inwardly, Don gave thanks. For once the translation came understandably through its different stages. And to his benefit.

Cortes said, "On my faith as a gentleman, I can't believe it. You are not even an Indian. You are not even of this country."

And Don said evenly, "Nevertheless, I am a nephew of the Emperor and hence, obviously, a member of the royal family. Can you say as much?"

The eyes of the conquistador shifted. He was too new in the city to wish to take chances. He was not ready to move as yet.

He said, "Very well, Don Fielding. We shall look further into this matter. But for the time we recognize your status."

Pedro de Alvarado growled, "You mean the dog is to go free? Por Dios! He has killed my brother, Gomez."

"That will be all, Pedro," Cortes said. "I said, *for the time*."

Pedro de Alvarado, his eyes glaring, shoved his sword back into its sheath with a snap. Gonzalo de Sandoval, who was standing next to him, chuckled and Alvarado turned his glare in that direction.

Motechzoma, bewildered by all this and physically trembling, said in Nahuatl, "Malintzin, we have long had a tradition in this land that it was once blessed by the visit of a great god, our lord Quetzalcoatl, who revealed to his chosen people, the Toltecs, great discoveries to make them happy and to make their lives easier. After many years of peace they enjoyed with him, evil ones expelled him from Tula and he departed to the east vowing to return in the year One Reed. This is the year One Reed. You come from the east. Are you the god returned?"

Through Malinche, through Aguilar, this was repeated to Cortes, somewhat garbled.

The Captain-General deliberately evaded.

He said, "I come from across the seas. I am the subject of a great lord, Emperor Charles. When he heard of your existence—such a great prince—he was anxious to have me come and meet you and to invite you to become a Christian. Later we will explain the only true religion to you so that you can be converted. And later, too, perhaps you will desire to become a liege of His Majesty, who is the greatest lord in all the world.''

This too was translated, once again in garbled form. Malinche simply did not have the concept of feudalism, nor of Christianity, for that matter. Inwardly, Don Fielding groaned. However, he knew very well that the Captain-General was not going to accept his services as an interpreter. Cortes wouldn't have trusted him to repeat any conversation accurately. All Don could hope to do was talk it over with his new relatives later, though by the looks of the Tenocha war chief, Motechzoma was in no shape to assimilate anything complicated. His worst fears had evidently been realized. He thought the Spaniard was the returned god Quetzalcoatl, come to lead the people as once he had long centuries before. Both Cuauhtemoc and the Snake-Woman had contempt in their eyes, though they attempted to hide it before the strangers.

Still in a dither, Motechzoma gave commands for the presents to be brought and personally hung a chain of gold around the necks of each of the conquistadores in the room. There were other ornaments of gold, silver, and featherwork, and he also gave orders that each Spanish soldier and each of the Indian allies be given clothing of cotton. Don wondered how long the supply of Tenocha precious metals was going to hold out at this rate. The First Speaker had been distributing it wholesale to the invaders ever since they had landed.

When at last the meeting was ended, the Tenochtitlan delegation filed out again.

And when Don passed young Sandoval, that one said, mockery in his eyes, ''For the time, Don Fielding. For the time.''

When he passed Malinche, her face was without expression.

When he passed Fray Olmedo, the priest said sadly, "And have you become one of the heathen faith, my son?"

Don said, "No, Padre," and marched on.

In the square the delegation broke up, the individuals heading for their respective quarters. Don walked beside Cuauhtemoc.

He said, "And what did you think of that?"

"Much of it I did not understand."

"That is because much of it was not understandable. Malinche and the Spanish interpreter garbled it."

"What is it, then, that Malintzin wishes? He makes great protestations of friendship. I fear that my uncle will be taken in by him."

Don looked at him from the side of his eyes.

The other said, "My uncle has always been fearful of the gods, beyond most men. I too am fearful of gods, but especially those I cannot see. There is something strange about gods who look almost exactly as you do yourself."

Don laughed. "You are learning, brother; you are learning." He added sourly, "However, I doubt that your uncle is."

"Our uncle," Cuauhtemoc told him.

"Yes, of course. The Spaniard's name is not Malintzin; it is Hernando Cortes and in his land they have very strange ways. Each man serves, almost as a *tlacotli*, as a slave, a chief above him. Ultimately one arrives at the very highest chief. In the land of Hernando Cortes that chief is named Charles. If Cortes serves him well, he will be highly rewarded. If he fails him, he will be killed."

"Sacrificed?"

"No. Just killed. Cortes wishes to serve his chief by making all in this country, not just Tenochas but all the tribes, slaves to the Emperor Charles."

"But why?"

"So that they can force you to work the mines, build houses and temples for them, till the soil so that they themselves can live lives of plenty without need to labor."

The Indian was horrified. "But that is criminal!"

Don groaned inwardly. How did you, even an anthropologist, describe class-divided society to a primitive communist? Above all, how did you explain that it led to progress? That to have scientists, scholars, and artists, you had to have a leisure class that had the time to create. Yes, the present-day Spain produced freebooters such as Cortes and Alvarado, but it also produced Cervantes and in due time Goya, Velazques, El Greco, and Murillo. Would Leonardo da Vinci ever have done his work if he'd had to put in ten or twelve hours a day tilling a field? Would Michelangelo?

How did you explain the need of a class-divided society to one to whom the conception is monstrous? For a million years man's institutions had remained comparatively free, basically democratic, as the institutions of these Aztecs were basically democratic. And progress was practically nil. With the coming of classes and of leisure time for the few, man's potential blossomed until, in Don's own time, there was potential aplenty for all, certainly plenty compared to this age. There were problems to be ironed out in distribution, yet the plenty was there.

But how did you explain the institutions of slavery, feudalism, or classical capitalism, not to speak of its later developments, to a free savage?

You didn't.

They were approaching the buildings of the Eagle clan.

Don said, "Among your people, are there any who speak the Tlaxcalan tongue?"

"Why, yes, giant brother. It is very similar to our own. They speak Nahuatl."

Are there any who speak any other languages, such as Mixtec, Zapotec, Tarascan?"

Cuauhtemoc was puzzled. "But yes. When the pochteco go to far lands for trade, it is necessary that they be able to speak to the people. Thus it is that they sponsor schools where young people are taught foreign tongues."

"Young people, eh? Good. Now, are some of these young people better students of foreign tongues than others? That is, do some of them speak several languages; are some able to pick up a new one much better than most?"

"Why, giant brother, I assume so. I know of some who can make themselves known in four or five different tongues."

They were passing through the entry to the quarters of the Eagle Clan now.

Don said, "All right. I want you to try to find me six of the best students of foreign languages in the schools. They must be courageous, very intelligent, and take to language quickly."

"But why?"

"Because we need a spy service." He twisted his face in irritation. "Especially do I need one, because I'm not long for this world unless I know, from day to day, what our Spanish friends are up to."

"I do not understand."

"It isn't necessary that you do right now. Find me the six and bring them to my quarters. It is most important."

Something else came to Don Fielding. "Look, now that I am a member of the Eagle calpulli, will land be assigned me that I must farm?"

The other looked embarrassed. "But you are a teteuh."

"Like hell I am! I want to carry my share of the load."

"It has been decided, in council, that in view of your strange discoveries of the longbow, the use of the litters that roll, and the other things that you have taught us, that you be given priest status and thus need not work in the fields but be supported from the common stores.''

Oh, oh. Here was the class-divided society he had been thinking about in its embryo stages.

So he was still a ward of the government. Now, agnostic as he had always thought himself, he was a priest. How many priests, he wondered, were agnostics?

''Get the lads to my room, blood brother.''

They turned up in surprisingly short order. Two of them he dismissed as too old. He wanted kids. Nobody noticed kids.

The four remaining were from differing clans. So far as he knew, none of them had ever seen him before. At least, not up close. While Cuauhtemoc stood against one wall, fascinated, Don had the four squat on the floor before his stool.

He said, ''The teteuhs—though in truth they are not teteuhs—speak a strange tongue. Now listen carefully. Their word for *yes* is *Si*. Their word for the opposite is *No*. Now, repeat that.''

They repeated, their eyes bright.

He shook his head. ''No. You must speak with a softer tongue.'' He repeated the Spanish affirmative and negative.

He gave them twenty words that night before he dismissed them.

Then he turned to Cuauhtemoc. ''See that all four of them are assigned as servants to the Spanish. Instruct them that they are never to reveal that they can understand a single word of what is being spoken. Above all, do not let Malinche know that they understand *any*thing. She is the brain, as well as the tongue, of Cortes. He does not understand Mexico. She does. Within a week, the boys will be proficient enough that they will understand small things they overhear. Within a month, I'll have them revealing everything that Cortes and his bullyboys discuss among themselves. The Spanish have the arrogance of all conquerors. They speak their own language openly, not believing that those about them understand, since they themselves are too lazy to learn the language of the people they conquer.''

Cuauhtemoc looked at him consideringly. "I do not understand much of what you say. But I have never understood much of what you say, giant brother. I will make the arrangements. And I think it possibly well that I too learn this new tongue.''

"Welcome to the class," Don said.

After the other had left, Don Fielding had a twinge of conscience. The Indians could use the spies in their coming conflict with the invaders, but he knew that their cause was doomed to failure. In actuality, his big motivation was to keep up with his own fate. When Cortes finally decided to deal with him, and that was only a matter of time, he wanted warning. He could still flee the city and attempt to find refuge with the Tarascans or whomever. At least he might prolong his life for a year or so. *Survive, survive!*

The Spanish lost no time in getting about their business. They spent the second day of their visit in strengthening their defenses. They blocked up every street entry into the tecpan save one, and for that one they built a heavy door of thick beams. It was, Don Fielding realized, the first wooden door ever seen in Mexico. They requisitioned stores of corn and other food far beyond daily needs, obviously building up a reserve. They also requisitioned a large number of huge pots and had their Indian porters fill them with water from the central reservoir in the middle of the plaza. These were evidently stored away as well. In the days that followed they were to add to this food and water over and over again, to the astonishment of the Tenochas who couldn't understand their motivation.

Don explained it to Cuauhtemoc.

"They are laying in supplies, in the case you attack them and they have to withstand a siege.''

His new blood brother was shocked. "But we have received them with open arms. We give them all that they require. We give them all that they ask for. My uncle, Motechzoma, refuses to thwart the teteuhs in any manner." The young Indian took a deep breath and added, "He has become an old woman before them."

Cuauhtemoc was maturing rapidly these days, Don noted. He laughed considerably less often.

Don looked at him. "How many of your people are talking thus?"

The other held silence for a long moment, then said, "Many. But many others are as fearful of the teteuhs as is he."

"They have good reason to fear," Don growled.

Each night, he gave his classes in Spanish to the young linguists and to Cuauhtemoc who sat in on the lessons and proved almost as good a student as the teenagers. Don Fielding was surprised at their aptitude. It went even faster than he had expected. But then, that was always the case. If you speak one language, it is difficult to learn another. But if you have already gone through the experience of learning three or four or even more, then acquiring a new one is comparatively simple. In his own time, such people as the Swiss and Danes, who were raised speaking several languages, had little difficulty in picking up another.

During the day, his charges worked in the tecpan, cleaning up, doing errands, submitting to whatever indignities the Spanish inflicted upon them, and kept to themselves the extent to which they understood the words of the invaders. At night they spent several concentrated hours of drill under Don Fielding.

Largely, he kept to himself and out of the way of the conquistadores. Although Cortes had ruled that he was *for the time* not to be touched, Don didn't trust the tempestuous Alvarado, nor his three remaining brothers, for that matter. He suspected that Pedro de Alvarado, and all the

rest of the Spanish army as well, had precious little respect
for the Tenochas, even the royal family, or for Motechzoma
himself, though they believed him to be emperor, or at
least king, of all Mexico.

On the second day after their arrival, the Spanish began
to case the town.

Their Indian allies they left in the tecpan, having no
desire to precipitate any outbreaks between the Tlaxcalans
and the Tenochas, hereditary enemies for generations. But
in groups never smaller than ten, and fully armed and
armored, they explored all aspects of the city, almost
touristlike, Don thought grimly.

They went up and down every street, every canal. The
horsemen rode up and down each causeway, keen-eyed.
Others rode out and completely circumnavigated the lakes,
visiting Tetzcuco, Tlacopan, and all the other towns and
villages in the valley of Mexico.

Some of them ascended the higher pyramids in both
Tenochtitlan and Tlaltelolco, and from Cuauhtemoc Don
Fielding learned that some of the soldiers made sketches of
the town from these vantage points.

His new blood brother was mystified at this.

Don sighed and said, "They are making their plans to
take over the city. They wish to plan routes of retreat in
case of disaster. They wish to map out the vantage points
to seize. They want to discover where your . . ."

"Our," Cuauhtemoc reminded him.

"Yes . . . our arsenals are. You see, they are much
more advanced in the arts of war than are the Tenochas.
They plan thoroughly. They do it well." Don paused and
then added, "And they will win and destroy this city and
your . . . our people."

Cuauhtemoc said emptily, "This you know, my giant
blood brother?"

"I—believe it to be so."

"Again you foresee the future. You are a magician, but still I am a man and must fight."

"Yes, of course."

"What do they do next?"

"They will capture your uncle, the First Speaker, and hold him captive in the tecpan." Don Fielding was again drawing on his history.

The other's eyes were wide. "But why?"

Don made a gesture of resignation. "Because they believe that he is the only chief of your confederation. In fact, they believe him to be the chief of all the lands of which you know—or they pretend to believe that. I truly do not know, but so they report back to the Emperor Charles in Spain. They believe that by capturing Motechzoma they have captured the government of Tenochtitlan."

Cuauhtemoc was still staring at him blankly. "But why do they think that?"

"Because that is the way it would be in their own country. If the Emperor Charles was captured, he who accomplished it would have all Spain and all the Holy Roman Empire in his possession."

"I do not understand."

"No. I know. But if you think me a magician or not, very shortly the Spanish will take your uncle and hold him in the tecpan as a captive."

"Very good."

"What?"

"Of what use is he to the Tenochas? He has become an old woman. He fears the teteuhs. Of what use is a First Speaker who fears the enemy?"

Don looked at him. "You're learning," he said. "It probably won't do you any good, but you're learning."

Nevertheless, Don Fielding felt it his duty to warn both Motechzoma and the Snake-Woman. After all, they had done him the honor of adopting him into their clan, the greatest honor of which they could conceive. Inside, he was a mass of confusion. He knew what was going to happen, that the Spanish were fated to capture the city, but here he was trying to thwart developments that he knew to be history. Well, he had tried to reason that out before and had come up a cropper.

He walked from his own room to the quarters the Tenocha war chief had taken over for his offices. As usual, there were no sentries, no guard. Such a thing as a bodyguard had undoubtedly never occurred to these people, except possibly on actual campaign or in battle. Perhaps he ought to suggest it.

Motechzoma, in his legless chair, was dictating to several scribes who squatted on the floor and wrote and drew with colored inks on *amatl* paper. When a message was completed, the large sheets of paper were folded so that they looked something like a book.

The First Speaker looked up at Don's entrance; neither the Snake-Woman nor any of the other members of the Tlatocan high council were present. He didn't seem surprised at Don simply walking in on him. Evidently, the government of the Tenochas operated on a very informal basis, Indian-style. Any member of the tribe, certainly any member of this calpulli, was free to confront the Tlacatecuhtli at any time.

Don said, or at least began to say, "I came to warn you that . . ."

There was a clatter of arms and armor outside and Don Fielding winced. He had miscalculated. The Spanish were acting before he had expected them to. He had thought it would be several more days.

Captain-General Hernando Cortes, in full armor and accompanied by five of his officers, including Alvarado, Sandoval, and Bernal Diaz, came striding into the room, his face in wrath. Behind him came Malinche and Aguilar, and outside, Don Fielding could see a squad of the Spanish footmen armed with pikes and swords.

Motechzoma looked apprehensive.

Malinche said to the secretary-scribes. "The god orders you to leave the room."

They beat a hasty retreat.

Cortes, still glaring at Motechzoma, rapped to Aguilar, "Tell him."

Aguilar addressed Malinche in Mayan, a few words. And she turned to Motechzoma.

"The god has been informed that your people have done a great evil."

She went on to tell the other that the Captain-General had left a garrison under the command of Juan de Escalante at Vera Cruz. When Quauhpopoca, and it wasn't quite clear to Don if this individual was a Tenocha tribute collector or a local chief, tried to get the Totonacs to pay the same taxes they had before the coming of the Spanish, the Totonacs revolted and asked aid of Escalante, who marched out with his forty soldiers, all he had fit to fight, his two cannon, and two arquebuses. Quauhpopoca had roundly defeated him, chased the Spanish back into Vera Cruz, and accepted the submission of the Totonacs. Juan de Escalante and several others of the Spanish garrison had been killed.

At this point Motechzoma denied that he knew anything of the matter.

Cortes, and Don Fielding had about decided that the rage was an act, thundered, "Give him my command!"

His command turned out to be that Quauhpopoca and his accomplices be turned over to the Spanish and that, meanwhile, Motechzoma be held hostage in the Spanish quarters.

That took some arguing. Cortes now simmered down to the point of saying that the other wouldn't truly be a prisoner but an honored guest. He could take over any quarters he wished. He was free to conduct his government, and any of his officials could come and go, carrying out his commands. He could bring as big a staff as he wished.

The translating and retranslating went back and forth and, to Don's understanding, about half of it came through confused.

Finally, Pedro de Alvarado and Sandoval drew their swords. "Skewer him if he protests," Alvarado growled.

Although this wasn't translated, the meaning was obvious and Motechzoma paled. Some war chief, Don thought. If the other had shouted, a thousand Indians would have come on the run.

But Motechzoma was demoralized beyond all ability to rise to the occasion. His shoulders slumped in defeat and he made a motion of acceptance. These, after all, were gods.

The Captain-General, his face elated, snapped, "Make arrangements for his litter, Doña Marina!"

Malinche turned and left. She was evidently picking up Spanish rapidly.

Cortes turned to Don who had remained quiet through all this. His eyes narrowed, "And I think you had better come along as well, Don Fielding."

Chapter Fifteen

All right. He had just inwardly criticized his adoptive uncle for lack of backbone. Put up or shut up, Don Fielding.

But he knew full well he would never even get his gun out before the swords of Alvarado and Sandoval pierced him through. He was helpless. Hang on to life! Something might come up.

The litter arrived and Motechzoma, who had given in completely, mounted it. The Spanish gathered around tightly, desperately, and the march to the tecpan began.

As they progressed through the courtyards of the buildings of the Eagle clan, various of the First Speaker's kin looked up in surprise, but no one raised a hand, or even a shout. They must have thought, Don realized, that this was but one more visit of the Tlacatecuhtli to the inscrutable teteuhs, who were so full of surprises.

The same applied to the great square which they crossed quickly and without incident.

In the tecpan, the whole invading host was standing to arms, Spanish and Indian allies alike. The men at the artillery had smoldering lengths of rope in hand. The crossbowmen had their bows cocked, quarrels in their grooves. The musketeers stood at vantage points, arquebuses at the ready. In the center of the main courtyard, the horsemen, armed with lances, were mounted and ready to go.

They had expected trouble, Don could see. It must have been an unbelievable relief for it to have come off so easily. They were probably dumbfounded. Could anyone imagine Emperor Charles the Fifth being captured so easily?

Cortes snapped orders that "His Majesty" be given any quarters he desired and anything else that he wished, short of leaving the building. The dejected pseudo-monarch was led off by a fawning Sandoval and a properly respectful Malinche.

The Captain-General turned to Don Fielding and eyed him speculatively. Don held his peace. It was the other's ball.

Cortes said, "My faith, I should execute you and have done with it. But there are some aspects about you that mystify me. None of your story holds together. So we will postpone your fate until I have time to dig further into your impossible tale. Bernal!"

Bernal Diaz stepped up. "Yes, my Captain-General."

"He is your responsibility. This palace is free to him. However, he is never to leave it save in your company. And he is not to leave the city under any circumstances. Otherwise, since he claims to be a gentleman, we will accept his parole if he gives it. Well, Don Fielding?"

Don sighed and said, "I give my parole. So long as you are here in command, I won't leave the . . . the palace without Captain Diaz and will not leave the city without your permission."

Pedro de Alvarado growled, "You are going to give this murdering dog permission to roam at will?"

Cortes said, "For the time, Pedro. Curb your temper. We have much to do. Come, let us examine the defenses. I trust no one save myself in such matters."

Cortes and his officers went off, and Bernal Diaz looked at Don Fielding in amusement.

"Well, my tall friend, what brought you to this?"

Don snorted. "As though you didn't know."

"Believe me, on my faith, I don't! Only that you were the death of one of our people, Gomez de Alvarado. Personally, I never thought highly of Gomez; nevertheless, he was a countryman and part of the army."

"He entered the room in Cempoala in which I was sleeping and attempted to put me to the sword, as the expression goes."

The other looked at him in disbelief. "Why? You are not even a soldier. You were of no danger to our expedition."

Don Fielding sighed. "Undoubtedly, your good Captain-General looked forward to a period when he might wish new lands to conquer—lands to the north. He didn't want me taking off for my own country and warning them of his presence on the scene. Actually, he needn't have worried, but he didn't know that."

Bernal Diaz considered it. "Well," he said, a certain admission in his tone, "had Don Hernando decided on such an action, Gomez would have been the man to carry it out. Come, we'll find you quarters."

Don said, "I lived here for a few days before your arrival. If you have no objection, I'll reoccupy my old room."

"Why not? So you lived here before. By my beard, you are full of surprises, Don Fielding. What would you be doing in the palace of the Great Montezuma's father, King Axayacatzin?"

Don led the way toward the room he had formerly occupied.

"It's not a palace," he said. "It's the nearest thing they have to a hotel, combined with their administrative offices."

"What is a hotel?"

"An inn."

"An *inn*." Bernal gestured. "An inn this size? Why, it will house thousands."

"It has to," Don said, realizing full well that the other put no credence in what he was saying. "In this city they have no other place to put up visitors. Delegations, embassies, merchants, all have only this building in which to sleep and eat, and of course, such people come to this city from all over . . . New Spain."

They reached his former room and found it occupied by some twenty Cholulan porters. Bernal shooed them out contemptuously.

He stood in the middle of the room, hands on hips, and said, "No chairs, no tables, no beds. They have much that is magnificent, but they live like Moors."

"Have you ever seen the way Moors live?"

"Why, no, but I have heard."

"Well, these people don't live on the level Moors do. Their culture is not nearly so advanced."

The other scowled. "You say strange things, Don Fielding, and a great deal that is hard to understand."

Don said, "Speaking of furniture, I have a stool and a small table and various odds and ends over in my quarters in the house of the Eagle calpulli."

"The where?"

Don said, "The palace of the Great Montezuma."

"Very well. Most likely we will be able to have it brought. There will be a great deal of things brought, I assume, when the Great Montezuma moves his belongings and brings his people." He added apologetically, "Whether or not you will be alive long enough to need your things, I cannot say. But it is my belief that the Captain-General wants to know considerably more about this land of yours, and even if what you say about the attempt to assassinate you is correct, now he need not be in any hurry. You are completely in his power."

"And have even given my parole as a gentleman," Don

said dryly. He sat down on the floor, leaning his back against the wall, and crossed his long legs.

Bernal scowled at him. "I detect sarcasm."

Don couldn't help saying, "In my country the law says that a contract made under duress lacks validity."

The other shook his head. "You seem to speak excellent Spanish, but much of what you say holds little understanding."

Hernando Cortes seemed to be in no hurry insofar as Don Fielding was concerned. Bernal Diaz had probably been correct. Don was completely in the Captain-General's power and the other could take his time in deciding just what to do with the mysterious stranger who claimed to be from the north.

The Spanish leader kept his promise to Motechzoma in reference to his freedom to conduct his government and his head men to come and go as they wished. Don realized, as the Captain-General did not, that bringing the war chief here was not as upsetting to the Indians as all that. Motechzoma was simply returning to the building that housed the official offices of the administration. They had always conducted their government here, and he had lived here since becoming First Speaker. Snake-Woman, the full Tlatocan and numerous other chiefs, including representatives from other cities, came and went, carrying on the affairs of Tenochtitlan and the confederacy.

It was on the day following the kidnapping that Bernal said to him, "Come see something, Don Fielding. God's truth, it is a sight to make a saint's eyes pop."

Don followed him to a point where two musketeers stood guard before a door. By the looks of it, it had been sealed up, and evidently the inquisitive Spaniards had wondered why and chipped away the plaster.

Bernal said to one of the guards, "Let us take a look at the treasure, Diego."

The other scowled. "The Captain-General has forbidden . . ."

"Oh, come now, Diego, my old friend. Every man in the army has been in there. If anyone approaches, call out and we'll leave immediately."

"Very well, Bernal, but just a few minutes."

Bernal led the way into what became immediately obvious to be the treasure room of the Tenochas. Gold, silver, jewels, in a thousand forms, were everywhere, along with the highly praised featherwork, mantles richly embroidered, and various other items of Indian wealth. Bernal had been right—a saint's eyes would have popped. Certainly, Don's did. He had no manner of estimating the value of it all, but it would certainly have amounted to many, many millions in his time.

It must have taken centuries to accumulate.

Diego, the guard, hissed, "Bernal, quickly! The Captain-General!"

Don and Bernal Diaz hustled from the place. It would be all Don needed to have the suspicious Hernando Cortes find him in a treasure room.

They hurried outside and ducked around the corner, Assistant Professor Donald Fielding feeling like a grammar-school child lurking in the faculty lounge.

They stood with their backs to the wall and could hear the approach of several persons. The voice of one was obviously that of Hernando Cortes, and then Don could recognize that of Malinche, then that of Motechzoma. There was another voice—Aguilar, undoubtedly.

Through the interpreters, Cortes was unctuously telling the fallen war chief, "It would be well, great king, if you sent a token of your respect to the Emperor Charles, my liege lord across the sea. So it was that when, by accident, we discovered your treasury, the thought occurred to me."

There was such an element of greed in the conquistador's voice that Don Fielding flinched.

And there was nothing save depression and submission in Motechzoma. He said listlessly, "Take it, Malintzin, and let it be recorded in your annals that our people send this present to your chief."

Bernal hissed between his teeth when the message was fed through Malinche and Aguilar.

Motechzoma said hopefully, "And now, Malintzin, that you have in your possession practically all of the gold and silver in Tenochtitlan, you are free to return to your own land."

And the Cortes response to that was, "Ah, but unfortunately, great king, our ships have all been sunk and it will be necessary to build new ones. I have given orders that this be done."

"If you wish, I will make arrangements that great numbers of our people be assigned to help you so that your departure can be hastened."

Malinche said, "Unfortunately, the Tenochas do not know how to build the ships of the teteuhs. It not as though they were to hollow out logs for canoes."

Evidently, the group then turned and returned from whence they had come.

That evening, as Don Fielding sat at his rickety table, allowing dejection at his situation to seep over him, the mat at the door was pushed aside and Cuauhtemoc entered. He was dressed in nothing save a loincloth and was barefooted. Obviously, he was in his equivalent of being incognito. Like many conquerors of a people of other face, the Spanish professed not to be able to tell one Indian from another. They probably thought the young warrior simply one of the many servants with which the Tenochas had provided their unwelcome visitors.

He chuckled lowly and said, "And how does it go with my giant brother?"

Don said in a whisper, "Are you safe here? Aren't you

afraid that if the Spanish recognize you, they'd try to seize you as a hostage as well?''

The other shrugged it off. ''I have been raised to be a chief of war of our clan and would look over the manner in which the teteuhs have fortified the tecpan, for already some of the younger chiefs talk of taking action against them. We know now that they can be killed, as other men can be killed, for Quauhpopoca and his men killed this teteuh Escalante. Besides, I wished to see how my blood brother fared.''

''For the time, I am all right,'' Don said. ''It seems as though the Captain-General, Cortes, can't quite understand me and wishes more information before deciding what to do.''

''None can understand you, blood brother. However, you could escape over the wall at the back and into the canal. I would await you there in a canoe.''

Don shook his head. ''Where would I go?''

''You would return to the home of the Eagle clan. Where else?''

Don shook his head again. ''I gave my word to Cortes that I would not leave the tecpan. Besides, if I did try to hide in your buildings there, it would simply be a matter of time before they found out. I suspect that the girl, Malinche, is already organizing her espionage throughout the city. Her spies would bring in the information.''

His friend thought about it. ''Perhaps you are right. And your presence here gives us our own opportunity to spy on the teteuhs—if you can survive.''

Don said unhappily, ''Yeah. If I can survive. For the moment, that largely depends on keeping out of the sight of Alvarado, the man you call Tonatiuh, the sun, because of his red hair. He and that young snake, Sandoval.''

Cuauhtemoc said, ''There was one other reason for which I came.'' He stuck his head out the door and whispered.

And Don's four students of Spanish slithered in one by one. He blinked his surprise at seeing them.

Cuauhtemoc, obviously pleased with himself, said, "We have come for our nightly lesson in the tongue of the teteuhs."

Don Fielding shook his head in despair. "Was school ever held before in such circumstances?"

He kept out of the way, to the extent that he could. What was the old phrase—out of sight, out of mind? Hernando Cortes had plenty on his mind. If he wasn't reminded of Don Fielding, he might postpone indefinitely a showdown with the mysterious stranger. Still, Don couldn't imagine why he hadn't been summoned long before this.

In the night hours he held his classes in Spanish. Cuauhtemoc turned up about one night out of two. The youngsters were outstripping him. Don was continually astonished at their progress.

Don Fielding didn't witness the tragedy of Quauhpopoca, that unfortunate who had made the mistake of killing Escalante and the other Spaniards, thus proving that the so-called teteuhs were not immortal.

Cuauhtemoc told him about it. The Indian chief had been brought up from the coast and turned over to the Spaniards. Some fifteen of his subchiefs and his son were with him.

The Captain-General had killed two birds with one stone. He pressured the demoralized Motechzoma into emptying the *tlacochcalcos*, meaning, literally, "the houses of darts," in other words, arsenals, in the vicinity of the great *teocalli* square, of their arrows, javelins, and other weapons. These he used for the bonfires which consumed the victims.

On top, to humiliate the Tenocha war chief still further, he put Motechzoma in irons on the charge that he had been the one who instigated the battle in which Escalante had been killed. Motechzoma, probably more bewildered than anything else, had submitted without even an argument.

When the whole thing was over, the Indian population, by appearance, was as confused as their war chief. In fact, most of them evidently assumed that the execution had been ordered by Motechzoma. Malinche had seen that that idea got around.

Cortes reentered the apartments occupied by Motechzoma, personally removed the leg irons, and embraced his captive, telling him that now all was settled. Cuauhtemoc, as flabbergasted as his uncle, must have been at all these proceedings, but hadn't the vaguest idea of what it was all about.

Don Fielding had little to tell him beyond the fact that it was part of the conquistador's plan to take over the whole country and part of the delusion that Motechzoma was king of all Mexico, or New Spain, as the invading army was already calling it.

Don said, "And how are the Tenochas taking all this?"

"We grow increasingly restive."

"I would expect so," Don said.

What could he say to this friend, this blood brother? He knew what would eventually transpire. The bloodbath, the complete collapse of the Indian power, the enslavement of not only the Aztecs but all the other Indian inhabitants, the decimation of the population under the Spanish lash in the mines, in the smelters, in the building of churches and cathedrals, palaces and haciendas. He knew what was going to happen. What could he say? Nothing. There was nothing to say.

It was only a few nights afterward, when he was conducting his class in Spanish for his little group of potential spies—well, more than potential, since they already had an amazing amount of the language—that he saw the rug which covered the doorway to his room stir.

He jumped to his feet and headed for it. Brushed it aside.

Stared out.

He could see a figure dashing away—a small one. The Cortes page, Orteguilla, the one he had caught trying to steal his pistol. He hadn't seen much of the eleven-year-old since his enforced stay with the army. Cortes had assigned the boy to Motechzoma, and he was the only one in the Spanish forces that had picked up a bit of Nahuatl.

He turned and snapped to his students, "Go quickly! We have been discovered."

They scooted from the room.

It was Gonzalo de Sandoval who came to get him, two footmen with pikes backing him up.

The young conquistaror was amused. As usual, he wore a velvet cap rather than the helmet most of the Spanish hatted themselves with night and day. He took it off and made a flourishing bow.

"Don Fielding," he said with his slight lisp, "the Captain-General invites your attendance."

"How courteous of him," Don muttered hopelessly. "But tell him I have a previous engagement."

"I beg your pardon?" The young dandy cocked his head.

"Nothing," Don said wearily, coming to his feet.

He walked side by side with Sandoval, the two footmen bringing up the rear. His mind raced, desperately seeking an alibi.

They reached the set of rooms that Cortes was using for both living quarters and offices, and entered, leaving the two pikemen to join the balance of the sentries in front. Hernando Cortes was not making the mistake Motechzoma had. He had sentries and guards aplenty.

Inside, Cortes sat at an improvised table, in his usual military folding chair. Present were Fray Bartolome de Olmedo, the inevitable Malinche and Aguilar, and one that Don recognized as Francisco de Terrazas, Cortes's major-domo and secretary. He sat at a smaller table to one side, a portable military desk with writing materials before him.

Cortes said coldly, "Is there anything you have to say before I order you hanged?"

Don Fielding pretended puzzlement. "But what is the charge?"

"My faith, you're a cool one. The charge is that you have been secretly teaching these Indian dogs the Spanish language."

Don held his two hands out, palms upward, in a gesture of surprise. "There was no secret about it. I thought you would be highly pleased. It was but a method of spending my time. I told you I was a scholar and teacher. What else would I do to pass the hours away?"

"Please me?"

Don Fielding indicated Malinche and Aguilar. "Your staff of interpreters is inadequate and you need them constantly at your side. Suppose you were to send an expedition to some other town under, say, Captain Sandoval here. You could not afford to let your own interpreters go along. So then, how would he communicate? Even the four I am training are too few. Eventually, of course, every Indian in New Spain must learn Spanish, but for the present you need many interpreters."

"This makes reason, my son," Fray Olmedo said to the army head.

Cortes said, "Why these secret classes at night?"

"Because during the day hours these boys work at their tasks around the building here. There is no secret. They had no time for lessons."

"My faith, you have a glib tongue," the Captain-General growled. "Something comes to me, what with you claiming to be the nephew of the king and being able to teach to the Indians. You must speak Nahuatl."

"Yes, of course."

"You never mentioned the fact."

Don pretended bewilderment. "No one ever asked me."

The Captain-General, irritated at that, said, "Speak in the accursed language to Doña Marina."

Don looked at the girl and said, "I wish to thank you for warning me there in Cempoala. You saved my life."

There was a sad something in her voice. She said softly, also in Nahuatl, "I saved it again, here in Tenochtitlan, Don Fielding. The others wanted you executed. I persuaded my lord, the Captain-General, to save your life so that we could learn more of your strange land to the north."

The girl turned back to Cortes and said in very poor but understandable Spanish, "Yes, my lord, he speaks Nahuatl."

The conquistador grunted and turned back to his captive. "This nation of yours—is it large?"

"Yes. At least twice the size of all New Spain."

That caused pause in the other, but he said, "Are all of the people as tall as you and do all look like you?"

"No. I am somewhat more than average height. We have many nationalities. We even have Moors—blacks. Yes, we certainly have blacks."

"They make good slaves," Terrazas put in.

"Maybe they used to," Don said. "Not anymore. Yes, we have many nationalities, even some Puerto Ricans, as I already told you."

"Poor shipwrecked souls," Olmedo murmured, crossing himself.

Don agreed to that, at least in part. "Yes, many of them are *poor* souls and on relief."

Cortes said, "Tell me, what language do you speak in this country of yours?"

He was treading on thin ice again. The English of the year 1519 was not the English of his own era; however, it was probably near enough to it that if any of these knew Englishmen they might recognize it. English was out. He said carefully, "We speak many languages, but one that practically all our people learn in their youth is, uh, Pig Latin."

Chapter Sixteen

"Let me hear you speak in this tongue," Cortes demanded.

Don gave him a few sentences of Pig Latin, in which he covered his opinions of the legality of the relationship between the Captain-General's mother and father and also his sexual preference for little boys and animals.

Cortes shook his head. "Gibberish. But now we come to the question, Don Fielding. Doña Marina has suggested that if, perhaps some years from now, I head an expedition north, you could accompany us as a guide and interpreter."

Don looked at the girl and understood that for some reason she was again sticking out her neck to rescue him.

He looked back. "Yes. I would be glad to."

Sandoval said mockingly, "Why? Surely you realize it would be a military expedition. Would you betray your own people?"

Don's mind began to race again. He took a breath and said, "I am not interested in war or politics. I am a teacher and scholar." He looked at Fray Olmedo. "It would be most interesting for me to see Fray Olmedo and Padre Juan Diaz bring their message to my people; in fact, it would be impossibly interesting. When I was last in my country, I came to the conclusion that my countrymen could use a little faith . . . of some sort or the other.''

Cortes looked at him narrowly. ''But the good Father has informed me that you are not a Catholic and that you even refused to take instruction from him—not to speak of being baptised.''

''While it is true that I have not taken instruction from the Fathers, thinking them much too busy to waste their time upon me, I have asked many questions of the men and have on occasion read some of the religious material the more pious carry. Thus I have assimilated a good deal of the message.''

Cortes looked at Olmedo.

The Fray eyed Don quizzically and said, ''My son, how many brothers and sisters did Our Lord have?''

Don was on shaky ground. So opposed was he, intellectually, to organized religion that he had acquired less than even average of his contemporary beliefs in the field. He said carefully, ''Our Savior had no brothers and sisters, Father. Mary, the Mother of God, died a virgin and was immediately taken into Heaven where she joined the Holy Trinity—the Father, the Son, and the Holy Ghost.''

His fingers were crossed. He hoped he had got that right. He knew that some of the Christian sects believed that Jesus had brothers and sisters and they had quotes from the Bible that seemingly proved it. But he remembered vaguely that other sects, and he thought the Catholics among them, or at least he hoped, believed that Mary died childless, save for her immaculately conceived son.

Fray Olmedo turned to Cortes. ''This man has been studying our faith, as you can see. Undoubtedly, he truly desires that the holy message be brought to his country.''

Cortes thought about it and came to a conclusion. ''Very good; for the time we will continue on the present basis. That is, on your parole you have the freedom of the enclosure here. However, you are not to leave it except in the presence of Bernal Diaz and you are not to leave the city without my own permission.''

''And my classes?''

''Continue them. And the boys will be released from their daytime duties to attend. The sooner we have their services, the better.'' Cortes looked at the priest. ''Father, as soon as they have sufficient Spanish to understand, you and Padre Diaz must take over their instruction so that they can be baptized and pass on the message of the Holy Mother Church in this dog's language the Indians speak.''

So, now he was free to continue his class and in the open at that. Nevertheless, a great deal of it had lost its point. The Spanish would be aware that the Indian boys understood them and would guard their language. On top of that, Cuauhtemoc would not be able to attend.

In fact, on the very next day Cuauhtemoc was almost taken as a spy himself. Chiefs and other officials were free to come to the quarters of Motechzoma and consult with him, but they were not given a free run of the areas devoted to the Spanish and their Indian allies. The sentries kept a careful eye upon them.

Cuauhtemoc, pretending to be one of the servants, had been ranging about with increasing lack of care. He was checking out the placing of the cannon, the stationing of the sentries and guards, the rooms used to store weapons. He was checking out, too, the morale of the Indian allies. The some four hundred Spanish were nothing without their Indians, who numbered several thousands. Although the whole army had seen Cuauhtemoc in Cempoala, he had found that, dressed in a loincloth and barefooted rather than in his finery as an ambassador, none recognized him.

On the occasion in question, he actually walked brazenly past Hernando Cortes, who was going along in the company of Malinche across a courtyard before the quarters of Motechzoma. The Captain-General didn't blink an eye in recognition although he, above any of the others, had been face to face with the young Indian for at least several hours in Cempoala.

But Don Fielding, to one side, saw a look of questioning come over the face of Doña Marina. She cocked her head slightly to one side, turned, looked thoughtfully after the nonchalantly receding Cuauhtemoc, then turned back to her Captain-General companion. She was obviously still thinking about it.

Don knew that although she had stuck out her neck for him, for whatever reason, her sympathies were all for the Spanish and she was sleeping with Cortes. She was as competent at intrigue as anyone in the invading army's camp and in many ways superior to them since they were working in a strange country peopled with a strange folk most of whose ways were incomprehensible to the Europeans. She was the power behind the throne and as interested in the overthrow of the Tenochtitlan power as any of her white masters. In short, she was poison to Cuauhtemoc, deadly on contact.

As soon as he could do so unobtrusively, Don hurried after his Indian friend. He overtook him in the courtyard once removed from the one in which Malinche had spotted him.

Don darted a look around. No Spanish were present. He put a hand on the other's arm. "Cuauhtemoc! Get out. Get out immediately. Malinche has recognized you. Her spies will have let her know that you've been raised to war chief level. She'll know you are spying. Get out!"

Cuauhtemoc looked at him and laughed softly. "So you are blood brother indeed, my giant friend. You risk being seen with me, although your own position is not as though you were comfortably taking your bath. Thank you and farewell."

He headed for the gate.

Moments later, a squad of the Spanish came trotting through, Malinche beside them urging speed.

Her Spanish was getting very good, Don decided. Shortly, Aguilar, as the middle man, wouldn't be required.

As she passed him, she shot him a questioning look but then hurried on.

His own life went into a routine. Evidently, orders had gone out. With the exception of Pedro de Alvarado and his brothers, Don Fielding became reasonably well received by the rest of the army and especially so with Fray Olmedo, though Padre Diaz seemed to continue to hold reservations about him. There was also a something about Sandoval which was difficult to put his finger upon. He got the feeling that the young conquistador knew that he was playing a part—or various parts—and was out to unmask him. Thus far, Sandoval hadn't sufficient evidence to present a case to his leader and fellow townsmen. Orteguilla, the page, loathed him, Don knew, and it probably went back to when he had caught the kid out in Cempoala. Well, it wasn't a bad average in an army of four hundred. Bernal Diaz he got along with excellently, and Avila was at least always pleasantly courteous.

He had his troubles. On the third day after his reconciliation with the Captain-General, he wandered into a courtyard in which the Spanish soldiery, an eagle eye being kept on them by Padre Juan Diaz, were melting down the Aztec treasury, insofar as gold and silver were concerned. Historically, he knew it had happened, but when he saw it in actuality, he was horrified. It was all going into the melting pot to be poured into ingots—little gods, ornaments, decorations, plate, jewelry. The soldiers sat there with their knives, prying out the jewels, tossing the remaining metal into the iron melting pots, laughing and jesting.

Don was aghast.

Bernal was among the others. He would make a trip into the treasury to issue forth with a load of the worked precious metals and toss them to the ground to be sorted out.

Don blurted, "You're being fools. The gold is worth more in its form as art objects than it is melted."

Bernal laughed at him. "Who in Spain would wish such ornaments? Besides, it is more easily transported this way." He tossed a delicately worked pendant into the bubbling pot of gold.

Don turned to the priest. "Surely an educated man such as yourself is opposed to the destruction of these beautiful objects."

Around his neck Padre Juan Diaz had a foot-long religious cross gaudily worked with semiprecious stones, gold, and silver. It was a slob of an ornament. In Don's day it would have been called camp.

The priest held it up proudly and said, "This is the only true art, my son. All else is worthless." He gestured at the Indian goldwork on the ground. "These are but heathen geegaws, and it is well that they be destroyed. They would offend the eyes of His Majesty in Spain."

Don was more shaken by the affair than he had expected to be. He had reconciled himself to the fact that Tenochtitlan would fall and his Indian friends go down with it—all in the name of inevitable progress. Was this the progress he anticipated?

But it was the following day that really got to him.

He came upon Fray Olmedo, assisted by a dozen or so of the soldiers, burning the Indian archives. The tecpan of Tenochtitlan was not only its administration center, the home of its principal chiefs, and what amounted to a gigantic hotel, but it also contained the national library.

As a student of Mexican history and anthropology, Don Fielding had studied the Mexican codices that had come down to his time. They had numbered less than a dozen and were scattered about the world's museums, and most of them he had to peruse in reproduction, though he had seen the originals in the National Museum in Mexico City. In actuality, there hadn't been even that number of Aztec codices; the sum total included Mayan books, some of those actually written and drawn after the Conquest, such as the Codex Mendoza. Unfortunately, the few that had survived were usually on subjects of comparatively little interest to the scholar—astrology, say, rather than history.

Now he could see these literally priceless volumes going up in flames, thousand upon thousands of them. It was as though somebody deliberately burned the Library of Congress in Washington. No, it was much worse since the contents of the Congressional Library were practically all duplicated elsewhere. But these were all *originals*. There were no copies run off on printing presses by the thousands. And now, there never would be. . . .

His eyes wide with horror, if not disbelief, he put a hand on the priest's arm.

"Father Olmedo, these Indian books are priceless. They contain the history, the medicine, the arts, the governmental system, the sciences of these people. To destroy them is barbarism. They contain all the knowledge that the Tenochas have accumulated in centuries."

For once, Olmedo was less than kindly toward him. He held up his Bible. "All necessary knowledge is here contained, my son." He indicated the burning codices. "These are the work of the devil!"

"But how do you know?" Don said desperately. "You can't read them. If they are preserved, some day scholars will be able to decipher them and a considerable knowledge will have been gained."

"What knowledge?" the other said scornfully. "Of what use are the beliefs of these savages? So long as such vile books are allowed to remain to them, the true word will be ignored."

Don Fielding slumped. He turned away, not being able to stand the sight.

In his own day, any one of the Indian books would have been worth a million dollars to any library or museum in the world. A million? No; the sum was meaningless. No scholar could put a price on an Aztec codex. Some things have no price. They have value, yes; but not price.

This, then, was the progress the Spanish were bringing to Mexico? As he stumbled away, he was so sick that he all but vomited. He knew his history. The melting down of the Indian art and the burning of the books shouldn't have hit him like this. He knew it had happened. He knew it would also happen when the Spanish hit Yucatan and found the tens of thousands of Mayan books. However, *seeing* it happen was another thing; it was the difference between hearing about a grisly accident and seeing it in slow motion.

Matters were developing rapidly. With what they thought was the Tenochtitlan government (Motechzoma!) in their hands, the Spanish began to consolidate their position. They got hold of the tribute lists of the confederation and determined which cities that the Indian armies had conquered provided gold to Tenochtitlan and her allies. To those that were nearest, they sent out expeditions both to pick up whatever additional gold and silver was on hand and to check the source of supply, the streams and mines from which the previous metals were extracted.

Sandoval was sent on down to Vera Cruz to take over the command of the force there, now that Escalante was dead. Which was a relief to Don Fielding. The dapper young conquistador was almost as keen to eliminate him as was Pedro de Alvarado and his brothers.

He had barely finished one of his classes in Spanish one day when Bernal Diaz came in and said, "You wouldn't be a carpenter by any means, would you?"

Don eyed him blankly.

Bernal laughed. "Or a blacksmith, or shipwright, or toolmaker, for that matter."

"I'm a teacher."

"Then you're safe. The Captain-General is combing the

army. I too am safe, and as Lord Jesus Christ is my judge, it's a relief. I've never been anything save a soldier."

"What are you talking about?"

"Don Hernando becomes uncomfortable about our position here. We are completely surrounded by water, and these Indian dogs can even cut the causeways by removing the wooden beams that bridge them periodically. So our Captain-General has decided to build four brigantines about forty feet in length apiece and with sufficient capacity so that if we must retreat, they could carry us and the horses to the mainland."

Don said, "How about your Tlaxcalan allies?"

Bernal Diaz seemed surprised that he should ask. "Undoubtedly, they could fend for themselves."

"Undoubtedly," Don said with sarcasm.

Bernal said, "It happens that Martin Lopez, one of the footmen, is an experienced shipwright. Pedro and Miguel de Mafla are carpenters who have worked at shipbuilding before. Hernan Martin is a blacksmith capable of turning out the stools needed. It is amazing the diversity of trades in our small army. Pedro Hernandez was also a blacksmith before leaving Spain. Juan Gomez de Herrera has had experience caulking ships. On my faith, we shall have a fleet in no time at all. And then the Captain-General plans to send the shipbuilding crew down to Vera Cruz to build a caravel."

Don frowned. He hadn't known about this, either from his history or current gossip. He said, "What for? He beached or scuttled the ships he had. Now he builds a new one?"

Bernal laughed and winked. "It is necessary to bring over to our cause the Emperor and his court. Don Hernando plans to send to Spain the royal fifth, thus cementing our position."

"Did you finish melting down the Indian gold?"

"Why not? Let me tell you, Don Fielding, there is a

great satisfaction in realizing that the portion that is mine will make me wealthy to an extent I have never dreamed of before.''

A germ of an idea was growing in Don Fielding's mind. A mere germ, but there. It had been sparked by Bernal's description of the workers that Cortes had found when it became necessary to build his brigantines. And side by side with it was another germ. Only germs, as yet.

He said, ''You dreamer, you.''

Bernal eyed him. ''What do you mean?''

''Come now. Do you really think you will receive this fortune?''

The other held a long silence and his face was less friendly than Don had ever seen it. ''What do you mean?''

Don scoffed. ''On this expedition the army has already several times managed to acquire large amounts of gold and silver. Come now; how much of it did *you* wind up with? How much do you have right now, right as of this minute?''

Bernal growled, ''I have been unlucky with the dice.''

''But when they split the spoil—Cortes, Alvarado, Sandoval and the others—what came to them, and what came to you?''

''The Captain-General is the head of the expedition. His share is a fifth. The other captains all contributed ships and horses, money and weapons.''

Don said sarcastically, ''So their share is larger as well. And then, of course, the emperor gets his royal fifth. On top of which, it is oh-so-necessary to spread around a few bribes in Spain to gain the support of important members of the court. When all is done, what kind of a share do *you* get, Bernal Diaz, all you who stand and fight and bleed in the front rank, who die for the greater glory of these gentlemen? Where do you stand when the loot is distributed?''

In sudden anger the other turned and strode off.

Don looked after him thoughtfully. He wondered how well the initial seed had been planted.

Shortly afterward, Cortes sent an expedition down to Vera Cruz to pick up some of the fittings, sail and rope that he had stripped from his destroyed fleet. Martin Lopez requisitioned a sizable number of Indians and took off for a grove of oak that the Spanish had located on the mountainside. It would take Spanish carpenters working with iron saws to make the final planks, but the Indians could chop down the trees and do the initial trimming.

With their continued success, the Spanish were becoming increasingly arrogant. They swarmed up the pyramids, thrust the protesting priests aside, and overthrew the Indian idols, sending them crashing down the steps that led up to the temples. Most of them shattered on the ground below, to the horror of both priests and tribesmen.

Cortes also forbade any further sacrifices. At least that was a step in the right direction, Don decided grimly. The Spanish were taking precious few such steps, their basic motivation being greed.

Malinche's spies brought word that Cacama, the Tlachochcalcatl of Tetzcuco, was organizing a revolt against the Spanish. Four of the other lake cities were in on the conspiracy. The Captain-General struck with characteristic duplicity, speed, and ruthlessness. A couple of boatloads of armed men were sent to Tetzcuco and to a house into which Cacama had been lured. They seized him, lowered him into one of the boats, and brought him back to Tenochtitlan and the Spanish quarters where he was thrown into irons. The next steps were to send out expeditions to arrest the chiefs of the other towns involved, and they too were thrown into chains and imprisoned in the tecpan. The revolt, for the time at least, was suppressed.

Ordinarily, Don Fielding knew, the Tetzcucans would have elected a new head chief, but the Spanish didn't know this, thinking the Tlachochcalcatl to be a hereditary king. Cortes insisted that Motechzoma, as emperor, appoint a younger brother of Cacama to be the new king. And Motechzoma, as usual bewildered by the Spanish demands, acquiesced. The Tetzcucans, probably equally bewildered, accepted the stripling Cuicuitzca as their supposed king and gave him lip service, but in actuality they ignored him and appointed their own new leader.

It was shortly after this affair that Malinche appeared at Don's door while he was in the middle of one of his classes. He came to his feet. As always, she was dressed in her Mayan-type *kub*, the single piece of decorated cloth with holes for the arms and a square-cut opening for the head and looking somewhat like a chemise. Underneath she wore a lighter white cotton petticoat, highly and colorfully embroidered and fringed. About her shoulders was draped a *booch*, somewhat similar to a stole. And as always, she was barefooted, her jet black hair in braids.

She said, "My lord, the Captain-General, desires your presence in the quarters of Motechzoma."

He dismissed his class and turned back to her. It was time to plant another seed, somewhat similar to the one he had used upon Bernal Diaz. Perhaps he wasn't quite sure what his goad was, but he was playing it instinctively now.

Don said softly, "And how does the campaign go to bring new freedoms and a better faith to your people, Malinche?"

Her chin went up a bit. "My name is now Doña Marina."

He nodded. "Although the army has been here in Mexico for the better part of a year, you are one of the few who have been baptized. I understand that the reason was that the Captain-General didn't want to take the chance on sleeping with a heathen. Now that he has taken on other mistresses does he have much occasion to bring you to his bed?"

She frowned slightly and her large dark Indian eyes took on a vague, almost pathetic quality. She said, so low that he could hardly make it out, "My lord, the Captain-General, is so busy that he has little time for any activity save his work."

"His work being to secure all the gold and other valuables that he can get his hands upon and in treading down everyone who gets in his way. Did you witness the burning of Quauhpopoca and his chiefs and son? Did you witness the imprisonment of Cacama and the others, their sole offense being that they wished to resist the Spanish?"

"They stand in the way of bringing the true faith to all the land."

"Twenty years after the Spanish have succeeded, the population of all the land will have been reduced by two-thirds. What good is it to have a new faith if you're dead?"

"How do you know?"

"I know."

"Through your history?"

"Yes."

The girl was far from stupid, as he had already discovered. She said, "I asked Fray Olmedo the meaning of the word, and he told me that it was the knowledge of things past. But you attempt to look into the future."

"I can't explain it to you, Malinche, but I'll tell you what I'll do. I'll tell you something that will transpire within the fairly new future. A new Spanish fleet will appear near Vera Cruz and it will contain something like one thousand soldiers. They will have come to arrest Cortes and to take over this expedition, so that they, instead of Cortes, can acquire the gold here."

"I don't believe you. The emperor in Spain would never lift a hand against his loyal subject, my lord, the Captain-General."

"Very well, we'll see." He turned to go.

She said, her voice very low, "A moment, Don Fielding."

He turned back to her, questioningly.

Her eyes were on the floor as she said, "Do that to me again, which you did in the temple at Zempoala."

At first he didn't understand. Then he did. And with it came another understanding. Now he knew why she had taken his part on more than one occasion.

He tilted up her chin and did a better job than he had the first time. Her mouth was unbelievably soft and eager under his own.

Chapter Seventeen

They were all there—Cortes, his captains, and Pedro Hernandez, one of the army secretaries, and a public notary to boot. And Motechzoma, the Tenochtitlan high council, and representative chiefs from Tlacopan and Tetzcuco and even some of the other towns in the valley.

The Indians, who, on the face of it, hadn't the vaguest idea of what was going on, periodically exchanged looks of puzzlement.

Pedro Hernandez was reading from a lengthy paper which looked to Don like some sort of legal document. He droned on and on, and Don Fielding finally got the drift of it. Motechzoma was pledging his fealty to Emperor Charles the Fifth and accepting him as the liege lord of all the domains controlled by Motechzoma.

The Spanish stood around looking, to Don, like nothing so much as a pack of wolves. And the Indians stood around looking like nothing so much as a group of Indians being read to in a language they didn't understand.

When Hernandez was through, Cortes said to Malinche, "Tell the king what has been said and have him sign, with his royal seal, the paper."

Don suspected that Malinche's capability to understand the whole thing was almost as limited as that of the other

Indians present. However, she did better than he had expected.

She said in Nahuatl, "The teteuh says that he wishes you to accept the friendship of the great chief across the waters and be as though you were a member of his tribe."

Cortes said tightly to Don Fielding, "What does she say?"

Don told him.

Motechzoma was looking puzzled, as he invariably looked puzzled these days.

Don said to him, "If you sign that paper, then you are of no more value to the teteuhs. And all the lands that belong to your people will belong to the great chief across the waters."

Cortes snapped to Malinche, "What did he say?"

She darted a despairing look at Don, then took a deep breath and in poor Spanish said, "He urges Montezuma to sign the paper with his seal."

Inwardly, Don's stomach did a double turn. Pedro de Alvarado, in the background, was glaring hatred at him.

Motechzoma said, to both Malinche and Don, "But why is it necessary? What does it mean?"

Malinche said hurriedly, in Nahuatl, "It is to bind your friendship with the great chief across the seas."

Don said, "It is to make *tlacotli*, slaves, of all your people."

In continued bewilderment, Motechzoma said, "But how could that be? My putting my seal as Tlacatechtli on that small paper make the Tenochas *tlacotli*? They are not *tlacotli*; they are free tribesmen. There are few *tlacotli* in all the land—kinless, clanless ones."

Don said, "The teteuhs do not know this. The customs in their own land are different than in Tenochtitlan. Most of the teteuhs are *tlacotli* to their great chiefs."

Motechzoma moaned.

Cortes said suspiciously to Malinche, "What does this Don Fielding say to the king?"

Malinche said, her voice low and the words coming slowly, "He urges him to sign the paper."

So, my dear, Don thought, you betray your lord, the Captain-General, for the sake of one who kisses you, rather than holding you in contempt as an Indian wench not worthy of the treatment to be devoted to a white woman.

Cortes said harshly, "Inform the king that I have pressing matters and that I cannot wait on this the balance of the day."

She did so, though in slightly more conciliatory words.

Motechzoma groaned again. His fellow chiefs were staring at him in open contempt. They had heard Don's opinion, and although they didn't completely understand this matter of fealty and liege lords, they didn't like the situation one bit.

Cortes snapped impatiently, "Well?"

Motechzoma turned wearily to the Snake-Woman. "My seal."

Tlilpotonque looked at him emptily for a long moment, his intelligent face cold. At long last he took from a pouch a seal carved in the form of an Eagle in green jade. He handed it over.

The public notary supplied the ink.

Motechzoma made the impression, then sighed deeply, as though in relief.

So far as Cortes and his officers were concerned, all of what they called New Spain was now a fief of the Emperor Charles. There was elation on their faces, triumph in their eyes.

Cortes came to his feet, the document in his hand. He made a sweeping bow, flourishing his velvet cap. "Thank you, Your Majesty!"

He marched from the room, his officers, laughing and

chattering their relief, following him. Malinche, after a quick look at Don, went too.

Tlilpotonque turned to Don. "Kinsman, what does all this mean?"

Don said hollowly, "I told you. In the land from which the Spaniards come, they have different customs, different laws. In their belief, all the Tenochas, and all the people of all the lands, are now their *tlacotli*."

"Are they mad?"

"No, they are not mad. And now they have accomplished what they wanted. I make this suggestion to you. Do not return to the tecpan again, assuming that they will even let you depart at this time. They have the proof they need to submit to Spain, making it legal in their courts of law, and you are the sole witnesses to the transaction. As such, you are potential trouble-makers for them. They would not hesitate for a moment to imprison you as they have Cacama and the others, or even to kill you."

"But we have done them no harm," Motechzoma blurted. "We have given them all that they have requested. Why do they not return to this far land across the seas whence they came?"

Don said, "Don't you see? They have no intention of ever returning."

"But the teteuh pledged his word. As soon as they built new ships in which they could travel."

Don said grimly, "To take a silly phrase from the old stories of my land: Malintzin speaks with a forked tongue. They are building their new ships here on the lake, not down on the beaches of the eastern sea. Does that mean nothing to you?"

Motechzoma moaned. "Malintzin said that they are for pleasure, to sail about the lake."

If it hadn't been so deadly serious, Don Fielding could have laughed.

Instead, he looked at the Snake-Woman. "I suggest that

you and the others leave, before it occurs to Cortes—
Malintzin—to detain you.''

When they were gone, he looked at Motechzoma in
compassion. ''They won't let you leave. If there is some
manner in which you can escape, I suggest you do so.''

But the other had lost all remnants of decision, fortitude,
self-respect. He shook his head mutely.

If the Spanish had been arrogant before, they knew no
bounds now. Hernando Cortes let Motechzoma know that
now New Spain was a fief of the Emperor Charles Fifth,
and it was only suitable that all the towns pay tribute of
His Majesty, and hence the Spanish should accompany the
Indian tribute collectors to each city in Montezuma's domain.
The tribute collectors were especially instructed to urge
those areas that produced gold or silver to intensify the
production of the metals.

While these various expeditions were under way, the
construction of the brigantines went on, and in surprisingly
short time they were launched. They mounted a bronze
cannon on the prow of each, and on the maiden voyage of
the largest of the four the Captain-General made a point of
taking Motechzoma along with him. They set off at full
sail down the length of the lake and from time to time
touched off the cannon. Cortes made his point to the fallen
war chief. The canoes of the Indians lacked both the speed
and the firepower of this awesome vessel.

Don Fielding finished his Spanish class of four and took
on another group, if for no other reason than to fill his
hours. This time he located ten youngsters and, besides the
Spanish classes, introduced them to both Arabic numbers
and the Latin alphabet. The Indians, surprisingly enough,
had developed the use of the zero in their numbering
system, but the unit dots and bars of five they used were
too clumsy for much in the way of mathematics. Nahuatl
lent itself well, as a language, to the alphabet, and shortly

the boys were writing their language in Latin script with a verve.

The teenagers he had already graduated were pressed into service as interpreters, although Cortes still depended usually on Malinche. He knew he could trust her but was cautious with the Tenochas.

When, for whatever reason, Malinche wasn't available, the Captain-General sometimes called upon Don Fielding as an interpreter. Thus it was that Don was present when the first news of the Narvaez expedition came through. The girl was off on some errand involving the requisitioning of supplies for the Spanish and Don was summoned.

The meeting took place in Motechzoma's quarters, which was passingly surprising in itself. In the relationship between the Captain-General and the imprisoned First Speaker it was usually Cortes who summoned the Indian into his presence when communication was called for.

Now there was something out of place in the demeanor of Motechzoma, and Cortes had obviously detected it, since his eyes were narrow and calculating. Seemingly, there was more backbone in the war chief than Don Fielding had thus far seen, even before the kidnapping.

The First Speaker said, "Now, Malintzin, you will be able to return to your home across the seas."

Don translated.

"Why do you say that?" Cortes demanded.

Motechzoma brought forth a large piece of the Indian *amatl* paper which they utilized for messages and handed it over.

Scowling, Cortes unfolded the paper. On it were drawn nineteen ships. Below them were drawn horses, cannons, men, crossbows, and arquebuses.

The Captain-General looked up. "What is this?"

"Off the coast of the eastern sea have arrived more teteuhs. My messengers have counted them and sent the information to me. There are ten cannon, eighty horses, eighty of the teteuhs who carry guns, one hundred twenty teteuhs who carry crossbows, and perhaps a thousand others. So now you will have ships in which to return, O Malintzin.''

The mind of Hernando Cortes was obviously in high gear. He had no idea of whom these men might be, but they outnumbered him at least two-to-one and they had eighty horses to his sixteen.

He spun on his heel and strode quickly from the conference room. As he went, he shouted out orders to soldiers in the vicinity to round up all his captains who were in the city. Sandoval, of course, was in Vera Cruz, de Leon and de Rangel were off with fairly large groups of the Spanish garrison collecting tribute. The army available was at about half-strength.

Don followed along, largely through curiosity.

Cortes reentered his headquarters and banged down into his chair, his face working.

He snapped to the page, Orteguilla, the only one of the Spanish who had any Nahuatl at all, ''Go find Doña Marina. Tell her to come here immediately.''

Pedro de Alvarado came hurrying in, his face questioning.

The Captain-General snapped, ''Get a man off on our fastest horse to Sandoval in Vera Cruz.''

''What has happened?''

''Nineteen ships, off the coast. I want a detailed report. Who it is; what they want. Sandoval will know what I require. In fact, he has already probably sent a message, but since he has no horses, it will take forever to get here.''

The other captains came trooping in, one by one, apprehension already on some faces, as though by extrasensory perception the consternation was spreading.

Cortes gave them all he had. ''The question becomes, are they from Spain—reinforcements from the Emperor? Or are they from Cuba, seeking to displace us?''

"Aiii," Olid complained fiercely. "Just when everything was going so well."

They remained on tenterhooks for two days before the message from Sandoval got through, and it was not the horseman who brought it, but an Indian runner. By coincidence, Don Fielding was again present, Cortes having just used his service in some transactions with the Tlatocan high council. Cortes was beginning to get suspicious about the fact that they no longer came to this building to administer the city and seemingly no longer found it necessary to consult with Motechzoma for his orders.

Sandoval, in his letter, minced no words. The expedition was under Panfilo Narvaez and had been sent by Governor Velasques of Cuba to arrest Cortes and take over the expedition. The governor was furious over the manner in which Cortes had usurped the expedition and bypassed him to deal directly with the court in Spain. He had assembled a new army and the figures that had come through Motechzoma were substantially correct. There were thirteen hundred of the newcomers, ten cannon, evidently all of them larger than anything Cortes had at his command, and eighty horses. Eighty!

The ships had anchored off Cempoala and Narvaez was making that town his base.

Then came the Sandoval touch. He, of course, was based in Vera Cruz and had but forty men capable of bearing arms. Narvaez hadn't even bothered to march on him but had sent envoys to demand the town's surrender. Sandoval promptly arrested them and was rushing them to Tenochtitlan trussed up in hammocks and carried by Totonac porters working in relays and traveling night and day. They couldn't make as good time as the runners who had brought the message, of course, but they should make the run in about four days.

The situation was too tense for humor and Avila was the

only one to laugh. "That Gonzalo," he said. "By my conscience, he would not fear the devil. Forty men at his disposal and he risks the wrath of an army of thirteen hundred by arresting its envoys!"

Cortes looked around at them, wanly. "Opinions, anyone?"

They were fighters, not thinkers.

Malinche said finally, "My lord?"

He looked at her a bit impatiently. "Yes?"

Her Spanish by now was quite good. She said, "Are these new teteuhs as hungry for gold as all you others?"

Olid growled, "All Spanish are hungry for gold, Doña Marina."

"Then, my lord," she said to Cortes, "perhaps this is the weapon to use against them."

All eyes were on her.

She said, "If I understand correctly, you have at your disposal quantities of gold beyond that which any of you have ever seen before. It will do you no good if you are dead or imprisoned. So why not use it?"

Diego de Ordaz said darkly, "By my beard, we have worked and fought for that treasure for a year and more."

She looked at him, her eyebrows high in a very feminine sarcasm. She repeated, "What good will it do you if you are dead or imprisoned?"

Cortes said, "What do you propose?"

"That when these envoys arrive that Sandoval sends, meet them with full honors. Make friends of them. Apologize for the manner in which they were trussed up in hammocks. Explain that there is plenty of gold for all. Tell them that it would be a mistake to upset the situation here by fighting among yourselves. Then load them down with riches and let them return to the camp of this new teteuh, Narvaez. Send him friendly messages and, with the messengers, send still more gold to be distributed among his captains and men."

Silence fell as they thought about it.

She said, "Among this great number of teteuhs, are any of them your friends or blood kin?"

Pedro de Alvarado grumbled, "How could we know?"

"The messengers you send could find out. These in particular should be given presents of gold."

The Captain-General shifted in his chair unhappily. He, more than any of the rest, disliked the idea of giving up any of their loot.

He said finally, "We could send Fray Olmedo as a messenger. He's a priest; Narvaez would not dare lay hands on him. And he is acquainted with practically every Spaniard in Cuba. He would know whom to attempt to win over through bribery."

Alvarado said, in argument, "They must be the dregs of Cuba. When we gathered up this army of ours, we took the best men on the island, most of them veterans of the Indian fighting in Hispañola or Puerto Rico, many of them veterans of the European wars or those against the Moors. And we have been fighting since first we landed in Yucatan and Tabasco. One of us is worth a score of them."

Cortes shook his head. "Brave words, Pedro, but on my faith as a gentleman, no Spaniard is worth twenty other Spaniards. Twenty Indians armed with stone weapons, yes, but not twenty Spaniards, or even three or four. No, Doña Marina is correct. We must use diplomacy. Pedro, send messages to de Leon and de Rangel and to Sandoval. Order them to rendezvous with me on the road to Vera Cruz. You will remain here with seventy men and four hundred of the Tlaxcalans. Your orders are to remain here in the palace, as quietly as possible. Do not issue forth from the gates. We wish the city to remain tranquil. I will leave Doña Marina with you, since I will have little need of an interpreter. One of the Indian boys Don Fielding has taught will suffice for me. And, Pedro . . ."

"Yes, my Captain-General?"

"Nothing is to happen to Don Fielding. I have future need of his services."

Pedro de Alvarado sucked in air as he shot one of his patented glares at Don. "Yes, my Captain-General."

When Hernando Cortes marched out from the city, he had but seventy men with him, and no Indian allies. The Tlaxcalans made it clear that though they were willing to mobilize for him in an attack upon the Tenochas, they would not fight teteuhs armed with cannon, crossbows, and arquebuses backed by cavalry. By the time he picked up the forces of the other captains, including those of Sandoval, his small army numbered some three hundred and thirty. Three hundred and thirty against an enemy that outnumbered him by a thousand, and with superior firepower! Whatever else he was, Hernando Cortes was no coward.

On the second day after Cortes left, Don Fielding looked up Bernal Diaz and suggested a stroll in the great square.

Bernal didn't like the idea. "The Captain-General wished us to remain here in the palace."

"You forget that I am a nephew of the king and a citizen of this city. Far from provoking the people by my presence, they will be glad to see me, and it will give an air of the tranquility Don Hernando wished to be expressed."

Bernal was not convinced, but: "I'll ask Alvarado," he said.

Pedro de Alvarado, impatient at being left out of the action, was too busy biting his nails to give a hoot. He granted permission, but warned them to go no farther than the city square.

The two strolled around, Don noting the increased antagonism in Tenocha citizens at the sight of Bernal Diaz. There was open hatred in some faces.

Bernal said, "On my faith, I should teach some of these devil-worshiping dogs a lesson at the point of my sword."

Don said dryly, "I wouldn't recommend it; we'd never

make it back to our quarters. Besides, remember the Captain-General's orders. Nothing to upset the tranquility . . .''

When they reached the vicinity of the huge buildings which housed the Eagle clan, Don spoke nonchalantly to one of the young men walking past them. "I would see my blood brother as soon as possible," he said pleasantly, in Nahuatl, not raising his voice.

"I will give him the message, kinsman," said the Indian in the same tongue.

Don's luck was holding; the other was an Eagle clan member.

Bernal Diaz looked at him suspiciously. "What did you say to him?"

"I passed greetings of the day. He is a slight acquaintance."

"You are a strange one, on my faith. It has never been clear to me how you could possibly be a nephew of the great Montezuma."

"It is a long story," Don told him.

They returned to the tecpan and Don retired to his room and waited.

Cuauhtemoc showed up in surprisingly short order. He was dressed in his usual disguise, barefooted and wearing nothing but a loincloth, as though he was one of the Indians utilized by the Spanish who were too lazy to perform their own menial tasks.

Don pulled the mat securely over the door and the two of them sat on the floor.

Don said, "We must speak quickly since the tecpan is now in command of one who hates me and very possibly I am spied upon in hopes that I will commit some act that will give him any excuse to kill me."

Cuauhtemoc nodded. "Very well, my giant brother. Speak."

"How goes the feeling among the people about the Spanish?"

"They hate them, but they fear them more."

"I see. And how do you and the young chiefs feel?"

"We wish to fight. We and the members of the confederation in Tetzcuco and Tlacopan."

Don accepted that. "All right. Now, this is what has to be done. First, your high council must depose your uncle Motechzoma and elect a new chief of war of the confederation."

The other took him in, wide-eyed. "This is within our traditions. Any chief can be disposed if he is incapable of fulfilling his duties. But no Tlacatecuhtli has ever been removed from his office in our annals."

"He is worthless to you and the time for action is upon us."

Cuauhtemoc sighed. "You would not have known my uncle before the coming of the teteuhs."

"I am sure. But now he is worthless to you. As you said once before, he has become an old woman."

"Yes. And then?"

"And then we need a spark. Something must happen to enrage the people and allow the fighting to begin. There are only seventy of the Spanish now in the city, so it will be easier for the people to find the courage to attack them. Once the step has been taken, they will continue to fight when the others have returned from the eastern sea."

"What kind of a spark?"

Don Fielding was not a man of violence. He had never been. In his own era, he had seldom gone to the movies or watched television shows. They were too replete with violence. He hated war; he even detested sports that involved death, such as bullfights.

He sucked in breath and said, "Some must be killed so that the people will rise in anger and attack these invaders."

Chapter Eighteen

There was a stirring at the mat which covered the door. Don Fielding jumped to his feet, snatched his Beretta .22 from its holster, and flung the mat aside. It was the page, Orteguilla, the one Cortes had loaned to Motechzoma and the sole Spaniard in the expedition who had a smattering of Nahuatl.

"Good God," Don snarled. "Every time I have a private conversation I find one of these Spanish kids under my feet!"

Orteguilla, his eyes wide now, turned and darted away.

Don brought the gun up and drew a bead on the boy's back. But then he lowered it again and shook his head. If it had been a man—perhaps. Things were desperate.

He grabbed up his entrenching tool, attached it to his belt, returned the gun to its holster. Cuauhtemoc was also standing by now.

"Quickly," Don snapped. "We must get out of here. The boy will report the talk of revolt to Alvarado, the one you call Tonatiuh, the sun. He'll have his excuse to execute me. And you with me. What is the best manner to get from the tecpan?"

He led the way out the door.

Cuauhtemoc said, "But all entries are guarded."

"Which is least guarded?"

"That to the canal to the rear of the buildings. It is there they unload the canoes which carry the supplies for the teteuhs and their allies."

It was the area where most of the Tlaxcalans were quartered and Don didn't know it very well. But they hurried in that direction.

At the small dock two Spanish soldiers were posted. Both of them looked bored. They were armed with swords alone, in both cases sheathed. Don knew one of them slightly, Juan Sedeno.

Don Fielding came up and said to him, "Juan, Pedro de Alvarado wants to see you."

The other looked surprised. "Me? Why? I'm supposed to be on guard duty."

Don shrugged. "I wouldn't know. He seems awfully upset about something or other. Listen . . ."

From the center of the tecpan came shouts and the clatter of men running in armor.

"Por Dios!" the soldier snapped. Holding his sword scabbard in his right hand so that it wouldn't trip him up, he started for the tumult at a run.

Don Fielding turned to the other, opened his mouth as though to say something, but then let his eyes widen. He looked beyond the soldier at the canal, packed as it was with the transport canoes.

"What's that!"

The Spaniard spun and stared.

The oldest wheeze in the world, Don thought as he pulled out his entrenching tool and clipped the other on the back of the neck, immediately below the helmet.

"Quick," he snapped at his Indian companion and jumped into an empty canoe.

He sat in the bottom, knowing he was worthless with paddle or punting pole. It was Cuauhtemoc's ball now and the other went at it with a vim. He headed straight across the narrow canal for the community house there. As was common in these buildings, an arm of the canal went directly into the establishment for landing stages inside.

Just as they darted into the narrow entry, a crossbow quarrel banged into the masonry. Don involuntarily ducked. They jumped onto the landing stage.

"They'll be after us in moments."

His companion laughed exuberance even as he led the way. "I spent my boyhood playing around these buildings, my giant brother. If they can catch us, they deserve to!"

They ran through a maze of corridors, courtyards, arches, and in moments Don had lost his sense of direction. They came upon another canal, evidently on the far side of the building, and confiscated another canoe. In moments, Cuauhtemoc had it under way at full speed up the canal.

"We cannot go to our home," he said. "There the teteuhs might seek us out and the people are not yet ready to resist them. We will go to the home of the Turtle clan. Their chief, Tetlepanquetzaltzin, is a great friend of mine and hates the teteuhs beyond all others." He laughed his exuberance again. "Except for me."

Don said, "Does that boy, Orteguilla, know you? Has he ever seen you with your uncle, Motechzoma?"

Even as he paddled, the other thought about it. "I do not think so. I hope not, for tomorrow I lead the dancers in the great square before the temple."

"What dancers?"

"It is the beginning of the feast of Toxcatl in which we dance and make merry in honor of the god Huitzilopochtli. Tonatiuh, the sun, has given permission to my uncle to hold it."

"No," Don said.

Cuauhtemoc looked at him in surprised questioning.

Don said, "If you dance in that enclosure, you will die."

"But it is a great honor to lead the young warriors in the

Dance of the Serpent. It was undecided who to choose and I won out over Ocuitecatl when Xochitl, the high priest, sided with me.''

"If you dance in that enclosure, you will die the same day."

"You know this, giant brother?"

"Yes."

The Indian sighed. "And you say you are no magician."

They spent the night in the community house of the Turtle clan and with the friend of Cuauhtemoc. While they sat around and talked, word came that there had been a fight between Cortes's men and those of Narvaez. Cortes had won hands-down.

"It wasn't much of a fight," Don told them. "The weapon used was gold. But now the ranks of the Spanish are more than tripled."

The shoulders of the two Indian chiefs slumped at that.

"Then we are lost," Cuauhtemoc said lowly. "For even with the lesser number of teteuhs, the people are afraid to rise."

"Not quite yet," Don said. He looked at his friend. "When you are preparing to march out to war, how do you summon the warriors?"

"Why, the priests beat the great drums from the top of the great pyramid."

Early the next day, Don and Cuauhtemoc ascended the pyramid from the far side so that Spanish sentries on the walls of the tecpan could not detect them. They hid in the temple at the top, to the surprise of Xochitl and his priests, and peered out the doorway at the proceedings below.

The dancers in their barbaric finery began to assemble early, excitement in the air.

"That is Ocuitecatl," Cuauhtemoc said glumly. "He will lead the young warriors in the Dance of the Serpent. It was to be my honor."

A large group of the Spaniards came over from the

tecpan and stood around as though curious to watch. Don noticed that they were strategically placed at each of the entrances to the temple enclosure, but evidently none of the laughing, chattering Indians did. He was sick inside. It was a fiesta; there was not an armed Indian in sight. The Spanish, as always, wore their swords and armor.

The singing and dancing were well under the way when Alvarado gave the signal. At each entry, the Spanish set guards, shoulder to shoulder. Then the balance of them, swords swinging mercilessly, began the attack with cries of "Santiago, and at them!"

Don sat down, his eyes on his feet.

Cuauhtemoc stared at him. "You knew this was to happen?"

Lowly, Don said, "Yes. I knew it was to happen."

"And you didn't warn them? Some of them are our kin, blood brother."

"I know," Don Fielding said in agony. "But we needed our spark." He turned to Xochitl, who had, for once, horror in his face rather than madness.

"Begin the sounding of the great drums," Don told him.

By noon, the Spanish and their allies were under full siege. The square was packed with screaming Indians launching veritable clouds of arrows, javelins, stones from slings. From the top of the pyramid, archers were able to see down into the tecpan courtyards and no man was safe to issue forth from cover. On the walls, the Spanish cannon fired over and over again, cutting bloody swaths in the ranks of the attackers, but still they came on.

In the buildings of the Eagle clan, the war chiefs held a conference. There was one chief from each calpulli, four head war chiefs from the four divisions of the city, one head chief from Tlaltelolco, the sister city of Tenochtitlan, and one each from Tetzcuco and Tlacopan, the other two members of the confederation.

The first item on the agenda was the election of a new First Speaker, Motechzoma being replaced. The position fell to Cuitlahuac, member of the Eagle clan and a brother of Motechzoma.

He was a warrior born. He came to his feet, eyes flashing enthusiasm. "We will now go forth and storm the tecpan and kill or capture them all!"

A shout went up. Arms were brandished. Somewhat to his surprise, Don noted that several of them, besides Cuauhtemoc, bore longbows.

"Here we go," he muttered under his breath. He came to his feet and held up his arms. All knew him and fell silent.

"No," he said.

Cuitlahuac scowled. "But you too are their enemy. Why do you not wish to rush in and destroy them all?"

Don said, "Because Malintzin will soon be on his way back. With him are fifteen hundred Spaniards, and they have many guns and almost one hundred horses. If we kill Alvarado and his seventy men at this time, Malintzin will remain on the mainland and invest the city, and the other tribes will come over to him in large numbers because all of them hate your confederation and wish to participate in the looting. With that many men and all his guns, he will eventually triumph, no matter how valiant the Tenochas."

Cuitlahuac said fiercely, "When he comes, we will sortie out and overwhelm him."

Don shook his head. "As you are now, you cannot prevail against horsemen and against cannons, no matter how much you outnumber him."

"Then what are we to do?" the Snake-Woman demanded.

"We lay siege to Alvarado. And for the time, we take up the bridges in the causeways so that he cannot possibly fight his way out. We let him send messengers to Cortes, though we do not let them know we are aware of the fact that he has done so. Cortes will come to the rescue. The bridges will be replaced so that he can enter. We will suck him into the trap. Then we will take up the bridges again; all the allies will be summoned, and we will decimate him. His horses are worthless in the city, with all its canals, and the cannon almost so, since there is so much shelter for us. He will try to escape, but we will be upon him. No matter how many of the Spanish we destroy, however, they will come again. We must so defeat them at this time that it will take long for them to recover. We must have time to prepare for future attacks.''

Tlilpotonque, the Snake-Woman, said emptily, ''There are many of these teteuhs in the lands from which they come?''

''As many as the grains of corn in your distant fields, my brothers. *But they are not teteuhs*, which you should know by now. Calling them that name makes the people fear them, since who wishes to fight gods? We must spend every moment of our time in preparation to meet them, for they will come again and again, even though we defeat Malintzin.''

The assembled chiefs thought it out. Obviously, in this first flush of enthusiasm in battle, their whole instinct was to polish off the immediate foe, but on the other hand, the confederacy had not gained its position of supremacy, militarily, in Mexico by being less than efficient warriors. Don's arguments were obvious.

Cuitlahuac said, ''Then what do we do for the present, Magician?''

Inwardly, Don Fielding thought, *I've put it over. God knows what this will do to the history books*. Aloud, he said, ''The first important step is to seize the brigantines, the great canoes of the enemy.''

Cuauhtemoc produced his Eagle Knight regalia from a deer hide shoulder bag and dressed quickly. Enthusiastically, he said, ''We will fire flaming arrows at them. We will burn them and sink them to the bottom of the lake.''

Don shook his head again. "No. That we must not do. It will cost the lives of many, but they must be seized. Now they ride at anchor with guards upon them. In the middle of the night, when matters are most still, thousands of canoes must sally forth and the ships be overrun. They must be captured, and all the Spanish upon them. They must not be slain, if there is any possibility of not slaying."

"Why, Magician?" Cuitlahuac, the new war chief, said.

"So that they can be sacrificed to the gods and thus win merit for us!" Xochitl screamed.

Don Fielding would have to have it out with that one later. Now he had enough problems on his hands.

He said, "Because to destroy the brigantines would be madness. Later we will need them. We will need all of the things the Spanish have brought if we are to resist them. For the time, we are unable to utilize these large canoes, but we must learn. The Spanish on them know how to use them. We must capture them so that we can force them to show us how to use the sails and the galley oars—and the cannon, for that matter, since not even I know how to use the cannon."

Don turned to Cuitlahuac. "Meanwhile, it is necessary to curb your warriors somewhat. Besiege the Spanish, yes, but do not expose yourselves to the cannon and the arquebuses. It is brave to dash full into the mouth of the guns, but a brave man is of no use to us if he becomes dead. Instruct them to fight from cover. If the Spanish sally forth, retreat quickly before them, showering them with missiles, but do not, at this point, meet them face to face, man to man. Their weapons are too superior. Against your missiles they have defenses, their armor, but even the best of armor sometimes fails against a sharp obsidian point."

He looked at Cuauhtemoc. "Your longbow is such that it can sometimes penetrate the best of mail or even a steel breastplate. It would be well if you put your bow-makers to producing them as rapidly as possible and your best bow-men be put to instructing the archers in the new method of firing.''

Cuitlahuac, the new war chief, was obviously somewhat put out by this comparative stranger usurping his position of command, even though he might be a magician beyond all magicians that had ever been known. He said, ''If we are not to destroy these large canoes of the teteuhs and we cannot sail them since we know not how, what are we to do with them?''

''Pull them with your canoes to some place in the lake where they will be safe. Not Tetzcuco because the Spanish army will come through there upon their return from the eastern sea.''

''This you know?'' the war chief of Tetzcuco demanded.

''This I know.''

''And you claim not to be a magician,'' Cuauhtemoc chortled.

The raid on the brigantines came off as Don Fielding had scheduled. He stood on the top of the pyramid and watched, the night being bright enough under the moon. The slaughter was stomach-churning, but the Tenochas, like the Spartans before them, preferred to die in battle. The cannon blew them down by the scores, but they continued on. Happily, each ship had a guard of no more than four or five. Pedro de Alvarado simply did not have the manpower to provide more. They were overwhelmed and towed off by the victorious, whooping Indians.

And the siege as well proceeded according to the plan Don Fielding had outlined. The messengers to Cortes were allowed to escape. It was noted that they were Tlaxcalans rather than Spanish. Alvarado was not risking any of his precious men and, in his eyes, the Indians were expendable.

A couple of times the Spanish brought Motechzoma out onto the rooftops to order his people to stop resisting the

Spanish and to return to their homes, but he was met with jeers and Alvarado gave that up.

Several times, the Spanish footmen sallied forth to try and disperse those who were tormenting them, night and day, with the arrows and slung stones, the javelins and pellets from blowguns. But the Tenochas, under instructions, melted away before them, and the casualties taken in the open were not worth the game. There was hardly a soldier now who had not at least a few wounds. Largely, they were minor, due to armor and the low quality of the Indian firepower, but over the days of combat, one by one the Spanish were losing their effectiveness.

Don Fielding had been amazed at the degree to which Cuitlahuac, the Snake-Woman, and all the rest of the Tlatocan high council had allowed him to dominate their decisions. It didn't stand up to reality. He was, although an adopted member of the Eagle clan, a stranger and, by admission, no warrior, not to speak of being a chief.

The understanding came with his confrontation of Xochitl, the high priest.

For some time now, most of the other high chiefs had no longer been calling him magician.

The crisis was upon the capture of the seventeen Spaniards who had been on the brigantines. Cuitlahuac, the new First Speaker, the Snake-Woman and Don Fielding and Cuauhtemoc, who had led the assault on the ships, were all who had been present.

Xochitl, insanity in his eyes, had been for sacrificing the white men on the pyramid of Huitzilopochtli so that the Spanish still remaining in the tecpan could witness it going on—an indication of things to come so far as their own lives were concerned.

Don said emphatically, "No!"

The head priest was furious and his mad eyes blazed. Don was beginning to realize why he was head priest: there was religious strength in insanity. But he was surprised the other had enough stability to hold down his office.

"The gods demand it!" the other screamed.

Don shook his head. "We need them to teach us the things they know."

"They must die! Their hearts!"

Cuauhtemoc looked at the priest, his face ultimately stoical, and gestured with reverence toward Don as he said, "Are you blind, so that you cannot see? His face is white, paler than any of those we thought teteuhs and now know are in truth devils. His beard, when he allows it to grow, is black, as I can witness. To mystify us, perhaps, he tells us he comes from the north, but in truth he has come from the east. He has led us in defense against the devils from across the seas. He foresees the future, correctly as all know. He can bring fire from his fingertips. It is the year One Reed. Would you fly, then, in the face of our returned Lord, Quetzalcoatl?"

Part Four

Chapter Nineteen

Donald Fielding closed his eyes in pain. Successively, this agnostic had worn the titles of magician and priest, and now he had made the ultimate. He was being hailed a god.

The face of the high priest, Xochitl, had sagged at Cuauhtemoc's words, though by the expressions of Cuitlahuac and the Snake-Woman they had already accepted, within themselves, what the younger man had proclaimed: Don's divinity. Don Fielding was the returned god Quetzalcoatl, leader of the Toltecs who owned this area before the coming of the Tenochas. The tradition was that the god had promised to return in time of crisis and resume the leadership of the peoples.

Xochitl gaped at Don. Finally, he got out, "But he does not claim to be the god. When first Malintzin landed on the coast, we thought him to be Quetzalcoatl. We called them all teteuhs. Now we know them to be devils instead."

"I am not Quetzalcoatl, nor any other teteuh," Don said. "I am simply a man."

Cuauhtemoc's look was both friendly and tolerant. "Perhaps he does not even know it himself. The ways of the gods are strange, as all men are aware."

Don gave up. By the looks of the priest, he was

undecided; nevertheless, he was taking no chances. For the time, at least, he gave up his fight to have the captured Spaniards sacrificed on the altar of Huitzilopochtli.

Cuitlahuac said respectfully, "We will continue to take your suggestions. Even if your words are correct, and as you claim, you are not the returned god—still, as a magician, if you are no more, your advice has been good and we will continue to heed it."

The Snake-Woman nodded acceptance of that.

He moved back into his room in the buildings of the Eagle clan and gave instructions for a new table and stool to be made for him. He simply couldn't think well sitting or squatting on the floor.

That night he tried to bring order to his thoughts. For the past few days he had been working as though instinctively; one development led to another. He had met each problem as it came up as best he could. But now he had to face the reality of it all.

Ever since he had been thrown into this other time, he had agonized over the question of whether or not it was possible for him to change history. Now? Now it was no longer a question; he already had changed history. And it was not in a minor way. In history, the Indians had burned those brigantines and they had sacrificed every Spaniard they caught.

Always before, he had thought the Aztecs doomed. In his era, history told him that they had gone down and that the Spanish had completely destroyed their culture and imposed their own upon Mexico. When he found himself in this time, he had accepted the fact. But now the question was upon him. Was it possible to prevent the defeat of the Indians?

He had found them more desirable as a people than the Europeans. In many respects he found their society more advanced. Certainly, their institutions were more democratic than were the feudalistic Spanish.

He had, in spite of himself, managed to build up a great deal of prestige with the Tenochas. Would it be possible to bring them from barbarism, avoiding chattel slavery and feudalism, into a more advanced society, still retaining those of their institutions that were desirable?

It came back to him now that Cuauhtemoc, or someone, had told him that the Toltec god, Quetzalcoatl, did not desire blood as Huitzilopochtli, the Tenocha god, did. So that solved that. So long as they thought him divine, there would be no more sacrifices.

He fell asleep, wondering at how much impact he could have on this age, and whether or not it was really desirable that he attempt it. Should he stand aside and let the Spanish overwhelm these people? Or even if he tried his hardest, could he help prevent it?

They were taking too many casualties. The trouble was, the Tenochas were warriors, not soldiers. They fought largely as individuals and in the heat of combat paid little attention to their chiefs. For that matter, the chief himself was more likely to be in the thickest of the fray, paying little if any attention to what his supposed followers were doing.

They would dash valiantly up to the wall of the tecpan and loose one of their inadequate javelins, an arrow, or even a stone from a sling. And the Spanish up on the walls would coolly pick them off with crossbows or arquebuses. Or if a large enough group assembled, one of the cannon would blast them down.

Don was no soldier, but he had read a great deal of history and he knew enough about warfare to realize that the Tenochas had insufficient firepower.

He had Cuauhtemoc bring the captured Spanish before him. There were twenty of them in all. Besides those captured on the brigantines, several more had been taken on Alvarado sorties. About half were wounded to one degree or the other. They were bound and well guarded. Don knew only two or three slightly.

One he knew as Gaspar Sanchez hissed at him: "Traitor!"

Don had to laugh. "Traitor? Did you labor under the illusion that I was a free member of your army? I was in danger of my life every moment I was in your vicinity."

"You're a white man, yet you side with these heathens."

"I'm a heathen myself," Don said mildly. "But let us get to the point." He looked around at them slowly. "The priests wish to sacrifice you to their gods. I imagine you've heard of the procedure. You're taken up to the altar in the temple atop the pyramid and your body is stretched across it. Four of the priests hold you, your back over the stone. Another takes a stone knife, cuts open your chest, and pulls out your heart. *While you watch.*"

Most of them reacted as might have been expected. Brave men they undoubtedly were; concede them that, Don thought. But even a brave man does not look forward to a gruesome death.

Nevertheless, one cool-looking redhead spat on the ground in a demonstration that his mouth was not dry at the contemplation of his fate. He said, "Well, why do we not get around to it? By my Lady, it grows wearisome trussed up in the temple dungeon."

Don looked at him. "Because I talked them out of it."

Silence fell over the twenty.

Don said, "It was not easy, particularly after your massacre of the unarmed dancers."

"Pedro de Alvarado was informed that they planned an uprising, a revolt," one said.

"As men who call themselves soldiers—and Spanish gentlemen—one might have expected you to wait until such a revolt materialized, until you were confronted with an armed army. However, that is not the point. The point is that I have saved your lives, and they will continue to be in no danger, if you pay my price."

Sanchez said, "What price? On my soul, it is obvious that we have not an ounce of gold among us."

"In the fighting we have captured various weapons, especially on the ships. We have cannon, arquebuses, crossbows, swords, and pikes. It is not convenient to use the cannon at this time, and we have not the time to learn the correct use of the sword. However, we wish you to teach us to use the matchlocks and the crossbows. The brigantines were well stocked with powder, shot, and cross-bow quarrels."

"Are you mad?" said one that Don recognized as Bartolome Garcia by name.

"No. Let me finish. Any who so assist us will not only be granted his freedom when the war is ended but will be awarded with fifty pesos of gold." In actuality, Don Fielding did not know what fifty pesos of gold was worth in the Spain of this age, but he knew it was a fortune.

They goggled at him.

Finally, one rasped, "We are not traitors to our Captain-General, our Emperor, and our Lord Jesus."

"Well spoken," Don said, nodding. "Does anyone disagree? If you were released and rejoined your comrades, do you believe that any of you would wind up the war with that much gold, or would the Emperor, Cortes, his captains, and the other high-placed confiscate it all, or almost all?"

Most of them glared at him.

One of them rasped, "And if we do not accept your offer, we are to suppose it is the sacrificial altar?"

Don looked at him coolly.

Another said, "And how do we know you will keep your word? These Indians are treacherous savages."

Don said, "It is a strange statement to come from the lips of men who participated in the slaughters of Cholula and here in Tenochtitlan against unarmed men who had not bothered you. However, my name is *Don* Fielding. I am an *hidalgo* in my own land. I do not lie and I pledge you my word.''

They still remained silent, although there were furtive glances at each other.

Don said, ''Very well. You will be placed in separate rooms, one man to a room. Each will have a guard posted at the door. If any one of you wishes to speak to me secretly, alone, and in such manner that your fellows need never know, unless they assume the same position, you need only say so to the guard and he will bring you to me.''

He sent them off.

Cuauhtemoc had gone through all this in silence, standing off to one side. He said now, ''What did you say to them?''

Don told him.

The other shook his head. ''None will accept your offer. I do not admire the teteuhs—the Spanish—but they are brave warriors.''

''That they are, but they are also sixteenth-century Spaniards. Their real god is yellow metal.''

All twenty were recruited. When they saw each other, there was a certain moment of shamefacedness, but they were all there. Don sent for the captured weapons.

From the first, the Tenocha warriors took to the crossbows. There were four of them in all, though one needed repair and the job was not too successful. The arquebuses were another thing. There were three of them and the Indians were afraid of the noise. Besides that, they were too new to the clumsy muskets, and one of the new Indian musketeers overloaded his piece. He managed to kill himself and two others when it blew up.

Don stationed them on the pyramid which overlooked the tecpan, along with the crossbowmen and those who already bore longbows. They dominated what had become the fort of the enemy—four crossbows, two remaining arquebuses, and the longbows. Below, the Spanish and their Tlaxcalan allies had to keep out of sight, out of the courtyards, which hindered their activities considerably.

Alvarado was no novice at war. He retrained his cannon and soon managed to level the temple. But this led to no casualties at all. The Tenochas simply retreated to the far side of the pyramid and popped up once more as soon as the gun had been fired. The early model cannon were so primitive that it could be clearly seen under these circumstances when one was ready to be fired—seen, and guarded against.

Don suggested to the war chief, Cuitlahuac, that no more frontal attacks be made on the tecpan fort, that all fire against it be directed from other buildings in the vicinity, and particularly the pyramid. It was against all Indian warfare traditions, but Cuitlahuac was receptive. He liked the idea of sucking Cortes into the trap. It would have been comparatively easy to rip up ladders and take the place by storm, but they wanted *all* of the enemy, not just this handful. Orders were given that if the Spanish sortied again and attempted to take the pyramid top, the defenders fade away before them, scurrying down the opposite side, rain missiles on them from all directions, and then reoccupy their position when the Europeans were forced to return to their safer quarters.

Time was running out and daily messengers came with word of the progress of Cortes coming up from the coast. But Don Fielding had the long view in mind. He took one of the crossbows to the craftsmen in Tlaltelolco and gave them instructions to duplicate it as best they could. The one major shortcoming was that the actual bow on the Spanish models was made of steel, which gave the weapon its great power. All the Indians could use was wood. Don recalled that the Mongols, or some other people of antiquity, strengthened their bows by gluing a heavy strip of rawhide the full length of the back. He didn't know exactly how it was done, but he passed the idea along for experimentation.

Cuauhtemoc had become Cuitlahuac's right-hand man and was invariably in the first line. He had become the most accurate archer and spent long hours on the pyramid bedeviling the Spanish and their allies with his arrows.

Conscious of logistics, as the Indians weren't, Don Fielding had Cuitlahuac send messengers and porters to every town in the immediate vicinity to trade for arrows and javelins and other military supplies, and also to request that each town begin all-out manufacture of additional quantities of these. Cuitlahuac and the Tlatocan put up an argument when Don insisted they barter for these things rather than confiscate them. For a century, the Tenochas had dominated this area with a strong and ruthless hand and were used to taking what they wanted.

No more, Don told them. Cortes was recruiting new allies. The defenders of Tenochtitlan couldn't afford to antagonize anyone. If the wily Captain-General could bring a couple of hundred thousand Indians to his colors, the city was lost. Tenocha fences had to be mended. They didn't have the time now to begin the operation, but at least they could refrain from further antagonism.

The message finally arrived that the Spanish were about to enter onto the causeway. Cuitlahuac sent out the orders to replace the beams in the bridges. No efforts were to be made to hinder the advance of the Spanish army. All canoes were withdrawn from the vicinity; all warriors were instructed to keep themselves hidden.

Cortes, riding in the lead at the head of his cavalry, must have smelled a rat. But for the better part of a year now, his contempt for the Indians had grown. The messages from Alvarado had been upsetting, but then, Alvarado had now but fifty Spanish and four hundred Indians at his disposal. The Captain-General had the largest army the Europeans had thus far mobilized in the New World and it was well-equipped by the standards of the day.

While they were still on the outskirts of the city, he had the trumpets peal, and his military band struck up a lively march. From the beleaguered tecpan came the blast of cannon triumphantly welcoming them.

The Spanish march made a brave display: the horsemen, the musketeers, the crossbowmen, the long lines of footmen with pikes; the Indians drawing the guns; the long lines of Tlaxcalan and Totonac porters with the supplies; the alert Spanish rearguard, so that no attempt could be made on the train.

All was silence. They filed down the causeway until it became the main street which entered upon the great square. The new recruits from the forces of Narvaez darted apprehensive looks about, but the veterans of Cortes were more philosophical. They had been in this town for months. They knew it and they knew its inhabitants. The Indian dogs were no match for white men!

Cuitlahuac, Cuauhtemoc, and Don Fielding stood at the top of the pyramid watching the parade, their faces empty of expression.

When all the newcomers had filed into the tecpan and the gate closed behind them, Don said, "Sound the great drums. And from now on, let them continue sounding night and day from the top of every pyramid in the city."

Cuitlahuac said, looking at him, "Why? It will keep us from rest at night."

"It will keep *them* from rest even more so. At least we know that they are our drums and indicate our belief in victory." Don added in English, below his breath, "It's known as psychological warfare."

Cuauhtemoc said, "And we will keep up the attack, night and day, as well!"

Don shook his head. "No. As soon as night falls, we pull our warriors back, as though they have gone home to rest. Each night we do this. But secretly we post reliable warriors, ones that can be trusted not to sleep and not to leave their posts. Let these sentries each have conches. When the Spanish attempt to escape, let the conches sound and let every Tenocha in the city spring to arms."

He turned to Cuitlahuac, "Send out messengers to every tribe in all the valley and even beyond. Have every warrior who will serve you come to the city as well armed as can be provided. When the Spanish sally forth and try to return to the mainland, it will be the crucial point. We must capture and destroy as much of that army as we can so as to earn time for ourselves."

Cuitlahuac said questioningly, "How do you know they will sally forth and try to escape? They are much stronger than they were before."

"Because here in the city they cannot maneuver their horse troops and it is too easy for our warriors to hide from them. Cities are not good battlegrounds for armies—as the Nazis found out after they were sucked into the ruins of Stalingrad."

The two Indians frowned puzzlement at him.

He said, "It is not important. Malintzin will undoubtedly fight for a few days. He will sally forth into the great square. He will not be able to comprehend the fact that he is now on the defensive and his position is untenable. When he does make his sorties, attack with all your might. He must be shown that retreat to the mainland is his only alternative. When he does so retreat, we have him. The bridges will be removed and without boats he will not be able to cross the canals."

Don turned to Cuauhtemoc. "Let one warrior out of ten be armed solely with the long poles with loops of rope on the end with which to pull the horsemen off their mounts."

He had wanted to introduce *la reata*, the lariat, to the Tenochas for this purpose, but knew he had no time to train them. Besides, he didn't have the slightest idea of how to throw a lasso himself. Possibly he could work it out eventually, but it was always time, time, time. He was fighting time.

The kettledrums began to sound from one pyramid, then from another; soon the whole town was arumble. Before it was over, Don was going to regret he had ever made the suggestion.

The warriors began to congregate behind the shelters they had improvised all about the tecpan. Others appeared upon the top of the pyramid on which the three stood. Don noted that there were more men now with longbows and several with the new crossbows the craftsmen were making. The fire against the tecpan began.

The new crossbows weren't as good as the Spanish ones by any means. Don doubted that they were even as efficient as the longbows, but they were better than the inefficient weapons the Tenochas had earlier. Once again, time was going to count here. The Indian workers were excellent and every crossbow they turned out would be better than the last. The quality of firepower would improve as the days went by.

Don had been right about the sorties.

Suddenly the huge wooden gate the Spanish had built in the tecpan opened, and Cortes and at least eighty horses came charging out, lances couched. They dashed valiantly across the square, lancing, swinging their swords mightily, and most of the warriors scattered before them. Some stood and fought; of those who did, most died.

But from all directions came the clouds of arrows and javelins—from the rooftops, from the temple and pyramid tops, from behind the shelters, from the doorways of the community buildings.

Armor protected the Europeans, but not completely. Here and there a man or horse went down.

The Spanish charged completely across the square, cutting and lancing, their battle cries ringing on the air, calling upon this saint or that. Behind them, from the tecpan, the cannon roared and arquebuses boomed.

"Waste of powder," Don muttered. "They don't have enough targets."

His eyes narrowed as he saw a Jaguar Knight, with one of his improvised loops on the end of a long lance, dash out from a point of concealment and flick the noose over an unsuspecting horseman's head. He jerked, and the horseman crashed to the ground in a great clatter of armor. The Indian dashed forward, pulled an obsidian knife from his waist, and slashed the other's throat. Pedro de Alvarado galloped up and lanced him.

Don shook his head. But at least the device worked.

Cortes, Sandoval, and about twenty of the horsemen were heading at a gallop for the pyramid. They flung themselves from their steeds and, swords in hand, began the ascent.

"Let's get out of here," Don snapped.

Cuauhtemoc glared at him. "No. We'll stand and fight."

"Like hell we will," Don said. "We're the command staff; we can't afford the luxury of standing and fighting. If anything happens to us, who is going to tell the warriors what to do? Let's get out of here. Around to the other side!"

Cuauhtemoc, his longbow in hand, eyed the Spanish coming up the pyramid's side. "If we stay, we die?"

"Yes," Don said. "Come on!"

"This you know, my giant brother?"

"This I know," Don lied. For all he really knew, they might have made a fight of it and even have thrown the ascending Spanish back, but he couldn't take the chance.

He was no militarist, but he knew you didn't risk your general in a battle. Alexander had charged at the head of his Companions, the Macedonian heavy cavalry, but by the time of Caesar, the military had evolved beyond that.

They scampered around to the far side of the pyramid and began the descent. Let the Spanish capture the top; they'd find nothing but the abandoned kettledrums, and kettledrums in Tenochtitlan were a dime a dozen. There'd be a new set of them banging away within minutes after Cortes and his men had abandoned the untenable position.

The fight continued in the square for more than an hour, and then a trumpet sounded and the horsemen withdrew to whence they had come.

"Big victory," Don grunted. He gave instruction to have the fallen Spanish weapons gathered up.

The Indian warriors were filing back into the positions they had been driven from, and the heavy fire of arrows, crossbow quarrels, stones, and javelins was resumed. The top of the pyramid was reoccupied with its vantage point overlooking the main enclosure of the enemy and the many courtyards.

Don didn't envy the Spanish position. He even felt a qualm or two for some of those below. Bernal Diaz, Avila, Fray Olmedo, and, of course, Malinche.

He turned to Cuitlahuac who was again standing next to him on the pyramid top.

"Above all, cut off their food; cut off their water. Let no canoes from the tecpan leave for the mainland and let no canoes from the mainland join them. At night, as well as day, allow them no access to the canals in their canoes."

He sought into his memory for details of ancient warfare.

He said, "Saturate pieces of cotton with oil that will burn, bind them to arrows, and fire clouds of them into their quarters."

He thought some more. "The bodies of those who have

died—do not burn or bury them. Let them stand in the sun for a few days. When they are covered with maggots and stinking, throw them over the walls into the tecpan.''

Cuitlahuac stared at him, obviously repelled. "This is necessary?"

"Everything is necessary to defeat the Spanish."

"This is not the manner in which the Tenochas have forever fought their enemies."

"It sure as hell isn't," Don growled out. "This is total war. If I can start an epidemic in that camp, we've got it made. It's known as biological warfare."

Chapter Twenty

Captain-General Hernando Cortes simply couldn't get it through his head that the city was no longer his. For the next few days he fought it out. Over and over again, the Spanish sallied forth—sometimes the cavalry alone, sometimes both horse and foot.

They soon found it was best to confine themselves to the great square. The moment they got into the narrower streets, rocks dropped down upon them from the flat rooftops like a rain. If they dashed into the houses to flush out the foe, the Indians fled over the roofs or into canoes in the canals.

Cortes sent Ordaz to reconnoiter the Tlacopan causeway with four hundred footmen, and they were driven back after losing eight soldiers to the howling, screeching Tenochas who swarmed everywhere. They reported the bridges removed.

And always the kettledrums boomed, all but driving the Spanish to madness.

In desperation, the Captain-General had built three wooden towers from the top of which his soldiers could fire onto the rooftops. They wheeled them out at early dawn and before noon all three were in the hands of Cuitlahuac's braves, occupants either dead or prisoners.

The Tenocha forces were continuing to accumulate captured weapons, especially swords, lances, and pikes, but also a few crossbows and even a couple more muskets. The latter were immediately pressed into service. The others were stored in one of the rooms of the Eagle clan buildings.

During one of the rare pauses in activity, Don stared down at them. It came to him that even though the Indian warriors did not have the time to learn proper use of the sword, even improperly utilized it was better than the *maquauhuitl*, set with its obsidian blades. The Tenocha sword wasn't so bad when the warrior first went into action, but after a few snipes at Spanish armor, the blades shattered and the weapon was little more than a club.

Don said to his constant companion, Cuauhtemoc, "Take these long knives of the Spanish and distribute them among those of your warriors who love most to use the *maquauhuitl*. At first they might seem awkward, but they will prove more effective against the footmen and the horses."

Cuauhtemoc frowned unhappily, "These are not the traditional weapons of the Tenochas."

Don grunted at that. "Well, we'd better start some new traditions then. Because we are never going to win a war against men with steel weapons while we carry stone ones."

The other gave up. These days he seldom argued with this new blood brother of his. One seldom argues with gods.

From their command post on the top of the pyramid, Cuitlahuac, Cuauhtemoc, and Don Fielding watched the progress of the battle. It had been going on four days now, at a pace that seemed almost impossible to maintain from the viewpoint of the Spanish. Surely, almost all of them must be wounded by now. Don tried to think of some new tactic that would break their morale to the point where they'd attempt to desert the city. He had to get them out in those causeways, into the canals, where they'd be helpless.

It was the cavalry that gave him the most trouble. The horsemen, and the horses as well, were highly armored and the warriors had practically no defense against them. The Spanish lances took a terrible toll and the Tenochas could do little but run from them, only to be speared in the back.

Somewhere, Don had read that horse should not charge footmen. Why not? The Spanish must have read: *disciplined* footmen. But still, why not? Why shouldn't cavalry charge foot?

His eyes narrowed and he turned to Cuauhtemoc thoughtfully. "Come with me," he said and led the way down the pyramid back to where they had stored the captured Spanish weapons.

There were some thirty lances and more than that number of pikes. The lances were half again as long as the pikes.

Don said, "I want you to locate sixty of your bravest warriors. They must be absolutely fearless in battle and never have been known to run in the face of the enemy."

"All we Tenochas . . ." Cuauhtemoc began.

But Don Fielding held up a hand. "Some men are braver than others. I want the bravest in all Tenochtitlan. You will be their chief. Assemble these sixty warriors here in the courtyard."

Don Fielding had never held a spear in his hands in his life, but he managed to get his message over. He demonstrated.

"You advance in a straight line, two deep. Thirty of you in front, bearing these shorter spears, thirty in the second line, bearing these longer spears. You keep your line straight. No man dashes forward before the others, no matter how valiant. No man drops behind.

"When the Spanish ride at you, at the command of your

chief, the first line drops to one knee and their spears are grounded, like this, butt on the ground, the point extended upward at a slant, like this. The second line holds its spears firmly, at breast level, extended over the shoulders of the warriors who are kneeling. The charge of the horses is received with no man giving way, even though he go down to black death under the hoofs, the swords, or the spears of the enemy.''

These were highly experienced fighters, all Eagle Knights, the most highly experienced in Tenochtitlan. They immediately got the idea. Don wasn't thinking in such terms at the time, but at that moment the first primitive phalanx was born in Mexico.

They drilled for the balance of the day, impatient to be left out of the combat sounds which could be heard from the square. Now that they had the idea, they could do a better job of drilling themselves than he could. Don left them and returned to the pyramid vantage point.

It was upon this day that Hernando Cortes decided to utilize diplomacy in view of the fact that force was proving inadequate. Don found later than it was Malinche who made the suggestion.

During a lull in the fighting, a small group of soldiers with shields came up on the walls of the tecpan surrounding Motechzoma, who was in his full regalia as the First Speaker of the Tlatocan high council. Evidently, he hadn't heard that he had been deposed. He held up his hands and the firing fell away completely, from both sides.

He held that position and finally the Tenochas left their shelters and gathered beneath the walls or stood on nearby rooftops fully exposed.

From the pyramid top, Don and his two Indian companions could barely make out the former chief's words.

If the fighting stopped and the beams were returned to the bridges over the causeway, Malintzin and all his army would march out of the city and back to the sea where they would take their ships and leave this land forever.

Somebody called something from the crowd that Don didn't catch.

Motechzoma answered that Malintzin himself had given his word.

The crowd stirred, whispered, murmured.

Don said, "No." He said urgently, "We've got to end this."

Cuauhtemoc said, "But they promise to go. That is what we wish."

"He'll leave only temporarily. He's getting desperate and wants out. He'll regroup his army at Vera Cruz, get more reinforcements, and then return stronger than ever. We must inflict more casualties upon him. Many more. We must wound him as badly as we can."

The crowd was still stirring. The Tenochas had not gone unharmed in this past few weeks of fighting. There was not a clan in town that hadn't lost its scores of warriors.

Don said flatly, "They're listening to him. After all, he was their respected head war chief for years. Fire on him, Cuauhtemoc."

"But he is an Eagle, a member of our clan! He is my uncle, our uncle, our kinsman."

"But all he can think of is getting the Spanish out of the city, in hopes that all will return to be the same as before. It won't. You can never go back, and certainly *he* can't. Fire on him, Cuauhtemoc! If we don't, all is lost. Tenochtitlan is lost. The warriors must be kept at full fighting pitch."

Cuauhtemoc said, "You know this to be the truth, giant brother?"

"Yes. I know it."

The other turned to a group of nearby slingers. "Bring him down before he says another word to influence the people."

Their slings spun. A shower of stones rained.

The Spanish soldiers below, who had been guarding the former war chief, had lowered their shields when it seemed as though his message was being received. He staggered back, hit several times.

A cannon boomed and the crowded Indians scattered for cover. Motechzoma was carried away by the soldiers.

Cuauhtemoc looked emptily at Don Fielding. "You know all. Is he dead?"

Don shook his head in negation. "No. He lives, but the Spanish will kill him when they retreat. This is the final straw. He is of no more use to them whatsoever. He has, in their eyes, signed over to the Emperor Charles the Fifth all of New Spain. But his people have rejected him. He is of no use any longer and they will murder him."

"When will they attempt to flee?"

"I don't know. One of these nights, but which one I don't know."

"I thought you could foresee the future."

"Some of it. But . . . this I cannot explain to you . . . but the future I can foresee is being changed. I myself do not understand. But every day that goes by, it is being changed more. How much longer I will be able to foresee anything at all, I do not know."

The Indian shook his head. "The ways of the gods cannot be understood by man."

"They sure as hell can't," Don muttered in English. "And usually they can't be understood by the gods, either."

The Spanish took their final bitter pill two days later. Cortes, thinking that they had broken the back of the Indian resistance, sallied forth with forty of his horse and possibly eight hundred foot, leaving just enough of his force in the tecpan to man the walls and to preserve a reserve of horse in case of emergency. He was, on the face of it, out to deliver such a crushing blow that the city's defenders would be demoralized.

At the far side of the square, Cuauhtemoc's Eagle Knights were drawn up in their simple phalanx, each man about three feet from his neighbors to each side. Behind them a drummer beat out the march, an innovation that Don hadn't thought of. Evidently Cuauhtemoc had.

Cortes shouted his battle cry, swung his sword, and led his horsemen on the charge.

He had without doubt never seen Indians so arrayed. Not in Cuba, not in Hispañola, where he had once campaigned against naked savages; not in Yucatan, Tabasco, or Tlaxcala. But it obviously never occurred to him that they would stand fast upon the impact of the cavalry.

Cuauhtemoc snapped a command; the beat of the drum changed and his men came to a halt and dressed their lines. The Spanish were but a few yards away. He snapped another command. The drum broke into a staccato. The first rank knelt and grounded the butts of their pikes, the spearheads at a forty-five degree angle. The rear rank extended their lances over the shoulders of the first.

Don Fielding was too far off to see the expression on the face of Captain-General Hernando Cortes when the reality of the situation hit him, but it must have come as a shock. Cavalry should not charge disciplined footmen. The axiom had been laid down long hence. But it was too late to reverse the charge now. The Spanish hit and impaled themselves on the spears, going down almost to a man before it was through.

The Captain-General, bearing a charmed life, was one of the few who survived. He staggered back, his horse dead, Cortes badly wounded in one arm.

The new-born phalanx had taken its casualties. Possibly half of them had gone down. But so great had been the soldier's debacle that even the Spanish foot were demoralized. They covered their own retreat with crossbow and arquebuses, but their hearts weren't in it. They were driven, helter-skelter, back to the tecpan fortress.

Don was atop the pyramid with Cuitlahuac.

He said grimly, "Have the drummer increase the tempo of the kettledrums. And then summon the council of the war chiefs. Tonight the Spanish will attempt to break out and reach the mainland."

"Are you sure?"

"No. But if I was Malintzin, that is what I would do. His army must be demoralized and a good number of them wounded. He knows that after that success, tomorrow there will be two hundred warriors instead of sixty in our phalanx, and the next day, two thousand. Armed, of course, largely with lances tipped with obsidian or flint rather than with steel, but still more than a match for his few men."

The full complement of war chiefs was in the dining hall of the Eagle clan's buildings. The process had been slow so that Don Fielding hadn't particularly noticed it, but for all practical purposes he had taken over the prerogatives of Cuitlahuac, the First Speaker. Not that the other took umbrage. He was enough of a commander not to argue with success, and this tall white man they now called Quetzalcoatl was giving them successes with his new weapons, his new tactics.

Don stood, flanked by Cuitlahuac and Cuauhtemoc, while the others squatted Indian-fashion on the floor.

He said, "Tonight, most likely the enemy will try to retreat to the mainland. Thus it is that the Tetzcucans and the Tlacopans and the rest of the allies, instead of returning to their own towns in their canoes for the night, must remain ready for the big fight. The Tlacopans will remain at their end of the causeway; when they hear the sounds of battle, they must dash down it and join the fray, preventing the Spanish from crossing. The Tetzcucans will all be in canoes on each side of the causeway, and they will drag down the enemy and carry them off."

"Ha! Later to be sacrificed to the gods," one of the allied chiefs chortled.

Don ignored him and went on. "We wish to capture as many of the Spanish as possible and the horses as well. Do not kill either a Spaniard or a horse unless absolutely necessary. The Tlaxcalans it would be best to kill, since those that escape will come back another day, using our new tactics perhaps. The Tenochas will remain in the city and pursue the army down the causeway from this end, once again capturing as many as possible."

The Snake-Woman spoke up. "But how can they possibly expect to make the mainland when the bridges have all been raised?"

"They have built a portable bridge in the tecpan. They plan to carry it with them. Each time they cross a break in the causeway they plan to put the bridge down, have the whole army file across, then pick it up again and carry it to the next break."

"How do you know?" Cuappiatzin, chief of the House of Arrows, demanded.

"I know," Don said. He added, "There is just one more thing. When the retreat begins, capture Malinche. Above all, capture Malinche unharmed! She is the strongest weapon in the Spanish arsenal."

"But she is only a woman," someone blurted.

"That makes no difference. She doesn't have to fight with a sword; she operates with her brain and it is the most dangerous brain in all the land. In the abilities of that girl lie the downfall of this city. *Capture Malinche*."

Later, when the war council was over, Don took Cuauhtemoc aside.

He said, "How many Tenocha women still remain inside the tecpan with the Spanish?"

The other wasn't sure. "Perhaps a hundred. They were offered to the army as servants when the teteuh first arrived. Now they are kept on, in spite of themselves, as tlacotli slaves."

Don thought it out. "So the Spanish are quite used to

having these women about. Would it be possible to smuggle one more in?"

"But why, giant brother?"

"I want to get a message to Malinche."

"It should be possible. In spite of our blockade, a few canoes get through to the teteuhs, bringing them food and other supplies. When we catch these, we kill them, but still a few attempt it, mostly women who have become infatuated by a teteuh and would do anything for the man she loves." He considered it. "Yes, she could enter with a canoe-load of food and undoubtedly the Spanish would welcome her. What is the message?"

"Malinche is to be told that the Spanish cause is lost. She has probably already come to that conclusion. She is to be told to drop behind when the Spanish retreat begins and to hide in what was formerly my room when I lived there. She knows where it is. She is to be told that the message comes from me."

"But why all this?"

"For two reasons, Cuauhtemoc. First, as I said, she is the most dangerous person in the Spanish army, save only Malintzin himself. Second, she is the woman I love."

"Perhaps I understand, my giant brother."

Don Fielding's prediction was correct. The Spanish army, shaken by the day's defeat, chose that night for its dash for freedom.

From the top of the pyramid, well concealed, Don, Cuitlahuac, and Cuauhtemoc watched. The moon was still bright enough that they could make out the movement of the column below, which was maintaining a ghostly silence in spite of its numbers.

Sandoval—Don thought he recognized the slim figure— led with a small group of horse and about two hundred Spanish foot. Cortes himself was evidently in command of the center, in which went some of the cannon and most of the baggage, probably including most of the treasure, Don decided. Pedro de Alvarado brought up the rear with the better part of the infantry.

When the full column had departed the buildings which they had converted into a veritable fort, Pedro de Alvarado spurred his horse around and reentered. Don's eyes narrowed; he didn't like that.

He said quickly, "There are three branches in the causeway before they reach Tlacopan. Let the full Spanish army get over the first one, then sound the conches. Then mount the attack. And remember, above all, capture as many as possible and as many of the horses."

He stood, preparatory to descending the pyramid.

"Where do you go, brother?" Cuauhtemoc said.

"I am no longer needed for the time. All will be complete confusion until dawn and past, and it is only midnight now. I am going down into the deserted tecpan."

Cuitlahuac looked at him strangely. He said, "To rescue my brother, Motechzoma, Cacama, and the others?"

"Perhaps, if they are still alive," Don said, and left.

The column had already disappeared down the street which led to the causeway, making remarkably little noise as it went. He darted across the square and into the entry, his Beretta .22 in one hand, his entrenching tool, unfolded, in the other.

He gave another silent prayer to whoever looked after agnostics that there would be no Spanish stragglers who had possibly dropped behind to acquire one last ingot of the gold that Cortes had been forced to leave behind in the tecpan. There had been plenty, according to history.

He tried desperately to remember the route to his former room. He had never been over it before at this time of night. He made several wrong turns but finally found the courtyard.

He called desperately, "Malinche! Malinche!" Not knowing, actually, if she was here or not. Had her disillusionment with those she once thought gods reached a point

where she would desert them? Had her regard for Hernando
Cortes cooled to the point where she would give him up
for a comparative stranger who had but twice kissed her?

Her form materialized in the doorway. She had one fist
to her mouth, obviously frightened.

"Don Fielding!" she whispered.

He hurried closer. "They're all gone," he said. "They
have all fled."

"No, they haven't," a voice rasped from behind him.

Don spun.

It was Pedro de Alvarado, his eyes glaring as they
always glared when he looked at Don Fielding. His sword
was naked and dripping with blood and there was an
additional dark stain on his armor. He looked as though he
had been literally wallowing in blood.

"So," Don said flatly. "Motechzoma and the other
prisoners are no more."

Alvarado came forward with deliberation. "And soon
neither will you be, Don Fielding." He took in Malinche.
"Nor you, traitoress."

Don brought up his Beretta and emptied its clip into the
other. He had no time for aim.

The small bullets splattered harmlessly on the oncoming
swordsman's armor, giving him only a slight pause to
register his astonishment.

Alvarado stabbed, but Don, more through pure luck
than anything else, faded to one side. He made a back-
handed swipe with his entrenching tool and managed to
miss as well. He dropped the gun to the courtyard floor,
swearing at himself inwardly for not having aimed at the
other's face. With that many shots in the magazine, he
should have hit the swordsman at least once. Once would
have been enough, in the face. He switched the entrenching tool from his left hand to right and stood back, crouched.

Alvarado was an experienced swordsman and had undoubtedly in his time come up against many a far-out

weapon, but obviously he had never seen anything like the folding spade. It must have seemed a strange combination of battle mace and short sword. He eyed it for a moment before boring in again, his saber in practiced position.

Don wasn't going to get out of this one, he knew. It was all very well his having finished off the assassin in Cempoala, in the darkness of the small room, and all very well his having clipped the sentry in the tecpan while the other's back was turned, but this was an experienced swordsman, veteran of a hundred person-to-person combats. A bloody damned sure-enough Spanish hero.

He hissed over to his shoulder to Malinche, ''Run!''

Pedro de Alvarado laughed aloud and in joy and came lunging in.

And an arrow transfixed his throat.

Chapter Twenty-One

Cuauhtemoc said, "I, too, saw Tonatiuh reenter this building, my giant brother. I have just been to the room where Motechzoma and the others were held in chains. They carried their chains to the afterlife."

Don Fielding sat down on the steps which led up from the courtyard to the level on which his former room was located. He looked back. Malinche stood there. She hadn't run. Face it, he told himself, she's more of a fighter than you are. Hell, he wasn't a fighter at all.

He said, "Thank you, blood brother," his voice shaky.

Cuauhtemoc said, and the question was not rhetorical, "For what?"

It was at that moment that the kettledrums, for the first time in a week, fell silent. And then the conches sounded the attack.

The Indian chief said quickly, "I must go. The battle begins."

Don came to his feet, complete exhaustion upon him. "Yes," he said, picking up his small gun again and reaching for his diminished box of shells.

"No," Cuauhtemoc said.

Don looked at him.

Cuauhtemoc said, "We cannot risk you in the fight. It is

as you said on the pyramid. Some cannot be risked, and you have proven over and over again, giant brother, that you cannot be risked. For in you lies the only hope of all the lands.''

Don opened his mouth to protest and closed it again. There was simply nothing to say.

Cuauhtemoc turned quickly and hurried away.

The girl looked at Don Fielding. ''Would you, then, let your blood brother go into the fray against the teteuhs and you refrain?''

His shoulders slumped in dejection. ''Yes,'' he said. ''He is expendable. I am not. It is not easy.''

''I do not know what your words mean.''

''No, of course not.''

He turned. ''Come. I'll take you to quarters in the house of my . . . clan.''

''I am not sure I wish to go with you, Don Fielding.''

From the distance came the blast of cannon, the booming of arquebuses, shouts and screams, above them all the hooting of the conches and the ululations and shrillings of pipes and whistles, the battle music of the Tenochas.

''I'm afraid it is too late to change your mind now,'' Don told her, the utter tiredness still in his voice. Thousands would die or be wounded tonight. Was it history . . . or his machinations?

He took her to the home of the Eagle clan and saw that she was given quarters and then returned to his own room and flung himself on his bed. If possible, he was going to have to get some rest. There was a multitude of things that had to be done the next day.

But the thought came to him before he fell into exhausted sleep: there is no doubt at all now; history can be changed and is being changed. In the history he had studied, Pedro de Alvarado survived the battle and lived later to become the conqueror of Guatemala. Malinche had remained with the Spanish army continuing to be its tongue and the alter ego of Hernando Cortes.

Just before he fell off into sleep, a memory came back to him from school days. The memory of the so-called Dichotomy. Zeno had propounded it some five hundred years B.C. According to the Greek philosopher it was impossible to cover any given distance. The argument: First, half the distance must be traversed; then, half of the remaining distance; then, again half of what remains, and so on. It followed that some portion of the distance to be covered always remains and therefore reaching a goal was impossible. It was not until comparatively modern times that the mathematicians solved the paradox. The Greek had assumed that any totality composed of an infinite number of parts must, itself, be infinite, whereas the later mathematicians decided that an infinite number of elements make up a finite total. But the point was that although the Greeks could not explain the paradox, and supposedly had logical proof that motion was impossible, that didn't prevent them from utilizing motion. So it was with his time travel paradox. He couldn't understand it and doubted if anybody else did, in any age, but if he understood it or not, he was utilizing it, willy-nilly.

In the morning, the battle over and the remnants of the Spanish army retreating in exhaustion up the side of the lake to the north, the war chiefs of the victorious Indians held another council.

Cihuaca, Tlacochcalcatl of Texcuco, was all in favor of immediate pursuit.

"No," Don said. "In spite of the fact that we have killed or captured at least two-thirds of their force, we are still no match for them in the open field. Their discipline and training gives them too much the advantage and they still have some horse cavalry."

Don's domination of the Tenochas was greater than of the allies, who didn't know him nearly so well. Cihuaca was stubborn. "We can descend upon them in all our numbers and end them once and for all. We could come around the other side of the lake and waylay them at Otumba."

"No," Don said. "We aren't ready for them yet. We have to build up our phalanx, acquire better weapons, recruit more allies." He turned to Cuitlahuac. "This is my advice."

The First Speaker turned to the Tetzcucan. "The forces of the confederacy will not pursue Malintzin."

Cihuaca was infuriated. "Then the forces of Tetzcuco alone will do so and win all the glory and plunder."

"That is your right," Cuitlahuac said evenly. "We wish you well."

The Tetzcucan stormed out, followed by his subchiefs.

One of the other allied chiefs said, "We have taken many prisoners and many horses. Now is the time to turn them over to the priests of Huitzilopochtli so that they may be sacrificed."

Here they went again. Don shook his head emphatically. "No. There is to be no more human sacrifice. You have seen the advantage of our sparing the first twenty prisoners. They teach the warriors the use of the weapons of the Spanish and we must continue to use them. The others can teach us the use of other things the Spanish have but we have not. You saw the advantage of using the spears tipped with steel rather than obsidian. What if one of our prisoners can show us how to obtain steel—or gunpowder?"

Most of them didn't like it, though the Tenochas present had already accepted the situation.

One said in irritation, "We can at least sacrifice the captured deer upon which the teteuhs ride."

"The horses! Are you mad? Sacrifice them! We must learn to *ride* them as the Spanish ride them. We must use them to pull the new wheeled vehicles I have introduced.

We must learn to breed them and fill the land with their descendants.''

Xochitl, the head priest, obviously put out by Don's rejection of sacrificing the captured white men, said, ''No man in all the land has ever ridden one of these animals. It is not the way of the Tenochas, nor the Tlacopans, nor the . . .''

''That's too bad,'' Don said grimly. ''But ride them we will. We must learn.''

The Snake-Woman said, ''I agree with you that it is best not to kill the teteuh prisoners. We can force them to teach us their secret arts. However, this does not apply to our traditional enemies, the Tlaxcalans. These can be sacrificed and we have captured perhaps a thousand of them.''

Don was still shaking his head. ''No. They too must not be sacrificed.''

Even his supporter, Cuitlahuac, was taken aback by that, and Cuauhtemoc as well.

Cuitlahuac said, ''But what can we do with these people? If we keep them, they eat our food and take up room in our quarters. If we turn them loose, they will return to Tlaxcala and one day come back to fight us again.'' It was the same argument that Cuauhtemoc had given Don once before.

Don said, ''We'll put them to work, helping us repair the city and to build new fortifications. We'll put them to work on the roads which must be widened and improved so that the new vehicles can utilize them. We will feed them as well as we feed our own people and clothe them and see that they have adequate shelter. Then, when the war is over, we will turn them loose and let them return to their own land where they will tell the people how well they were treated and the great advances we have made. For, you see, sooner or later we have to make our peace with the Tlaxcalans.'' He added under his breath, in English, ''The whole thing is known as good propaganda.''

The war chief of Tlacopan was indignant. "We will never make peace with Tlaxcala."

Don looked at him. "Yes, we will make our peace with all the tribes in all the lands, since only in this manner can we repel the attacks of the Spanish."

He had his way, but they were grudging.

The prisoners were housed in the tecpan, under ample guard, and Don and Cuauhtemoc went to supervise the recovery of the equipment of the Spanish army. Much of it had been dumped in the lake on both sides of the causeway and would have to be fished out, but a great deal had also been abandoned by the fleeing foe in the city streets or on the causeway top.

Cuauhtemoc happily told him about the events of the night before. In moments after the first onslaught of the Tenochas, the Spanish army had stopped being an army and had become a hysterical mob, each man for himself. The Indians in their canoes came up alongside the road and charged the causeway. They would grab a foe bodily and wrestle him down into the lake where other canoemen would haul him out and carry him away. The humanity was so packed that it was all but impossible for either side to wield their weapons.

When the fleeing mob of Spanish horsemen, Spanish foot, and Indian porters reached the second breach they were without means of crossing it. The portable bridge had become stuck after having so much weight on it, including the heavy cannon, and it was impossible to bring it up as first planned. Those who reached the breach first stopped, but those behind pushed them on so that hundreds fell into the lake, complete with baggage. Shortly there were so many bodies, especially of the Indians, that the balance could cross over on them. And as the mob continued its flight, the cannon were abandoned, the crossbows, the arquebuses. Lances, shields, pikes, and even swords were thrown away, the better to run.

And always the canoes debouched their warriors to take more prisoners or to slay. The crowding was such that hundreds fell off the causeway and into the waters, some to drown, some to be picked up and hauled away.

"It was a great sight," Cuauhtemoc wound it up in satisfaction.

"It must have been," Don said, shuddering.

He enumerated the things he particularly wanted rescued. All the cannon, all the weapons, all the armor, all the tools. All the gold and silver that had been recovered. All these were to be taken to the tecpan and stored.

At the mention of taking the gold and silver back to the tecpan, his companion looked at him in surprise. "Then, you too have this strange hunger for gold that the other teteuhs do?"

"No," Don said grimly, "but we'll need it later to deal with them and other Europeans. It is the most precious thing in their world, save life itself. The greater quantity we have, the better."

The rescue operations well under way, they returned to the tecpan to check the prisoners.

Don was surprised and elated at the fact that thirty-three horses had been captured. He had them temporarily housed in the improvised stables that the Spanish had built.

Cuitlahuac had rejoined them and they reviewed the prisoners who were standing and sitting about the largest of the courtyards in the enclosure. There were a hundred and forty-two of them, counting the twenty men that had been captured earlier in the fighting. Don recognized quite a few, including Padre Juan Diaz, the soft-spoken Avila, and even the page, Orteguilla. Most of them were wounded to one degree or the other, but the majority were still on their feet—still on their feet and portraying in their faces despair, resignation, defiance, and hate.

Don had his original table and stool brought, along with

writing materials, and sat himself down at it. They watched him numbly, silently.

To the prisoners, Don said, "Your lives have been spared, due to my intervention. If you give your parole, pledge to try not to leave the city except upon my orders, you will be released upon the termination of the war. Form in a line. I wish the name of each man and his former occupation, if any, previous to becoming a soldier."

Disbelief on their faces, since they had all expected to die on the altars in the temples, they lined up.

Don said to the priest, "Your Bible, please, Padre."

He put the Bible on the table, next to his paper, and took up the pen.

"First man. Name and former occupation."

"Garcia de Olguin. I was formerly a seaman."

"Put your hand upon the Bible and swear that you will not attempt escape."

"I swear."

"Next man."

"Pedro de Mafla. Carpenter."

"Good." Don went through the routine again, then called for the next man, without looking up.

"Gonzalo de Sandoval. Gentleman. And I will not give my parole, particularly to a man who broke his own."

Don looked up. "Indeed? In actuality, I did not break my oath. You forget the wording of my parole. It applied only so long as the Captain-General remained in the city. He was gone when I escaped. If you will not give your parole, you will be isolated and kept under strict guard."

"So be it," Sandoval said mockingly and turned and joined those who had already been processed.

The next man said, "Bernal Diaz. I have been a soldier since becoming an adult. I am willing to give my parole."

Don said, "I am glad you survived, Bernal. Next man."

The next man said, "Juan Diego."

The name was Spanish, but the voice wasn't. It was

thick and accented. Don looked up. For a moment he was surprised at seeing a black. The other wasn't dressed as a soldier, but rather a servant. Then Don, remembering his history now, blanched. The black man's face was badly pockmarked.

Don shot to his feet and snapped to Cuitlahuac, "Let this man go free! Immediately. Turn him loose and let him follow after the Spanish army. Have criers go before him and to each side, but not approaching near and let them warn all away."

His Indian companions were staring.

"He carries a dread disease from over the seas. If it spreads, it will decimate the city."

"Why not kill him?" Cuauhtemoc blurted.

"Even his corpse cannot be touched. Drive him from the city, immediately! And let no person come near him!"

He turned to the bewildered black, who could sense he had started something but had no idea what. Don snapped at him, "You are free to go! Leave immediately! Avoid coming near any person!"

Stumbling, the man hurried away, followed at some distance by two warriors with spears. Cuauhtemoc shouted orders for criers to get out in front of him and clear the way.

Don sank down into his chair. Smallpox! It all came back to him now. A black servant with the Narvaez forces had brought it to Tenochtitlan, and the Indians, with no immunity to the European disease, had died like flies. Eventually, they had gotten their revenge, perhaps. The Europeans had never run into syphilis before, but it was rife among the Cuban Indians, who obligingly passed it on.

When they were all through, he found that he had some sixty-five men who had held trades before joining the Spanish expedition. They represented quite a cross-list— most, though not all, of use to him. He even had a former glassblower from Florence, Italy. Not all of the Cortes army came from Spain. There were Italians, French, Portuguese, and even a couple of Greeks. And one, possibly the most precious of all, was a wheelwright.

Only three—Sandoval, the priest, and the little page— had refused the parole oath.

He leaned back and regarded them.

"We now come to the reason why you are still alive, although you are men who kill your prisoners. When you were in command of this city, you gave nothing in return for that which you took. You brought these people none of the advances Europeans have made. Now, instead of taking, you are going to give."

"They did not pledge that in giving their paroles," Sandoval called out.

Don ignored him. He said, "You carpenters are going to teach the people European carpentry. You blacksmiths, how to work iron and other metals. You former miners are going to teach them to make superior wagons to the ones I have already tried to build. You former seamen are going to teach them to sail the four brigantines we have captured. You . . ."

Sandoval called out, a sneer in his voice, "No, they are not, for this would make them traitors. It would enable the Indians to repulse the forces of the Captain-General more efficiently."

"That is exactly my purpose, friend," Don said grimly. He turned his eyes back to the others. "When the war is over, all who have cooperated, whether a captain, a gentleman soldier, or a footman in the ranks, will receive fifty pesos of gold and be allowed to return to his home in Europe if he swears never to take up arms against this land again."

Air sucked into the lungs of all but a few.

Sandoval said, "They would be traitors."

"But still alive." Don looked at him and laughed scorn, and brought up the argument he had used before. "If you had won the war, how many of these men would have received the deserts promised them? You, Sandoval, yes. And perhaps the other top captains, and most certainly Cortes who was to get a full fifth, as commander of the army. And the Emperor with his royal fifth. But the others here?'' He laughed his scorn again. ''All know the Captain-General by now. He is willing to betray anyone. If, after all that Motechzoma did for him, he was willing to send Alvarado to murder that innocent fool, how can you trust him?''

He turned his eyes back to the men. ''If you wish, when the war is over, to remain here, you may. You are free to take wives and become valued members of the community. You remember your former lives in Spain and in Cuba, where you were, at least most of you, considered dregs, as soldiers are almost always so considered with contempt. Here you would be free and honored by the people to whom you will bring so much. But that is your decision to make. To stay or to take your gold and return home. I will let you sleep on it for the night. Tomorrow I will want your response. If you don't wish to cooperate, you will share the fate of Sandoval and receive no pay when finally you are released. Meanwhile, I suggest you elect a committee to represent you in your relationship with the chiefs of Tenochtitlan and with me.''

Sandoval said, ''As senior captain of the army present, I will represent us.''

Don snorted at that. ''There are no more captains. The men will elect your representatives. Have a committee of at least three by tomorrow. Now, do you have sufficient physicians to tend your wounds, or do you desire the assistance of the Indian medicine men? Their medical science is probably at least as well advanced as your own.''

They wished to leave themselves in the hands of their own people and Don, through Cuitlahuac, saw that captured medical supplies and equipment were released to them.

He had his first volunteer immediately. Bernal Diaz approached him as he stood to leave, and said, "I accept your words about Cortes and the fact that we footmen would receive little in reward when all was through. However, I am not a carpenter or blacksmith, nor do I have any other art than that of war. Of what use can I be to you?"

Don sighed and said, "If you don't do it, somebody else will. On top of that, the end justifies the means, and the end you had in mind when you came here was to become wealthy."

Bernal frowned. "The end justifies the means?"

Don said wearily, "I have some others just as good. Such as: do unto others before they do unto you; and whatever grifter first thought up the idea of patriotism put ninety percent of the human race on the sucker list."

Bernal looked at him questioningly and growled, "Many of your words I do not understand, Don Fielding. But I accept. I will teach the use of the sword to your men."

The address to the Tlaxcalans was made by Cuauhtemoc and it went even easier than Don's to the Spanish. And they were as astonished as the latter had been. They had expected the sacrificial knife and there were few of them who had looked forward to pleasing the gods, particularly since most of their gods differed from those of Tenochtitlan.

The conception of parole was foreign to them and Cuauhtemoc had to explain an institution which had been unknown to him as well until this morning. They all accepted and Don suspected that they would turn out to be at least as honorable in keeping their sworn word as would be the Europeans.

When all was agreed, Don said to Cuitlahuac, "Take two of them. Feed them well. Give them as many presents of the type they would appreciate most as they can carry and turn them loose.''

The war chief fixed his eyes on him in surprise. "And why would we do this, Don Fielding?"

"Because already we wish to begin to woo the Tlaxcalans away from Malintzin. We want them to know that their people are being taken care of here in Tenochtitlan. Each ten days that go by, we will release another two, with presents. And the Tlaxcalans will soon begin to realize that we are not their true enemies. On top of that, Cortes and the other Spanish cannot refrain from their arrogance and before long the Tlaxcalans should begin to weary of them.''

"It shall be as you suggest.''

After he returned to his room, he looked up Malinche to see if his orders had been followed and she had been given suitable quarters and arrangements made for her other needs.

She looked at him coldly. "I cannot honor a man who would allow his blood brother to go into war while he remained behind, though he is the largest man in the land and unwounded. The Captain-General I have turned my back upon, but at least he was no coward.''

Don looked at her quizzically. "Did not the priests Olmedo and Juan Diaz remain behind when the army went into combat?"

Her head was high. "You are no priest.''

Don sighed. "I am afraid I am more than a priest, if I wish to be or not.'' He turned and left her.

Chapter Twenty-Two

In the morning, he returned to the tecpan and had the Spanish assembled again. They had elected their committee. It consisted of Padre Juan Diaz, Avila, and Sandoval. So Sandoval had had his way in spite of what Don Fielding had said the day before; he was one of the army's representatives.

The priest acted as spokesman.

"Despite my words of entreaty and those of Don Gonzalo de Sandoval, approximately half of the men have decided to accept your offer and turn traitor to the Captain-General and their emperor."

Don spoke to the assembly. "All you who have decided to cooperate, step to this side of the enclosure. All who have decided not to, step to that side." He indicated with his hand.

When the division had been made, Don addressed those who had turned him down. "You who have not given your parole will be forced to remain confined and under guard. The rest of you have the freedom of the city; however, in view of the fact that you have the antagonism of the people and the fact that you are unarmed, I suggest that you not leave the tecpan. If unwilling to cooperate, you will be fed on hard rations, the simplest of Indian food. If any of you change your minds, contact me.''

He had an inner feeling that most, if not all of them, would come over in time, especially when they noted how their collaborating comrades fared.

He went over to the other group, which was headed by Avila.

He said, ''Divide yourselves by occupation and let each group quarter themselves together. Those men who are the single representatives of their trade quarter themselves alone. There are plenty of rooms here. Repair to it and take up those that apply to your trade, if any, and take them to your quarters.''

Alonzo de Avila stepped forward. ''Some of us have no trade. I was a gentleman farmer on my family's estates outside Avila. What can I do?''

Don said with satisfaction, ''A great deal, my friend. You are a superlative horseman. You will teach our men to ride. You undoubtedly bred horses on your *finca* in Spain. You will also help supervise the breeding of the mares that we have captured.''

Avila was taken aback. ''Teach the Indians how to ride?''

''You can teach me, too. I've never been on a horse in my life. All of you gentlemen who know horses will participate in a concentrated effort to train our men not only to ride but to fight with Spanish weapons from horseback. We have thirty-three horses. Each horse will be assigned four students, and the horses will be pushed to whatever point is consistent with their health all day long. As soon as one group of students has satisfactorily learned all you can teach them, you will be assigned to another group. I want every warrior between the ages of eighteen and twenty-five to learn horsemanship.''

''What do you say, giant brother?'' Cuauhtemoc asked. Don told him.

"But why so many? If there are but thirty-three of these horses, why do we need more than thirty-three braves to ride them?"

"Because we'll get more later," Don said grimly. "We'd better."

"Very well, I accept," Avila said.

"Traitor!" Sandoval called out sneeringly from the other side of the enclosure.

Avila turned, his face dark. "I shall demand satisfaction, Don Gonzalo." He started for the other.

Don grabbed the man's arm. "No, you don't. There'll be no dueling, no fighting between you men. For the time you are no longer gentlemen; you're working men." Under his breath he said in English, "The damndest bunch of proletarians ever assembled."

When they had all dispersed, he stood there and thought about it for a moment. First things first. But what was first? In actuality, he was getting a better start than he could have hoped for. To build the four brigantines, the Spanish had brought up tools from the coast and those that they didn't have had been made by the blacksmiths and other toolmakers right here in Tenochtitlan. Most of these had been rescued from the causeways and the lake, and divers were bringing in others continually as the recovery effort continued.

He sought out the blacksmiths and took them to the room in which the Spanish armor and that of the horses had been piled.

"Your job will be to melt this stuff down, or whatever you do to it, and to make tools for the other occupations, such as saws for the carpenters. I'm going to send some of the Indian metalworkers over to be your apprentices. Each of you will have four apprentices, and part of your job, the main part, will be to teach them everything you can. Do not abuse them. As soon as they've learned that, you'll get a new batch of apprentices."

He thought about it. "I'm going to start a school. We have four Indian boys who speak Spanish. They'll be the teachers and teach you all to speak Nahuatl. The school will be for three hours each morning and attendance will be compulsory for all Spaniards." He considered it some more. "We'll have other classes taught by Spaniards to instruct more students in this language. However, the most important thing is for you people to learn the Indian tongue as quickly as possible."

He rounded up the wheelwright and took him over to the room occupied by the carpenters. He had hit the jackpot with them. There were three.

He said, "Initially, you'll work on building wagons or carts, two-wheeled carts. If you need additional tools, see the blacksmiths. I believe they already have a jury-rigged smithy here; if not, they can make one. The Indians will supply them with charcoal. Draw on them for whatever additional tools you need, nails and so forth. Use iron products just as seldom as you can; our supply is very small. I'm going to send you Indian apprentices, four to each of you. Perhaps they'll be able to show you how to substitute wooden pegs or copper nails for iron ones."

Through all this, Cuauhtemoc and several of his warriors had been following Don around, comprehending little, but sometimes being able to help out running messages or whatever. Now a messenger came up and spoke to the Tenocha chief.

Cuauhtemoc said to Don, his voice upset, "It is as you foresaw. The Tetzcucans mustered all their forces and sallied out and met the retreating teteuhs at Otumba, at the head of the lake. In spite of how weak the teteuhs were and in spite of the small number remaining, it was a great disaster. The war chief, Cihuaca, was killed and many, many of his chiefs and warriors."

Don swore. "Damn, this is a setback for morale. And just when we were riding high."

The other said, "A council of the chiefs has been called."

The government of the city and the confederation was still being conducted in the Eagle clan building. It had been decided, at least for the time, to continue to allow the captured Spanish and Tlaxcalans to occupy the tecpan since they were used to it.

When Don and Cuauhtemoc strode in, the others had already assembled. There was a new something in all faces. Don didn't realize it at the time, but with his calling of the shots in his confrontation with the now-dead Tetzcuco chief, his credit rating had zoomed. There was no doubt in any mind now of who he was. Quetzalcoatl returned to help his people in time of great crisis, as long prophesied.

There was another thing he didn't realize at the time. A life-long believer in the democratic ethic, he had just become the all-powerful dictator of Tenochtitlan and the Mexican valley confederation.

The Snake-Woman said respectfully, "You have been told of the Tetzcuco disaster. Tell, us, O Don Fielding, what will develop now?"

Don took a deep breath. "I cannot foresee as well as once I could, since things are changing so rapidly."

Cuitlahuac said softly, "Look forward as best you can, Don Fielding."

"Very well. As best I know, Malintzin will return to the Tlaxcala cities and be welcomed by them. The Spanish army will rest but a short time, recovering from their wounds, and then begin to prepare to return. New ships will land at the coast bringing new supplies, new arms, and more horses because the word has gone out to Cuba and Spain that there is great wealth here. Within a few weeks Malintzin will begin his campaign to gain new allies. Even cities and tribes that have long been under the control of the confederation will go over to him. He will

not be able to operate as well as he did when he had
Malinche with him . . .''

"We must kill that accursed woman," Cuappiatzin
snarled.

Don looked at him coldly. "Are you, then, mad? In her
head is more information about the Spanish than any person in Tenochtitlan, save the captured Spanish themselves,
and she has come over to us of her own will."

The Snake-Woman said, "Then what are we to do, Don
Fielding?"

Subconsciously, for the past week, Don Fielding had
been mulling this over. He was no authority on socio-
economics. Certainly he was no politician. The ground he
was on was as shaky as though an earthquake was under
way.

He said, "We must change the nature of the state."

"State?" The Snake-Woman said blankly. Don had
used the English word, since there was no equivalent in
the Nahuatl of this period.

"A concept with which you are not as yet acquainted,"
Don said. "It was first developed far, far from here by a
man named Cleisthenes in a city named Athens and, at
approximately the same time, by a chief named Servius
Tullius in a city named Rome."

"You speak words of the gods, since we know not what
you mean," Cuitlahuac told him.

"No, of course not," Don said. "This, then, is what we
must do. The confederation of the three tribes must be no
more."

A sigh went through the assembled chiefs.

"But . . . but . . ." Cuauhtemoc blurted. "This has
been our strength. For many generations we have been
strong through our three tribes fighting together."

Don looked at his blood brother and nodded. "But now
we need additional strength. Now we need to include in
our new confederation all the tribes of all the lands."

They gaped at him blankly.

All right. He had the ball; this was no time to let go of it.

He said, "From now on, we shall call all the lands of which we know by the name of Mexico. We shall call our new confederation the Aztec Republic and we shall invite all tribes near us to join. If some will not, we will march upon them and force them to join."

They were still blank.

Cuauhtemoc said, "What is Mexico?"

Another chief demanded, "What is Aztec Republic?"

Don said, "You people sometimes call yourselves Mexicas. So all the lands will be called Mexico. Aztec is a name others give you, or will give you. I cannot explain this. It is not a word you use yourself, but we will use it." He hesitated before adding a clincher. "It came to me in a dream."

A sigh went through them. He was a god. His dreams could not be ignored.

The Snake-Woman said, "But how will we make this new Aztec Republic?"

"Messengers must be sent out to all the cities, all the tribes in the valley, at first. To the Culhuacans, to the Azcapotzalcons, to the Xaltocans, and all the others. All must be invited to join the new republic."

"And what tribute do we demand?" Cuitlahuac said.

"None. All members of the new republic will be equal and free. Each tribe will send to Tenochtitlan, our capital, two . . ." He was making it up as he went along now. ". . . two senators, a type of chief who speaks for his tribe's interests. No tribe will have more, no tribe less."

He licked his underlip. He had to have more government than that. Besides, Tenochtitlan had a considerably larger population than most of the valley tribes and hence had a right to more representation.

He said, "And each clan, in each tribe, shall send one

subchief to a council that we shall call, uh, . . . the General Assembly. And each subchief shall have equal standing in the General Assembly.''

They were goggling at him, but he pressed on.

"The Senate shall nominate the First Speaker, but for him to be elected, the General Assembly must vote. Each tribe shall govern itself internally, as in the past, but all the chiefs of the republic will be nominated by the Senate and elected by the General Assembly.''

He was still improvising.

"At least during the present crisis, the Senate must always be in session, but the General Assembly must meet . . . uh, at least twice a year to pass upon their decisions. The Senate shall be as the present Tlatocan high council is here in Tenochtitlan and shall make all decisions involving the republic. The First Speaker will execute such decisions. But all must be ratified by the General Assembly when it meets. The General Assembly can change all.''

There, damn it, was the basic constitution of the Aztec Republic! Let them change it. Let *them* come up with the necessary applications. Let *them* decide what additional offices need be established. It was, at least, a basis for welding the warring tribes together.

They squatted there in dumb silence, assimilating it.

"No tribute from the many we have conquered?'' Cuitlahuac said finally.

"No tribute. From now on, anything we bring to Tenochtitlan from other tribes will be as a result of barter. We must make things here worthy of trade. And we shall. Already I have begun instructing the craftsmen in how to manufacture many of the devices of the Spanish. Other cities and other tribes will be anxious to acquire these things.''

The Snake-Woman said hesitantly, "Don Fielding, Tenochtitlan is the greatest city in all the lands. In what you propose, she will have no more senators than, say, Tlacopan, which is but a town.''

Don nodded. "But Tenochtitlan has twenty calpulli, twenty clans. And her sister city, Tlaltelolco, has six more. So, between you, there will be twenty-six representatives in the General Assembly, which is the ultimate ruling body. How many clans does Tlacopan have?"

"Six."

The Snake-Woman, and all the rest for that matter, were thoughtful. This was not as big a shock to them as it might have been. Their institutions were democratic. This was little more than an extension of them; the clan nature of their society was not being disrupted, nor was their local government.

Cuitlahuac said, "And the office of First Speaker will be drawn, as for so long, from the Eagle clan?"

Don smiled and copied the Aztec "who knows" gesture, holding one hand palm-up with a rocking motion. "Perhaps, but not necessarily. The Eagle clan has long produced capable war chiefs and administrators, but in the future the First Speaker of the republic shall be nominated by the Senate and elected or rejected by the General Assembly. The term of office will be six years rather than life. Any member of the republic is eligible." He decided, while he was at it, to get a blow in for women's rights. "*Any* adult, male or female."

They laughed at that, of course. Obviously, he was jesting.

And then they studied his expression and thought some more.

Finally, Pizotzin, a chief from the town of Culhuacan said, "And when all this has been accomplished? When all the tribes of the valley have been brought into the new . . . republic? What then?"

"Then we go beyond the valley. We go to Cholula, to Toluca, to Huexotzingo, and all we invite to join the new republic."

They were aghast.

Cuitlahuac said, "But these are long-time enemies! For many years we have fought them. My lord, we have *always* fought them; it is a cherished tradition. . . ."

"No more; you will find other sports. All must be brought together. And in time we will go on to the tribes of Michoacan, the Tarasca, the Huaxteca, and even to the Mayans. No matter the distance. All Mexico must come to the republic if we are to defend ourselves against the Spanish. As it is now, they destroy us one by one."

Even Cuauhtemoc, his strongest adherent, was floored. "But why should they join us? Why should they wish to belong to this . . . republic?"

"Because, through our pochteca traders we shall send them our new products. Knives of iron, such as the Spanish now have, and other tools. Vehicles with wheels, new weapons. To those such as the Mayans, who live on the sea, we will teach how to build the ships that sail by the wind. They will see the great advantages of belonging to the new republic. And those that do not come in at the first, for whatever reason, we will force to join."

The war chiefs nodded at that.

The Tlacopan, who invariably seemed more bloodthirsty than the rest, liked that idea. "And loot them and demand tribute!"

Don shook his head negatively. "No. Merely defeat them in combat and then insist they join the Aztec Republic and send their senators and representatives of their clans to Tenochtitlan."

Xochitl, who had remained ominously silent through all this, demanded, "And destroy their gods and make them accept ours!" His eyes were mad again. Don knew he was going to have continuing trouble with this one.

"No," he said. "Each tribe will be free to worship whatever gods they wish, though there shall be no human sacrifice throughout the republic."

He had said enough at this stage, he felt.

He said, "And now I leave you to your debate. But remember this. It will be as I say: *All the tribes will be united, or all will fall.*"

A long sigh went through them. He had never made a prediction that hadn't come about.

Don Fielding turned and left the conference hall.

He spent the balance of the day working on the preliminaries involved in getting his Spaniards under way. Orders were given to build an enclosure in Chapultepec embracing a good deal of that mainland area. It was for the horses, both for their graze and a location for the riding school.

He consulted with his four miners. All were from Asturias in Spain, where they had worked both in the coal and iron mines. One even had some smelter experience. Don Fielding knew very little indeed about iron and couldn't have recognized any type of iron ore for that matter. He would have given his weight in gold for the Hoover translation of Agricola's history of metallurgy, but the notion made him smile. At the moment, Agricola was a young schoolmaster in Germany who would not write that book for another thirty years. Don explained their needs as well as he could.

One of the men, Diego Garcia, looked thoughtful. He said, "There is iron ore just south of Cholula. I saw the signs as we marched past. How much, I do not know, since I was not particularly interested at the time. But there is ore there."

"I know nothing about extracting iron from the ore nor turning it into steel," Don said. "Can it be done with charcoal?"

"Yes," one of the others said. "But that won't be necessary. I went with Olid to Toluca, when we were in possession of this city, on an expedition to collect gold and silver. I saw a vein of coal about halfway there, up in the mountains."

"What would you suggest? How many porters would

you need to bring the required coal and ore here so that you could begin smelting it?''

Diego Garcia shook his head. ''The better way would be to build your smelter where the ore is. Transport the coal down there, and when you've got your raw iron, bring it back to the city.''

''All right. You four will be in charge of the operation. You will be given all the manpower you need to produce all the iron you can possibly turn out. Now, come with me.''

He took them to the room in which the recovered gold and silver were deposited. There were also some scales which the Spanish had used to split the loot, back when Hernando Cortes was still in control of the city.

Don said, ''Weigh out three portions of the gold into piles of fifty pesos each.''

They regarded him quizzically for a moment, but then proceeded to do so. Fifty pesos turned out to be a respectable amount of gold. Don took up each pile, took it to a far side of the room, and laid it against a wall.

''This is yours,'' he said. ''To be given to you when the war is over. If you are completely successful in your project, there will be a bonus. We all know that if I allow you to leave the city, you will have your opportunity to escape and rejoin the Captain-General. However, if you do, you will never receive this fortune. Not even if Cortes manages to recapture the city, because if he does, I'll have *all* the treasure spread across the deepest part of the lake.''

The eyes of the Spaniards glinted greed.

''We gave our parole,'' Garcia complained. ''But how do we know that you'll keep your word? Or even if you wished to, how do we know the Indians would let us leave with our share?''

''The Indians do not care about gold and silver beyond using them for ornaments. As for me, I don't care for it either. Gold and silver have brought more trouble to the world than possibly any other single thing.''

He ran into a hitch, though. When he checked with Cuitlahuac and Cuauhtemoc, it was to find that his expedition to the area of Cholula with its iron deposits was out of the question. Cholula and especially Huexotzingo, which was nearby, were both enemy country. The coal was no problem. In that direction the Aztecs controlled, but workers sent to Cholulan territory would surely be attacked.

Don's face worked in irritation.

He said, ''All right. We've just this moment created a standing army. I want you to muster two thousand warriors from Tenochtitlan, two thousand from Tetzcuco, and one thousand from Tlacopan. They will be under arms at all times and must not return to their fields so long as the war continues. Others will have to do their work, and they will be fed and equipped from the common supplies of their cities.''

He considered it for a moment. ''They will be drilled in the method that I taught the other day. The phalanx, in groups of one thousand. But there will be one difference; our depth was too shallow. Instead of standing two-deep, they will stand three-deep. Perhaps we'll find that four-deep will be better, or even five. The men in front will carry short spears and shields. The second row will carry a spear half again as long and a shield. The third row will carry a spear twice the length of the short spears and a javelin to throw, but no shields. As many of the first rank as possible will be armed with the swords we have captured from the Spanish; the rest will have to rely on your own obsidian swords until we have managed to produce good Mexican steel.''

He looked at Cuitlahuac. ''I am not a warrior. You will have to work out the details yourself. Hurry as much as possible. When you feel the men ready for combat, we march on Cholula and Huexotzingo.''

"But this is only five thousand men," the other protested. "What of the rest of the warriors?"

"They will act as auxiliaries to the phalanx, on both sides and to the rear. With longbows, with the captured crossbows, and the arquebuses, they will keep up a galling fire on the enemy, while the phalanx advances."

"And the cannon?" Cuitlahuac said. "By that time we should have learned the use of the cannon."

Don shook his head. "We can't afford to expend the powder yet. It is bad enough to use the arquebuses. We're saving the cannon for the return of Captain-General Hernando Cortes."

Chapter Twenty-Three

He spent part of the next day in Tlaltelolco, the northern part of the twin city, in the section of town largely devoted to the pochteca traders and with its special temple to Yacatecuhtli, Guiding Lord, god of commerce. He was accompanied by Tlilpotonque, the Snake-Woman, and a group of Don's aides, a force that was rapidly accumulating from subchiefs and scribes, messengers and porters. Cuauhtemoc was busy drilling drill sergeants who could take over the task of shaping up the five-thousand-man phalanx.

They began by explaining the new Aztec Republic to the gathered men of primitive commerce. That is, the Snake-Woman did. For one thing, Don wanted to listen to find whether or not the whole concept was clear to Tlilpotonque himself. After all, Don Fielding had been over it only once.

But the other had the idea, and although Don felt it necessary to embellish a bit, the Snake-Woman did a good job. Afterward, Don took over.

He said, "By tomorrow morning, I want every pochteca in Tenochtitlan on the roads. You will go as traders, as always, but you will also be ambassadors of the Aztec Republic. Everywhere you go, you will explain that there

277

are to be no more raids on their cities and no more tribute, ever, if they join the new Mexico, the Aztec Republic. Each city that wishes to join must immediately elect its two senators and its representatives from each of its clans and send them to Tenochtitlan for our first . . . our first congress. Make note of each tribe that refuses to join; let it be known that they have incurred the displeasure of the Aztec Republic, the greatest confederation in all the lands.'' He thought of something, hesitated, sighed a sigh for agnosticism, then added, ''And the returned Quetzalcoatl.''

There was no surprise evinced at the last. They knew who he was, all right, all right. Under his breath, he muttered in English, ''Religion is the opium of the people.'' But he needed to give them the extra lift.

He said, ''The largest expedition must go to the Tarascans to the north.''

The Snake-Woman said, ''But except for the Tlaxcalans, these are our greatest enemies.''

Don nodded. ''So I understand. However, they must become our friends, instead. We need them. They are the greatest producers of copper in Mexico and the best workers of that metal. We can use it for hammers and other tools that we must not waste our iron upon. As traders, the pochteca will be able to enter their area safely. It is doubtful that they will wish to join the republic as yet, but the seed will be sown. What do they value most that is here in Tenochtitlan and Tlaltelolco?''

''They value most what *we* do well. Ornaments of jade, the precious green stone, cacao, tobacco, and rubber, which comes from the south. Also they value our . . . Aztec . . . featherwork and various herbs and medicines which we bring up from Tabasco and the Mayan country beyond.''

''Very well. Gather up all of these things in the city and send them with the pochteca to Tzintzuntzan, their capital. In return, we wish all the copper they have on hand, in any form, and any other metal they have.''

Every eye in the building goggled at him.

Snake-Woman blurted, "But these are the very things we cherish most."

"No more. Now we treasure freedom. Those goods are of no value whatsoever if the Spanish return and conquer us. We need the copper more than we need luxuries. We need guns instead of butter."

"I do not understand your last words."

"It is of no importance. Also tell the Tarascans that we wish still more copper and will trade them our most precious possessions for it. Urge them to intensify their mining of it."

He thought for a moment. "In each area into which the trading expeditions go, take those items they desire most, though we strip the city. Trade always for metals, any kind of metals they have." Unconsciously he was using more of their gestures, crossing his wrists to indicate "trade." One day, far to the north, other tribes would call it "sign talk."

Damn it. He knew they had tin here in the Mexico of this time. History told him so. But he couldn't remember from which area it came, nor, for that matter, what it even looked like. He needed tin for bronze. Pure copper was too soft.

He considered some more and said, "And in each area you come to, request that they widen and smooth the roads. They are to be made at least three times as wide. Soon the new wheeled wagons will be using them. Also, request that they double the number of shelters along the roads. Soon there will be a great increase of traffic. Soon large numbers of people will be using them, not just traders and ambassadors, as the new Aztec Republic gets under way."

Complete with his staff, which seemed to be burgeoning by the hour, he returned to the tecpan and brought together all the prisoners who had been farmers before soldiers. There were a considerable number of them, more than any other category. The gentleman farmers he eliminated, delegating them to training the Aztecs in European weapons and drill or to the newly created riding school.

The remaining peasants and small landholders he divided into two, those who were actual farmers and those who were specialists with animals.

He instructed the first group to repair the blacksmith shop and toolmaking smithy to have several plows made, utilizing as little steel as possible. When these were done, they were to go to the mainland and instruct the Aztecs in field agriculture. They were to draw upon the horses to the extent necessary but also to try to work out a method of using manpower, if possible.

He took the remaining contingent to the zoo, which had once been the pride of Motechzoma and the other members of the Eagle clan. They went through it with care. The Aztecs had done a good job. Almost every animal and bird known to Mexico was represented, including the long-tailed quetzal.

His Spanish companions were nonplussed, not getting it at all.

After the conducted tour, Don said to them, "All right. What can be domesticated?"

They all took him in blankly.

Don pointed. "That's some kind of a goat, isn't it? I hardly know a goat from a sheep."

One of the farm-raised Europeans, a Rodrigo Reogel, said grudgingly, "It is a mountain goat. We saw them on our way up from Vera Cruz. They are very wild; we were able to shoot none of them."

Don said, "Could they be domesticated and used for milk and meat?"

Reogel peered at him, as though Don was kidding. "Why?"

"Isn't it obvious? These people have neither enough milk nor sufficient meat in their diet. I thought the goat was one of the most efficient animals ever domesticated.''

Although they were soldiers all, a farmer-born never quite loses all of the instinct. They were intrigued.

One said hesitantly, ''It might take a long time. The newly taken ones could never be trained, but if you started with the kids . . .''

Another said, just as hesitantly, ''You would have to breed for larger udders if you wished milk. It would take time . . .''

''Then the sooner we start, the better,'' Don said decisively. He turned to one of his aides. ''Send orders out that the hunters are to be sent into the hills to capture as many of these animals as possible—unharmed. Both male and female, but particularly female. Use huge net traps, if you must.''

He turned back to his farmers. ''Now, of all the other animals you have seen, which do you think best lend themselves to domestication?''

Reogel said definitely, ''Those geese. They are wild, but clip their wings and in a few years you would have excellent eggs, excellent meat.''

Don made a gesture to a secretary. ''See that the hunters capture alive as many of those birds as possible and bring them to Tenochtitlan.''

One of the other Spaniards said, ''Those peccaries, or whatever they call them. They are very similar to pigs. I once tasted their meat. It is similar to pork.''

Don said to his Indians, ''Where do they come from?''

One said, ''To the far, far north.''

''Send an expedition to acquire as many as possible—alive.''

''What else?'' he said to the Spanish, who were becoming increasingly fascinated by the whole prospect.

''There are also mountain sheep. What they taste like, I could not know. But they should yield a fairly good wool. What is all this for?''

Don said, "The wool we can also use. But the big project is building up the protein content of this diet. In the long run, we'll wind up with a bigger people."

They continued through the zoo, and as they went, Don talked less and listened more. These were pros who had gotten the fundamental idea and, with their backgrounds, instinctively liked it. The prisoner and warden atmosphere evaporated. They had the feel of the thing. Mountain goats, mountain sheep, various fowl, wild pig; it all obviously intrigued them. What, Don wondered vaguely, brings a man farm-raised to become a soldier? They even studied the bison, the American buffalo. But that set them back. It was the nearest thing to a horse, or a cow for that matter, that they had seen in Mexico, but none would admit to a desire to domesticate it. Not that it was particularly important. Don had no idea how far north you had to go before you could capture the lumbering plains dwellers. He did know they could be domesticated, even saddled and ridden.

He assigned one of the Spanish-speaking Indian boys to the farmers and returned to the tecpan. They had enough on their hands to last them indefinitely and were interested enough to carry it through on their own. He would assign them a subchief or scribe to see that their needs were fulfilled and then let them develop it their own way. One good thing about this set, they wouldn't think of themselves as traitors. If the Spanish won out, any work they had done would redound to the Spanish cause.

At the tecpan he rounded up the Spanish sailors and sent them with double the number of Aztecs to get the ships and begin the process of training the Indians to sail them.

He discussed glass with his sole glassblower and found the other was of the opinion that he could improvise equipment to turn out a rather low-quality product. Don gave him the go-ahead.

Several of the Spanish gentlemen had attended the university in Salamanca, Spain. He made them teachers in his rapidly expanding school and instructed them to introduce the metric system, among other things.

He queried around among the Indians, particularly the pochteca traders, who were by far the most traveled of the Aztecs, and described petroleum to them. And, yes, they were aware of the black stuff. About three days north of Vera Cruz was a place where it bubbled up into the lakes and rivers. It could be scooped out and would burn. Sometimes it was thicker and could be used as black paint.

"Tar," Don said. Very well, he gave his staff orders to outfit an expedition carrying large pots to go and acquire a large quantity of both. Wasn't there some other form in which petroleum turned up in nature? Asphalt? He didn't know.

That brought something else to mind. How did you make kerosene from petroleum? Distillation, wasn't it? He knew nothing about petroleum products and nothing about distillation. However, he ran into luck once more. Two of his farmers had worked in the vineyards in Spain and one knew how to distill wine to make "spirits." Don put him to work building a still, acquiring the copper for the coils from the market in Tlaltelolco. The blacksmiths worked it into tubing.

He was working, these days, sixteen hours a day from dawn until dark. He would have worked later still, but the only type of illumination was torch and that was inadequate for paperwork. Possibly the petroleum would end that. How did you make a lamp? Hell, the Greeks had solved that one!

More of the Spanish were coming over to him daily as they saw the advantages of collaboration. They were opportunists to a man, Don decided grimly. He had given his collaborators a superior diet, better quarters, and had even allowed them women. When they had been in command of the city, many of the soldiers had acquired Aztec mistresses. Some of them had even had their girls baptized and married them. Don now encouraged these to return. The non-collaborators were not allowed this privilege.

His clothes were really rags now. At long last he took them to the quarters where the seamstresses worked to be duplicated as best they could. He introduced them to the concept of the button-hole and button.

And then he ran into Malinche. She was evidently as clever with a needle as the next woman.

The city by this time was an armed camp. Most men of military age carried arms and participated in daily drill.

Malinche said, her head high again, "And you alone in all Tenochtitlan wear clothes like these, carry no shield or weapons, in a time when the city prepares to fight for its very existence?"

He sighed and said, "Yes, I alone, Malinche."

"When the time comes, even women will fight. We will stand on the rooftops and throw large stones on the invaders. Where will you be then, Don Fielding?"

He looked at her in sour amusement. "Out of the way of the fighting, if possible," he told her levelly.

He had come to peace with himself on the subject. Let war be fought by such as Cuauhtemoc whose profession it was. If Mexico was to be dragged by the scruff of the neck from a Neolithic culture into the sixteenth century, Don was not expendable. At least he—unique in the world of 1519—had been vaccinated for smallpox!

Assistance came from an unexpected source when the pochteca expedition returned from Tarascan country with the copper and other metals. The trading mission had met with all-out success, and the several hundred porters who had gone along were weighted down with copper and smaller amounts of other metals, including gold, silver, and even a little lead.

Botello Puerto de Plata, the supposed astrologer of the Spanish army, had listed himself as a soothsayer as his former occupation when Don Fielding had taken roll call.

However, when Don called on the blacksmiths and the miners to look at his collection of metals and tell him if they recognized tin, the dark-visaged Botello came along.

He pointed at some of the ingots. "That isn't silver. It's tin."

Don looked at him. "How do you know?"

"When I was a boy, I was apprenticed to an alchemist."

"An alchemist! For how long?" If there was anything Don needed it was a chemist—no matter how primitive a chemist.

"For but two years. He blew himself up. But at least I know the metals. He was attempting to produce gold from the baser ones."

Don turned back to his blacksmiths. "I assume that none of you know how to make bronze from copper and tin. You'll have to experiment at the proportions. As soon as you come up with a suitable hard product, we will begin the manufacture of bronze spear- and arrowheads. We will send you more metalworkers and you can train them, scores of them. Train them in shifts. At this time they need to learn to make nothing save spear- and arrowheads."

Don turned back to the subchief who had captained the expedition to Tarasca. "As soon as some of the other trade groups have returned from the south, acquire more of the things the Tarascans desire and return to trade for more of this tin."

"It's name is *amochitl*," the pochteca said. "And there are other areas where it is found, particularly near Taxco, to the south."

Don turned to one of his secretary-scribes. "Get a list of all tribes that mine amochitl. Send expeditions to acquire all we can, as well as all the copper. Promise anything; barter anything for it; urge the people to intensify their attempts to get both of these." He added under his breath, "We've just left the Stone Age and entered the Bronze Age; Iron, coming up."

From time to time messengers came in with news of the Spanish. Don had been right. New ships appeared, one or two at a time, once a small fleet of three. The Captain-General was acquiring his reinforcements and new supplies. And then the word came that Martin Lopez, the shipwright, was constructing brigantines in the Tlaxcan river. Don Fielding had expected that but was dismayed that it was getting under way so soon. He couldn't remember from his former reading how long it had been between the Cortes retreat to Tlaxcala and his return, but he had thought he had more time than this.

The Aztec chiefs were flabbergasted at the news. They couldn't imagine what the Spanish had in mind. How could they possibly get the small ships over the mountains to the lake near Tetzcuco? However, Don knew the story. The Spanish would first build the brigantines, then dismantle them and haul them all the way on the backs of the porters. Then they'd assemble them in the lake near Tetzcuco.

That brought something else to mind. The still was now in operating order. Don had the Indians bring large amounts of pulque, their drink fermented from maguey. He stood and watched as the veteran vintner ran the first batch through. Tequila had been born.

But Don Fielding wasn't, at least at this point, particularly interested in introducing distilled potables to the Aztecs, or even to the Spanish, who could probably handle it better. He had his distiller run it through again and again until he got as close to pure alcohol as he could get.

Then he went to his glassblower and had him blow several narrow-necked bottles of about a quart capacity. The glass was crude in appearance, and not transparent, but useable. When these were completed, he filled two of them with the alcohol and stoppered them with rags.

He summoned Cuitlahuac and some of his chiefs and assembled them in the great square. One of the smaller structures was of wood, a minor temple to some forest god.

The Aztecs were mystified. Don took out his matches, lit the rag, which protruded slightly from one of the bottle necks, and quickly heaved the alcohol bottle at the wooden structure. He kept his fingers crossed that it would work, especially this first time. It would be a hell of an anticlimax if he had to make two tries.

It worked. The bottle splattered up against the wooden wall, the alcohol splashed every which way and immediately took fire—colorless shimmering heat waves that ignited the wood.

Don threw his second bottle with equivalent results. The building was ablaze. He turned to the Aztec chiefs who were staring, bug-eyed.

"What . . . what is it?" Cuitlahuac blurted. "Magic of the gods, that you have water that burns?"

"It's the first Molotov cocktail," Don said in satisfaction. "And the Spanish have some surprises coming when they bring those tar-caulked brigantines down here. But no, it isn't magic. It is a new weapon which I will show your people how to make. We need more young men to learn to make glass and to distill pulque." He thought about it. Perhaps kerosene or gasoline would be better, if he could only figure out how to distill them. What was fractional distillation? He knew the words, but that was about all. If he only had time!

By now, all of the Spanish had been seduced from their patriotism, such as it was. Only Padre Diaz and the page, Orteguilla, held out, and neither of them was of the slightest importance. Even Sandoval grudgingly succumbed, gave his parole, and volunteered to help train the Indian warriors to ride. The first class of horsemen had already graduated and a new group was being rushed through the course.

An idea came to Don Fielding and he discussed it with

Cuitlahuac and Cuauhtemoc. One of their spies from the coast had reported that a ship had brought in ten new horses for the Cortes forces and that they had immediately been marched inland. It was bad news; the Spanish cavalry was building up again from the low point it had hit during the debacle of the causeways.

They had the boys who had learned horsemanship brought before them. They were the youthful cream of the Aztec host and Don Fielding's heart sank at what he was going to have to propose.

He said, "Fifty of you will go to Tlaxcala. You will move only at night. Each day you will hide so that the whole distance you will not be seen. This is of the utmost importance. Our spies have brought us sketches of the quarters where the Spanish army is housed, including the stables of the horses. The Spanish have grown careless, since they now trust the Tlaxcalans completely and feel that we, the enemy, are far away. Just before dawn you will creep up upon the sentries. There will probably be only a few; they'll be sleepy and not alert at that time of the morning. Half of you will rush them. The others will fling yourselves on the horses, not taking time to saddle them, and dash off. If possible, stampede those that cannot be taken."

They were watching and listening stolidly. On the face of it, most of them were being sent to their deaths.

Don took a deep breath and exhaled. He said, "Some of you will die. Possibly all of you will. However, you must realize that even if we succeed in stealing two horses, it means two more for us, two less for them. So important are the horses in the battles to come that it might mean the difference between defeat and victory. Now, then: We want fifty volunteers."

Cuauhtemoc said, "But these are Tenochas. All wish to participate."

"We need only fifty. A larger number is too clumsy. Those who wish to go, raise a hand."

All hands went up.

"As I told you," Cuauhtemoc laughed.

Don said, "Only fifty go, and those, perhaps, have the best chance to survive since one moon from now we will again make the same attempt, and by then, of course, the Spanish will be more alert."

Don Fielding looked at his blood brother. "I will leave the details to you."

Chapter Twenty-Four

The smallpox hit the following day.

And Cuitlahuac, the First Speaker, was among the very first. He had been complaining of fever and aching for three days; now he was prostrated and an eruption broke out all over his body.

Don Fielding held a doctorate, but most certainly not in medicine. He knew no more about medicine than to prescribe aspirin for a headache, but he knew this must be the virulent disease. Vaccine? He hadn't the vaguest idea of how to prepare smallpox vaccine and he knew precious well that neither did any of the Spanish physicians. The Europeans were largely, though not completely, immune, since they had been subjected to it for centuries. For the Aztecs, it was unadulterated death.

He could think of nothing save isolation. The people must not be allowed to nurse one another.

He bit out his ruthless commands to the Snake-Woman.

All who showed even the first symptoms must be driven from the city. All. Even the First Speaker. They must go up into the mountains and none be allowed near them save only those who also had the disease. Porters could be sent up to them with food, but these must not get to within a thousand meters.

Cuauhtemoc said dismally, "Then there is no hope?"

"Very little, for those who have it. Some will recover. They will then be safe and never contract the disease again. They can nurse the sick, and eventually, they can return to the city."

"What else do you know of this dread sickness, giant brother?"

"Nothing," Don said miserably.

They had the medicine men continually checking every house in Tenochtitlan. At the first sign of symptoms, the victims were sent up into the hills. Perhaps a thousand in all. Don knew that many of them were probably not infected and were being sent to where they would be. But there was nothing for it. Men, women, and children were sent off wholesale. To their deaths, most of them, he knew.

Cuitlahuac died up in the mountains.

By this time, all of the valley tribes had been brought into the Aztec Republic. They couldn't have done otherwise if they had wished, but none of them wished. For the first time in almost two centuries, they were free of the domination of the former confederation, free to participate in the type of comparative affluence of the Tenochas. Their senators and clan representatives flooded into the capital. Quickly enlisted, too, were such nearby cities as Toluca, some forty miles to the west.

And then they began to arrive in a flood as the pochteca traders hit the towns, over three hundred in all, that had formerly suffered under the confederation's campaigns. Don had no illusions. They were joining up, at this stage of the game, either in fear of the new Aztec Republic or in relief by the fact that there was to be no more tribute and no more demand for victims for the former sacrifices.

The first Congress was held. Hesitantly, confusedly, but held. And Cuauhtemoc was elected First Speaker.

Then it came back to Don Fielding. The name of his

blood brother was variously spelled in the twentieth century—Guatemoc, Guatemozin, and even Cuauhte-moctzin. History had the youthful war chief as the last of the Aztec "emperors."

We'll see about that, Don decided grimly. Given his plans, there would be a good many First Speakers in the future history of Mexico.

The five-thousand-man phalanx had reached a degree of training that was going to have to do. Cholula and Huexotzingo had both refused to join the republic. In fact, they had united in a confederacy of their own and let it be known that they supported the Spanish and were ready to ally themselves further with the Tlaxcalans. Don needed that iron ore—and the sooner, the better. He had put his Spanish miners to work on the coal seam in the mountains with a sizable contingent of Aztecs, but now that mine was well under way. The Europeans could leave it in the hands of their Indian apprentices. Apprentices learned much faster than slaves.

Don Fielding suggested the attack be undertaken and the new First Speaker mobilized. Don wanted to go along, on the off-chance that he'd note some improvements that could be made in the new method of war, but for once his blood brother refused.

"The enemy is numerous and there might be disaster. It is a new method of warfare for us. You cannot be risked. If I go down to black death, a new First Speaker can be elected. But if you die, we cannot elect a new Quetzalcoatl."

"Once again, I am not Quetzalcoatl."

Cuauhtemoc looked at him in amusement. "Yes, you are, though perhaps you know it not. But even if you were not, you are just as good. You are the hope of all Mexico and must come to no harm."

As the army marched out, Don stood on the rooftop of the Eagle clan buildings and watched. It made a brave display. The ranks of the phalanx were quite orderly and straight. The auxiliary warriors who followed in their thousands were almost universally armed with the new longbows and crossbows. There were some twenty armed with the Spanish arquebuses. That reminded him. He wondered if any of the Spanish musketeers or cannoneers knew how to make gunpowder. He'd have to find out; their supply was short. They had captured quite a bit when they took the four brigantines, but the rest in the possession of Cortes had largely been fired in the fighting. Some of what remained had fallen into the lake from the causeways and had been ruined.

A voice from beside him said archly, "You do not go?"

He looked at her.

Malinche said scornfully, "Every able-bodied man in Tenochtitlan marches on Cholula except you."

"That is correct," he said. "Actually, I did want to go, to observe, but Cuauhtemoc, the First Speaker, would not let me."

She laughed scornfully at that and turned and left. He looked after her. As ever, her figure was desirable even under the sacklike dress. Don Fielding had the normal amount of sex drive, and he had not known a woman since his arrival in this other time.

Sandoval made his play while the army was gone. Indian-fashion, every able-bodied man was a member of the Aztec host and in a war the whole town participated. Don was going to have to change that, he knew. He couldn't let all his activities grind to a halt every time the organization went into combat. He was going to have to organize a large standing army.

Of the thirty-three horses, twenty-five went with the army, Indian warriors proudly on their backs, carrying European lances and European swords. The other eight horses remained for one reason or the other, including the fact that several were mares heavy with colt. Sandoval and two of the other gentleman cavalrymen rounded up four of the horses, the four in best shape, and rode them into the city and to the Eagle quarters. They had managed to acquire swords.

Somehow, too, they had found out where Malinche was quartered, perhaps by questioning one of the women married to a Spaniard. They marched in, bare swords in hand, seized her, gagged her, bound her hands behind her back, and then headed for the quarters occupied by Don Fielding.

Don, for once, was alone. His entourage was all off on the road to Cholula. He sat on his stool, going over paperwork. There was plenty of it. He was going to have to figure out some method of shoving more of it off on someone else's shoulders.

De Leon held Malinche, who was staring wide-eyed and trying to struggle, while Sandoval and Olid bounded into the room.

"Prepare to die!" the slight swordsman shrilled.

Don Fielding knocked his stool over backward and retreated to the far side of the room. Breathing deeply, he assessed the situation. It was obvious. The three wished to kill him and to smuggle the invaluable Malinche back to the forces of Cortes.

He tried to keep his voice calm. "You gentlemen all gave your parole and swore to it on the Bible of your religion."

Sandoval laughed softly, even as he began to shuffle forward, his sword extended. "The good Padre Diaz absolved us of that oath and has given us indulgence for all that we do."

Don Fielding brought forth the Beretta. He didn't want to shoot any of these men. He needed them, and it would set a bad precedent with the other Spanish.

He aimed the gun at the other and said, "I warn you that this is a gun. You wear no armor. Come any closer and I fire. Release the girl immediately and return to your quarters."

Sandoval paused long enough to laugh at that one. The Beretta was smaller than a man's hand. It couldn't possibly be a gun. There were no guns that small in the Europe of the period.

"By my soul, you are ever a cause for amusement, Don Fielding," he said mockingly in his slight lisp, and came on again.

He was still laughing when he died. Don shot him twice in the vicinity of the heart. The young soldier fell forward onto his knees and then flat on his face.

Don turned the gun on de Leon and Olid. "This weapon fires many, many times. You would not live to count every shot. Release the girl and drop your swords or you are both dead men."

They gaped unbelievingly at their fallen comrade, thinking of the two rapid shots.

"Drop the swords," Don repeated.

They dropped them. Don marched them back to the tecpan after they had unbound Malinche and taken the gag from her mouth. His face expressionless, he instructed the girl to take the reins of the four horses and lead them into the Eagle buildings. He could make arrangements to have them taken back to the mainland later.

In the tecpan there were some of the few Aztecs in town who could bear arms at all. They were older men or cripples from past wars who had been unfit for the march. Don had them confine de Leon and Olid and Padre Juan Diaz as well. He didn't even bother to have words with the priest. The hell with it.

The battle with the forces of Cholula and Huexotzingo, as Cuauhtemoc described it later, was over almost before it had begun. The phalanx stood in the center, five thousand strong. The crossbowmen stood to one flank, musketeers to the other; in battle the flanks of a phalanx must not be turned. The longbowmen were to the rear of the long lines of spearmen, sending showers of arrows over their heads.

The thousands of the enemy charged in an undisciplined mob—Indian-style. And failed completely to break the advancing lines. Around the right flank charged the cavalry and made for the rear where they cut through the enemy there like a sickle, rounded up Tlaquiach and Tlalciac, the two Cholulan war chiefs, and hauled them off. Cuauhtemoc ordered the drums to beat the charge and the phalanx pressed on the double.

And all was soon over, save the agreement to join the republic and send their senators and clan representatives to Tenochtitlan. The Aztecs had lost exactly twenty-three men, their foe over two thousand. It was in utter disbelief that the remaining enemy learned that their cities were not to be looted, no prisoners were to be taken for sacrifice, and no future tribute was to be demanded. Their coming over to the new republic was heartfelt.

Don Fielding immediately dispatched Diego Garcia and the other two miners to seek out their iron ore. When they reported the deposits ample, he turned over to them six of the new wagons and six horses to draw them. He would have to spare the horses, though he hated to take them out of the riding school.

The loss was balanced by the fact that the horse-raiding expedition against the Spanish in Tlaxcala was successful beyond his wildest hopes. His young horse-thieves managed to get back with eight of the steeds. They had scattered, after the raid, and now straggled in one at a time. Then the balance of the raiders, those on foot, continued to dribble in for almost a week. They'd had twenty-nine casualties in all, which was not as bad as Don had feared, but bad enough. They also revealed that two more horses had been killed in the fighting, which at least deprived the enemy of them.

While the smelter was still in the process of being built, hundreds of the Indians participating, Don Fielding looked up the Spaniards who had been on the arquebuses before their defeat. There were twelve of them in all.

He said, "Do any of you know how to make gunpowder?"

Gonzalo Sanchez, scowling puzzlement, said, "We all know how to make gunpowder, of course. We are trained musketeers."

That surprised Don. "You do, eh? Can you make it, here in Mexico?"

"Of course. Given the materials."

Ah, that was the rub.

Another said, "The Captain-General has already made powder here in New Spain."

"He has? But where did he find the saltpeter?"

"You mean nitre? That is not the difficulty. There are plenty of deposits of that. Horse dung, bat dung—but nitre from dung is more likely to grow damp. Yet we can manage. Charcoal is, of course, no problem either. It is sulphur that is the hardest."

He knew there had to be some rub. Sulphur was mined, he knew. And Mexico was a big exporter in his own time. But where did it come from in this country?

Gonzalo Sanchez said, "Not even that is too much of a problem, if you are willing to lose some of these Indian dogs. When we passed that steaming volcano, Popocatepetl, the Captain-General dispatched Diego Ordaz and nine men to ascend it and see if it was possible to find sulphur in the crater. The trip was difficult and dangerous; smoke, sparks, cinders belching up, but they found plenty of pure sulphur there, caked inside the lip of the volcano. Get your Indians to go down for it and the making of powder will be simple enough."

"Very well. It will be done, somehow. Six of you will participate in this endeavor. Prepare yourselves to go out prospecting for bat caves. Two more of you will go with a group of Aztecs to Popocatepetl. You'll have to be there to show them initially just what it is you want."

He looked at them speculatively. "Do any of you know how to make arquebuses?"

Two of them were gunsmiths—if one stretched a point.

"Given the materials," one said. "You need good steel or, on my faith, the damned things will blow up on you the first time you fire."

"We'll see if we can't achieve steel sufficiently good," Don told him. "Meanwhile, I'll sketch out the gun I want. And one more thing that may be just the thing to lob a Molotov cocktail, express, long-distance." He was smiling.

Manpower was one of their difficulties. He needed a large standing army and simply hadn't enough men to do the necessary farming and other work basic to the economy and at the same time do the mining and manufacturing, the studying, the learning of new weapons and tools. He suggested to Cuauhtemoc that subchiefs already trained in the phalanx be sent to each of the new member tribes. The smaller tribes would provide divisions of one thousand men to be drilled, the larger towns, divisions of two thousand. How to make longbows and crossbows would be taught them and, as soon as steel was available, swords. Bronze arrowheads and spearheads would be rushed to them as soon as possible.

He figured it out. If they had three hundred towns at their disposal and each contributed their share of warriors, he would have at his disposal the better part of half a million trained men. With a force like that, he wouldn't need advanced weapons, even though he had one in mind. They could trample the Spanish to death on their landing beaches.

He had all of the arquebuses brought to his room and studied them. There was precious little to study. It was the simplest of mechanisms—a wooden stock with what amounted to an iron pipe mounted on it. A simple trigger device, when pulled, lowered a smoldering piece of hemp to a touchhole.

Don Fielding knew mighty little about early guns, but he didn't like the looks of these and he wouldn't be able to spare enough steel to make very many of them, anyway. He sat down at his desk and attempted to sketch something more adapted to the combat he anticipated. He came up finally with a double-barreled blunderbuss with a barrel about two feet long and a short stock. When he finished, it looked like nothing so much as a sawed-off shotgun of the Capone era in Chicago. He planned to put as many of them as he could in the front ranks of the phalanx. When the battle was joined, there would be time for only two volleys. No attempt would be made to reload. Two volleys, one from each barrel, then the guns would be dropped to the ground to be recovered later, after the battle. Loaded with the equivalent of buckshot, they would yield a fire-power such as this continent had never seen or imagined. He could almost pity the Spanish troops. . . .

He had the two gunsmiths brought to him and asked their advice. They had never seen any such thing, but, they conceded grudgingly, there was no particular reason why they could not be made.

"Very well," Don told them. "Get the blacksmiths to provide you with enough metal to make the barrels. Bronze should be adequate for the trigger; we must conserve iron. Make your prototype. By that time iron from Cholula should be coming in. What I want done is this: You must train one group of Indians to make the wooden stocks, another group to make the barrels, another group to make the ramrods you load with, a group of their metalworkers to make the triggers, and finally still another group to assemble each of these into the final gun. Each Indian does but one task; each part is made identically, so that they could actually be changed from any one weapon to any other."

"A strange manner in which to make guns," one of them muttered.

"It's known as an assembly line," Don said. "Mass production is coming to Tenochtitlan. It has to. We haven't much time. But there's one thing even simpler in some ways," he added, pulling another sketch atop the stack. "Do you recognize this?"

After another long pause, the usually silent one snorted. "Ah, *roqueta*? It lacks accuracy and distance."

"Right, it's a rocket—just a seamed tube with a cap, a guide stick of bamboo, with a pottery nozzle, and packed with slow-burning gunpowder. I think the powder should be rammed in damp, with a long, tapering hole up the middle. You may have to add charcoal. We'll soon have plenty of gunpowder to try it with."

The other gunsmith was squinting. "But what is that fat, finned arrow on its front?"

"Another rocket," Don said grinning, "with a delay fuse."

"We will only entertain them," said the talkative one.

"We'll entertain the hell out of them if we manage a range of several thousand meters," Don rejoined. "Just try it and keep me posted. Two-stage rockets were an idea whose time came a lot later than it should have."

Plainly, they thought this last notion to be crazy. Just as plainly, they knew that orders were made to be followed.

After they had gone, he sat there wearily. It had grown dark and he had dismissed his staff. He was always tired now. He couldn't remember back to the time when he wasn't tired.

He stared down at his sketches illuminated only by flickering torchlight. He wished the iron would start coming through so that he could get into the manufacture of swords. He had about decided to introduce the Roman shortsword, rather than copying the more difficult Spanish saber. Less metal would be required and they should take fewer man-hours to produce. Besides, proper use of the Spanish sword required considerable time-consuming practice, while the Roman shortsword was fairly similar to the maquahuitl with which his Indians were familiar.

He considered again the introduction of the heliograph

for communications and wondered if his glassblower could make mirrors. If not, possibly bronze or copper could be utilized. Or fine gold leaf! Ghengis Khan's Mongols had used a system of flashing signals from hilltop to hilltop. There was no reason why he couldn't establish such a system, semaphore as well. When a Boy Scout he had learned both the Morse Code and semaphore, but he'd forgotten them both at this point in life. But it was no problem. He knew the theory in both cases and could devise an equivalent of Morse in a matter of hours. How did it go? 'E' was the most common letter in the alphabet, so you made that one dot. What was next, 'A'? He didn't know, but it was a vowel, so you could make that one dash. He imagined that it was the second most widely utilized letter.

He pushed that aside for the moment and looked back at some of the other sketches. God, he was tired. He wondered vaguely if it would be possible for him to introduce the steam engine, if he could recall how the damned thing was valved. Or even the internal-combustion engine, assuming they located oil and learned to refine it. Perhaps a diesel engine. Weren't they supposed to be the simplest? He didn't know. For all practical purposes, he knew little of mechanics. Well, if he ever found time for experimentation, he could give it a whirl. But not now!

How about electricity? What was a wet cell? You had something like a rod of lead and a rod of copper suspended in some kind of acid. Was it sulphuric acid? He wondered if Botello knew how to make sulphuric acid. It seemed to come back to him that the old alchemists had known the acid by some other name—oil of vitriol, or something. But what if he did manage to generate a current of electricity? What would he do with it? Not in a million years would he be able to come up with something like the radio or even the electric light. Telegraph. Now that was remotely possible—remotely.

He began sketching a Viking longship. For use here on the lake, it seemed to him a more efficient ship than the Spanish brigantines. If he could teach them how to use oars, why not? They'd have it made. He sketched in a sharp bronze ram on the prow. They would mount one cannon on the bow of each ship, but otherwise the fire-power would consist of crossbows and the newly planned blunderbusses, if they had the time to get them into production and the powder with which to load them.

As he sketched, he thought, how about the flintlock? These muskets the Spanish used were primitive in the extreme. Could he devise a trigger based on flint and steel causing a spark, rather than depending on a smoldering piece of heavy string?

He didn't hear her enter.

She stood by the side of his table and looked down at his work.

She said, "I have been talking to Cuauhtemoc, the First Speaker. You bring the things of the teteuhs to the Aztecs, do you not?"

"Yes. And possibly other things as well. Things that the Spanish do not know about as yet."

"This is why you cannot be allowed to go into battle? You must bring these things to our people. No one else can do it and it must be done above all else."

He was weary beyond weariness. Tired. Tired. "Yes, that is the reason. And I have no time for your scorn, Malinche. Please go away now. I need time; I need . . ."

"Cuauhtemoc says that you need *me*." Very softly.

"Oh, he does, eh?" Don cut it off short and thought about it. "Well, I suppose he is right, Malinche. I do need you. I've been too busy to let myself think about it, but I suppose I've known for a long time that I need you."

She said, her dark eyes down, "You may do to me that thing you do with your mouth, if you wish." She pursed her lips for a kiss.

He sighed. He did wish. It was simple as that. She moved into his room that night.

In the morning the wagons of iron began to arrive from Cholula. Don sent orders to build more smelters and requested of the senators from Cholula that as many of that city's people as could be spared be sent to work them, and in the iron and coal mines. He sent word to his Spanish foremen to begin looking for new deposits of both iron and coal.

Several new and larger smithies had been erected in the tecpan. Indian apprentices, not just from Tenochtitlan now but from all over the republic, were swarming there. Their job was to learn and take the new techniques back to their home cities. The tecpan was rapidly beginning to look like a manufacturing complex rather than a set of government buildings. Don was going to have to requisition some more buildings. Possibly the temples would do it. How could the priests resist, when the cause was the saving of all Mexico?

Swords, lance tips, guns, tools with which to make more tools—all began to pour out.

To the extent he could, Don continued to apply his assembly-line technique. In the past, an arrow maker would go through the whole process by himself, from chipping the obsidian or flint, to making the shaft, to attaching the feathers with glue, to binding on the arrowhead with gut and glue. In a day's time a good arrow-maker might turn out as many as three arrows.

Now a score of metalworkers pounded out the bronze or iron arrowheads. Another score trimmed feathers; another score devoted full time to the shafts; another group assembled the finished parts. Women, it turned out, proved most deft at this last in particular. Don was leaning ever more to the use of women in his primitive factories. When he got time, he told himself, he was going to have to make a pitch for equal rights. Oh, Sweet Jesus, did he have a lot of postponed projects!

He had Bernal Diaz summoned one morning. The sturdy Diaz proved as receptive as any of the Spanish prisoners and was one of those who had sensibly taken an Aztec wife. Don Fielding suspected that Diaz would choose to remain in Mexico after the war and had considered suggesting to Cuauhtemoc that the man be adopted into one of the calpulli. He was a likable sort, tough and straight as an arrow shaft.

He said, "Bernal, how would you like to begin thinking in terms of making a voyage to Cuba or Hispañola? We're not ready for it yet, but it wouldn't hurt to start thinking about it a bit."

Bernal squinted at him. "Cuba? You mean now? I don't understand."

"No, not quite yet. If Cortes defeats us, of course, all is off. But if we defeat him, we will immediately march on Vera Cruz and attempt to capture the men and ships there. I then wish to send an expedition to Cuba, well laden with gold and silver, to purchase a good many things we need here. Cows, for instance; pigs, burros, chickens, goats, sheep, seed of European grains and fruit trees. I want all the books we can buy . . . except religious ones. I want every kind of tool available. I want samples of every kind of weapon that you failed to bring on this expedition."

"They would seize your ship when it landed."

Don shook his head. "I don't believe so. It would be pointed out to them that many, *many* more of our ships will soon arrive to trade—or to raid, if that's the way the bastards want it. We plan to pay well for all the purchases and the market we provide is all but endless. We want thousands of cows, thousands of horses and pigs, sheep and goats. Why, the market is such that all Cuba would become wealthy by raising these things or importing them from Spain for resale."

Bernal was thoughtful. "So what is it that you wish me to do?"

"Consider all your comrades and select ten of them to man the ship. We will also send some of my Aztecs. You will be captain."

"How do you know we will not seize the ship and the gold you give us to trade with?"

Don grinned at him and laughed. "Because your shares of gold will remain here and, for the ten of you, it will be worth a great deal more than the amount you take with you. It would not pay you to attempt to rob us." He paused, then added, "There is one other aspect of the voyage to Cuba."

"Yes?"

"When you arrive, you will spread the message of the great wealth available here. Start the rumor among crafts-men that there are many positions for their trade, with the highest pay anywhere in the world. We welcome colonists, so long as they have some trade, some skill. This recruit-ing is not for gentlemen, judges, lawyers, or priests, but for honest, working men."

"I see." Bernal Diaz was obviously intrigued at the idea, and then he proved that Don's suspicions had been correct. He said slowly, "When you took the paroles of the army, you promised that when the war was over, they could return to their own lands, complete with the gold you also promised. This truly will happen?"

"Of course!"

"Then I make this suggestion, Don Fielding. Do not send those who wish to go back to Cuba. Send them back to *Europe*, laden with their riches. And let them spread the word that you desire craftsmen, alchemists, watchmakers, metalworkers, and all the rest. Some of our army came from countries other than Spain. In fact, almost every country in Europe is represented. Your colonists, as you call them, would come from everywhere—those who were adventurous—and for your purposes, if I interpret them correctly, you wish adventurous, curious, inventive minds.''

''I see you are with us,'' Don told him. ''If you remain, possibly you can conduct another mission for us on the west coast. There is another great civilization to the south, the Incas, even richer than Mexico. Soon we must contact them. They too must prepare against that son-of-a-bitch, Pizarro. We'll send them the wheel, the use of iron, gunpowder, and all the rest. We here in Mexico cannot afford to allow the European governments a foothold in South America any more than in North.''

He added in English, under his breath, ''In another age we called it the Monroe Doctrine.''

Aftermath

The messenger came from the coast some six months later. He bore one of the old-time type messages with both hieroglyphics and paintings.

Cuauhtemoc and Don Fielding stared down at it. They'd been expecting something like this, and preparing.

Painted on the parchment were some fifty ships riding at anchor in Vera Cruz harbor. But these were not brigantines and caravels. Don recognized them. He had seen paintings and prints of the Spanish Armada. These were galleons, heavy transport vessels, the heaviest available in Europe at this time for the carrying of horses, heavy cannon, and military stores. In the background were troop transports. These ships were clearly not from Cuba, but a direct reply from Spain. The galleons were tall enough to have three decks of cannon.

"They'll wallow like pigs when they try to get away," Don said.

Cuauhtemoc frowned. "I do not think they came with the idea of going away. Look at these figures: many horses, crossbowmen, cannon—"

"That's why I had those two-stage rockets built," Don said. "Even with the coarse black powder we're producing, we can pound the bastards beyond cannon range from our

307

rocket carts, and flaming oil payloads will put them into panic.''

"By now, lord, their troops will be engaging ours.''

"Several thousand of theirs against double that number of ours," Don Fielding replied, "and we've got more Molotov Cocktails than they can handle.'' He sighed and stood up. "Let the conches sound and the drums be played, Cuauhtemoc. Send messengers to muster the full host from all the Republic.''

Cuauhtemoc faced his mentor. "This, then, is what you have said would be the moment of truth?''

Don Fielding's eyes were shining. "It is. With our own cavalry and rocket artillery, with half a million warriors, it should be a truth the Spaniards learn with bitterness.''

Here is an excerpt from *Killer*, by Karl Edward Wagner and David Drake, coming in January 1985 from Baen Books:

Rain was again trickling from the greyness overhead, and the damp reek of the animals hung on the misty droplets. A hyena wailed miserably, longing for the dry plains it would never see again. Lycon listened without pity. Let it bark its lungs out here in Portus, at the Tiber's mouth, or die later in the amphitheater at Rome. He remembered the Ethiopian girl who had lived three days after a hyena had dragged her down. It would have been far better had the beast not been driven off before it had finished disembowelling her.

"Wish the rain would stop," complained Vonones. The Armenian dealer's plump face was gloomy.

The tiger whose angry cough had been cutting through the general racket thundered forth a full-throated roar. Vonones nodded toward the sound. "There's one I can't replace."

"What? The tiger?" Lycon seemed surprised. "I'll grant you he's the biggest I've ever captured, but I brought back two others with him that are near as fine."

"No, not the tiger." Vonones pointed. "I mean the thing he's snarling at. Come on, I'll show you. Maybe you'll know what it is."

Beasts snarled and lunged as the men threaded through the maze of cages. "There it is," Vonones announced, pointing to a squat cage of iron.

"You've got some sort of wild man!" Lycon blurted with first glance.

"Nonsense!" Vonones snorted. "Look at the tiny scales, those talons! There may be a race somewhere with blue skin, but this thing's no more human than a mandrill is. The Numidians called it a lizard-ape in their tongue— a sauropithecus."

It seemed as good a name as any for the beast. It was scaled and exuded an acrid reptilian scent, but its movements and poise were feline. Ape-like, it walked erect in a forward crouch. Its eyes looked straight forward with human intensity, but were slit-pupiled and showed a swift nictitating membrane.

"This came from the Aures Mountains?" Lycon questioned wonderingly.

"It did. Came with a big lot of gazelles and elephants that one of my agents jobbed from the Numidians. All I know about it is what Dama wrote me when he sent the shipment: that a band of Numidians saw a hilltop explode and found this animal when they went to see what had happened."

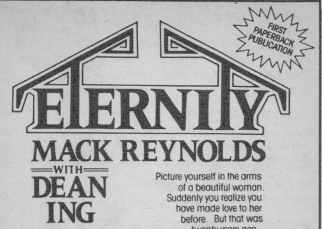